# THE HUMAN LEGION
#### ◄◄◄ FREEDOM CAN BE WON ►►►

### THE
# BATTLE OF
# EARTH
— PART 2: RESTART —

## Also by Tim C. Taylor

Marine Cadet (The Human Legion Book 1)
Indigo Squad (The Human Legion Book 2)
Renegade Legion (The Human Legion Book 3)
Human Empire (The Human Legion Book 4)
War Against the White Knights (The Human Legion Book 5)
The Battle of Earth Part1: Endgame (The Human Legion Book 6)
The Battle of Earth Part1: Restart (The Human Legion Book 7)
After War (Revenge Squad prequel)
Hurt U Back (Revenge Squad Book 1)
Second Strike (Revenge Squad Book 2)
The Midnight Sun (A Four Horsemen Universe novel)
The Reality War #1: The Slough of Despond
The Reality War #2: The City of Destruction

## Writing as Crustias Scattermush (YA science-fantasy)

Treasure of the Last Dragon
The Ultimate Green Energy

## Also in the Human Legion Universe by JR Handley

The Demons of Kor-Lir (Sleeping Legion prequel novella)
The Legion Awakes (Sleeping Legion book1)
Fortress Beta City (Sleeping Legion book2)
Operation Breakout (Sleeping Legion book3)
Insurgency: Spartika (Sleeping Legion book4)

# THE
# BATTLE OF
# EARTH

— PART 2: RESTART —

# TIM C. TAYLOR

Human Legion Annals
—Book 7—

HumanLegion.com

# —— Recon Team ——

I wish to thank our Recon Team for this book, who bravely scouted out the first draft, searching for hazards. This book is much better for their generous assistance.
                                                    — *Tim C. Taylor*

Brian Anderson
Lynda Card
Reed Fallaw Jr.
Mike Garst
Andrew Jackson
Marc Morris
Steve Salas
Will R. Smithers
Brent Spurrell
Andrew Stafford
Michael Tompkins

# The Battle of Earth
## Part 2: RESTART

Published by Human Legion Publications
All Rights Reserved

**HumanLegion.com**

ISBN: 978-1721591121
Also available in
eBook editions.

The author wishes to thank all those who supported the making of this book. In particular, Paul Melhuish for allowing me to raid his vault of filthy Skyfirean vernacular, Hans, Mike, JR, Melissa, Donna Scott, the wonderful recon team volunteers (sorry for blowing a lot of you up), and the loyal supporters on humanlegion.com.

For a free Tim C. Taylor starter library, join the Legion at humanlegion.com.

# —— PART VI ——
# GODDESS
# OF THE
# CAMUVELLAUNI

# —— Chapter 01 ——

**Arun McEwan**
**Aboard unidentified starship**

How the frakk did I get here?

From his wheelchair, Arun looked around the sparsely equipped compartment into which he and the other survivors of the *Hotchelpis* had been dumped, plucked from the ship during its death dive into the surface of a ruined Earth city. How had he wound up here? He'd lay money on Aelingir and the other Jotun crew asking the same question. By his side, Springer was beaming distrust at the woman who had set this up, and she was doing so with such intensity that he expected her eyes would soon burn with the lilac glow that would reveal her true identity.

Arun might be wondering how the frakk he got here, but Springer would have a different question in her mind, one aimed at the woman in front of him with the smug smile, so annoyingly beautiful. How the frakk did *she* get here?

He willed Springer to keep calm. Her voice had been altered, her leg regrown, and the plasma burns that had melted her face were now covered by the colorful scales produced by an alien skin parasite. The galaxy believed Springer was dead, sacrificed by Arun to the White Knight Emperor. She was Lissa now, his fearsome Wolf bodyguard. And Lissa had no personal history with Lee Xin.

Springer finally noticed his attention and tore her glare away from Xin.

As for Xin herself, she acted as she always did, as if she had known how the course of events would run ever since they'd met centuries ago as cadets.

Silence hung over the compartment as everyone seemed to be catching their breath to absorb what had just happened, even the young woman who'd plucked them from certain death on the *Hotchelpis*. Grace had oozed confidence when she was on her rescue mission, but now she was fiddling with her ponytail, mouth agape in some kind of delayed shock. She wore the black uniform of the Human Legion but the gold sunburst on her left lapel was not a rank insignia he'd ever authorized.

How was he here? Because the young woman with the same eyes he saw every time he looked in the mirror had teleported them. Teleported! Tele-frakking-ported. How was that possible?

He was on a starship sitting in a wheelchair, and Xin was wearing a dress. A dress.

It was a beguiling shimmer of deep blues that changed color tone as its folds wrapped beneath her breasts and fell to her ankles. What was that, silk? Wool? Plastic? Hell, he didn't know. He'd never seen anyone wear a dress on a starship before, because such clothing didn't work well in zero-g. For that matter, dresses didn't come fitted with exo-muscles, air supply, extra armor over the vital organs, or fuel cells designed to connect up to SA-71s. Which was why Xin had never previously had any use for such impractical garments. Not when the two of them had been together, anyway. But it was the way Xin's dress flowed languidly to the deck that astonished Arun most. The dress was specifically cut not only to flatter her figure, but to work in the gravity they were currently experiencing in this compartment.

Gravity.

On board a ship.

Where the hell was he?

And how could he use any of this to kill Tawfiq Woomer-Calix and liberate Earth from the New Order Hardits?

As his mind snapped back to military considerations, he cast a critical eye over Xin's five escort guards who had joined the Littorane Marines already present. They dwarfed her in their ACE combat armor, and their leader had kept eyes on Arun since he arrived.

Were they prisoners here?

Time to find out. Time to recruit allies and kill Hardits.

"Dress suits you," he told Xin. "You look… stunning."

"You don't," she replied. "You look like crap." She nodded at Grace. "How did you two get along?"

9

"Hello, my name is Grace," Arun replied. "Would you like to not die?" He shrugged. "We didn't have time to get beyond that to play happy families. And we *are* family, aren't we? I'm not just imagining all this."

Grace removed her glove and shook his hand. Her fingers were thin, almost delicate in their lack of burns and gnarling, but her grip was assured. "No, Father. This is real. And please don't listen to Mother. She can't help her obnoxious streak. You put up with it for centuries, so you know better than me. Beneath her snark, she's overjoyed to see you again. Been talking about little else but you for months."

Xin laughed. "Grace has your stubborn streak, Arun. And your impulsiveness. Not to mention your flights of fancy, and" – she flashed him a wicked grin – "your deep affection for aliens. Frankly she's a dangerous liability to all who come near her. I'd exile her to the exterior maintenance teams if I could, but I can't help myself but love her, despite the multitude of reasons she gives me not to. Just like…"

Her expression tightened, and she didn't finish her words.

Arun's heart and mind scrambled to make sense of what he'd just seen and heard. Neither could gain any traction. Xin had left with half the fleet, but it wasn't because they'd stopped loving each other. Xin had opposed the treaty Arun had negotiated with the White Knight Emperor that continued the ritual of the Cull. Secretly, Arun had opposed it too, which was why he'd cheated — the Cull victims being given disguised DNA and fresh identities as Wolves. It was a secret that would come out one day, but not yet. The strong dictated to the weak in the Trans-Species Union, and the Human Autonomous Region was not yet robust enough to force the Emperor to turn a blind eye to Arun's subterfuge.

He had never doubted he had made the right decision, but it had cost him his wife, his daughter, and his happiness. On any other matter, he'd have confided his secret with Xin, but not this. She had opposed his stance on the Cull for years before the treaty, and spies were everywhere. If she'd suddenly softened her opposition to his position, it would have caused suspicion that would soon have reached the Emperor's ears.

Beside him, Springer was back to glaring at Xin.

And Xin was glaring right back.

Some things never changed.

Awkward didn't even begin to describe this. Despite everything, his heart jumped in excitement to see Xin alive. She'd aged. In fact, she looked older than him now — maybe by twenty years — but she was still the most beautiful sight in the universe. Ever since he'd met her in novice school, his heart had been entangled with hers in a way that defied all the laws of nature, logic and decency.

*We had our years,* he told himself. *And they were good ones. I don't love you anymore, Xin. When the battle for Earth is over, all I want is to disappear into obscurity with Springer.*

In perfect unison, both women turned to regard him. It was like being swept by twin security beams — a harsh scrutiny that easily penetrated his shell of desperate lies.

He couldn't stop loving Xin any more than a star could will itself to switch off its nuclear fire. It had never occurred to him that Xin felt the same about him, but now he saw her afresh after so many years, he finally understood that this had always worked both ways.

Springer's Wolfish exterior had clamped down on her facial expressions, but he could see it plain as day in her eyes that she'd always known too. Ever since that day they'd met in novice school, Springer had seen the chains binding him with Xin…

"Yeah, this is super awkward," said Grace.

It was foolish, but despite the Legion uniform that Grace wore so comfortably she looked as if she'd been born wearing it, Arun couldn't help but think of her as anything but a child. By her age he'd led a rebellion, killed thousands, and as for the pleasures he'd enjoyed with Springer and with her mother by that age… He grimaced. This wasn't going to be easy.

"Again with the awkward family reunion," Grace said, "but I think your shaggy friends need some attention."

Arun followed her gaze to the slumped Jotuns who looked a sick bunch. Aelingir was holding her head, groaning.

"We are ghosts," Aelingir wailed. "We left our indivisible souls behind. We're dead and yet we persist. My soul was lost in the crash of the *Hotchelpis,* and yet this remnant you see before you can think and hold discourse with you. There is a word you humans use that I finally understand. We are the *undead.*"

Xin rolled her eyes at the Jotun general. "And to think your species used to terrify me when I was a kid. Turns out you delicate Jotun flowers aren't tough enough to make your way in the big bad galaxy. No wonder your race surrendered yourselves as slaves to the White Knights for so long."

The Jotun crewmembers rose menacingly to their full seven-foot height and gave Xin an ominous low growl in defiance of her escorts who were now aiming their weapons at them.

Despite the *slikkk* of Jotun claws unsheathing, Xin completely ignored them back.

Aelingir snapped an order at her subordinates and they reluctantly settled down. For now.

"You're so full of drent," Springer accused Xin. "Your words are cheap and untrue, and we all know it. We already know you're an utter ass-hat, so what exactly are you trying to prove by insulting my comrades?"

"And you're worst of all," Xin told Arun, ignoring Springer and with sudden anger in her eyes. "You put your faith in Jotuns, and this regressed, half-human Wolf creature. Pathetic. Time for you to man up, husband dear, and learn there are far more deadly powers in the galaxy than these six-legged teddy bears, and those giant newts that purple-mopped spacer girl used to swim around with."

"Don't let her get to you," Arun warned Springer.

"Me?" Springer snarled at him. "We've been here less than five minutes and already you're orbiting her little finger."

Finally, Xin deigned to acknowledge Springer. "Don't you dare speak to my husband like that!" Guard Sergeant, if this degenerate Wolf utters one more word, shoot her dead."

As Aelingir's groans grew louder, and some of the other Jotuns joined in, Arun wheeled his chair in front of Springer and lifted his arms to sit squarely in the line of fire.

Then he thought about Xin's words and dropped them. "Wait," he said to Xin, "are we still married?"

Xin looked puzzled. "I assume so. Have you married again?"

"No."

"Divorced?"

"You took my child and my heart. And while you were abandoning me, you took half the Legion fleet with you. It sure felt like a divorce."

"But did you get a legal separation?"

"I never saw the point."

"That's what I assumed. Then you and I are still married, and I am not debating our personal affairs with this regressed security Wolf."

"Leave off Lissa. She's more of a hero than you'll ever be."

"Oh, so you're sleeping with her, I take it?"

"Yes."

Xin jerked as if slapped. "Disgusting. I see you're still the alien-faggot, Arun. I don't know why I'm surprised."

"Mother!" Grace snapped. "I know we're not here to reconcile, but neither are you helping our cause by rekindling old fights."

Arun winced to see the supreme effort it took Xin, but she eventually managed to compose herself. "Quite so, my dear," she said. "You always bring out the worst in me, McEwan."

"I know," he said. "So why don't you clear off? Let me sort Aelingir out while you cool down and get your daughter to teach you how to behave in public."

"Dad's right," said Grace. "It's not as if they're going anywhere."

"Very well," said Xin. "I grant you five minutes to play your charade. Everyone out!" She gave an indulgent grin at Aelingir. "When you've finished powdering your snout, I'll be waiting just outside."

She left, drawing all of her escort in her wake. Last to leave was her combat-suited guard sergeant who lingered at the door. The blackness of the Marine's helmet visor pointed at Arun as if an accusation.

"Didn't you hear what your mistress said?" snapped Arun.

The Marine popped her neck seal and withdrew her helmet, shaking free her long blonde ponytail.

Recognition registered instantly in Arun's head. He'd grown up with this Marine, but those eyes… they looked so dead. What sights had she seen since the Legion split?

"Don't play games with her, Arun," said Majanita. "Xin is trying to avoid a war with you." She brandished her SA-71. It was the old model with the grenade launcher beneath the railgun that they'd trained on back when she, Arun and Springer were cadet dorm buddies. Majanita's was loaded with three of the deadly flattened cones, the launcher's firing mechanism humming audibly as it went live. "Some of us are not so squeamish."

Threat duly issued, Majanita followed her president outside, leaving the crew of the *Hotchelpis* in relative privacy.

# Chapter 02

**Springer**
**Aboard unknown ship**

*I always knew it would end badly, dear.*

*Shut up, Saraswati. Nothing's ended.*

*Shut up! How dare you? I bet Arun never talks to his AI that way.*

*No, I'm sure he doesn't. But Arun and Barney have lived inside each other for so many centuries they're practically a single personality, whereas… Oh, I get it. You're distracting me.*

*Now she gets it. Don't rule yourself out of the picture, my girl. The last time you decided Xin was a rival, you picked up your ball and walked away for two hundred years. Now stop acting like a moody teenager and make people respect you.*

Springer dismissed Saraswati from the upper reaches of her mind and plugged herself back into the situation. Arun had wheeled himself over to the Jotuns who were talking animatedly amongst themselves. She hurried across to join them.

"Have you heard of teleportation tech?" Arun was asking Aelingir. "Even in rumor?"

"No. Never. Instantaneous movement – the implications are thunderous."

"But did we move?" queried Ensign Skalzan. "Perhaps information was transmitted – as with any FTL communication – and we were recreated at our destination."

"Unlikely," said Aelingir. "We did not appear to emerge inside any kind of fabricator machine."

"This compartment is an empty box," said Springer, "with no indication of its purpose. It resembles a room in a virtual environment that has yet to be dressed with decoration, function or texture."

"Are you saying you think we're experiencing a guided hallucination?" said Arun. "Or that we've been virtualized?"

"I'm saying we don't know drent about what's just happened. Why don't we take what we're told as a working version of the truth for now?"

"Agreed," said Arun. "But I need to know if you've a problem, Aelingir. Divided souls. Undead. That's not what I want to hear in my senior command officer."

The Jotun lifted her lips on her wicked fangs. "It is a theoretical worry," she said. "But I don't think it applies here. I am certain that if our bodies were still on the *Hotchelpis* then they perished in the inevitable crash. We are information, General McEwan. The essence of who we are — our souls if you like — is pure information — the cells of our bodies are but ephemeral particles. Whether we are virtualized, copied into recreated bodies, or the matter of our flesh has indeed been what you call teleported, then it makes no difference. I recognize my own soul. It is intact. I am me."

"Good to hear it. If only all theological arguments were so quickly resolved."

"General Aelingir," said Springer. "I apologize for pushing you to adopt this ruse."

"Apology accepted, *Lissa*." The Jotun rose to her full height and gave a low growl — just a reminder of how easily the muscular alien could rip her to shreds in moments. "Don't fail us again. It is fortunate for all our sakes that I have established such an effective rapport with your species. I could perceive the instant antipathy between you and former Colonel Lee. This is potentially very dangerous and entirely unprofessional. It's not even as if you've ever met the individual before, is it?"

"No, General," said Springer with head bowed. "I have never met Lee Xin." She turned to Arun. "Sorry, sir. It won't happen again."

He gave her a long, searching look — as if he wasn't himself guilty of being knocked wildly off course by the reappearance of *that* woman – but gave her a nod and a brisk smile.

"Okay, listen up, people," he said. "Let's not beat ourselves up for reacting when the universe suddenly changes all the rules. But now we need to focus. I need to feed the battle computer that your people, Aelingir, planted inside my head. It hungers for data. So far, all it has is speculation. Meanwhile, our people in the European Pocket are dying and Tawfiq Woomer-Calix isn't. General Aelingir, kindly lead us out to meet our rescuers."

The party left, Arun wheeling himself behind the Jotuns. He made no protest when Springer grabbed the handles behind his chair and began pushing him.

*That's better*, said Saraswati. *That's using your brains. So long as you're holding onto his chair, you can't punch that treacherous bitch. Wait for your moment.*

*Oh, I will. I should have killed her when I had the chance at the Second Battle of Khallini. I won't make that mistake again.*

# —— Chapter 03 ——

**Arun McEwan**
**Aboard unknown ship**

Turned out that Xin wasn't waiting outside in the passageway. They were courteously escorted under armed guard to a conference room with chairs and a large oval table, none of which were bolted to the deck. Along the way he seized every opportunity to peer inside compartments, storage canisters and into every status viewscreen. He ran his hand over the bulkheads and felt the strange vibrations pulse through the ship, felt them through the wheels of his chair too. This wasn't the first time he'd been on a ship that hummed that way.

It had been his first combat tour, or so he'd thought. Aboard the Human Marine Corps troopship *Beowulf,* supposedly en route to the frontier war with the Muryani – although in reality under the control of rebels in the imperial civil war – his battalion had been woken unexpectedly in deep space. *Beowulf* and sister ship *Themistocles* had fought with and disabled an unidentified vessel. Arun's Indigo Squad was tasked with boarding and seizing the mysterious ship.

That the ship was there at all was far beyond strange. Starships – hell, even stars and planets – were infinitesimally small motes in the vastness of the black. Ships never chanced across each other in interstellar space.

And when they captured this ship and renamed it *Bonaventure,* as if doing so would make it theirs, the mysteries began to pile up.

Most mysterious of all was the human crew who called themselves Amilx. Arun had been a kid, high on adventure, but even he could tell that the Amilxi crew hadn't wanted to be there at all, hadn't wanted to fight. To them, this encounter was a complete FUBAR disaster.

And then one of the wounded crewmen had called him General McEwan.

They'd all laughed at the time. Arun a general? Ridiculous. The Human Marine Corps was officered exclusively by aliens, Jotuns in the case of Arun's regiment. The idea of a human officer was so ludicrous it wasn't even considered subversive to be joking about this man who'd called Arun a general.

And now Arun had been a general for most of his life.

Later, after Arun raised the Human Legion from the ashes of his Marine Corps battalion, another peculiarity of this 'Amilx' began to look less like a coincidence and more like an invitation, or possibly a warning.

AMILX. Arun McEwan. Indiya. Lee Xin.

He'd put that out of his mind when Xin had deserted him. But now they were back together again, and still Springer had no part in that name. What did it mean? Destiny was catching up with them all, and he felt sure he would soon learn the truth.

But to practical matters: was he aboard another Amilxi vessel?

The ship looked to him like it had started life as a Purify-class destroyer, one of the Littorane-designed backbones of the Legion Navy. But if he was right, then it was something very different now. For a violently warlike species, Littoranes had a strange obsession with harmony, and their design aesthetic reflected this with smooth lines that married form and function and made it look effortless — no mean feat in the endless struggle for real estate inside a warship. By contrast, this ship looked as if it had been gutted down to bare metal and then rebuilt and rebuilt again with random equipment taken from a score of different races.

And ladders. He'd discovered a lot of ladders.

Arun sometimes liked to joke bitterly that he was better off without his legs because he lived most of his life on starships where they were an unnecessary burden. But Legion starships spent 99.9% of their time in zero-g, and when they weren't you had better be inside an acceleration station or you would be crushed to death.

Now he found himself hitching a ride on Springer's back, as she traveled between decks, and trying not to bang his head on hatchways. Aelingir had offered to carry him in her middle limbs, but something about that seemed undignified, so she settled for carrying his wheelchair between decks.

But now he was here, staring across a table at Xin, with Grace, Springer, and the Jotuns waiting for him to begin.

"Where are we?" he opened.

"Aboard the *FRS New Frontier*," Xin answered. "We're currently running dark in orbit around Venus. Now it's your turn to explain something. I want to understand why Indiya ran away to hide around Mars leaving a Legion army behind on Earth for Tawfiq to play with."

Before he could reply, Springer asked, "Did you use time travel to reach us?"

Xin looked startled. Then angry. "Who is this Wolf woman?" she snapped at Arun.

"Lissa is my aide," he replied.

Xin nodded and rolled her eyes as she looked Springer over. "Figures. She's insolent, but you always did like that. Is Janna still alive? She was your first Wolf girlfriend as I recall."

Arun leaned over to put a reassuring hand on Springer's thigh. He felt her muscles lose a little of their drawstring tension. "Last I heard," he replied, "Janna was serving with the 7th Armored Claw, part of the defense of the Calais bastion and being pounded into dust by New Order theater artillery." He paused, wondering what had prompted him to lie when the truth was that, as far as he knew, Janna was on *Holy Retribution*, about the safest location in the Solar System. "She's probably dead now. Every second we waste time, that is more likely to be the case." Arun lifted his hands in an entreaty. "Please. Lissa is an integral part of my command team. My personal relationship with her is irrelevant to the war and none of your damned business. Now answer the frakking question."

"Yes, we have."

And there it was. *Time travel.* Ever since the *Bonaventure* he'd believed deep down that the mysteries hinted at by that ship would one day catch up with him. And now that they had, it was almost an anti-climax. He noticed that neither Springer nor the Jotuns looked surprised by Xin's answer.

"Then you are Amilx?" he asked.

Xin looked thoughtful. "That remains to be seen. My working theory – we are on the path to becoming the Amilx."

"What about General McEwan?" asked Springer. "Does he become part of this Amilx? The usual interpretation of the name as an acronym suggests that he will."

Xin glared. "That's none of your business."

"This is no time to be playing games," Arun shot back.

Xin turned fury on Arun, her eyes burning like the nuclear fire her strike armies had unleashed on the imperial capital. "I have *never* played games! It was me who kept your traveling circus you called the Human Legion on the road. It was me who came back here to rescue your sorry ass, and me who is about to save the Legion yet again."

"With the teleport?" asked Aelingir. "Can you teleport us back to our Legion ships?"

"Maybe," said Xin. "Maybe not."

"What kind of an answer is that?" said Arun. "If you can, then you are also capable of teleporting a strike team directly into the vital areas of any Legion ship. We'd be helpless. Were you hoping we wouldn't think that through?"

"The President means that we do not know," said Grace. "There's only been a single case where we've teleported onto another ship, and that was to rescue you from your shuttle. But your craft was crude, and we waited until your hull was practically unshielded before I ported on board."

"You…" Arun felt his eyes bulge. "You were a test subject?"

Grace raised a teasing eyebrow, exactly as her mother used to. "It worked, didn't it? Sure it was a risk, but it was the only way to get you out alive."

Arun rounded on the Xin. "You used our own daughter as a frakking test subject? She could have been atomized. What were you thinking of?"

It was Xin's turn to raise a teasing eyebrow in a perfect mirror of her daughter. "I was thinking of you, actually, Twinkle Eyes. Grace has inherited your penchant for insanity that you choose to call risk-taking. She also has your capacity for taking outrageous gambles and then seeing them come off successfully – usually. I suggest you learn to accept her as she is, just as I did... *with both of you.*"

Springer bristled.

"Oh, keep your scales on, Wolf girl. Grown-ups are talking now." Xin rose smoothly to her feet. "Calm down everyone and shut the frakk up." She winked at Arun. "Especially you. Let me explain everything my way."

# Chapter 04

**President Lee**
**Aboard *FRS New Frontier***

Xin paced, trying to calm down but finding herself relishing the look on Arun's face. "Yes," she told him as she walked. "It's artificial gravity. And, no, I don't feel like sharing that technology today."

So many strong feelings were swirling within her that they were blending into a fiery mix that was overwhelming her capacity to distinguish between them. She was hopeful, furious, deliriously happy to see Arun, and barely able to stop herself from ordering the carbine-armed Marines waiting behind her to open fire and give him the execution he thoroughly deserved.

Only one emotion rang clear as a bell. This Wolf woman, Lissa – Xin loathed her on sight. In fact, the feeling was so strong that she halted and looked within herself to try to understand why.

It wasn't jealousy of his current lover; Xin was absolutely sure of that. Xin hadn't expected or wanted Arun to remain celibate. It had seemed impossible, after all, that either would ever see the other. In fact, in moments of quiet reflection, she had prayed that Arun and Indiya had found comfort, solace, even a little happiness in each other. Neither was emotionally strong enough on their own, and she knew only too well that it was hellishly difficult to develop meaningful friendships with other people when you were a historical figure in command of millions of souls. In her entire life, she had only ever made a single friend that meant a damn, and he was sitting on the other side of her table.

So why did Lissa make her feel like a cat with its fur on end?

That the two were lovers was obvious from the moment she'd seen them, but how had they forged a connection so deep that their lives seemed to have fused? For two people to embed in each other so deeply took years, and Arun simply hadn't had long enough.

Lissa didn't make sense, and Xin didn't trust people she didn't understand.

She noticed that Arun had been signaling for his team to keep silent and wait for her to collect her thoughts. He hadn't forgotten how she operated.

He looked shriveled. Pain had etched lines across his face. He looked like a hideous statue transfigured in perpetual agony. She longed to rest her hand on his brow and sooth away Arun's hurt… and to don an armored gauntlet and smash his face to pulp for forcing her to leave him.

Again! Xin's gaze found itself resting on Lissa. Again, Xin wrenched it away to study Arun and his senior Jotun officer.

There was a little more white in Aelingir's fur, and a firmer set to her jaw. The way she kept her mid-arms out broadcast her distrust of Xin to anyone with the slightest understanding of Jotuns.

Aelingir's support, or at least neutrality, could prove essential to Xin's plans, so she took pains to show neither weakness nor disrespect toward the Jotun general. She winced. What had she been thinking of when she insulted the general earlier?

*Show no weakness*, she told herself. *Seize the moment with all six limbs. That's what they taught us.*

She stopped pacing and leaned over the table at Arun. "We left behind the smoldering battlefields of the imperial homeworld," she said. "And we left you, Arun, still pledging fealty to the White Knight Emperor like a feudal vassal lord paying homage to their monarch in return for granting the power of life, death, and taxation over land and subjects."

"Your opinion is already known to me," Aelingir told her. "The wounds you inflicted still fester within the spirits of many of my warriors."

Xin gave Aelingir a deep bow. "My apologies, General. What I had meant to say was this – when we had the Emperor at our feet, we disagreed on policy, but not on our aims. When I left with my followers, we still sought freedom for our races, never doubting that you were fighting for the same end. But for us that freedom had to come through strength, not compromise and negotiation.

"We traveled beyond the frontier. Outside of the Trans-Species Union we would establish a haven that would become a staging post, a test bed, a place of power and renewal from which we would grow until we would return and free all races from their bondage. Far Reach, we named this place. The best minds and ideas would hothouse in a cycle of innovation that would suck in the best from all around. No longer would we suffer the stultifying conservatism of the White Knights, nor the limits of the Hardits' xenophobia, although we count Hardits amongst our number. The Human Legion became a rallying cry to scores of suppressed peoples. A symbol of hope and rebellion. It still is, Arun, but Far Reach will become its focal point. For the Legion's heart to beat over the centuries, it requires a home, a center. It can't be the ruins of Detroit on Tranquility-4, or this shattered Earth where our human ancestors first walked. It will be Far Reach."

"That's a pile of drent and we all know it," said Lissa. "In the first place, we already have Khallini, and if you're looking for symbolism, Khallini is where the Legion chose to stand and fight as an alliance of many races against heavy odds, while this Far Reach is a drentball outcast planet that you ran away to."

"It is symbolic to *us*," warned Xin.

"And secondly, you can't have made it to this planet anyway. You haven't had enough time to do all this. The distances are too vast."

"How did you get here?" Arun asked.

"And who helped you?" added Aelingir. "The Night Hummers?"

Xin had to stifle a laugh because the thought of the Hummers made the general's fur tremble with anxiety. Arun probably still considered Jotuns to be inscrutable aliens; she could read them like a book. "I don't trust the Hummers either," she told Aelingir. "We were aided by a third party, a faction I believe to be deadly rivals to the Hummers."

Aelingir's fur shook. "You mean there's another species who can see through time?"

"Yes. Funny thing, though. Turns out it's—"

"Us!" Lissa interjected fiercely. "Humans."

The Wolf… Xin stared at her openly, looking for familiar features but finding none. The way Lissa had spoken to her with such resentment, though. That was very familiar. Xin had only ever met one person who'd felt such jealousy for her, and had done from the day she'd been assigned to Arun's unit in Novice School and ordered to watch over him. Even as novices, Arun had loved this girl, but he'd been blinded to what was obvious to everyone else by his obsession with Xin. Now Xin began to wonder whether *she* had been the one blinded by love.

Walking around the table to Lissa's seat, Xin placed her arms on the front of the Wolf woman's shoulders and stared into her eyes. They were brown – no tinge of violet – but physical appearances could be changed, and voices altered. "Arun and I knew one human who claimed she was visited by foreknowledge," she told this woman who went by the name of Lissa. "You could call them visions, if you like, although she always insisted they were not visual. Funnily enough, the Hummers say they experience their foreknowledge the same way. Her name was *Springer*."

The Wolf woman who called herself Lissa held herself rigidly. Arun clammed up too. That evidence was circumstantial at best, but the guilty way Aelingir scratched at the fur on her neck put the question beyond doubt. The Jotun was hopeless at keeping secrets, and Aelingir knew Lissa's.

Xin looked into those scaly whorls around Lissa's eyes that looked like Celtic knots, and resisted the urge to apply pressure from her thumbs to choke her windpipe.

So this was really Springer. Publicly executed in the Cull, but secretly refashioned and reborn as a Wolf. How many years had she and Arun tried to live apart before fate reconnected them? Knowing these two, they would have left it to the very last moment before the campaign for Earth. Idiots. They were perfect mirrors of each other.

The real world drained away, replaced by the memory of the day she'd left Arun, the yawning emptiness that had haunted her every night since. He could have trusted her. She was his wife, dammit, and he hadn't thought to share his secret. He'd let her split the fleet to protect a lie. A stinking deceit so flimsy even that drenting Jotun had seen through it. Mader chodding Zagh!

She turned the full glare of her fury on her husband.

He couldn't meet her gaze, looking down guiltily at the deck, as well he frakking might. And the worst thing of all was that Xin had to be complicit in the same pathetic deceit. She knew Arun. He wouldn't have set this up just for Springer; he'd have set up an escape line for as many people as he could. Thousands, more, would rely on the secret, at least until he felt strong enough to abandon the pretense.

"This *Springer*..." Xin said, practically spitting out the name in its owner's face. "If she truly did see the future, then it didn't do her much good. She could see her friends and loved ones in the future, but she couldn't see herself, so she cut herself away from her world, and hid like the selfish coward she was."

Springer – and there was no longer any doubt in Xin's mind who Lissa really was – clenched her fists and ground her jaw. *That's right, try coming at me now, bitch. You'll get a volley of railgun darts through those pretty scales.*

But Springer kept her cool. For now. "Maybe she was wrong," Xin taunted. "All that pain and isolation for nothing. Perhaps Springer was there all the time in those visions, *she just didn't recognize her appearance.*"

Aelingir rose to her feet, prompting a half-dozen carbines to be aimed at her heart. Undeterred, the Jotun barred her fangs and hissed at Xin like a faulty pressure valve.

"Act your rank," the general growled in direct human speech, bypassing her translator. "I believe Springer truly had the curse of foresight, but she is dead. Enough of her. You were describing your ally. Are you telling us there are more foresighted humans like Springer once was?"

"Springer was a mutant freak, gene-spliced with Hummer pseudo-DNA. I always presumed she was a one-off, a tool manufactured for a Hummer plan. As with all offshoots of the White Knights, Hummer genetic material is so transmorphic that it will bind with anything, but it still needs a framework to plug into. A Hummer could bond with the remnants of yesterday's dinner you left on your plate, but it couldn't give whatever disgusting life form resulted the ability to peer through the veil of time. But Springer could, because we humans all possess the latent architecture to see beyond conventional space-time. And not just humans. Kurlei have it too. The White Knights produced the Hummers through controlled mutation of this latent ability in their own kind. I think the humans I have encountered used technology to achieve the same ends."

"These humans," said Aelingir, "are *they* the Amilx?"

Arun interrupted. "There will be time to talk on such matters. Right now, I want assets. Your forces, Xin. Tech. Ships. Troops. Allies of the kind who can project force here and now in the Solar System. I want us to figure out how we're going to dust Tawfiq and kick the New Order off the Earth. I expect your new human allies to help."

"Allies? There is but one man. He calls himself Greyhart, and he is as human as Marines such as you and I are compared to the baseline natives of Earth. More so. I think he is an example of what humans will evolve into."

"Is he here now?"

"Maybe. He comes and goes at his whim. Mostly goes. What you need to know is that Greyhart is generous with knowledge and equipment when it suits his agenda. He is the reason we are here to save your ass."

"How convenient."

"We're talking not just seeing the future. We're using time travel in both directions, and anyone with such power can shape the universe for their convenience. There is no longer such a thing as coincidence. I don't like the smug veck and I sure as hell don't trust him. Since the moment we met, every time I utter a word, a little voice in my head tells me that I'm just a puppet reading from a frakking script."

"If he is human," said Aelingir, "then he can't want your species to be wiped out. He must want the New Order defeated."

"We are all of us reluctant allies in this," said Arun. "How big is your fleet?"

"I have two time-capable ships: *New Frontier,* which we are aboard now, and *Expansion*. Both are destroyer size and with a complement of 400 Marines in total, with dropships and enough equipment for three heavy-weapons squads."

Arun shook his head, incredulous. "Is that it? One understrength battalion?"

"The rest of my forces are decades away."

"Your two ships – their propulsion is conventional?"

"Same as your Legion tech, but add in time jumps and they're effectively FTL capable. We don't actually travel faster than light, but say you want to make a journey that takes twenty years, all you need to do is first wind the clock back twenty years and then start your journey early. Twenty years early."

"And to an outside observer," said Springer, "your journey appears instantaneous."

Xin shrugged. "It's not so very different from the momentum dumps that connect your X-Boats to the Klein-Manifold Region. Tricks like pulling 60-gees while tucking into a hearty lunch washed down with sweet tea *appear* to break the laws of nature. They don't. They only seem to when you don't get to see the big picture."

"And the artificial gravity?" asked Arun.

She rolled her eyes theatrically – and noted the smile that brought to Arun's lips. "That's just Greyhart showing off, though these Navy types are so used to it now, they would mutiny rather than serve aboard a ship that couldn't host a weekly bowling night."

"We need each other," said Arun. "We need your time-ships to outflank Tawfiq, and you need our numbers."

"And Greyhart needs us both," said Xin.

"We'll deal with him later."

"I've told you enough," she said. "As you're fond of saying, Arun, there's a war on. So if we've established at least that we're on the same side for the time being, let's hook in Indiya and your field commanders. I expect she'll be worrying about you."

"No," said Aelingir. "You need to understand that the human Legionaries have been infiltrated by the New Order. It acts like a surveillance nanovirus that hides in the bloodstream, but we cannot isolate the infection. However it works, our security is badly compromised. Tawfiq hears everything, and our infected personnel acting as traitors are unaware they are the security leak."

Grace looked horrified. "You're saying every human we meet is a potential carrier? Even my father?"

"Afraid so," Arun admitted. "I have frequent blood transfusions and every test the Khallene techs can think of, but it's possible. If I've passed it on to you, then I'm sorry."

"That's a risk we'll take," said Xin. "But unlikely. We suspected the existence of such an infection before I... split from your faction. We took steps to purge ourselves. Nonetheless, I agree with General Aelingir. It's best for now if we keep quiet about your survival and the presence of *New Frontier* and *Expansion*. We need to meet with Indiya in secret, face to face."

"Agreed," said Arun, gesturing to Springer to help him onto his wheelchair. "Let's go find Indiya."

Grace joined her father on the other side of the table. The poor dear looked uncharacteristically awkward, wanting to assist Arun into his chair, but Springer wasn't offering to share her task. Typical!

"I'll take them across in *Karypsic*," Grace announced. "And I'll go alone. They won't see it as a threat if it's just me."

Xin nodded her assent.

"Shouldn't you give her an escort?" Arun queried.

"No need," said Xin proudly. "She can take care of herself."

"And she speaks for you?"

"No, *she* speaks for *herself*," snapped Grace.

Arun looked at Grace, but she smiled sweetly. Dear Arun. He had a lot to learn about his daughter.

"I'm a civilian," Xin explained. "Your daughter commands our military forces."

"Grace? But she's—"

"She's impressive, yes. Or were you going to say *young*? Arun, she's no younger than we were when we'd kicked off our war of liberation. General McEwan, meet General Lee-McEwan."

"I…" He looked momentarily flummoxed. "I forget how young we were." He raised his hand and Grace shook it. "We've a lot of catching up to do. But first, we need to brief each other on…" His eyes blanked and then he looked back at Xin. "Wait, you're a civilian? *President* Lee?" He rolled that title around his tongue. "I thought that was just a new rank you'd dreamed up to outrank generals."

"Of course I'm a civilian. What did you think I was? A dictator? Everyone in the Far Reach Fleet was given an equally weighted vote. Yes, I was *elected*. Damn right I was. You should try it sometime, *General*. Or do they call you supreme commander these days?"

Xin allowed herself a little smile of triumph, because for once in his life, Arun McEwan had no answer.

# —— Chapter 05 ——

Arun McEwan

Aboard *Karypsic* bound for main Legion fleet

A thousand questions blazed in Arun's mind on the flight back to the Legion fleet around Mars. Who the frakk was this Greyhart for starters? The only evidence for his existence was Xin's explanation that he was behind the teleport, artificial gravity, and the time travel that Arun was already having to wrap his mind around as a practical means of waging war.

But Xin had a habit of stretching words to suit her means. Greyhart could be a fabrication. For that matter, Majanita and those Littorane guards could all be dead, the husks of their bodies kept alive by an alien parasite consuming their flesh from within that would soon metamorphose into void moths and flutter along the cold plasma streams between the stars.

One explanation sounded more ridiculous than the other, but both fit the facts, and to be honest, one was scarcely less plausible than the other.

And what of Grace? Biologically, she was in her early twenties, and there was no doubting the fierce intelligence and the even fiercer will that burned within that young body. Xin had always possessed an aura that seared so brightly that any lesser people caught in her penumbra had been dimmed to subservience, but their daughter's charisma was so intense that even Arun was feeling bludgeoned just by sitting near her in the flight deck of this vessel she called *Karypsic*, which looked to Arun like a heavily armed dropship.

As they headed away from the natural shield of Venus, Grace's hands danced over the flight controls with the surety of experience, while still following the discipline of making verbal checks with her AI co-pilot. But Grace as commander of an entire fleet when there were other officers with command experience? Was that another of Xin's tricks, sending Grace over with the *Hotchelpis* survivors as a spy who could bypass his suspicion?

A punch to his shoulder brought him out of his head.

"I don't have to be a Kurlei to know what you're thinking," said Springer, strapping herself back into the seat beside him. "The European pocket is shrinking every day. Tawfiq has reinforcements steaming in from out-system, and we failed to get the Hardit craft through the barrier to Indiya. We're too badly beaten to win this without taking some big chances. Remember, you trusted Xin enough to stay married to her for decades."

"Yes, but…" Arun grew some balls. If Springer wasn't avoiding talk of Xin, he certainly couldn't. "I know I did."

Springer shrugged. "So trust her one more time."

Grace opened a viewscreen that showed the troop compartment. Arun could see Aelingir sitting in silence with her Jotuns. There was enough room for a couple of the big aliens in the flight cabin, but Aelingir had ordered her people to absent themselves so that the humans could bond through ritual sniffing, as she termed it.

His Jotun friend certainly had a special way with words, but she was right that he needed a little time to figure out where he stood with the daughter who had been a talisman of his future with Xin last time he'd seen her, waiting inside her mother for a time when it would be safe to resume her pregnancy to term. Since detaching from *New Frontier*, though, Grace had been too busy piloting the war boat.

"General Aelingir," she said, "I am about to engage autopilot. Flight time to Mars will be approximately 63 minutes, though we will be challenged before then. I am transferring ship comms to your station while I concentrate on briefing General McEwan. Please acknowledge."

The Jotun swiveled the control panel in front of her and tapped at it with her mid-limbs. "I have comm control, pilot."

Arun winced. None of the Jotuns had acknowledged the ranks and titles assumed by Xin or any of her followers.

Grace showed no signs of noticing when she responded, "Forgive my need to reconfirm your earlier words, General, but I have not had the honor of serving alongside you."

"You doubt my competence, human?"

"I doubt interspecies communication in general, Jotun. Misunderstandings are commonplace across species boundaries until protocols are agreed, and mutual experience and trust established between individuals. I say again. I do not have the honor of working with you. Please confirm that you have the recognition codes to prevent your Navy comrades blasting us into vapor the moment we are detected."

"You should remain alert because I want you to give the codes first," Aelingir replied. "If we're very lucky, an alert officer will try to shepherd us out of sight as quietly as possible, without the need for any of us to reveal that we did not die when *Hotchelpis* crashed. If we encounter someone less alert, they are likely to hold fire long enough for me to identify myself."

"And if we're unlucky," Grace added, "they'll ignore the fact that *Karypsic* is obviously not a Hardit design and open fire anyway. Risk understood, General. The briefing will be an intense mental activity. I am not sure how conscious of outside events I will be. Please stay alert."

"Acknowledged."

"Intense activity? What the hell are you planning?" Arun said, as Grace cut the view of the Jotuns and unbuckled herself from her seat.

"It's quicker to do than to explain." She walked over to him – even this dropship had artificial gravity – and narrowed her eyes at him. "You don't trust me, do you?"

"I don't trust your mother."

"She warned me you could prove dangerously stubborn."

"What did you expect?" Springer shot at her. "Your mother will want to be in charge as soon as we've done with Tawfiq. That much is obvious, but that's in the future. Arun, Xin hates the New Order every bit as much as we do. Trust Xin's hatred."

"You can whisper sweet nothings to your *personal aide* once we're through," Grace told Arun tersely. "First, I need to reprogram the battle computer inside your head. You need to understand the capabilities of my people's forces, and then you need to tell us what the battle plan should be."

Arun shook his head. "Indiya is in operational command. That decision is for her. Let's wait."

"Admiral Indiya is one of many excellent field commanders at our disposal," Grace counted. "But we only have access to two leaders with organic battle computers in their heads."

*Two!* Arun's eyes widened, and he saw his daughter in a new light. The smooth skin free from scars and the pull of age, the brightness of eyes hard yet undimmed by the horrors he had witnessed at her age, and the effervescence that bubbled like a mountain spring from every aspect of her: he'd been so mesmerized by her youth that he'd failed to see the suppressed tension that pinched her features. Springer and Indiya had both described the same look about him, and now he could see it around Grace's eyes. It was as if a bomb in her brain had been held in stasis a tiny fraction of a second after the explosion started, an instant before her skull was going burst to open into a gray-red mist.

There was a computer inside Grace's head, a battle planner AI somehow encoded inside the messy organic mechanisms of the human brain. Arun was no longer unique in this universe.

He unbuckled himself and reached across to brush the hair at her temple with fingertips that trembled at this first physical contact. "Does it hurt?" he asked.

"Always. Does yours?"

"Not as much as the legs."

She nodded her understanding. How had his daughter grown so old before he'd even met her? "You can rest soon, Dad. I promise." She laughed. "I don't mean I'll wrap you up in a shroud and give you up to the void. I mean the liberation of Earth will free you from your responsibilities so that you can…" Her gaze flicked to Springer to whom she gave the peace offering of an attempted smile. "So you can find peace, Dad. Wherever you choose to seek it. It's one of the reasons I made Mother come here."

Her gaze drifted away to consider memories that felt impossibly alien to Arun, and then her expression hardened. "We're wasting time. Come, let me brief you properly."

She pressed her forehead to his and began to speak rapidly in staccato bursts of unpunctuated raw information. He'd never heard anyone talk that way before, but to him it made perfect sense.

# ——— Chapter 06 ———

**Arun McEwan**
**Aboard *Karypsic* en route to Mars fleet**

Time travel.

Time frakking travel!

Grace was still chattering away in human machine code, trying to brief him, but Arun's mind had snagged at the possibilities of being able to move through time and wouldn't release him.

Time traveling soldiers could land at an enemy position five years before it was built and bury a nuke deep underground with a multi-year timer.

Or make it personal. Track down Tawfiq's parents and kill them before the vile creature was born. And murder her grandparents too for good measure.

If teleportation were perfected to penetrate ship hulls and ground installations, then munitions could be deposited at every enemy command and control center simultaneously. The enemy's ability to fight back would be blasted into oblivion before they even knew they were under attack. Unsatisfying as revenge, but Arun would settle for its brutal efficiency.

Even with the teleportation he had seen, Marine boarding teams and special forces commandos could be placed just outside target objectives. And when combined with time travel, once these teams had carried out the mission, they could go back again and carry out more missions at another location and another, and all apparently simultaneously. It was like an infinite force enhancer. Of the 400 Marines Xin had with her, by combining time travel with teleportation, she may as well have 400 billion.

But how would repeating the same activity affect biological ageing? Arun had lived for over two hundred years, and although most of them had been in cryo suspension, he still felt every one of them in his bones. Could you make yourself younger with time travel? Did you age even faster?

As for those successful time travelling special forces… what present day would await their return? If the past had changed, surely so too would the present.

Every question he asked of time travel heaped paradox upon paradox.

Inside his head, he felt the battle computer that had been planted there by alien conspirators long ago, trying to absorb these paradoxes and beat them into a manageable shape. His mind interpreted this machine as titanic engines of brass and copper that were currently turning with such enormous angular momentum that they threatened to rip his brain to pieces. And the reason they were so out of control was because these colossal internal forces were freewheeling, unable to engage because they lacked the vital pieces of information to work. The technology Greyhart had given Xin – at least, according to his working assumption that what he was being told was true – had gotten Xin here, but without knowing any details, she may as well have been transported by magic. From a military point of view, it was like having ultra-high yield fusion bombs without primers: the potential was there to blow a planet into a trillion pieces, but without that missing component, they were just so much high-tech junk.

*Dad!*

Xin knew his mind would need more data to work on, and deliberately hadn't supplied it. She also needed his help, or else she wouldn't have let him go free. All of which meant that Greyhart was holding back from Xin's people too. Interesting. But why?

*Dad, snap out of it!*

He had precious little info on Greyhart, and all of it was second hand. Nonetheless, everything he knew pointed to this person being a showman. Greyhart wanted to assemble his team of primitives; Xin, Grace, Arun and the others were the bombs that he was going to set off in a time that presumably was in Greyhart's past. The time traveler would show up in person and prime his bombs by supplying the missing info. It was the one thing Arun's battle computer brain was sure of.

*Arun!*

Then another realization grabbed him by the shoulders and shook him violently; so hard that the back of his head hurt as if it were slamming into something hard and unyielding – a sign, he assumed, that his battle computer was struggling but was nonetheless delivering something of value. Hummers versus time-travelling human. Rivals. If future humans were getting involved, why now? Why here? Why him? Hummers were deeply involved in the battle for Earth on Tawfiq's side too. That was what was slipping into his head. The reason this Greyhart character needed them to fight his proxy time war here and now was because with the help of her Hummer allies, Tawfiq could time travel too!

The realization was so shocking, it felt like a punch to his face.

Then another punch, harder this time and straight to his solar plexus.

He gasped through a half-collapsed windpipe and opened his eyes on the looping colored whorls around Springer's eyes.

His lover was out of her seat and fending off his daughter's attacks with one hand while shaking him roughly with the other. Aelingir and her Jotuns had mysteriously appeared on the flight deck, looking on with interest, but unwilling to intervene in this bewildering all-human affair.

Arun couldn't speak, but he phrased his question at Springer eloquently with his furrowed brow: *what the frakk?*

"I told you to wait until Indiya was here before activating that wretched thing in your mind." Man, was she angry at him! "Only she can safely bring you out of your stupid frakking fugue state."

Grace stopped fighting. Springer relaxed. For a moment, there was calm. It lasted about a second.

"There's a problem," said Springer. "You need to talk to Caccamo. Now."

Arun shrugged. *Why?*

"Because his X-Boat squadron is about to blow us all into atoms," she replied. "Something about not transmitting friendly force identifiers and using code phrases known to the enemy." Springer passed over a transceiver and clicked it on. "Just tell them who you are."

"I'm in a good mood," said Arun's old friend, Caccamo. "Which means you have another thirty seconds to identify yourself before I open fire. Or you could power up your weapons and I'll end you sooner."

Arun flicked off the transceiver. "If we broadcast my voice, Tawfiq will soon know I'm here and alive." He hesitated, and then remembered that he was at least one step ahead of everyone else here. "Which is even worse than we thought because Tawfiq has time travel too," he explained, and switched the device back on.

Grace went white with horror. Interesting – she hadn't figured that out.

"Twenty seconds," said Caccamo. "Unless I get bored sooner."

Grace took the transceiver and replied to Caccamo. "We don't trust the security of this channel," she told him. "Nor of the security of your squadron. It is of the utmost importance that my passengers do not trigger the voice identification of any spies or AIs listening in, so they are speaking through me, a neutral third party."

She grinned at Arun. "If you have any dirty secrets on Caccamo, Dad, now's the time…"

"You're as unconvincing as a Tallerman in a Tutu," Caccamo told them. "Out of time."

But by then, Arun had already whispered the words Grace should say.

# —— Chapter 07 ——

**Grace Lee-McEwan**
**Aboard *Karypsic*en route to Mars fleet**

"Do you remember playing Scendence back in Novice School?" Grace asked, voicing Arun's words.

"Of course," Caccamo replied, sounding unimpressed. "Everyone had to play Scendence."

He was biting, though. Grace's stomach lurched with excitement, before remembering to continue. "I'm thinking specifically of the games to choose who would represent the battalion in the regimental Scendence championships."

"What of them?"

"Do you remember one endurance competition in particular? Competitors were strung upside down in a freezer room. Last one to stay conscious would win."

"I'm impressed. But not convinced. What you describe was a common format for endurance competitions."

Grace had no reply. Not yet. Her dad was still whispering it to her, and he was practically buzzing with the same excitement she felt. Mother always told her that her life had never been dull around Dad. They must have been wild together.

"Out of ideas?" said Caccamo. "What a shame. You're out of time."

"Lullabies!" shouted Grace.

"I was only playing with you," said Caccamo. "I want you alive until you've talked. Then you can die. Boarding teams are on their way. Resist or power up your weapons and I will... lullabies? Wait a minute..."

"You used lullabies to lure me into sleep. I said you were a chumpwit idiot for always believing the drent Menes Hecht told you, but his idea worked. I shouted and cursed until I was hoarse. And then I dozed off. Your

41

greatest secret, Laban Caccamo, is that you are blessed with the most beautiful singing voice in the Legion."

"Holy sweet crap! Don't say another word about the old days. Just answer my questions. Is your pilot competent?"

"I could outfly you, Caccamo."

"Hmm. We'll see about that. Form up behind and follow my lead. I'll guide you in and wrangle you some privacy. Cut all comms. Pull down the blinds. Go as dark as you can. When all this is over, you can buy me a drink."

"Roger that, flyboy, but my choice of venue. Going dark."

One of the X-Boats left formation and flew just in front of the dropship. Grace took *Karypsic* off autopilot and fell in behind.

"Did you just flirt with my childhood friend?" Arun asked her.

"No, Dad. I was only relaying your words, remember?"

# —— Chapter 08 ——

**Fleet Admiral Indiya**
**Admiral's Quarters.**
**Legion flagship** *Holy Retribution*

It was a desperate gamble.

But Indiya hadn't felt she had a choice.

So why was she watching the launch of the two time missions from the cocoon of her flooded quarters instead of from her flagship's CIC, or her own flag command deck?

She was hiding from her own decisions, and everyone in the fleet must realize that by now.

Let them! The two little boats would be entirely on their own once they jumped back in time – or activated their upstream time intercalators as Greyhart described it, quite possibly a term he'd invented for his own amusement. There was nothing useful she could do in CIC other than perform the spectacle that was the purple-haired human with gills.

"*Karypsic* and *Saravanan* are away," said Admiral Kreippil, jiggling his bulk in the warm water that flooded her compartment in order to nudge her from her stupor.

The commander of the First Fleet was only performing what he saw as his duty in keeping such a close eye on her. That didn't stop her resenting him for being right.

Indiya didn't answer but took the hint. She'd been staring at the aft bulkhead. Now she activated the view screen that covered much of it, and set up a selection of feeds that showed the two strange craft leaving Mars orbit to put a little distance from the fleet before jumping.

They even bore strange names, which Greyhart insisted had been carried by significant individuals, and might just make a material difference to their endeavors. If they were successful, the names would be celebrated for

43

thousands of years. Would that embed them in reality? Strengthen them by binding to whoever had first carried those names?

Maybe. She had nothing to offer but guesswork. It was up to Arun and Grace now.

Arun's vessel, the *Saravanan*, took point. It was a modified L-51 drop capsule. Indiya had dispatched many thousands of these from orbit around a score of planets. They resembled an artillery shell the size of a tree trunk and would carry a half-squad of Marines plus limited equipment. They could be recovered for reuse, but essentially they were just hollow shells fired down to a contested planet's surface.

Following was *Karypsic*, captained by Arun's daughter. Grace described it as an augmented attack dropship, but with its sleek lines, dart-like nose, and three nacelles like an aircraft's tail fins, it looked far too delicate to be a dropship.

In about three minutes, they would have put enough distance from the fleet to jump.

*Three minutes.* It was just enough time for a conversation that had been years in the making.

"May I ask you a question?" she asked Kreippil.

"Of course."

"When holy war was declared by your queen and her priests, the Littorane thirst for battle terrified me. But that was many years and countless campaigns ago. Do you feel your ardor has abated, Kreippil?"

"Never!" He thrashed his powerful tail in the water, but then abruptly calmed. "Though the ache in my tail never abates either. My muscles still function, but age has seeped the strength from my old bones."

"I don't know I can keep going," said Indiya in such a tiny voice that maybe it wouldn't carry through the water. Perhaps she wouldn't need to follow through with this conversation.

"You must," the Littorane insisted. "I know your secret that the Legions who follow your commands do not even suspect. You are a great war leader, Blessed One, but not a warrior. You are more of a thinker. An engineer

44

perhaps. Yes, I believe you would much prefer to work alongside your compatriot, Finfth."

"Engines are his specialty," she replied. "They have always fascinated me too. Do you know that for relaxation I sometimes theorize designs for FTL travel? I never tell anyone. It would be one more impossible burden upon me."

"Nor should you tell others. It is your escape. When this war is won, perhaps the Goddess will renew you as an engineer and thinker. I suspect she is planting those wondrous ideas in your mind as beacons of hope, but she will not release you from your burden as war leader until you have fulfilled the role she has ordained for you."

Kreippil and his divine roles! Indiya suddenly thought of Xin. What role had the Goddess planned for the traitor?

With unconscious mental commands, Indiya brought up more views of nearby space in which the two frigates Xin had brought were parked under the guns of the Legion fleet. Far Reach ships, they called themselves: *FRS New Frontier* and *FRS Expansion*. From the outside, they appeared to follow the conventional cigar-shaped design, but they were anything but conventional. According to Greyhart, he had supplied each of these warships with two intercalators: one to jump back in time, and one to make the return jump to when and where the ship had started. Those devices were now on *Karypsic* and *Saravanan*, which meant in theory that the two parent ships were now at Indiya's mercy.

But she didn't trust Greyhart.

And she trusted Xin even less. She had sent out her daughter to command *Karypsic* but was herself still aboard *FRS New Frontier*. What was she doing there? What was she plotting?

She turned her attention back to the smaller craft, unwilling to confront the instinct that screamed at her to seize the Far Reach ships by force.

"Look at them," she said to Kreippil. "Those brave soldiers venturing into the unknown to do battle across time! It is extraordinary. The impossible. As is the reappearance of Xin and her traitors. Today, the

45

universe is suddenly more complex, and it is my responsibility to understand it all. Whom to ally with? Whom to war upon? What are the implications once I have reassessed everything we have done and planned to do? My mind begs to be spared these responsibilities. Time travel, artificial gravity, and the other wonders I saw for myself long ago on the *Bonaventure*, are marvels to be explored and explained. I feel their pull keenly, but I cannot tell you of strategic implications and tactical advantages. My mind will no longer go there."

"Admiral Indiya, you have teams around you to advise. You listen to their analysis and then you lead. We shall follow."

Indiya shook her head. "I lack the courage to make decisions anymore."

With efficient swings of his tail and paddle-like limbs, the old Littorane swam between Indiya and the screen. "You are no warrior, My Lady. The crushing weight of leadership places heavier burdens upon you than anyone in this holy army, and yet you endure without complaint. You are the bravest individual I know."

"I don't think anyone's ever called me brave before, Kreippil."

The old Littorane raised his head and tail in deep obeisance. "Then I am at fault. I did not mean my words idly. You are the best of us, Indiya."

"Your words do me great honor, my friend. But if there is truth behind them, I do not feel it. The only reason I float here looking into these screens is because I lack the courage to tear myself away."

"You can, and you must. According to Greyhart, it will at least be quick. Instantaneous, he says. They will disappear and then reappear in the flick of a tail. You must endure just a few moments longer."

"I don't think I can. Help me, Kreippil. Take command. Let me be a figurehead and nothing more, because I cannot do this any longer."

"I refuse."

Indiya felt her face heat with anger. "And yet you shadow my every move. If not you, then CSO Arbentyne-Daex. You're lying in wait for the moment when I crack. Well, wait no longer."

"I do not deny it. I have been concerned for your well-being since the start of the campaign to liberate this system, but your words today carry a despair I have never heard in you, My Lady. How long have you felt this way?"

"How long do you think? Twenty hours. You were there, Kreippil. Twenty hours ago."

Before she could berate her friend further, Indiya's mind tingled. It was a comm chime of sorts, but it was a unique form of transmission that piggybacked off unsuspecting entangled comms and was used only by her kinfolk augments. Of the other augments, Fant was dead. Tizer long-since lost on Tranquility-4, and Finfth would never bother her at a moment like this. It could only be one person.

"You know how to pick your moments," she replied, forming the words in her mind. "I'm hearing you, Furn."

"Greetings from Khallini. Well, to be honest, warnings."

"What's wrong? Another attack on the command hub?"

"No, something's up closer to you. I have a few contacts in Fleet Signal Intelligence and I don't like what they're saying."

She watched an image of *Karypsic* accelerating away, on the cusp of time jumping. At a time like this, she hadn't the strength to be angry with Furn. The augment was forever plotting, inserting his data tentacles into every opening. But she knew his heart, and while he had done evil, she knew his spirit was not so much malevolent as easily misled.

"I'm just watching," he protested against her unspoken accusation. "I'm not plotting. Indiya, I've been locked in a bubble under the ocean for decades. I need to see the galaxy, or my mind will blow, but I think I've just spotted someone else who *is* plotting. I'm seeing signal traffic from your vicinity to the outer Solar System, and it's trying hard to go undetected."

"Hardits?"

"Negative. At least, if it is, then it's not using their tech signature. I've never seen it before–"

"Hardits innovate like hell," Indiya interrupted. The conversation was being conducted at the speed of thought, but *Karypsic* was about to jump, and this was no time for yet more mysteries.

"Hardits can be highly inventive," Furn admitted, "but they still have distinctive modes of thought. This is different, Indiya. If you put me on the spot, I'd speculate that the transport and encryption protocols share a common ancestor with the old Human Marine Corps comms. Have you encountered a third party? Imperial renegades? Another Littorane religious cult?"

Mader Zagh! Xin! Liar! She said she'd only had two ships and Indiya had believed her!

"Thank you, Furn. I owe you. Tell no one."

"Happy to help. Pop in some time. I could use company."

"I will," Indiya replied and cut the link.

She allowed herself a half-second to let the anger flow through her veins, dispelling the funk that had been claiming her.

Looping in Kreippil so he could hear, she contacted her senior flag officer in CIC. "Hood, raise the *Saravanan*. I need to speak with…"

But Arun and his team had jumped, the drop capsule shimmering briefly and then… And then the vacuum of space rushed in to claim the sudden absence and the *Saravanan* had never been.

"Stop the *Karypsic*," she shouted. "Fire on her if necessary, Hood, just stop them."

"Stand by," Hood replied.

Before her in the water, she felt Kreippil trembling with frustration at not understanding Indiya's sudden change of heart, but he trusted her and so kept his peace for now.

Which meant he was a fool. Indiya had proven today that her judgment was faulty. No one should trust her.

Too late. Now it was the sleek *Karypsic's* turn to shimmer and disappear…

And come back.

Greyhart had said the flickering was not real. It was an illusion spun by primitive minds to protect them from what they had not evolved to comprehend. He claimed he could not see the effects of a time jump, but he felt using other senses.

But *Karypsic* had been somewhere, all right. The dropship was on fire. Two of its nacelles had been shot away, one was bent over at right angles, and a jagged wound scored right through the hull as if something had tried to rip the craft open. She could actually see smoke, flames and the frantic movement of people on the inside of the *Karypsic*, the atmosphere contained by an unknown mechanism.

And of *Saravanan*, there remained no sign.

The return mechanism on Arun's craft had never activated. Which meant it had been destroyed. Or faulty. *Or sabotaged.*

"Dad? Are you there?" It was Grace, of course, her normally eager voice ragged, as if savaged by the horrors she'd escaped. She was broadcasting on a crude radio transmitter. "Are you okay?" she implored. "We've lost sensors and comms. Lost a lot of good people too. I need to know you're safe. Dad?"

It would have been a trivial matter to hook into Grace's signal and answer her, but Indiya did nothing. She didn't know what to say.

She had authorized a desperate gamble.

And it was going terribly wrong.

# —— Chapter 09 ——

*20 hours earlier*
Fleet Admiral Indiya
Gymnasium, Deck 23, Legion destroyer *Pavonichi*

She had screamed with delight when Caccamo pulled strings she never suspected him planting and revealed that he'd brought Arun and Aelingir back safely. But when Indiya raced to meet the veteran squadron leader, she discovered he had brought poison with him.

Perhaps that judgement of Grace was premature. Indiya dimly remembered a time when she had thought the best of people, but only a fool would regard anyone associated with Lee Xin with anything but the deepest suspicion. With this living blood connection to Xin leaving Arun wide-eyed and giddy with happiness and fear, she had to regard him as compromised too.

In a stroke, a gulf now separated her from her closest ally. It was now all down to her to bring the long war to a winning conclusion.

And then she heard the explanation of how this so-called Far Reach Fleet had traveled faster than anyone in recorded history.

Here they were again. The Legion's high command – or at least part of it – debating another dramatic shift in the winds of war. Now there were even more powerful enemies to contend with; some currently masquerading as allies, and some too mysterious to classify.

Command decisions were normally forged around the central axis of Indiya and Arun, with his meat-encoded battle computer allied to her many cognitive augmentations. He set the overall strategic direction of the Legion, and she was in operational command. It had been that way almost since the beginning.

And she had lost him.

Indiya watched Arun as he floated in the gym hall of this unremarkable Gliesan destroyer. He kept close to one of the sweeping poles from which the winged Gliesans would practice aerial maneuvers when the ship was under acceleration. He was closer still to the daughter of the greatest traitor in Legion history, close also to his aide, Lissa. Indiya had long suspected them of being lovers, but a change had come about the large Wolf after their time down on Earth. Lissa had grown more assertive, speaking openly as if she were a senior commander herself, and not an aide there to wrangle sense out of her tired master, much the way Indiya's faithful Kurlei, Arbentyne-Daex, did for her. Indiya couldn't explain why Aelingir of all people deferred to this new right to speak that Lissa had assumed.

For Lissa to act like Arun's loyal attack dog would be understandable – through no fault of their own, most Wolves were lobotomized thugs, after all – but she was speaking more like a trained diplomat, deflecting the calls from Legion Council members to torture the truth out of Grace and launch an immediate attack on Xin's two warships so her mother could be put on trial and executed before the day was over.

And those calls to war on the Far Reach renegades had come thick and fast.

Watched constantly by elite Gliesan Marines who circled the commanders at a respectful distance, Kreippil had argued strongest for war on Xin. Normally, the Littorane would look first for support from Indiya, but not this time. He didn't need her backing. Xin had betrayed holy sanction and must pay the price for blasphemy.

"You've hardly said a word," Indiya told Arun bitterly. "Have you better things to do?" She looked poison at Grace.

Her old friend looked momentarily stung by the bitterness in her voice. That was something, she supposed. She'd reached him at some level. "I have tried to explain," he said. "We've been shepherded. We are here at a time and place of someone else's choosing, wound up and ready to go, but we need our toymaker to release us. The best thing we can do at this moment is wait. I don't expect we'll need to wait much longer."

"Bravo, General," said a man's voice directly behind Indiya. She turned. "You are more perceptive than I imagined, though I fear your talent for tortured metaphor rivals my own."

It took a while to focus her eyes on this person who had appeared from nowhere. It was a human man. Or maybe *men*. He was blurred, as if a composite built from multiple versions of the same individual, and just being near him made her mind hum with static. She held out the palm of one hand to indicate to the Gliesan Marines that they should hold their fire.

"Grace," she asked, "is this him?"

"That's Greyhart all right," said the woman, and in her voice rang loud and clear the same joy of adventure Indiya had heard in her parents when they had all been impossibly young. "Hang on, everybody," said Grace. "This is going to get interesting real quick."

———

**Arun McEwan**
**Gymnasium, Deck 23, Legion destroyer *Pavonichi***

Greyhart floated behind Indiya with his arms out and a beaming smile, inviting the attention of the Legion Council. His appearance seemed to be actively resisting description; it was... *averaged*. Height, build, skin color and facial features were all middle of the human ranges Arun had encountered, and he had seen variations on the human design that extended far beyond anything that had emerged naturally on Earth. The only characteristics that came across distinctly were that the intruder was male, and that he wouldn't stop grinning.

Arun loathed Greyhart on sight.

*Why can't I see him clearly?* he asked Barney.

*I've been pondering the same question,* replied the AI embedded in his neck. *I've compared notes with Saraswati. Springer is not perceiving him the same way. The differences are small but confirmed. We can't explain it. After this encounter, I want you to hook me up with Aelingir via her AI, so we can compare the data both of you are recording from your optic nerves. I suspect aliens will see Greyhart very differently.*

*Any ideas on how to trap him? Or kill him if we need to?*

*Arun, the man just appeared in the middle of a compartment locked down under tight security in a starship in the middle of the Legion fleet. Anyone who can do that might as well wear a pointy hat and carry a staff, because it's magic as far as I'm concerned. If he becomes threatening, you could try pointing a gun and shooting. Somehow, though, I don't think that would do you much good.*

*Fair point. Let's see what he has to say.*

"What kept you, Greyhart?" said Arun. "Lose track of time?"

The man bowed in acknowledgement like a frakking court jester.

"I don't like people who manipulate me," said Arun. "We're your puppets, right here where you've summoned us, but I don't guarantee we'll perform as you intend. I'm guessing that if you could shape your past however you wanted, you wouldn't feel the need to reveal yourself. You need us, but you can only manipulate us so far. Am I right?"

Greyhart's grin evaporated. "You alone can dimly perceive the truth, McEwan, and that's because I'm not the only manipulator here. You blame the Jotuns for implanting a battle planner AI inside your head – neat trick, by the way, and lucky for you that I doubt I would learn it by dissecting you. The Jotuns were bio-engineers of choice for human subjects, but it was not a Jotun idea to do this, and it was not placed within you for... Oh, and I perceive one in your daughter too. Now, that is highly revealing. But I digress–"

"The Hummers," said Springer.

"Indeed," Greyhart started to reply, but then he froze like a video image that had lost transmission. Suddenly, he was back again, but his image had changed. Now he wore a mud-spattered greatcoat, a bulky woolen garment with a military rank Arun didn't recognize embroidered on epaulettes and cuffs.

*What was he wearing before?* Arun asked Barney

*Before when? He's wearing a military greatcoat, British Army pattern, circa 1918. Always has been.*

*He wasn't a moment ago.*

*I checked the data in your audio-visual memory. Whatever you think you saw, Arun, you didn't.*

"Yes, the Hummers," this revised version of Greyhart told Springer, studying her with interest. "A species with which you yourself are also intimately linked, Miss Lissa."

"Now it's starting to make sense," said Arun. "The thing inside my mind has given me an edge all my life. It's helped me make the right calls in the Legion's wars, but it always seemed a ludicrously complicated asset to store away in someone's head. Why not simply provide us with advanced battleplanner AIs in a regular processor block? But it was never about the Human Legion's wars, was it? The Jotuns might have rewired my head, but they did so because the Hummers wanted to prepare me against you."

"Indeed, although their meddling might also help you resist *them*. The Hummers have their own agenda, you see. And they are enjoying their own civil war at this period in time. What you hypothesize may well be true but is not relevant to your current agenda." He spread his arms to encompass the assembled group like a cheap theatre actor. "Questions, people. I have time to answer a few."

"Are you human?" asked Kreippil.

"Broadly speaking, I am."

"We always knew the Hummers can peer through time," said Aelingir, "now I learn humans possess similar abilities, as was always suspected. White Knights, Jotuns, Achaeans, Cienju, Tuskers and others all broke the contact seal around this planet because we heard rumors of time travel technology. We found nothing but warlike apes. If you could hide from such intense scrutiny, so might others. Who else possesses this advantage?"

"The good general refers to the events of the twenty-second century that in my day is known as the Scramble for Earth," said Greyhart. "I am aware of several time-capable species. All nonhuman, but nonetheless all natives of Earth."

Barney detected Arun's confusion and chimed in privately. *He's either implying knowledge of alternative realities in which humans do not evolve, or events far in the future.*

Indiya was already ahead of Arun. "Dolphins?" she suggested.

"Dogs?" said Aelingir

"Dinosaurs?" Arun asked.

"Not dogs," Greyhart replied. "The other two, yes. Especially a derivative of *Dilophosaurus* that caused a lot of grief that resonates still." He floated across to Arun, despite the lack of any obvious sign of propulsion. "And that is why you can trust me over the Night Hummers. Everything you have ever done in your long life, McEwan, the friends and lovers who fell along the way, all those who died on every side because of your decisions in your wars, all that will never have been if humans turn out to have been dinosaurs all along. All the sacrifice will have been for nothing." He slapped a dismayed Arun on the back. "Welcome to my world."

"But… they didn't win," said Arun. "The dinosaurs, I mean. We evolved enough to contact species from other stars, and the dinosaurs and dolphins did not."

"All potential realities coexist simultaneously, General McEwan. The only reason I'm able to talk with you, and not with a super-intelligent highly evolved hedgehog, is because your reality wave function is stronger than that of the hedgehogs. A lot stronger, thankfully. I fought in the Reality War, dear boy. Trust me, you have no idea how fragile our species' existence really is."

"I get it," said Springer. "You're a time cop."

"No, madam. *Cop* suggests the rule of law, and the only law I uphold is the right for my people to survive. You and I are natural allies because I require your version of history – or something close to it – to prevail in order for the people of my time to exist."

"When is your time?" asked Indiya. "Who are your people?"

Greyhart said nothing, but he was still human, and Arun knew Indiya's many mental enhancements included pattern recognition that could read most people like a book. "You don't know, do you?" she accused. "All this… the speech you just gave, and you are completely adrift. Do you even remember your name?"

The time traveler appeared to flicker and then stabilized, this time wearing crude black garb with a white lace collar. "I do not, Lady Indiya. The name Greyhart comes from a character I once wrote in a story. Or perhaps I named the character after myself."

"I am quite sure I know my own name," snapped Indiya. "And the rank I have earned. I am an admiral, not a lady."

"Forgive me, Admiral. I speak too soon of a title you may wear in your future." He sighed, and Arun sensed the man was genuinely worn out. "I confuse your title because time war is a grueling strain even for those, like me, who are engineered to fight it. Even being around you people is like having exploding EMP grenades shoved up my nose."

The grin that had seemed such a permanent feature now reasserted itself. "Time's up!" he roared. "It's always a shock for mundanes to meet me, so I've learned to give you a brief little chitchat to get over your initial *oh my God it's a man from the future!* You've had your dose now – except for General Lee-McEwan who's had the dubious pleasure of a double helping. Now, it's time for you to get your bloody fingers out and act. As that worthy of the Far Reach Fleet has already explained, I retrofitted two of her ships with time travel capability. They are now at the disposal of you all to defeat Tawfiq, and perhaps thwart the Night Hummers to boot. Whatever we do will be dangerous, but for me to tell you what to do at this stage would be suicidal. Two ships. Range five thousand years. The further back you go, the less mass you can take. And the more widespread the change you make, the more likely you are to bugger up the present day. So keep it surgical, and keep it smart, but you must decide your target time and objective, and then I'll wind the clock for you. Begin!"

The Council leaped into animated debate, as they often did. They were talking over each other, but Arun let them be. He'd learned it was a phase they had to work through. He declined to join in, instead watching his daughter arguing with the Tallerman General Graz.

"Sorry to interrupt, General." It was Greyhart who'd snuck up behind him and rested a hand on his shoulder. "But have you by any chance encountered an Earth native? Male, short by your standards, and late middle age by now. Possibly goes under the name of Sergeant Bashiri Bloehn of the 163rd Brigade, International Federation Defense Force?"

"What if I have?"

"Well, I bloody well hope you have. I went to a lot of trouble keeping him alive so that you two could meet. Did he mention the Battle of Cairo in 2717AD?"

Arun gave up. It wasn't clear how he could keep secrets from a man such as this. "Yes, I met Sergeant Bloehn. Cairo was a failed uprising. It was launched too soon."

"A failure, was it?" Greyhart's raised eyebrow spoke otherwise. "Too soon?" The other eyebrow lifted. "That remains to be seen. And just to be clear, this isn't me interfering. I'm just offering a little advice. Perhaps you should speak with Bloehn again before you make a decision."

"What is your deal?" said Springer. "You tell us to tread lightly or we'll frakk up the future, but do whatever you want and I'll back you. It's far too dangerous for me to tell you what to do, but, hey, do you remember that Bloehn guy? You really need to speak with him."

The smile left Greyhart. "I envy the mundanes who imagine they stumble through time on a steady speed and heading," he said. "Being attuned to the true nature of reality is difficult and painful. Believe me, Lissa – it *is* Lissa at the moment, isn't it? – your own experiences are nothing more than glimpses of the terrifying truth of reality, and yet I know how much hurt they have caused you. Oh, yes, I know more about you than any of the others. How to explain my actions? I cannot, except by analogy. Imagine, if you will, a circus performer spinning plates. I cause dozens of plates to spin, and if any should fall to the ground, it would mean catastrophe. Yet I cannot spin the plates myself because if I should touch them, they would shatter. The plates must be nudged and coerced, but they must spin themselves."

"Why must you spin so many plates?" asked Springer.

Greyhart gave a sheepish grimace. "It is conceivable that in the course of my duties, I may have interfered a tad too much."

"No kidding," said Arun. "And if we're one of these spinning plates. We have to go back in time, because from Greyhart's point of view, we've *already done it.* The *Bonaventure* incident warned us when we were still kids. We're locked into this. All of us. Even Greyhart."

"I can say no more."

"And I don't want to rush into this," said Arun, "especially since I think Tawfiq could have her own ability to move across time." He peered at Greyhart. "Does she?"

Greyhart made a zipping gesture across his lips.

"We have Night Hummers serving aboard our ships as FTL data transceivers," Indiya pointed out. "Perhaps we should put Greyhart and one of our Hummers in the same room and see what happens."

"That would not work well for anyone," said Greyhart petulantly.

"I don't know," said Arun. "I'm going to have to think on this before we can proceed. Indiya – and Grace if you're willing – I suggest we go away and put our heads together before reconvening."

"No, no," Greyhart protested. "Thrice nay. Stay a little longer. You can't leave now."

Arun peered at Greyhart. "Now? Why does *now* matter to a man who can travel through time? You've lured us to this precise place and time. What happens next?"

From the ring of Gliesan Marines, Arun caught the faint whine of portable railguns charging.

Greyhart bowed. "Indeed I have, sir, but only to gratify my warped sense of occasion." He ignored the guns aimed at his heart and head and looked meaningfully at Indiya.

Arun followed the time traveler's gaze and noticed Indiya's face go vacant for a few seconds.

Greyhart gave a knowing grin. "History calls," he says.

"I'm receiving a communications hail," Indiya explained. "Claims to be from the Voice of the Resistance."

———

**Fleet Admiral Indiya**
**Gymnasium, Deck 23, Legion destroyer *Pavonichi***

Hating the feeling that she was no longer in control of her own destiny, Indiya routed the incoming feed to the speaker in her wrist block. Hell, it was hardly worth keeping anything secret from this Greyhart character who seemed to know what was going to happen in advance.

"Who is this?" she queried.

"The Voice of the Resistance," replied a neutral voice devoid of any accent or gender cues that Indiya could detect.

"Go ahead."

"Do not listen to him."

"Don't listen to who?"

"He has many names. The last he used was Greyhart. You alone among your people perceived the damage done to reality by the *Bonaventure* all those years ago. He will entice you to destroy the fabric of the universe. Send him away. His words are dangerous. Don't listen to them."

"*Bonaventure?* How could you possibly know that? You… you aren't even human, are you?" And there was that idiot, Dock, thinking the Voice of the Resistance had been Romulus. "Why should I listen to you?"

"I gave you Tawfiq's shuttle. Learn from it, and hurry! Tawfiq will unleash new forces in ten days. If she succeeds, she will be unstoppable. Your species will be eradicated. And so will mine. But you must beat Tawfiq your way, not *his*."

"Mader zagh! You've seen this outcome, haven't you? You've seen the future. You're a Night Hummer."

But the transmission from the Voice of the Resistance shut off abruptly. Greyhart glowed with smugness but said no more.

"Find the Earth soldier, Sergeant Bloehn," she ordered Caccamo over a private channel she'd set up with him in advance. "Send him to me. And while you're at it, ask the captain of this ship to supply food and drink. We're not leaving this spot until we've made a decision."

# —— Chapter 10 ——

**Fleet Admiral Indiya**
**Admiral's Quarters.**
**Legion flagship *Holy Retribution***

Flag Lieutenant Hood was giving Indiya an update on the *Karypsic* via one of her secondary cognitive threads. The dropship had lost a third of its mass, hull armor had been penetrated and partially sealed in several locations, and the ship was radiating significant thermal energy that hadn't been there seconds earlier. It wasn't an elaborate deception. The *Karypsic* really had been in a fight, and it looked like some of Grace's team hadn't made it back.

"Hello?" Grace was saying. "Can anyone hear me?"

A sudden realization slapped Indiya out of her stupor. Grace's broadcast was so unconventional, that possibly Indiya was the only one to have noticed it. She was detecting no replies from Xin or the Far Reach Fleet.

This woman needed her.

"I hear you," Indiya replied. "I'm sending medical teams. You are not venting atmosphere, but I can see the interior of your craft through your hull. Do you require damage control teams or engineering assistance?"

"Negative, Admiral. But we do need medevac."

Indiya organized the assistance while simultaneously relaying Furn's message of treachery to Finfth – the only other surviving augment in the fleet. She wanted an outside opinion she could trust, and Finfth didn't share the same hatred of Xin that she and Kreippil felt. Rational analysis told Indiya that there were many candidates other than Xin who might be secretly communicating with the outer Solar System.

"What I need most of all," Grace was telling her at the same time, "is to talk with my father. He needs to know what we encountered."

"Grace, your father hasn't come back."

"Dad?" Panic gripped the daughter of Arun and Xin. Then, without warning, *Karypsic's* full comms started up, and amid busy signal traffic between the damaged dropship and both Legion and Far Reach ships, Grace found time to adjust a nearby camera to focus on her face. "Admiral Indiya," she said, "are you seeing me?"

The girl's panic had been brief. While Grace stared into the camera with the antagonistic jut to her jaw she'd inherited from her mother, she was also issuing instructions to the incoming medical teams and was organizing her own damage control.

Indiya was seeing her all right. When she'd first appeared out of the blue, the irreverent optimism that had shone from the girl's cheeky smile was exactly like her father's. Indiya had almost been charmed. Now there was a focus about her that was almost cruel in its intensity. Just like her mother. Indiya realized she could never trust this woman, no matter how much she might admire her.

"Admiral?"

"I see you, Lee-McEwan."

"I know precisely what Greyhart told us," Grace said. "If my father's team didn't make it back then either they were unable to activate the return mechanism, or they did but it failed."

"I'm sorry, Grace, but I agree. We've lost him. It would be cruel to hope."

The younger woman hardened her expression, and Indiya saw the ruthless determination within her that would stop at nothing to achieve her goals. Grace's hair was matted with blood and dirt, and an unidentified fluid had spattered over her face and then been wiped away from her eyes. In stark contrast, the smartfabric of her uniform had cleaned itself. It was a pristine example of the simple black with gold insignia of the Legion Navy, the same uniform Indiya wore herself, as indeed did Kreippil. Indiya didn't consider Grace to serve in the same navy as her and Kreippil, whatever lies Xin might spin.

"You misunderstand," Grace told Indiya. "My mother often told me what attracted her most to my father." The girl spoke as if she were a parent soothing a troubled infant. "He's a survivor. Even as a cadet, he kept bouncing back, no matter what he did. No matter how risky his plans."

Indiya blinked. She didn't want to remember that far back. Too many memories lay buried there.

A change came about Grace; she softened and flashed her father's smile. "You didn't hear this from me," she said quietly, "but ever since my earliest memories, whenever Mother faced a hard choice, she always asked herself, what would Dad do?"

"Arun's gone," Indiya said firmly.

"And yet he always bounces back. Hey, maybe Greyhart has been rerolling the dice for Arun all these years until he lucks out enough to survive his mission. Maybe he's already made his killer roll, but it hasn't caught up with us yet. Or maybe your Littorane goddess wanted to keep playing with Dad for a little longer in her divine games. You can believe whatever you want, Admiral Indiya – I don't give a frozen frakk – but you should believe in *him*. Wherever he is, Dad will be fighting, trying to get back to you, and grumbling all the way. Don't give up on him."

Kreippil began bathing Indiya in a soothing flow of water from his tail sweeps. "The young human is correct," he said. "McEwan usually flounders, often in dark abyssal depths, and yet he always regains the surface."

"Stop saying that!" Indiya screamed. It was bad enough that they were trying to soothe her, but she could read the Littorane like a book and knew he was being deceitful. She knew why too. Oh, now it was becoming clear! Kreippil was glad to be rid of Arun. Indiya clamped her mouth and gills, and squeezed her eyes shut, trying to confine the rage within her.

These idiots who surrounded her could only see Arun as an icon, an idea – and maybe, in Kreippil's case, a rival – but Indiya had stuffed Arun's seventeen-year-old body into a cryopod and flushed out his blood to replace it with preserving fluids. She had seen him wither over the decades into a pain-filled old man, lonely and tired of life. Having been inside Arun's mind to help him out of the planning trance in which he'd determined the targets for *Karypsic* and *Saravanan*, Indiya suspected Lissa was really Springer back from the dead. Whatever physical comforts those two might offer each other, Arun and Indiya still relied on each other. The two of them had supported each other for so many centuries that they were like ancient lightning-blasted trees that had grown together, each needing the other to stand upright.

"He's gone," Indiya whispered and then the full horror of his loss slammed into her like a punch to the gut.

She bunched her fists, but that only seemed to focus and intensify the rage which spread through her and out into the world, haloing her in a flame of anger.

She felt her gills burn and her flesh boil.

Suddenly, she realized her physical pain was real, and reason reclaimed her sanity. Without daring to open her eyes, she connected her mind to the camera looking into her quarters, the same view shared with Grace. Indiya saw a distorted figure, clenched inwardly, but mercifully half concealed within a glistening shell of bubbles as her anger physically manifested to boil the water around her.

Kreippil was flapping his tail as hard as he could to circulate cooler water, and within seconds the water had shifted from dangerously scalding to merely hot. "Goddess protect us," he chanted. "Goddess protect us."

Indiya was okay. She'd lost her composure for a moment, that's all. Maybe it had been for the best, because she had no idea that the ever-present cloud of nanobots around her could produce such an extreme effect on the physical environment. Maybe she could use that as a weapon?

Arun was dead. Perhaps he'd lived his days out in the past with Lissa-Springer, but he was never coming back to the war. Indiya didn't have to pretend to anyone that surviving without him would be easy. All she had to do was lead the Legion to its final victory. Then she could fade to black.

The mental connection to the camera feed slipped away and she was forced to open her eyes.

"Admiral?" Grace's image was still there, displayed on the bulkhead, her face a mix of concern and alarm.

The woman's image flickered just long enough for Indiya to see a frown appear. Grace's mouth seemed to extend, her face grew hairier. Then Grace disappeared altogether, replaced by someone else.

Three eyes peered at Indiya down a jaw filled with fangs. "Goddess protect you?" sneered the Hardit. "Not this time, Kreippil."

*Tawfiq!*

# —— Chapter 11 ——

*Twenty-two years earlier. 2717AD.*

**Grace Lee-McEwan**
**Flight Deck.**
**Far Reach Dropship** *Karypsic.*
**Near Mars orbit**

The stars changed.

It was almost disappointing. The last time she'd traveled back in time, Grace had been frozen in cryo. And this time… she'd felt nothing. Not even a tingle in her stomach.

*Which is good*, she told herself, *because we've got a job to do.*

"Jackson, spool up the stealth engines and make us vanish pronto. Francini, using passive mode only, I want you to take a good, hard look at Mars. We just swapped a Human Legion fleet for a scattering of New Order bases."

She willed away the knot of tension she found in her shoulders. By her estimate, this was the most dangerous part of an audacious mission. If they lived through the next five minutes, they would have a fighting chance to get through to Tawfiq.

In order to blend into the surrounding environment, the stealth field generator needed to first *be* in that environment. And that left them vulnerable and visible while the systems reset themselves after the 22-year jump.

The other two flight crew, Jackson and Francini, went about their duties with calm professionalism, even though only Grace knew the nature of their mission, the need for secrecy having been paramount. No way in the world was she going to let herself be the only one who couldn't keep her cool.

Nonetheless, she had to take a deep breath to steady herself before asking, "Anything?"

"Stealth efficiency ten percent and rising," reported second-in-command, Ensign Andy Jackson. "We'll be like ghosts in twenty seconds."

"I'm getting low-level energy readings from beneath the Martian surface," said Petty Officer Massimo Francini from his station. "No spikes or pings."

"Good enough, thank you. Captain Lee-McEwan to all hands. I repeat, this is the captain to all hands. We have left Mars orbit in 2739 and emerged in the same position and velocity, relative to Mars, in 2317. The Legion Fleet we have left behind in the future, commanded by Admiral Indiya and General McEwan, has been heavily compromised by the New Order. They're riddled with some kind of surveillance nano plague they called the Blood Virus. That's why operational security has been so tight. None of you know what we're here to do, so listen up, because this is the big one. In four days, the survivors of the Earth Defense Force will rise up and make a strike against a key New Order facility in a city called Cairo. Our intelligence is that this will cause panic in the New Order high command who will be caught completely unprepared. Tawfiq will lock herself in her bunker while dispatching New Order reserves to meet the threat at Cairo. With communications severely disrupted by the attack, and rumors of uprisings, invasions and coups spreading like a virus, this is a unique moment of vulnerability for Tawfiq. Our task is to drop a strike team into the New Order capital of Victory City, where we shall take advantage of the confusion to kill Tawfiq Woomer-Calix and wipe out as much of the New Order high command as we can. If the situation permits, we shall wait and observe, to aid a general uprising should it occur and if we can make a material difference."

She gave her people a few moments to absorb the enormity of this vital mission. Just long enough for them to start asking themselves the question: why?

"Many years ago, at the gates of the imperial capital, the Human Legion split." She paused to consider her next words carefully. She hadn't been born then, but for many in the troop compartment the wounds from the rupture still festered. "Our dream was to push on beyond the frontier, and establish a new civilization, free of the Cull, at Far Reach. So why are we here in the Solar System? Given the painful memories of invading alien soldiers the Earth people have endured, only *Homo sapiens* personnel have been picked for this mission. That means for us, this is personal. This is the birthworld of our species, and yet I myself have asked, why should we help the world who gave away our ancestors as slave tributes? Here is my answer. If we don't stop Tawfiq in the twenty-eighth century, then the New Order will grow into an unstoppable plague that will one day engulf Far Reach. We are the descendants of a generation wronged by humankind. Let us right that wrong. Today we carry out this mission so that tomorrow our descendants – and, yes, the children of Earth too – shall walk the stars in freedom. That is all."

She glanced at the other flight crew, who appeared to have taken her words in their stride "Well?" she demanded of Jackson. "How did I do, Andy?"

"Very impressive," he replied, "although in my version of the future you're a general, not a captain."

She laughed. "Don't worry, Andy. We haven't screwed with history. I started off piloting boats like this. *Karypsic* might not be a ship of the line, but on a mission like this, she deserves to have a captain."

*Commanding a boat like this is also a position I know I've earned*, she thought, though she kept that to herself.

From the troop compartment, the commander of the Marine contingent chimed a comm request

"Go ahead, Morris."

"Captain, I mean no disrespect, but do I have the full picture here? I command three half squads of ten Marines. That's plenty enough to shoot the hell out of a few senior monkeys and blow up some high-value shit, but

68

you talked of supporting an uprising, a war of planetary liberation. I can do a lot with thirty Marines, ma'am, but that might be pushing it."

"My apologies, Lieutenant. You speak the truth. Once I decide we are safely clear of New Order listening posts on Mars, the command team will meet on the flight deck. But I will say this now. We are not alone in this endeavor, Lieutenant. We are one half of a pincer attack, and if the other mission succeeds, then our sister team will support us at Victory City."

"You mean the drop capsule? The one the flight techs were calling the *Saravanan*? You could maybe squeeze eight Marines in there, but they'd not have enough room to scratch their butts, let alone be fully equipped, not with all the real estate these time intercalators take up."

Grace grinned. "If I'm right, then those numbers will grow. By the time we hit Victory City, we should have millions of warriors by our side. We'll be hard pressed to give Tawfiq time to realize her defeat before she's torn limb from limb."

"Let's hope you're right, Captain. And if you're not, we still have thirty Far Reach Marines hungry to put an end to Tawfiq. She doesn't stand a chance."

"Amen to that, Lieutenant Morris."

Grace was relieved to sense the fragility to the lieutenant's bravado. Despite his words, he understood that this was not going to be easy.

But it had to be done.

———

Grace Lee-McEwan
*Karypsic*
Earth orbit

It took *Karypsic* four days to reach the target. The jump had shifted them 22 years into the past but kept them in the same location relative to Mars. However, Mars took nearly twice as long to orbit the Sun as Earth, and the two planets were now in very different positions relative to each other, meaning the dropship's journey to Earth took half the time it would have done in 2739. It was a small detail, but Grace was encouraged that the orbital arrangement of the planets matched the schedule Greyhart had described for the Battle of Cairo.

Boats of *Karypsic's* class normally launched an attack directly from orbit after disgorging from the bellies of larger craft. With a full troop compartment, and a journey time measured in days not hours, *Karypsic* was stuffed full of ripe bodies fired up for the attack but with nowhere to go.

But flare-ups were rare and they made the best use of their time in training and planning, with plenty of rest periods to enjoy games of poker, skat dice, and Danish murder. Alcohol, though, had been banned by Grace until their return.

Grace knew she wouldn't let these people down, and that included herself. This jaunt into Tawfiq's bunker was exactly the kind of escapade her parents had gotten up to in their youth, and she was determined to live up to their reputation, daunting though that would be to most people.

But she was Grace Lee-McEwan.

She wasn't most people.

Hour by hour, the blue planet of their ancestors grew larger in the viewscreens on every bulkhead. Grew larger in the minds of everyone aboard *Karypsic* too, as the moment of their reckoning with Tawfiq drew near.

They slipped through the orbital defenses, directly under the enemy's snouts, then dropped through the air their distant ancestors had once breathed.

To make a stealthed descent while neither burning up in flames, nor revealing your position, required exceptional piloting skills, and Grace knew she was the best in the fleet. They dropped safely below cloud cover, heading east over night-time Central Asia.

"The ground... it's lifeless," remarked Jackson. "I can hardly see anything."

"We're traveling through the night," Francini pointed out.

**Corporal O'Hanlon**
**Vengeance Squad**
**Approaching Victory Obelisk**

Gliding through the crisp early morning air in his Armored Combat Exoskeleton (Scout-variant), O'Hanlon was struck with the serene beauty of the place. Jumping out of a dropship in ACE armor was normally a loud and frantic experience, what with the fire coming up to swat you out the sky and the rain of dirt thrown up by explosions. True, this Victory Mall was peppered with shell holes, but that was from the New Order invasion many years ago, and they'd been softened into well-tended flowerbeds and the whole area grassed over. The only thing he could hear outside of his suit was a squadron of ducks coming in to land on the rectangular pool of water that stretched out to the west. And with his two buddies who'd dropped with him running silent, it appeared to be just him and the ducks.

This place wouldn't stay serene for long, though. Not if he had anything to do with it.

But first they had to take the obelisk.

He bled off speed and flung his hands wide as he smacked into the white marble about halfway up on the east side. Despite all the incredible stealth tech on the ACE-6(S) suit, as he waited for his grip to firm, he could still hear two soft slaps as Jintu and Bryan landed a little farther down the obelisk.

Then they were scurrying like geckos up the outside of the sheer tower, taking just over two minutes to get into position.

After he'd ascended a hundred feet, he deviated to the side of the pillar to check they were still unobserved.

Yep. Still just him, the ducks, and beyond the pool of water was the white marble of the target. Of the *Karypsic* there was not a sign… until the ducks suddenly ruffled their feathers, and gentle ripples spread out along the pool despite the absence of wind. The disturbance persisted for a few seconds before serenity claimed the scene once more. And that was the only sign that a 245-ton dropship laden with Marines had passed over.

That boat still gave him goose bumps

They'd come a long way since the crude drop pods the White Knights had begrudged their human Marines when he'd first started in this business.

He felt a hand bump into his foot and set off again for the top. Took him thirty seconds.

There were observation ports cut into the pyramid atop the obelisk. O'Hanlon stretched a finger just below the lip of the eastern one and extended an invisible camera from the fingertip.

Inside was a hollowed-out space. Looked like there had originally been a complex honeycomb structure, but that had been taken out for renovations being carried out to Hardit tastes. O'Hanlon couldn't give a frakk about the fancy leather strips that covered the floor, or fake rocks glued to the wall that would make it look like an underground cavern once they had been painted. But he did approve of their redesign: the open space meant he could look out both viewports at the same time, and he could also see the place was deserted.

He hauled himself into the open space and activated an SBN secure battle net link to the other two Marines.

"Set up the M-cannon at the west viewpoint," he instructed, and began retrieving components of the crew-served gun from the storage area inside his ACE-6(S).

"What kind of perverted frakks chose this for their carpet?" said Bryan.

Now the SBN was active, he could see her outline painted in his HUD busy unloading her part of the gun, just as they'd all trained on the way over from Mars. "Keep your mind on your task, Bryan. Let's get this baby operational before we start thinking of a chat over coffee and donuts, eh? It's just… *leather*…"

But it wasn't. He saw now that the rectangular strips of leather hadn't been dyed different shades of white and brown. They hadn't been dyed at all. It was human skin.

"Makes no difference," O'Hanlon growled, slotting together segments of the gun's tripod. "We're here to kill Hardits, and that's what we're gonna do."

"New Order Hardits, Corporal," Bryan pointed out.

She was young; born after the Legion split. But she'd learn. "I never met a Hardit I liked," he told her, "except ones I'd killed first. That's all I'm saying. Now, help Jintu activate the targeting system while I fix the barrel."

Another twenty seconds and the M-cannon was ready to fire.

Captain had ordered them to keep hidden, to keep their powder dry until she told them the time was ready to unleash on the enemy.

But O'Hanlon and his crew were ready now.

Boy, was he ready.

―――――

**Sergeant Kraken**
**Arrow Squad**
**Flying west over target zone**

"Arrow Squad, jump!"

A hole irised beneath Sergeant Kraken's boots and he fell through the underside of the *Karypsic*, the camo extrusion field sucking at him as he passed through.

Immediately, the squad SBNet established itself, and while his ACE suit sensors scouted for the presence of hostiles, he mentally called out the names of his squad that his HUD had found and labeled: Malgra, Fallaw, Spurrell, Raschid, Malinga, Bunny, Zsoldos, Thongsuk, and his sister, Giant.

The two siblings had grown up into the war. It was all they had ever known but they had survived it all, even a decade serving in Lee Xin's personal special ops team that had once rescued Arun McEwan from right under Tawfiq's ugly snout. And now they were jumping to end Tawfiq in the past, and on a mission commanded by the daughter of those two Legion generals.

It was a crazy galaxy, all right. He bit his lip and let his gaze rest over the pale blue outline his HUD was painting him of Giant falling like deadly snow.

She'd survived the war, but the cancer she'd developed in her second-tier brain augments would soon be the death of her.

"Will you look at that?" Giant said over a private channel. "Makes me wanna hurl."

She was painting the target in his HUD, the entry point down into the Hardit burrows where they hoped to find and kill Tawfiq. *I know you wanna get her real bad, sis, but you don't need to tell me where we're headed.*

But then Kraken saw what she meant. Their intelligence had been patchy; all they knew was to head for a statue of a seated figure set in a shrine behind a marble colonnade. Nothing prepared them for the sight in real life. Tawfiq Woomer-Calix sprawled arrogantly in a massive seat, glaring with contempt out of her three alien eyes at this human world, daring all to defy her.

"We're on it," he told her. "Tawfiq ends here, today."

By the time Kraken hit the ground, his knees bending only slightly to absorb the gentle impact, he had already read the ground and made minor updates to his squad's deployment orders by thinking them to his AI. Within seconds they'd all landed safely and were racing west to secure the target.

———

**Corporal Giant**
**At the base of the Tawfiq Memorial**

Giant hugged the white marble in the northeast corner of the temple her HUD labeled as the Tawfiq Memorial, keeping overwatch on the approach across the parkland from the north. Why the crazy monkey-frakk would name a memorial after herself when she wasn't yet dead made no sense, but was an inconsistency Giant's team was eager to correct.

76

In the distance she could see a few lights in human civilian buildings that must have predated the invasion. It felt strange to think that out there so close were human civilians, and that at the end of her life she would come home to Earth of all places.

*Earth was never my home*, she reminded herself.

She shook her head and groaned as a lance of agony shot through the diseased parts of her brain.

"You okay?" asked Fallaw, from his position twenty-five feet away.

"What's that Fallaw? You want to take me out for a coffee to cheer me up? Keep your eyes on the prize."

He was a good kid, Reed Fallaw, but he needed to stop worrying about her. She had wanted to run this mission with clean veins, but it looked like it wasn't going to be. She allowed her suit to administer a limited dose of targeted pain meds.

She took a moment to study the overhead view of the target area, which occupied the bottom-left section of her HUD.

Behind her and Fallaw, through the colonnade and up the steps to the central area of Tawfiq's temple were two hostiles. Her brother and the rest of the central team would have them in their sights, but no one was making a move until the enemy sensor system protecting the memorial had been taken out of action.

The two Hardits began to pace, perhaps feeling a chill in the early morning air, their muscles cramped after a long stretch of sentry duty. Giant waited patiently for the cyber team to finish their business.

*No hurry, guys. We've nothing better to do here.*

Tech-Corporal Malgra would be launching nano-infiltration raids on cameras, wiring and wireless data traffic channels, but Spurrell was the team genius, and didn't he know it? Brent Spurrell could code slice through alien software stacks and decrypt his way into the vengeful heart of an incoming missile and turn it upon its firer. If only he hadn't devoted his life to inflicting the most humiliating so-called practical jokes in the entire Far Reach Fleet.

"And the monkeys are blind!" announced Spurrell. "Thank you and goodnight."

"Way to go, code boy," said Kraken. "Take overwatch from Giant and Fallaw. Giant, when you're ready, let the fun and games commence."

As soon as they were relieved, Giant led Fallaw to creep up the stone steps of this obscene temple and advance on the two Hardits.

They were Janissaries, a bioengineered development of the Hardits optimized for war, just the same as the Far Reach team would seem like inhuman monsters to the civilians beginning to wake up around them in Victory City. They wore hooded cloaks in a brightly striped fabric that looked so fine that it wouldn't keep out a light breeze, let alone a volley of railgun darts, but Giant knew looks were often deceptive in the case of the Hardits. New Order armor cloaks were highly effective, and their secret had yet to be fully unraveled by Far Reach techs.

No matter, she knew how to deal with these jerks.

Keeping a wide berth, Fallaw and Giant walked behind the Janissaries, ignoring the stubby pulse guns the aliens kept at port arms.

Walking in front of the enemy's guns and trusting that your scout model Armored Combat Exosuit would hide you was something she had long become accustomed to. The suits and the AIs inside them were an integral part of the squad, and for the squad to operate effectively, everyone had to trust everyone else to do their job. If you couldn't trust your comrade or your equipment, you wouldn't last long as a scout.

Even so, Giant was sweating when she took up position directly behind one of the Hardits.

She had to wait a moment for her hands to stop shaking, then she withdrew the hardened ceramic needle sheath, which immediately compromised her scout suit's stealth integrity. Over to her right, she saw a similar needle appear out of nowhere near the virtual outline of Reed Fallaw. Any Hardit eyes watching would see this. The risk level just ratcheted up a notch. But the two tired Janissary guards kept their eyes facing outward, seeing nothing, despite the Far Reach team out beyond the memorial steps waiting for them to die.

Giant plunged the needle through the weak point at the base of the Hardit skull and up into the brain areas responsible for forming scent and speech communication. She clamped her arm around the alien, crushing its attempts to escape. It was screaming inside its head, but Giant knew her business and the parts of its brain it needed to scream out its mouth or omit a pheromone call of distress no longer functioned.

Giant released her arm and the Janissary fell to the marble floor, writhing. She let it be. No one would hear or smell it die.

Over to the right, Fallaw had dispatched his guard with equal efficiency.

"Clear," she said.

As Kraken, Raschid, Thongsuk, and Bunny ran up the stairs and into the memorial building, Giant and Fallaw unsnapped the carbines from their backs and advanced on the stone edifice that was supposed to represent Tawfiq's domination of the Earth. Close up, she could tell the marble from which Tawfiq was hewn didn't match that of her chair, which looked suited for humans not Hardits, although her tail poked through a hole cut into its rear. Makes sense, Giant decided. There must once have been a human figure that Tawfiq had replaced.

Giant's steps faltered when she wondered who would replace Tawfiq on that seat. President Lee? Maybe General McEwan or one of the Jotun commanders?

"I don't intend to live long enough to find out," she muttered to herself.

"Say again?" queried Fallaw.

"Just thinking," she replied. "My generation's done enough. It's only fair if we leave some thorny problems for you youngsters to figure out."

"Let's kill Tawfiq first."

"Copy that. It's what we're here to do. Ahh… bingo!"

Behind the statue's plinth was a thing of beauty: a trapdoor that led down to the Hardit warren. If their intel was right about this entrance, then it should lead them to Tawfiq's current location – locked up tight in her personal quarters about 1000 feet to the northwest and 150 feet down.

Malgra and Thongsuk worked their magic to melt the bolts and hinges locking the door in place.

"Hold position," called Lieutenant Morris. "I'm deploying with Blaze Squad." Giant's HUD lit up with markers for the officer and ten Marines of Blaze, plus an object of interest tagged with the label PFT: Present for Tawfiq.

They didn't have the numbers to take and hold the Victory City warren. This was a different type of operation; Arrow was to secure the entrance and Blaze would go kill Tawfiq. Failing that, they would give Tawfiq her 50 kiloton present, and get the hell outta there.

"Do it!" said Morris. Malgra and Thongsuk shook the door free of its hinges and picked it up. Giant peered down the hole and saw an elevator shaft. Within seconds, Spurrell had a hovercam inside and announced the lobby beyond the elevator was clear.

"You take point," said her brother.

In all the years they'd served together as brother and sister, they'd always watched out for each other, but they'd never given the other special favors. This time was different. Kraken had made sure she would take the lead, and everyone in the team knew why.

"Unlucky for you this is my last mission, Tawfiq," she said. "There's just one more achievement I want to unlock, and it's got your name on it."

With that, Giant jumped down the lift shaft.

---

**Grenadier Reed Fallaw**
**Beneath the Tawfiq Memorial.**

With a dull metallic clang, Reed landed beside Giant on top of the elevator cab. Together, they efficiently melted through its roof and jumped below into monkey territory, trusty SA-71s out and ready to blast the vile creatures into bloody scraps of pelt.

The place was clear, though, just as the hovercam had promised. It was a lobby, a clean and open space about fifty feet square with a broad corridor leading away to the north. Reed let his suit scan for explosives and signs of surveillance. He discovered neither.

"Cover the exit," said Giant as she took a moment to confer with the Marines topside.

Reed obeyed, covering the corridor with his carbine. The light was low but plenty enough to see that there were no monkey-vecks to shoot yet.

*Monkeys.* Reed cursed silently. The older Marines – Giant in particular – were old school in their attitude to Hardits. As Giant was fond of saying, the only good Hardit was skinned and used as a rug in a high-traffic area. But Reed had known Far Reach Hardits. There weren't many, and he couldn't say he liked them, but they were fair in their own way. He couldn't summon up the same kind of hatred for Hardits as a race, but he reminded himself of the tales he'd heard of Janissary atrocities.

*Murdering skangat Janissaries! Yeah that will do.*

Orange targeting brackets appeared in his HUD, indicating a possible threat. Then they turned red and a Hardit walked into view at the far end of the passageway.

"Contact!" he confirmed to Giant, though she should be seeing a threat warning in her own HUD.

"What's it doing?" asked the veteran corporal.

With a thought, he communicated his interest to his ACE suit, which magnified the image of the hooded Janissary walking toward him. It wore baggy fabric clothing and was armed with a pistol slung around its hips. In one hand it carried a cup of a steaming beverage and in the other was a small cannister with a short tube projecting from its lid.

"Er, Corporal, I think it's come out for a coffee and a…"

The Hardit plunged the tube into its nostril and snorted.

"And to indulge in recreational pharmaceuticals."

81

"That will be tarngrip tea chaser and a snort of halo dust," said Giant. "Waste the veck!"

Reed gave the murdering skangat a triple-tap to its head.

To counter the insufficient penetrating power of carbine darts against the latest Janissary armor weave, the Far Reach team had set their guns to automatically fire a rapid three-round burst. With the recoil suppression on max, the rounds would impact at almost the same point, and battlefield experience had shown this to be more effective than a single round of higher momentum. But whatever the creature in Reed's sights had been wearing, it wasn't armor fabric because it went down with barely a grunt, and both head and hood in tatters. Steaming tarngrip tea spilled onto the floor, mixing with its drinker's blood.

Reed and Giant advanced up the corridor, each of them alternately providing overwatch while the other rushed ahead. They made rapid progress, attaching sticky signal repeater nodes to the walls to keep the SBN link to the rest of the team via secure line-of-sight microwave beams. The progress was so rapid, that soon they were passing junctions and doorways that they simply swept past, making Reed's heart beat faster every time. There was no time to check for the enemy along every side passage, not enough Marines to hold the ground with any certainty even if they did.

Giant pushed on at a relentless pace. At first, Reed let himself be pulled along in the wake of her ferocious urge to close on Tawfiq. But with his HUD overlays bringing home that they were increasingly isolated from the rest of the Arrows who had also entered the burrow, nerves worried at his mind. Arrow Squad's role was to secure a way through to Tawfiq, not to take her out themselves. Had Giant gone off plan?

Reed was in the process of finding the right form of words to tell Giant to slow the frakk down, without getting a ceramic needle shoved through his visor, when she raised a hand, signaling him to halt.

She backed up a few paces, so she could touch suits with him and communicate by pulsed van de Waals forces, an ultra-secure comms channel.

"Keep to the plan," she said. It wasn't just words she was sharing; his HUD now highlighted the BEFOIs she'd spotted: Battlezone Environment Features of Interest. In this case, they were viewing slits cut into the walls. A HUD text remark pointed out that the air beyond those slits was rich with Hardit scent.

"Guard post?" Reed suggested.

"Or defensive chokepoint. I want you to stow your carbine and rely on your ACE magic to get us through."

"Shouldn't we check with Sergeant Kraken?"

Reed regretted the words the moment they left his lips. Interfering with the brother-sister dynamic was like poking a nest of vipers with your dick to see what would happen next, except ten times as dangerous.

"It's a fair question," Giant replied, though she said it as if she wanted to rip his limbs off. Slowly. "But I trust the sergeant's competence. He will be observing our situation through SBNet, and he's said nothing."

"Then I'm good to go," said Reed as he deactivated his carbine and snapped it onto his back. His suit absorbed the weapon.

For thousands of years, teams of alien techs from across the White Knight Empire had developed the forerunner of Reed's SA-71 carbine to work alongside the ACE exosuits. The suit's stealth capabilities extended to the gun, but the weapon remained a weak point in the endless battle to avoid detection, and any form of camouflage was only as strong as its weakest element. Legion and Far Reach techs had recently started to redevelop the old stealth tech – as had the New Order – and one improvement was to snap the carbine diagonally across the wearer's back and let the exosuit swaddle the weapon with invisibility.

It made a big improvement to your chances of remaining undetected, but if you needed to fire your gun in a hurry… then it didn't feel like such an improvement.

Fighting the urge to crouch low beneath the view slits – he knew it would make no difference – Reed walked along the passageway, clenching his fists to give his hands something to do.

They followed the corridor as it veered left and saw it terminate in a room filled with Janissaries and protected by a heavy blast door.

The Hardits seemed to be chatting amongst themselves happily, and given the strength of the musky odor that permeated Reed's helmet, this guard room – if that was its role – was permanently occupied.

And the reason Reed could tell all this... the blast door was wide open.

Giant tapped a hand onto his shoulder to allow a little van de Waals chatter. "If that's not an invitation," she said, "I don't know what is."

"Doesn't feel right. There's supposed to be a major attack, an armed uprising. Shouldn't they be on high alert?"

"Monkey-frakkers are the most ill-disciplined scum in existence. Give soldiering a bad name all over the galaxy."

Reed couldn't argue with that. Even so, this seemed too easy. Of course, with the blast door open, they could simply toss in a few fraggers and watch the bloodied fur fly. But if Giant wasn't suggesting that, then he wouldn't either.

"Copy that," he said. "So... we're just gonna walk right through that guard room and out the other side?"

"No, Fallaw. We're going to shoot the bad guys, but we're going to do it in such a way that we slaughter them before they know what's happening – before they can set off an alert. Once we're in, you head to the southwest corner, and I'll take southeast. On my mark, unsnap your SA-71 and we'll introduce the frakkers to a Far Reach crossfire."

Reed would feel a whole lot better tossing in a few grenades, but you never knew what you'd be walking into when you followed up your bombardment.

"What's the matter?" Giant asked. "Haven't you got the balls, Grenadier?"

"Sure I do. Maybe not like yours, Giant, but plenty enough for those monkeys. I just like throwing things first. Guess it's more than just my job title."

With every step Reed took closer to the guard post, the Hardit noises grew ever louder: low growls and long sighs blown down lupine snouts to vibrate rubbery Hardit lips. The translator system in his suit didn't volunteer a translation, which was no surprise because the Hardit language was continually splitting and its branches evolving into new forms. He was no expert on Hardit social norms, but they appeared relaxed to him. But for sentries in the middle of an uprising? Giant was right, they were an embarrassment to the soldiering profession.

By the time he'd walked over the blast door threshold, he was convinced the Janissaries' slovenly attitude was not a trick. Two of the Hardits were sitting in comfortable chairs, guns in their laps, seeming to watch Reed and Giant's approach but seeing nothing.

Another pair sat by the only visible exit, another open blast door that sloped down to the northeast.

A clear path through the cluttered guard post connected the two exits, wide enough for two Hardits to pass abreast. It passed at the center of the room through a transparent archway that looked to Reed like a 3D view-tank, and was displaying brightly colored ribbons slowly threading through each other.

Reed realized he'd hesitated with one boot rooted where the blast door's frame was sunk into the earth. He took a deep breath, and then advanced two clear steps into the room.

The sentries didn't react, and neither did the other Hardits, some of whom were drinking and chatting gruffly, but mostly they were staring at the ribbon patterns in the central archway. They reminded Reed of the soporific patterns you watched at night to distract you from the nightmares, but the aliens had ears erect and noses quivering with keen interest.

He was falling behind Giant, who was already halfway to the southeast corner of the room. So he sped up, giving the Janissaries as wide a berth as he could, which wasn't much because they were all around him.

Suddenly, the Janissaries came to life with roars, growls and hissing.

Spinning to face the center of the room, Reed reached behind to unsnap his carbine, but stopped just in time. The ribbons on the view-arch had frozen in place, and despite the species boundary, he understood immediately what he was seeing. Half the aliens were howling in delight, their tails high and lashing from side to side. Meanwhile the others had tails down and were fishing out plastic chits to hand to their happier comrades.

*Gambling.*

*A universal vice*, Reed thought. *I love it. Whoever said gambling's bad for your health obviously never went traipsing through an enemy guard post. Last chance to lay your bets, Janissary jackwads. This den's getting busted!*

The guards settled down and Reed hurried to his target position, but the final steps were almost blocked. To his right a pair of seated Hardits were enjoying mugs of tea, and to his left another was perched on a metal cabinet stripping and now reassembling its rifle. The gap between them was just arm's length.

His heart was thundering so hard that he was surprised the Hardits couldn't hear it with their sensitive ears. *Call yourself a grenadier?* he admonished himself. *Get the job done.*

Reed turned clockwise through ninety degrees and sidestepped through the Hardits.

With his knees almost brushing the chair where one was sitting, a sudden change came through the room and his heart seemed to stop. The Hardit in front of him shot to its feet.

Reed backed up just a few inches and reached for the needle that had put paid to the Janissary at the topside memorial. It wasn't much of a weapon, but he wanted its faster draw.

But he realized the Hardit hadn't seen or smelled him. It was gesturing at the archway with its tail as were many of its fellows. Reed chanced a look. The gambling show was over, replaced by a montage of images from an outdoor urban location of sunbaked and dilapidated human buildings. Soldiers in brown and green camo battledress were spilling out of a mix of civilian and military wheeled vehicles. They were humans. Smaller than

Marines like Reed, but he noted the determination on their faces and the familiarity with which they carried their weapons.

*So this is the Cairo uprising. No wonder the aliens weren't on high alert, we arrived too early.*

As he sidestepped away, he heard a roar of triumph directed at the battle scenes. His suit chimed in with a translation: "Humans die good!"

*Not as good as you butchering skangats.*

He was past the chair now, and about to take the final few steps to the position Giant had assigned him, when he felt something clatter against his back and saw the ears of every Hardit twitch at the noise.

*Frakk!*

Every Hardit snout turned his way.

But Reed Fallaw wasn't hanging around to make polite introductions; he'd already flung his head back and felt the satisfying meaty smack against a Hardit head. Before the Janissary who had stumbled into his back could react, Reed crouched low and spun around like an ice skater so he could bring his needle around and stab it into the Hardit's flank.

The alien didn't look like it was in uniform, but its clothes must have been spun from armor weave because Reed's needle snapped in two. It didn't even drop the gun that it had accidentally whacked against Reed's back.

Undeterred, he dropped the useless needle and stood up, thrusting from his exomuscle-enhanced hips as he grabbed the Hardit by its throat and lifted his arms to fling the vile creature back over his head. He overcooked it, though, and sent his foe flying up to bounce off the ceiling. No matter. That would do for now.

Janissary rounds sizzled through the air just over his head as he hit the deck, sliding away along the tiled floor on his belly like a penguin. By the time he slammed against the wall, he had unsnapped his SA-71 from his back and was bringing it around to the side. With a scrambling flip through one-eighty he was sitting back up against the wall with his carbine rails charging and pointing at the mass of Janissaries who were belatedly closing the blast doors, but still didn't know what they were facing. The ACE-6(S) was a dream.

"Ready with the lullabies?" queried Giant who was in the opposite corner, her presence not yet suspected by the Hardits.

"Ready as hell."

"Light 'em up, Grenadier!"

Giant was firing before she even finished speaking. With the ACE suits still stealthed, a human enemy would struggle to see where the fire was coming from, but Hardit hearing was on another level. They turned around to the corner where Giant sang them lullabies to endless sleep, and as they moved to face Giant's withering fire, Reed opened up with his own song.

Triple-tap lullaby darts left the muzzle of his carbine at 4600 feet per second, the relatively low speed being the cost paid for the near-perfect noise suppression. Even the normal muzzle flash of ionized air was absorbed into invisibility by the magic of the SA-71. Lullabies weren't a distinct round, but a different firing mode of the carbine itself. And they were damned effective.

The ammo bulb was uncannily abundant, and the recoil dampener a work of genius. Reed felt the mule kick of Janissary rounds hitting him, but the incoming fire was inaccurate because the enemy only knew his rough location, and with the doors now shut, there was nowhere for them to run.

Reed sat on his butt and took down any Hardit who looked about to fire his way. Then he took out any that weren't.

"I can see you," said Giant when the Hardits were all down and had stopped twitching.

*Damn!* He switched out his HUD overlays for a moment and saw himself in real-sight. When had those chunks been taken out of the armor on his thigh and shoulder? He ran a suit diagnostic. At least its basic functionality was still registering green, although armor integrity was compromised and stealth lost. "Can't detect any alarms," he said. "Do you think their weapons fire was overheard?"

A threat alarm icon flashed in his right peripheral vision and he twisted to face it.

There was a camouflaged door set flush against the wall ten feet to his right. Of course! It must lead to the spy holes they'd seen looking out onto the main passage.

The door was open a fraction, just enough for three yellow eyes to peer out from a Janissary surveying the slaughter Reed and Giant had made of its comrades.

Before he could finish getting to his feet, those sulfurous eyes focused their hate at Reed.

He reacted on impulse, lifting his right arm and firing his wrist-mounted micro-grenades through the doorway crack.

The Hardit slammed the door shut. Too late. The grenades it had shut inside exploded, shaking the guard post so violently, it kicked out a thick cloud of dust and dirt.

"Hmmm. Do you think they overheard that?" remarked Giant wryly.

"I can't help it, Corporal. I'm a grenadier."

"Guess nobody's perfect," she replied, gesturing for him to check there were no survivors while she covered the other two exits. "Giant to Kraken," she said, looping in Reed, "we seem to have revealed our position."

"No kidding," replied Sergeant Kraken. "We're right behind. Hold that position. Raschid and Spurrell will reinforce you. Then Blaze Squad will ghost through and move against the target."

"Roger that," said Giant.

The race to kill Tawfiq was on!

––––––

**Captain Grace Lee-McEwan**
**Holding station near the Tawfiq Memorial.**

"Well, this is fun," said Grace to *Karypsic's* flight crew. "Anyone think to bring some dice to play while we wait?" Even as she joked, she kept watch

89

on the tactical map showing Morris and Blaze Squad progressing deeper into the Hardit warren, and worried about the implications of the apparent absence of any support from her father's forces.

Ensign Jackson's signature belly laugh erupted from the co-pilot's seat. "Isn't this operation a gamble big enough for you General…? Sorry, *Captain?*"

*No*, she thought. *Not when my father took on the White Knight Empire with a few dozen half-trained Marines. And won.* But she pushed that idea down deep. The lives of her personnel were not hers to risk, and neither was the mission objective.

"Just messing with you," she said instead. "We've traveled back in time to kill Tawfiq in her own bunker. Anyone would think that was putting you on edge."

"Captain," said Francini who was plugged into the long-range sensors, "I'm picking up an energy spike below ground."

"Weapons fire?"

"Negative. Wrong signature. Also, it's deeper than our teams should be. And moving… moving toward Blaze Squad."

Grace hooked into Francini's view. *That looks bad.*

"Lethal Dancer this is Tawfiq's Bane. We're seeing an energy pattern below your depth consistent with maglev transportation headed your way from southwest. Over."

"Chodballs," replied Lieutenant Morris with feeling. "We don't see anything."

"Whatever it is has passed below you and is coming to a halt," said Grace with half her mind on the decision that might soon come her way. Did she abort and pull her team out while she still could?

"Lethal Dancer, how copy?" she asked when the lieutenant didn't reply. "Morris?"

"It's no use," said Jackson, "we've lost all comms except to the gun team in the obelisk. It's a jamming field."

Grace began rising *Karypsic* higher above the pool, heading for the roof of this fake temple to Tawfiq. "Jackson, update gun team on our situation. Captain to troop compartment. Get ready to drop with signal wire onto the memorial roof. You will secure that position and reestablish signals with Arrow and Blaze."

"Roger that," replied Sergeant Chen who commanded the Vengeance Squad reserve. "We're good for drop."

Below the *Karypsic*, the white stone steps of the memorial looked empty to Grace. With comms lost, Blaze Squad was as invisible to her as hopefully they were to the enemy, but she was reassured that there were no signs of the New Order either. "Ready to drop in 4… 3… 2… 1… Drop!"

---

**Sergeant Simpson**
**Blaze Squad. Nearing Tawfiq's quarters**

An urgent threat indicator pulled Sergeant Martin Simpson's head to his left and his SA-71 to his shoulder. Range 100 yards, four Hardits were dashing for safety along a cross corridor. They didn't make it.

Before Simpson could get off a shot, Salas acting as flank guard took them out with four triple-tap bursts. It seemed the Janissaries had not yet found a way to see an ACE-6(S) whose wearer wanted to stay hidden.

"This is only gonna get harder," Simpson growled to himself as he waved his squad onward, ever onward, toward Tawfiq. The relatively straight lines of the passageways beneath the memorial statue had turned into a nightmare warren of twisting confusion, with Janissary stragglers frequently darting just out of sight. Marine fire would catch a few, but after their initial shock at this human invasion, they would now be rallying. And as for the report from the captain that there might be reinforcements arriving deep beneath the ground…

"Keep moving!" urged Simpson and Lieutenant Morris simultaneously.

They advanced into tunnels that sloped deeper beneath the ground and became colder and darker. Simpson kept to the rear, continually assigning and reassigning his Marines to watch the many side tunnels they passed, and through which he fully expected Janissaries to emerge at any second. Lieutenant Morris took point with Garst and Tompkins, picking their way through the tunnels to Tawfiq. At the squad's center, pushing on a hover trolley, were Jones and Khatri. They would need luck to put a dart through Tawfiq's ugly skull today. The Marines had all acknowledged that, ever since the General had declared she was a captain for the duration and that they were going to win the Legion's battle with the Hardits before it had even started. Which was why they were bringing Tawfiq a present, just in case. A six-hundred-kiloton, quick-prime, cardioid blast pattern thermonuclear gift. Morris had even stuck on a gift tag.

Salas spotted movement and opened fire, missing. The defenders were grouping, and Simpson was convinced their response wouldn't be long coming. He looked at the PFT. It didn't look much, more like an oversized equipment crate with a simple control panel on its side. If they primed it ready to blow, getting out alive could get very tricky, which was why Blaze Squad were all volunteers. Even before they had known their mission, they had their reasons for being here, and none of those reasons mattered anymore.

"Update from Arrow Squad," said Lieutenant Morris over Squad Net, "signal wire is dropping down from the sky. Brace yourselves, Marines, looks like the captain's connecting us up and we'll soon have to endure her unique sense of humor."

Simpson grinned and tried not to be distracted by memories of the pranks Grace Lee-McEwan had played, but when his HUD reported a change to connection status it took him a few moments to register what it actually said.

= *Warning! Connection lost.* =

They hadn't re-established a link to *Karypsic*; they were now cut off from Arrow squad too!

He saw the other Marines falter – just half a step, but he knew these people and he saw the hope that they would make it out alive take a body blow.

"Simpson, I intend to ignore the other teams and press forward with all speed," the lieutenant said on a private channel. "Do you concur?"

Simpson made himself think through the limited options, because he knew Morris was seeking a genuine second opinion. "For all we know," he replied, "we'll hit less resistance pushing forward than heading back to the Arrows. I'm sure we're carrying these Fermi drills on our backs for a reason, sir. Once we've killed Tawfiq, we can drill an escape route up to the surface. It's our best chance. I concur, we press on."

"Thank you, Sergeant. I do hope we are not on a wild goose chase. The captain was extremely evasive about the source of our intel."

"We must be getting close," called Garst from a hundred yards up the passageway, "come take a look at this."

Simpson accepted the option displayed on his HUD to look through Garst's helmet-cam view. The passageways had increasingly begun to look like underground caverns hewn by pick and hammer through the bedrock, and here at a fork in the route, the left-hand path was marked by a pair of rocks protruding from each wall. To anyone approaching the fork, they displayed a pattern of three interlocking ovals made from glistening white crystals. The lower two were stretched wide into teardrop shapes, while the upper oval was smoothly symmetrical. The pattern was instantly recognizable: Hardit eyes. They looked as if they had been grown within the natural rock for millions of years.

Suddenly, the ground shook with the throb of a powerful motor close by. Simpson shook away Garst's cam view and kept still so his suit could identify the source of the noise. It seemed to be coming from below, but with this confusing environment, even the 6(S) could tell him no more. Then a metallic clang, like battleship hangar doors closing, brought the motor's rumble to a shuddering halt.

They ran down the left-hand path.

---

## Sergeant Simpson

"Almost there," cried Morris. "Just a little farther. It's a race against time now."

Simpson was backpedaling now; it slowed him down, but it meant he could face any attacks from the rear.

He gasped in surprise. Less than 30 feet away, a Hardit snout appeared in the passageway they had traveled through moments earlier. It looked straight through him. Frakk! Janissaries using stealth tech good enough to defeat his ACE-6(S). They could be all around him!

Then the flared tip of a tail materialized and pointed at the rest of the Blazers. With a sickening lurch in his gut, he knew what had attracted its attention.

Of course, the Hardits couldn't see through the human stealth tech any more than Simpson could see through theirs. But there was one party that was sitting out this little game of hide and seek in clear view of everyone: the Present for Tawfiq.

"I'll buy you some time," he said. "Kaur, you're with me."

"Good hunting," said Morris.

Simpson and Kaur retraced their steps halfway to the point where the Hardits had appeared, and now vanished once more.

"You ready?" Simpson checked of the grenadier.

"Yes," she replied with relish. "I've loaded nano penetrators, standard fraggers, concealment nerve clouds, and a flash bang to blind the little bastards."

"Just the way the Hardits love it. I'll fire first, and then you bombard on my mark. As soon as you've finished, we hightail it out."

"Copy that," said Kaur.

Simpson fired from the hip, not using his railgun this time, but the SA-71's x-ray beam mode. It was a bastard for draining his ACE's energy cell from the connector plugged into his suit, and it didn't deliver much stopping power, but as he counted to three while spraying the passageway with his ultra-high-energy directed beam, he was slaughtering the fancy tech the Hardits were hiding behind.

It worked! A comically surprised line of Janissaries appeared, hiding behind white plastic shields in an overlapping wall. Twenty yards behind the shield wall, the passageway was filled with nervous rifle-wielding Janissaries. By the way they looked at each other, they were suddenly wondering why their technology was failing all around them.

"Fire!"

At her sergeant's command, Grenadier Kaur launched a salvo of grenades from the launchers mounted around her wrists, which she held high as if she were about to dive off a cliff. Blinding flash bangs tuned to wreak maximum havoc with delicate Hardit vision burst simultaneously with nano shredders, which were designed to score tiny gashes through armor and facemasks, not that these Janissaries seem to have either. A second later, conventional fraggers sent shards of exotic metals through the enemy, and thick orange gas choked the passage with its poison.

Simpson and Kaur turned to run but were overcome by the hot wind that threw them 20 feet along the floor on their bellies. Once he'd caught his breath and waited for the thunder to stop echoing in his skull, Simpson checked they were both okay. Their suits were reporting no serious damage to themselves or their wearers, although Simpson had drained his power cell by his x-ray fire so much that his stealth mode had failed.

"Reckon the blast was constrained by the enemy's own shield wall. Eh, Sarge?" said Kaur as she got to her feet.

"I knew that," Simpson replied with a grin. "What, you thought I was bringing you on a suicide mission?"

Laughing, they raced away to join the others.

———

## Sergeant Simpson

"Breach team, go!" ordered Lieutenant Morris as Simpson and Kaur caught up with the rest of the squad. They were trapped at the end of the passageway, their progress halted by a shutter that carried the same stylized Hardit eyes as before, but this time in gold. The barrier looked ornate, but if the team hadn't yet penetrated it, then it must be sturdy indeed. The big question, though, was whether it was strong enough to protect what was beyond from the PFT.

Simpson organized Kaur, Salas, and Chinbat into a rearguard while Garst and Tompkins worked their magic on the door.

Wisps of poison gas stretched their tendrils to lick against the rearguard position, but there was no sign yet of another attack by the Janissaries.

"Fire in the hole!" he heard behind him, followed by an earsplitting whine.

"Yeah, baby," whooped Garst in triumph. "We're in. What the...?"

"Keep your eyes on the passageway," Simpson warned his rearguard, although he himself turned to see what had robbed Garst of his excitement.

It was a blast door all right. Six inches of metal sandwiched between decorative outer layers. But the breach team had gotten one side partially open. What lay beyond was concealed behind thick gray gas that was impenetrable even to his scout model armored combat exosuit.

"Prep our gift for delivery," Morris ordered the bomb team.

He'd barely finished speaking when heavy automatic weapons fire poured out from the smoke, rounds bursting into the Blazers. Simpson felt a sting on his thigh and he knew he'd been hit. Then again on his chest. A further round found his stomach.

His Marines were unhurt, he realized, because they been blasted by paint rounds, viscous fluorescent goop that cycled through color and temperature changes sufficiently to defeat any stealth technology. The Blazers poured darts and grenades through the doorway into the smoke until the paint rounds stopped coming, but the damage had been done. The Blazers were now defined as negative space, their Marine-shaped outlines a void beneath coatings of flashing slime.

"Shut down stealth mode," called Simpson. It was only a power-draining hindrance now.

"We get that bomb the far side of those doors and then we set it off immediately," ordered the Lieutenant. "Sergeant, make sure it happens."

"Yes, sir."

As the squad directed a steady fire into the room beyond, filling the passageway floor with sabots, Simpson crouched down alongside the bomb squad.

"It's primed and ready," said Tompkins nervously. Simpson couldn't fault the tremor in his voice. At least when this baby went off, it would not be a long goodbye.

"Yeah, let's do it," shouted Jones, and she began pushing the hover trolley toward the gap in the door.

"Coming through!" Simpson shouted as he raced ahead of Jones. "Hold your fire!"

They got to within a yard of the door when he realized something had gone badly wrong. The trolley had snagged on a hidden barrier and tumbled Tawfiq's present to clatter onto the ground amidst the heaps of chalky-white dart sabots. His heart skipped a beat, his gaze glued to the falling thermo-nuke. But it didn't go off. The bomb's primers were complex and heavily guarded against accidental triggering and cyber manipulation. But he did see what had tripped it to the ground. Janissaries. Scores of them! They were deploying from behind what he guessed was a wall of portable stealth shields, their hideous snarls and the swish of their maces filling Simpson's ears.

*Maces?*

"It's not the frakking days of yore," he shouted at a Janissary leaping at him with mace held high, and triple-tapped the veck in its face.

The Janissary was wearing hooded baggy clothing, but its face was uncovered. His dart should have shattered its skull, but the rounds bounced off, ricocheting off the thermo-nuke's case, which was now at the center of a furious melee between Janissaries and Marines.

The very much alive Hardit shook its head, as if a Marine railgun dart was no more than a minor irritation, and then pulled back its mace to swing.

The head of its weapon was constructed from a black metal, but its flanges glowed an ethereal blue that looked very familiar.

Simpson thrust his shoulder into the Janissary's swing, slamming into its wrist and weakening its grip. At the same time, he extended the assault cutters at the end of his carbine, causing monofilament needles to erupt from a ring extending around the muzzle. From the tips came the same blue glow, the secret of which the New Order had now discovered.

His foe had recovered its grip on the mace and was pulling it back for another swing. Simpson wasn't going to give it the chance. He thrust his cutters – *teeth* as the Marines call them – slowly but firmly into the Hardit's face. The needles hit an invisible barrier that had to be a force field, but Simpson pushed on through until the cutters slipped inside. It was like pushing through thick glue, but the sergeant put all his weight behind his carbine until the needles finally began to prick the Hardit's mouth. The Janissary dropped its mace and tried to pull itself free, but the same force field that had saved its life was now holding it fast against Marine teeth. Simpson spun his cutters, bringing them up to 3000 rpm. Liquefied Hardit splattered the convex interior of the invisible force field.

"Cutters in their snouts, Marines!" he shouted. "Cutters in their snouts."

Ducking under a swing coming in from his right flank, he smashed his new assailant in the gut with his carbine stock. As this Janissary stumbled, he thrust again with his teeth, filling another goldfish bowl with red slurry.

Around him, he saw Jones was down and Khatri was on her knees, sinking under a hail of mace blows.

*We'll just have to give you your present here and now*, he thought and dove at the nuclear bomb. As he moved, he felt a searing pain in his right shoulder as a mace struck home, cutting through his armor and deep into his flesh, making him drop his carbine. He ducked low and spun about to punch his foe, but although he got into position, his right arm refused to move. He dropped under a wild mace swing, using his left hand to grab the melee weapon by its metal shaft at the furthest extent of its swing. He wrenched it from the Hardit's grip and dealt his opponent a backhand strike in the top of its head, which brought a yelp of pain. It would have to be enough. With the melee ongoing around him, Simpson drove once more for the bomb and the control panel that was fortunately face up after the bomb case had toppled onto its side. All he had to do now was pray Tawfiq was in the blast radius, and punch in the seven-digit firing code. Preferably in that order.

*Six... Nine...* A Janissary rushed him from his right rear. He braced himself but carried on entering the code. Nothing else mattered now. *One...* The Janissary clattered into him, but Simpson rode easily underneath its momentum and reached for the control panel once more.

"Out of time," sneered the Janissary in a dialect his suit could translate. As he punched in the final code digits – *Two... One...* – he glanced up at the Hardit who had landed on the floor in front of the bomb. Simpson's heart drained of blood. The Janissary had its own fist-sized bombs, and they were stuck on the casing of Tawfiq's present.

*Eight...*

The Hardit bombs went off with a blinding flash, but Simpson didn't need to see to enter the final digit of the firing code. *Six!*

The control panel gave an audible click.

And the bomb did not explode.

Instead of hearing angels and the voices of fallen friends, he heard the sound of a Hardit screaming in agony.

Simpson blinked away the effects of the flash and saw what had happened.

The Present for Tawfiq was disintegrating. The inner core was still visible but corroding fast, but the case and the fuse had largely melted away. Hardit corrosion bombs. Had to be. The Janissary who'd planted them was paying the price. Its hands and forearms had vanished, and the flesh of its upper arms was unravelling to reveal bony stumps, which then dissolved in their turn.

The Marines had failed.

"We surrender," shouted Lieutenant Morris. "All Marines, cease fighting and surrender. That is an order."

The sounds of struggle had been dying away, but what Lieutenant said was unthinkable.

"We can't be taken alive," Simpson protested.

"I didn't say anything about being taken alive," Morris replied for all to hear.

Simpson grasped what the Lieutenant was asking them to do. "You heard the officer," he shouted. "Surrender to the New Order. They might treat us fairly."

The melee shuddered to a halt. The Far Reach Marines were bloodied but alive, overwhelmed by a wave of Janissaries who had swarmed over them, heedless to the enormous cost they had paid in their own lives.

"Fascinating," said a computer-generated voice from the smoke beyond the doorway.

By this point, Simpson was sitting within a ring of Janissaries, his right arm numb, and his knees shattered by mace blows. The ring of Hardits parted enough for him to see three figures emerge from the smoke. Two were alien creatures inside cylindrical life-support canisters that floated inches above the ground. The aliens inside were amorphous orange blobs inside a circulatory fluid system streaming with bubbles and ribbons. Night Hummers. As for the Hardit they flanked, Simpson had seen its likeness carved in white marble and seated on a chair in the topside memorial they had passed through.

"Humans from the future," said Tawfiq. "Quite fascinating. I look forward to learning more about you under interrogation."

A woman roared, and a commotion erupted further up the corridor. Simpson watched Grenadier Kaur rise to her feet, throwing off the sea of Hardits surrounding her and thrusting her arms at the New Order's supreme commander. It was a marvel that Kaur had found the time to reload her grenade launcher tubes, but Simpson could see the deadly cylinders locked in position around her wrists, ready to end Tawfiq once and for all.

So why wasn't Kaur firing?

The grenadier screamed in frustration, shaking her arms as if that would release the deadly cargo.

"One of the problems with fighting against Night Hummers," said Tawfiq, "is that sometimes they know what you're going to do before you do. Another problem is that they can do this…"

An invisible force lifted Kaur up off her feet, the sounds of her choking clear across the Squad Net. Then she was accelerated hard against the ceiling before dropping lifeless to the ground. Her status showed in Simpson's HUD as unconscious but alive.

Tawfiq strode amongst his prisoners, inspecting them with the same haughty disdain evident on the statue. The supreme commander came to rest in front of Lieutenant Morris.

"You must be the officer," she told him. "I wish you to know that you caught our defenses off guard. My mobile reserve followed your false orders deploying them to the southern polar region, and you sent the remaining reserves in this area chasing after ghost uprisings and reports of monsters emerging from below the ground. You were so effective at planting distractions that your contemptible little team punched clean through all my remaining Janissaries. I was a hundred yards away with my senior commanders, conferring on the status of your uprising of rabble in Africa, believing that had been the real aim of all this human activity. If you had arrived just two minutes earlier, you would have killed us all. It matters to me that you understand how close you came to success, and yet you still failed utterly."

"If we punched through your defenses," said Morris, standing proud, "who was it that attacked us with the maces?"

"Yes, now that is the truly fascinating part. My inner sanctum is on lockdown. I didn't order these soldiers to come to my defense. It was a warning from your era that summoned them here. They only just made it in time, almost as if you had arrived earlier than you were expected."

"What can I say?" Morris replied. "I don't like to be late." He cleared his throat. "I don't like to be dead either. You want to know more about us, Supreme Commander. I understand that. If you swear to keep us alive and treat us well, I will order the rest of the task force outside to surrender."

"I have dealt with humans for centuries," said Tawfiq. "You do not give up so easily. Why would you order your comrades to stand down?"

"The same reason that our task force commander will surrender when I ask her to. Because we can't bear to be separated."

"Explain yourself."

"The captain and I are lovers. I'll do anything to protect her, and anything to prevent us being separated."

"You humans are pathetic. That much I know to be true."

"You know it is," said Morris angrily. "The power of human love is what you corrupted to turn Romulus into the traitor who now serves you. Let me serve you the same way. Corrupt my love for the captain but let us live."

"Undeniably," said Tawfiq, "love is the greatest of human weaknesses. I was wise to eliminate that defect when I created my Janissaries."

"Well, don't just gloat about it," snapped Morris. "Every second we wait, the captain is more likely to escape to our own time. Take down your signal jamming and let me talk with her on the radio."

Tawfiq narrowed her eyes, deep in thought, but said nothing.

———

**Captain Grace Lee-McEwan**
**Holding station near the Tawfiq Memorial**

"Blaze Squad back on grid, Captain," observed Francini.

Grace had seen it, and was already asking herself the question: why?

With *Karypsic* in a slow holding pattern, not straying far from the drone holding up the signal wire, Grace had watched with mounting trepidation for signs of her missing Marines to reappear. Already, Arrow Squad had beaten back piecemeal counter-attacks, and with every passing second that Blaze Squad remained dark, Grace had been moving closer to the moment when she had to decide whether to rescue them, or abort the mission and move out with those she could still save.

And now, Morris, Simpson, and the others had reappeared, their suits reporting over easily overheard radio frequencies that they were bloodied but alive.

*And still deep within the target zone.*

Then it got worse. Grace felt the cold chill of defeat when her station received a broadcasted request for an audio-visual link. It carried the signature of Lieutenant Morris. She knew, then, that their gamble had failed.

With a heavy heart she accepted the signal and *Karypsic's* main screen filled with the view through Morris's helmet cam.

"Are you seeing this, Grace, my darling?" he said bizarrely, circling slowly so she could take in the scene of his final battle. "Please surrender. Tawfiq says we will be treated well. All of us."

What was Morris playing at?

His team had fought well, and many Janissaries had died under the ground beneath the dropship. But they hadn't traveled back through time to kill anonymous New Order foot soldiers; they had just one in their sights, and as Morris ended his camera tour, his view came to rest on Tawfiq herself, alive and gloating. To either side of the New Order supreme commander, and the creator of the Janissary race, was a Night Hummer in the cylinders they lived inside on Earth-like planets.

"Jackson!" she said grimly to her co-pilot, "those Hummers... can you give me the exact model of their life-support cylinders?"

"Already on it, Captain. Type-43 environment support capsules."

"Francini," said Grace, "load one bunker penetrator followed by a percussion bomb set to those capsules."

"Configuring bombs," Francini acknowledged. "Penetrator followed by Type-43 optimized percussion munition. It will take me 20 seconds to set up. Shall I add conventional explosives?"

Grace took a deep breath. Conventional bombs were unlikely to achieve much against a hardened Hardit defensive warren, but if they *did* get through… then she would be killing her own Marines.

"Please surrender now, darling," Morris said, "think of the children."

"Don't overdo it, Morris," she said under her breath, "you always hated the idea of having children."

"All I care about now," Morris continued, "is being reunited with my lifelong friend and lover. That's all that any of us here can look forward to now."

"Message understood," said Grace and then bit her lip to stop it trembling. "Francini, add conventional munitions to the bomb chute. Maximum yield consistent with giving Arrow Squad a fighting chance of getting back home. Strap in tight, people, we are about to become extremely visible."

She began rapidly entering flight course scenarios into her flight modeler. Jackson offered a few minor tweaks, but the automated systems and co-pilot alike confirmed that her instincts were spot on, in terms of flying if nothing else.

"What was it that Morris said to convince you?" asked Jackson.

Grace ceased her flight calculations. "His partner was my best friend. Died of some obscure alien pathogen. The Blazers all volunteered for a reason, Ensign Jackson. You knew that."

"Maybe your lover doesn't care for you as much as you pretend, Lieutenant." Grace glanced at the main screen and saw it filled with the face of their nemesis. Tawfiq's middle eye was wide with excitement and her lupine ears couldn't help but twitch either. The veck was enjoying this. "If you can hear this, human mission commander, respond now or be destroyed."

"Percussion munition configuration complete," said Francini.

"I have the lieutenant's revised coordinates now," added Jackson. "I am updating your flight calcs and auto-bombardier."

Grace established an unsecure link to Morris's suit, commandeering his external speaker. "I can hear you all right, you mangy wolf monkey." She enjoyed the way Tawfiq's ears closed in on themselves with annoyance.

Grace banked around the memorial that bore Tawfiq's name, and climbed rapidly, the inertial control systems limiting the 17g acceleration to a gentle pull against the back of her seat. "You win, Supreme Commander," she said through the commandeered speaker. "I'm coming down to you now."

"A wise choice," said Tawfiq, her mouth set to a toothy grin.

"Radar lock!" Jackson warned. "They've seen us."

*Karypsic* had climbed to 3,000 feet in moments; Grace hadn't expected such a maneuver to go unnoticed.

"Shut down all stealth cover," she told Jackson, "let them see us properly." To Tawfiq she said, "Before I come down, I want to tell you my name."

"Irrelevant," Tawfiq replied, the fronts of her lips now pulled high to show her gums – a Hardit in full gloat mode. "You will be assigned a number and scent identifier of my choosing."

"Captain!" warned Jackson, as *Karypsic* completed her inverted loop and began its dive bomb descent. "Don't reveal your name."

Tawfiq was gesturing ironically with her hands and tail, including her Janissaries in her little game with this silly human commander. "The slave species female wishes us to know her name. Shall we hear it?"

"Reckon she heard your warning, Jackson," said Grace as she extended *Karypsic*'s air brakes. "The monkey is intrigued. Aren't you, Mistress Tallfat Woomer Cat-Licks?" She grinned to see Tawfiq freeze in shock. "Yes, that's right. That's what my father called you when you first met." *Karypsic* was bucking now, the dropship screaming in protest as it fought to keep its nose from tracking across the innocent looking parkland Grace was aiming at. Targeting brackets on the main screen were narrowing fast. "Know my name, Tawfiq." The targeting brackets met, and *Karypsic* shuddered as its bombs shot away. "I am Grace Lee-McEwan, but you can call me Death." Missile lock alerts flared on the main screen. "Good hunting, Blaze Squad. Lee-McEwan, out."

*Karypsic* leveled out, or tried to but even this, the most rugged of spaceships, struggled to pull out of its 80-degree dive. It bucked, writhed and juddered, setting Grace's teeth chipping against one another. There were far safer ways of delivering munitions than using a spacecraft as a dive bomber, but this was their last chance to kill Tawfiq, and she'd had to risk everything on an accurate strike that wouldn't simply be shot out of the sky or deflected by a force barrier... Everything, including the margin of survival for the ship.

*Karypsic* fought valiantly to raise her nose above the horizontal.

But it wasn't quite enough.

The ventral nacelle, on which a force keel and a shield deflector were mounted, plowed into an empty expanse of grass in a northern spur to Victory Mall, which was shaking with the impact of *Karypsic*'s bombs.

Within milliseconds, automated safety systems jettisoned the nacelle to stop the ship flipping ass over tail, but Grace had to fight hard to calm the gyrating dropship.

Explosions burst behind them as the first salvo of Hardit surface-to-air missiles narrowly failed to track *Karypsic*'s wild movements and ripped into the park.

It seemed like forever, but it was less than two seconds before Grace had wrestled a semblance of control. They were trapped, flying north over the bombed-out ruins of a once-ornate stone building in a narrow rectangle of parkland surrounded on three sides by tall buildings. With speed brakes on full, the ship had an airspeed of 101 knots, and altitude of half a hand span. She was headed for a gap in the trees that fringed the northern end of the park. From there she would break through the road that squeezed through the eight-story high buildings at the north end of the mall.

Flying a spacecraft along a road? Tempting, but that was too risky even for her.

Just as she was about to attempt pulling up into a vertical climb – another risky option, opening up the engines to blast into the ground at point blank range – Hardit fire from the rooftops lashed *Karypsic's* upper shields. The explosive shells wouldn't penetrate, but without the deflector on the lower nacelle, if she climbed now, the enemy guns would rip out *Karypsic's* guts.

The alien thing in her mind, the battle computer, spooled up with a rampant eagerness to take on these tactical problems and provide optimal solutions.

"Pull up!" Jackson was screaming.

As she scanned the Hardit threat from the rooftops, she dodged *Karypsic* starboard to avoid hitting a statue ringed by ancient cannons. In another two seconds they would hit the buildings.

She didn't have time for Jackson or the battle computer. And, she realized with horror, she didn't have the option of the road either. A fence topped with downward facing guns stretched across the road. The guns swiveled around to track this incoming vessel.

It seemed they were out of options.

She grinned.

But not for her.

"Pull up!" Jackson called out again, but Grace was already kicking in a completely different maneuver. She activated the upper force keels and extended them forward, applying greater power to the port keel. The keels reached through to lower dimensions, which acted as a highly resistant hyperfluid – resistant enough to push back hard against the keels and apply a reaction torque to the ship. Then she kicked in with the gas. With her rear engines thrusting hard, the dropship *drifted*. The balance of forces was so delicately balanced, so easy to spiral out of control and into catastrophe, that

Grace stopped trying to think it through and slewed the ship around on raw instinct, trusting to the intimate connection she felt to *Karypsic*.

She'd missed being a dropship pilot!

The stern of the ship threatened to slide out to starboard, but every time it came to the brink, Grace caught the slide and charmed it back to her will.

"Yessss!" she screamed as they drifted around in a semicircle, using the statue as a pivot point.

Francini was quietly engaging the Hardit positions on the rooftops with the upper pop-up turrets. So was Jackson, when he could get a shot in from the guns mounted in the remaining two nacelles, but he was also screaming for his mamma at the top of his voice.

"Kinda noisy today, Ensign," Grace teased. "Is that terror or excitement I'm hearing?"

"I don't know," he said, taking out a pair of Janissaries on the grass who had been lifting dangerous looking tubes to their shoulders. "Both. Just promise you'll never pull this stunt again."

"How rude. See that statue of a man on horseback? He's holding out his hat to salute us." She withdrew the keels. "They were proper gentlemen in ancient days." And sped away in level flight. "Honestly, Ensign Jackson, anyone would think you'd never seen a spaceship pull a doughnut before. Right, let's see what damage Francini's done with his bombs."

———

**Sergeant Simpson, Blaze Squad**
**At the gates of Tawfiq's bunker**

"For the Legion!" roared Sergeant Simpson, and was immediately brought to the ground by mace strikes to his back.

"Freedom!" shouted another Marine.

"Far Reach!" cried another.

It fell to Lieutenant Morris to express it perfectly. "By the Grace of God," he declared to Tawfiq, "let this evil be expunged from the universe."

But the evil in question wasn't listening. Tawfiq was too busy cowering on the ground, her loyal Janissaries scrambling to form a pyramid around her, holding up personal force shields against death from above.

The passageway rang out as something struck the ground over their heads, A deep bass after-shock shaking Tawfiq's pyramid into a broken heap. It was followed by a high-pitched whine that seemed to be edging closer.

"Bunker penetrator," noted Morris.

The whine screeched so loudly that Simpson's helmet sprayed noise-dampening foam over his ears to limit the risk of permanent damage to his hearing.

"Good old suit," laughed Simpson. "But it's a bit late to worry about my ears."

The penetrator spooled down, its attempt to drill through to their level defeated by the New Order engineers who had built this warren.

But the Janissaries guarding the Far Reach Marines were still glancing up in alarm, maybe opening an opportunity...

The captain hadn't done yet. The world was suddenly stuffed with noise, perfectly tuned to a specific pitch, rich with overtones.

*Percussion bomb.*

The soundwave was all-encompassing. Simpson's insides seemed to liquefy and then dance to the bomb's deadly song. His vision kept glitching and his teeth hummed. But the percussion munition was not set up to kill him – painful though this was – it would have been calibrated to a specific resonance frequency. The single note that would kill its intended victim.

The Hardits all around were suffering even more than he was, hands held tightly against their sensitive ears. But they weren't dying either.

With his vision still flashing sparks, Simpson fumbled around the front of the nearest Janissary and felt for its mace handle.

Silent, inscrutable, and aloof, he'd ignored the Night Hummers whom Tawfiq had abandoned by the blast doors. Cracks appeared in the transparent tubes of the life-support tanks. The cracks spread to form black lattice work before shattering into an explosion of crystalline shards washed away by a flood of viscous liquid. The formless orange bodies of the strange aliens fell onto the glistening heaps of their ruined tanks and flapped pathetically, like landed fish.

Two more huge explosions shook the passageway, but the Hardit warren held strong, and Tawfiq emerged triumphant from beneath the shields of her Janissaries. Behind her, the Hummers were barely twitching now.

The captain had done her best, but it hadn't been enough. Now it was down to the Marines on the ground.

Simpson looked at the mace in his hands.

He dropped it to the ground. No, that wasn't the way.

"You failed," Tawfiq told Morris, walking up to him in triumph.

"Don't be so sure," answered the Lieutenant.

Tawfiq extended her hand toward the officer. It looked like she was holding a remote control, but the device gave a short staccato noise and then Morris's head... it just melted. The Lieutenant's torso crumpled to the floor.

"It's time," Simpson announced to the other Marines. "We're not leaving this place. You know what to do."

He shut his eyes and thought a command to his suit's operating system to alter the configuration of his power system. As he did so, he used the strength of his suit to stand upright, even though the human knees inside had been shattered.

The fuel cell for the Armored Combat Exosuit was a thing of wonder, an alien design still only partially understood by Far Reach and Legion techs. The tiny zero-point energy miner at its heart was a miniaturized version of the power plants that propelled starships across interstellar voids. Wonder though that was, its greatest mystery was the ability to dump the enormous heat generated by using some voodoo-science dimensional chicanery that Morris would never understand. All he needed to know was the Far Reach engineers' enhancement. The one that redirected the energy transfer back into an unstable closed loop.

"Now!" he shouted, and set his fuel cell to this new self-destruct mode.

As the Janissaries flicked their ears in confusion, trying to understand what this human was shouting about, Morris couldn't feel a change.

Was it working?

He thought he felt an itch in the band across his lower back in which the cell was planted, but it was difficult to tell against the roar of pain in his knees.

The itch grew into a searing pain that branded itself into his flesh.

Then the heat built in a positive feedback loop on a one-way ticket to overload.

———

**Sergeant Kraken**
**Arrow Squad**
**Below the statue of Tawfiq**

The marble floor of the Tawfiq Memorial shook beneath Kraken's feet, followed by a boom echoing from deep within the Hardit tunnels.

It had to be Blaze Squad. Had they done it? Had they killed Tawfiq?

There was no time for questions now. Giant was still at the bottom of the elevator shaft, and her suit was reporting hushed Hardit voices mustering beyond the turn in the passageway that led to the lobby beneath Tawfiq's statue. Whether or not their supreme commander was dead, these Janissaries would soon be rushing along that corridor to expel the human invaders.

Kraken reached a hand down the elevator shaft to his sister below. "Come on, Giant. Time to move out."

Her breathing was ragged in his ears, and her vital signs in his HUD were flashing red.

"No, brother," she replied. "It's time to stop running."

A Hardit grenade exploded in the lobby, but it was answered by a Marine carbine spitting darts.

*Frakk that! I'm not leaving you, sis.*

"Arrow Squad," he called. "I'm going back in. Link up with Vengeance on the roof."

He fell back down the shaft, spraying the lobby with darts as he descended.

The sounds of battle fell away, and the smoke cleared a little. Enough to see that amongst the heaps of Janissaries, debris from a partially collapsed roof, and the sea of dart sabots that spoke of the increasing Janissary pressure they'd fended off, there were currently no active threats.

Giant needed medical attention. She had lost a lot of blood, but somehow she was carrying on, hauling the bodies of Spurrell and Raschid over to the bottom of the shaft. Kraken knew exactly why she was doing this.

"Let me go," she whispered to him. "My choice. My way. I don't wanna drain away in a hospital bed with tubes sticking out of me and a crowd of long faces waiting for me to go."

"Stop that," he told her. "Let me help you."

She sat back in the elevator shaft while Kraken shifted Spurrell and Raschid to sit lifelessly beside her, checking that Giant had the access privileges to remotely command the suits of the dead Marines.

When he was done, he stood beside her, resting his hands on her shoulders. "Have you got my back?" he asked.

"Ever since the crèche," she replied. "And I'm not stopping now."

He jumped up and out of the shaft.

And into a firefight.

———

## Grace Lee-McEwan
*Karypsic*
**Victory Mall**

Grace hovered *Karypsic* above a flowerbed and let the twin heavy auto cannons in her nose play over the Janissary infantry and light vehicles streaming in from the north to engage her Marines at the Tawfiq Memorial.

Missiles and shells hammered away at the dropship's upper shields. They wouldn't hold out for long.

"O'Hanlon, report!"

"Watching and waiting, Captain. Just like you ordered."

"Keep your powder dry," Grace replied. "You'll get the chance. It's getting mighty hot here, but I'll be back."

Grace lifted the dropship and banked around to the memorial, keeping the upper nacelles and the vital shield deflectors they carried tilted toward the surviving Janissaries.

"Bogies headed our way," announced Francini. "Bearing 314, range just five klicks. Hugging the ground tight. They've launched missiles. Twenty of them."

"Thank you, Francini. By Horden's Hairy Hide, anyone would think these New Order Hardits weren't pleased to see us."

"Can't stop right now," she told her Marines at the memorial through *Karypsic*'s external speakers. "Be ready for pickup from the roof. Three minutes."

An explosion below ground rocked Tawfiq's statue on her marble seat.

"What was that?" Grace demanded of her squad leaders on the ground, using pulsed light flashes to cut through the Hardit jamming.

"Missile impact in ten seconds," warned Francini.

"That was Giant, Spurrell and Raschid watching our six," Kraken replied, smoke roiling out of the shaft behind the statue.

A lump came to Grace's throat. She could hear the ragged pride in the sergeant's voice.

"Understood," she answered him. "And I've got yours."

"Six seconds…"

"Ready countermeasures," she told Jackson.

"Four…"

*Karypsic* put a little distance from the memorial and then shot straight up in the sky, leaving in her wake a cloud of false target signatures.

Most of the missiles exploded prematurely, but six pursued the ship as it reached for the heavens.

———

## Grace Lee-McEwan

*Karypsic* shot through the air like a rocket, compressing the air in front of her into a fiery cone. The Hardit aircraft did their best to climb in pursuit, igniting afterburners and expanding fuel recklessly, but were outclassed. Their missiles, though, were another matter, closing fast all the way. Countermeasures put one off the scent, but the New Order battle techs had long experience of Legion defensive munitions and their smart missiles were already learning to defy the few tricks Far Reach had added.

Grace rolled the ship, to present the strongest shield deflection possible to the missiles that made it through. The shields still held, but they were now too weak to prevent damage penetrating. The missile payloads melted through armor and knocked out control systems with EMP bursts and cyber boarders.

But they were still alive, and the missiles were slowing. Failing. Their motors cutting out, leaving them to drop back down into the atmosphere.

Grace had flown them into the ephemeral heights of the upper atmosphere, where Earth's gravity still claimed a thin whispery cloaking of gas, but which was entirely inadequate for the missile motors designed to burn fuel in air.

*Karypsic* appeared to hang at the boundary with space, the blue arc of earth's atmosphere a beautiful sight on the horizon.

"We've been sighted," warned Francini. "An orbital defense platform, 400 klicks away."

Grace waited, leaving the ship vulnerable to the powerful New Order defenses designed to fend off full-sized warships. But she gambled that the platform's weapons were oriented outward. She had no choice; she had to be certain they had shaken off all the missiles from below.

The platform's painting us with a targeting laser."

*Karypsic* dove for the ground, the armor on her belly melting away fast as the Hardit orbital particle beam found her.

But as the ship descended, Earth surrounded *Karypsic* in the protective embrace of her atmosphere, shielding her with deflecting particles that defanged the Hardit beam weapon into powerlessness.

Halfway back to ground level, *Karypsic* exchanged fire with the pursuing Hardit aircraft who were still in their vertical climb. Did she hit one? The pass by flashed so quickly, Grace couldn't tell. And by that point her focus was entirely on making her rendezvous safely.

"And we are back," Grace told the Marines on the roof, as *Karypsic* glided into position ten feet above them. "Get back and strap in. I was away for 183 seconds. Apologies for being three seconds late, but we experienced a little turbulence."

She swapped her screen view to show the hold where Marines in their ACE-6(S) suits were jumping up through the egress portals to land in the troop compartment. The first wave scrambled away to the edges of the area to clear the space for their comrades to follow.

"Bogies are closing fast," reported Jackson. "And there's another flight of six approaching from the southeast. We won't load everyone in time."

Grace weighed her options. *Karypsic* might possibly survive an attack run by two flights of New Order fighters, but the Marines left on the roof wouldn't.

"Enemy aircraft inbound," she said through the external speakers. "Cease boarding. We will draw them away and pick you up from O'Hanlon's obelisk."

She sealed the egress portals and flew away, accelerating at maximum survivable thrust once she was a safe distance from the roof.

*Karypsic* ducked, weaved and corkscrewed violently, spraying out countermeasures in a dance she performed with the Hardit aircraft and air defenses over a 50-klick radius from the Marines she had left behind, but would never abandon.

She flew beneath the enemy fighters and clawed at them with the cannons in her nose and finished off survivors with her turret guns.

The Hardits were being slowly slaughtered, but *Karypsic* was sustaining heavy damage too. Her force keels failed, robbing her of maneuverability, and spraying high-pressure dimensional conduit fluids laced with highly unstable artificial elements that burned through her armor.

"Shield strength at nine percent and dropping fast," warned Francini.

"Another missile launch," added Jackson. "I think it's time to play our ace in the hole, Captain."

"You mean, we dumb apes get to play with that which we do not understand."

"Yep. Do you mind...?"

The tactical display was filled with so many missiles headed their way, it was difficult to read. "Be my guest, Ensign."

Grace saw her co-pilot beaming with excitement "Jumping...!" he said. "Now!"

Greyhart had deflected every question about the technology that propelled them across time. The *intercalators*. They were black boxes, with insides that were impenetrable, not only through heavy shielding but through a complete absence of conceptual understanding.

How the hell could they possibly work? It was only natural for Greyhart to keep that very secret.

And it was equally natural for the Far Reach Fleet to do whatever they could to learn about this impossible technology.

Every molecule in contact with the box that transported them back in time, and the much larger one that would return them to their time of origin, was constantly recorded and analyzed. Every fluctuation in the air current, every jitter in the power hook up could be important.

And the crews who had accompanied her and her mother on the trip back to Earth had been handpicked to include the brightest techs around.

So maybe – just, maybe – they'd found a way to jumpstart the upstream time intercalator, the device that took them back in time. Just a kick, that's all they could do. Perhaps travel back a few seconds. Maybe a minute. Just enough to put the pursuing missiles and fighters off their scent so they could collect the remaining survivors and go home.

Or maybe they would cause an explosion that would echo through all eternity.

They were about to find out.

———

**Sergeant Kraken, Arrow Squad**
**Victory Mall**

"Time to introduce yourself, gun team," said Kraken, turning to let off a burst of railgun fire at the Hardits hitting them from the north in suicidal waves.

"Roger that in spades, Sergeant," O'Hanlon replied.

Then the Hardits were upon him, and all Kraken could think of was the enemy, gripping his ankles with their tails, trying to sweep his legs from him with maces, and the two-handed pole arms that he'd seen slice clean through Thongsuk's left arm.

They were so damned close to the base of the obelisk, but the Hardits were swarming all over them in a confusing melee. Kraken daren't fire his carbine for fear of shooting his own, so it was down to assault cutters thrust into snouts, and the shattering blows from armored Marine fists. But even Kraken's suit-amplified muscles had tired. And he had the precious dead weight of Sergeant Chen's body hanging around his neck. And even if Chen didn't weigh much, her suit certainly did.

He screamed as a Hardit blade pierced the front of his right thigh. A left hook dealt the Janissary a stunning blow, but he himself had been brought to a halt. A pole arm swung from behind and struck him on the side of the knee and he almost crumpled.

"Not gonna take me alive, monkey-veck!"

Pushing down with his left leg, he toppled backward, hoping to crush the Hardit behind him. He went down as hard as he could. His weight combining with Chen's, he listened for the crunch of Hardit bones breaking.

But it was not to be. He did, however, feel the Janissary's pole arm being pulled from its grip as he pinned the alien beneath his back.

Kraken turned to fire at his assailant, only to see the Hardit's head explode as Andrew Stafford shot it through the back of its head, spilling its brains across the force shield that covered the enemy's face.

"Looks like O'Hanlon's bought us a little time," said Stafford, extending a hand to pull Kraken to his feet.

Kraken looked around to see the fleeing Janissaries had left behind swathes of Hardit corpses laid low by the devastating fire of the microwave cannon. Their internal fluids had been superheated, bursting ruptured organs to spray through eyes, nose and ears. And the zone of industrial devastation wrought by the M-cannon ended mere feet away from where Kraken had been caught in the confusing melee.

Unwilling to dwell on how closely he'd come to being cooked, he looked to the north, where the miniature New Order tanks that had seemed so threatening moments earlier were now lifeless, the crews broiled within. Only one mini tank still rumbled along the grass, headed away on a straight line that would take it past the temple to Tawfiq, from which smoke still rose from his sister's last stand.

"That was quite some introduction, gun team," he said.

"They're running like rabbits," O'Hanlon replied, "but there's more on their way. Don't hang around, Sergeant."

"Keep moving!" Kraken urged the survivors of the two squads. "No one else gets left behind, living or dead."

Before he set off, he checked the vitals for his squad. Half of them were showing up as wounded, and he was surprised to find he himself was marked in the same state, his suit having patched the wound in his thigh, and given his bloodstream something to persuade him to ignore his wounds. But even Far Reach Marines could only run on fumes for so long before the Piper demanded his payment.

Thongsuk had lost an arm in that last wave. His suit was patching him up too, but he was in a bad way. Stafford had seen it and was now carrying Marine and suit over his shoulder.

Kraken decided that wouldn't be enough. "Fallaw," he said, "assist Stafford. Get Thongsuk up to safety."

Satisfied everyone who needed assistance was receiving it, Kraken looked to his own safety and limped to the obelisk.

He stood at its base, contemplating what he was about to attempt. Between himself, Chen, and both their suits and equipment, Kraken was about to carry thirteen hundred pounds up a near-vertical stone face. It wouldn't be easy, and it wouldn't be fast, but he'd seen these latest scout model armored exosuits work miracles.

Maybe they would work one more.

Kraken hugged the obelisk until his suit registered a good grip, and then began to climb.

He'd scaled two thirds of the way to the top when a volley of Hardit bullets raked the obelisk. A bullet ricocheted off Chen's suit, chipping the obelisk inches from Kraken's hand.

A scream pierced the air below him as the gun team silenced the snipers, but a fresh spark of fear put new urgency into Kraken's exhausted limbs. If the Janissaries were now shooting to kill, he could think of few more vulnerable ways to present an inviting target than to squeeze all the survivors of Arrow and Vengeance into a tight space at the top of a pillar.

Hands splayed wide, he used the magic gecko grip to inch closer to the top.

"No time for sightseeing, Sergeant," teased a voice.

Kraken looked up and saw Stafford was just above him, trying to feed a rope into his hand. A rope secured to the top of the obelisk.

Why hadn't Kraken noticed Stafford descend to him?

Didn't matter. He grabbed the rope and let his suit's muscles take the strain as he abseiled higher.

Then an explosion below threw him off the wall, leaving him dangling with feet kicking over five-hundred feet above the ground. He looked down at the deep crater blown out of the parkland by what looked like a New Order artillery shell. Dirt and shattered Hardit limbs had been flung into the air and were now making their descent. The crater was a hundred feet away to the northwest, and if the enemy was willing to shell its own side in order to kill the Marines, they were almost out of time.

He climbed the rope with fresh urgency, now just 20 feet below the west viewport. Another shell landed. Closer this time – maybe 50 yards away to the southeast – but he was largely shielded from the blast by the obelisk.

"Don't get distracted, Captain," he said to himself as he hauled himself up the last distance, hand over hand. "You know how easily you get distracted."

"Surrender immediately or die!" came an amplified voice that flooded Victory Mall. Kraken froze. It was a human voice, coming from the Tawfiq Memorial.

*A human?* He shook away dark thoughts about collaborators and climbed for his life.

"The supreme commander has survived your mission of murder," said the human, "and prevails to fulfil her glorious destiny."

"Someone silence that jerk," Kraken called up to the top of the obelisk.

"You are cornered. Escape is impossible. This is your last chance. Surrender or... ahhhhh!"

"Die?" suggested Kraken as friendly hands hauled him and his precious cargo into the space at the top of the obelisk, where he tumbled onto a leather floor covering to join the remaining survivors.

With Sergeant Chen still over his back, Kraken checked the skies through both east and west viewports and saw nothing but empty blue.

"Where are you, Captain?" he whispered.

As if in answer, a fireball erupted on the horizon to the northwest, followed a few seconds later by the aerial scream of powerful engines headed their way.

———

**Grace Lee-McEwan**

*Karypsic* dove through impossible dimensions.

And then snapped back into comprehensible reality. Hard.

Grace was thrown against her harness, but the dropship's inertial compensators rapidly readjusted. Enough for her to regain control of *Karypsic's* flight controls and wait for the tactical display to recalculate.

When it finally admitted where and when they were, her heart leaped. They had jumped all right, but not back in time... they'd moved forward! About thirty seconds. How? Why?

"Holy mader zagh!" observed Francini.

"You got that right," said Grace. "But we're out of danger for the moment. Let's go for the pickup point."

There was a flash to the west, swiftly followed by the bark of an artillery piece. The *Karypsic* identified a battery in the process of deploying on the far bank of the river.

Grace banked the dropship to starboard.

"I'm sure Sergeant Kraken won't mind us making a little detour," she said, and checked the status of the dropship's air-to-ground missiles. Empty. "Francini, load a brace of fuel-air explosives for the bomb chutes if you please..."

———

**Corporal O'Hanlon, Vengeance Squad**
**Victory Monument**

The dropship circled around the Hardits down in the mall, nose down and delivering blistering fire from its nose cannon and the one remaining turret beneath its belly, the other having fallen victim to what O'Hanlon identified as beam weapon damage. Frakk! That was a space-borne weapon! What had *Karypsic* been up to?

The Janissaries were directing fire at the dropship, which was taking a terrible pounding. O'Hanlon did his best to relieve the pressure by firing at every heavy weapon he could see, but the M-cannon was not the machine of devastation it had been earlier. They were down to four functioning charge conduits, six having melted. Jintu was advising a maximum ten-second burst followed by a minimum one-minute cooldown, and Jimmy Jintu was not by nature a cautious man. The artillery shelling had stopped almost before it started, but indirect fire was beginning to range them from somewhere in the city. Most of the Marines with him at the top of the obelisk were leaning out the viewports firing down at Janissaries scaling the pillar. He was too busy to look himself, but when Jintu took a peek and said it was like crawling ants, it didn't sound good.

"At last!" whispered O'Hanlon. The *Karypsic* ceased its strafing hover and finally rose to the obelisk, coming to rest a short distance above the west viewport.

"Sorry to keep you waiting again," said the captain, tilting the dropship at a 45-degree angle so that her belly was presented to the viewport, and the shields on the smoking upper nacelles protected them from incoming fire. "Stopped off to have a chat with a New Order artillery battery," she explained as *Karypsic* dropped down to gather up the stranded Marines.

As Sergeant Kraken was ordering all remaining grenades fired into the Hardits, Jintu warned, "Armor headed our way from the southeast."

The grenades went off, engulfing the ground below the obelisk in smoke and far more deadly gifts, but the incoming fire only slackened slightly. And the noise vibrations from the dropship defying the laws of nature to hang in midair were so intense O'Hanlon could feel his brain melting. How Jintu could possibly know tanks were on their way was beyond him, but O'Hanlon knew from long experience that the man had a nose for danger.

"Shut the cannon down," he ordered his team. "Give it ten seconds to cool and then we'll reposition at the east viewport.

Jintu and Bryan waited for their moment while their comrades clambered out through the west viewport and, with a combination of amplified muscle power and suit motors, jumped up and through the egress holes and back into the bosom of their dropship.

Bryan detached the M-cannon's tripod from the floor, and with a fluid motion from long practice, O'Hanlon picked up the main assembly and carried it over to the new position, Jintu holding the power unit and heatsink, which were still attached to the main gun. While Bryan secured the tripod in the new position, and Jintu checked it was ready to fire, O'Hanlon looked out to see what threat they faced. But he saw only smoke clouds.

"We just lost two more charge conduits," Jintu reported.

"Quiet!" snapped O'Hanlon. Ordering the sounds of battle all around to go quiet was not so easy, but he detected a new bass note. A rumble through his feet. Armor. Heavy armor.

Sure enough, the smoke cleared enough to reveal huge armored vehicles using gravitics to hover a foot or so above the terrain on their advance from the east. The sound of cracking masonry hit the air as the formation of three tanks crashed through the domed building to the east, pulverizing it to white dust. They halted as their turrets traversed to aim at the obelisk and the dropship.

"Did you want a lift home?" asked the captain, her voice the most deafening point of reference in the entire battle zone. A moment later, the *Karypsic* floated into view above the east viewport.

"Get out of here," O'Hanlon growled at Bryan and Jintu.

They scrambled to obey. O'Hanlon cleared them from his mind.

*No one's getting out of here if those tanks fire.*

A single M-cannon, barely functioning, against three heavy tanks. It wasn't an even match, but maybe he could blind their sensors. Working as rapidly as he dared, he magnified the targeting image, aiming the cannon at the main sensor blisters mounted on the enemy turrets and on the front glacis armor near the co-pilot position.

"That's something they don't tell you in training," he said to himself, as he ran his beam over the blisters, finding them exactly where he expected them. "If you travel back in time, then even Hardit equipment specs are exactly what the textbooks say."

Infantry support caught up with the tanks and jumped up onto their bodies where they began deploying force shields to protect the sensor blisters. The Janissaries made tempting targets, but O'Hanlon told himself they would have to wait for another time, as he set the cannon to continuous fire and got ready to make his exit.

Gunshots suddenly went off just above his head. And more from behind that lashed his back with pain. He'd been shot! Warnings filled his HUD of the damage done to his suit and to his body. He looked up and saw Bryan and Jintu poking their head and shoulders out of *Karypsic's* belly, their carbines clearing the west viewport of Hardits who were clambering inside. Stafford was dangling out an egress hole by his ankles, holding his hand out to O'Hanlon. "Jump, you dongwit!"

But *Karypsic* was moving away.

Blind panic set in and O'Hanlon threw himself at Stafford, climbing over the M-cannon he had so carefully positioned, burning his foot and knocking the weapon over in his desperation to get away before his ride left.

He jumped into the air, pushing with his muscles and suit motors.

But he wasn't gonna make it.

As soon as he engaged his suit motors, he knew they'd failed. The Janissaries had shot them out.

O'Hanlon dropped through the air.

And so did the *Karypsic*. She came at him from above, Marine Andrew Stafford falling right out of the dropship to grab O'Hanlon in mid-air. Stafford was held by two Marines who were themselves dangling by their ankles.

A part of O'Hanlon noticed the flames flaring from *Karypsic's* upper nacelles, and the holes punched clean through the dropship's hull, but mostly he was too busy holding onto Stafford as their ride home spiraled to gain height.

As he dangled helplessly, the chain of Marine bodies gradually hauling him upward, he looked down and noticed something about the Hardit tanks that hadn't registered before. Their main turret armaments were not cannons as he had assumed, but lasers with full hemispherical elevation and traverse. These were anti-aircraft vehicles. They weren't in the clear yet.

———

## Grace Lee-McEwan

The countdown to the downstream intercalator dominated *Karypsic's* main screen, though the multiple threat warnings vied fiercely for attention. Eight seconds to jump.

"We won't make it," said Francini. "It's close, but we're still dead."

"You've got to juke us, Captain," added Jackson.

Six seconds.

Grace weighed her options.

Greyhart had volunteered almost nothing about the two intercalators, but he had insisted that once the device was engaged to trigger their return journey, *Karypsic* should maintain constant velocity in order for the device to precisely track their position, giving dire yet non-specific warnings about what would happen to those foolhardy enough to ignore his warning.

"At the barest minimum," he had told Grace under her questioning, "you must keep to an absolutely straight flight path."

So any evasive maneuver at this point probably meant jumping into a hell dimension, or pissing off the ancient gods buried within time itself. Something epically perilous.

On the more mundane side, three anti-aircraft lasers were burning a hole through the stern of her ship, and if they ruptured the fuel lines – which could happen at any moment – it would all go kablooey within milliseconds.

Then there were the two Hardit fighter formations trying to shoot her out the sky.

Grace balanced the suicidal against the certain death and tried to decide which choice meant which.

*Bugger what Greyhart tells us*, she thought, and deployed the force keels at 30 degrees to their space-time trajectory.

Shoving a force field through the gaps in reality to arrive unannounced in the lower dimensions was not a simple process. Nor was it remotely gentle. Safe deployment took several seconds.

Grace slammed out the keels in just 200 milliseconds.

It was like skimming a stone off the surface of a lake. *Karypsic* bounced off hard, disappearing from conventional space-time and instantly reappearing half a klick away. The enemy fire stopped.

Four seconds.

One of the nacelles had bent at right angles, the deflector shield it carried turning off automatically. The other nacelle had snapped off altogether and was plummeting to the ground.

"No great loss," Grace said, satisfying herself that Jackson had initiated the fire suppression systems and wrapped the craft in an emergency hull integrity force shield. "We stole that tech from the Hardits in the first place. They can have it back."

———

The countdown reached zero and the downstream intercalator fired.

When they had jumped back in time from 2739, the journey had been an anticlimactic nonevent.

The return trip... not so much.

*Karypsic* screamed.

A wound ruptured along her port flank, armor screeching in protest as the hull was ripped apart with a curious popping sound, as if metallic surgical stitches being ripped asunder. Then the inertial compensators failed, and Grace felt a lurching jolt, bracing for a crushing weight through her chest that never came.

She was weightless.

Which meant the engines were no longer thrusting.

"I can't get a fix on our position," Jackson reported.

"Sensor diagnostics report full functionality," said Francini. "But I can't see a frakking thing."

"Perhaps that's because we aren't actually anywhere," said Grace. "We are *nowhere*. Literally."

The wound along *Karypsic's* flank had spread to the flight deck. Grace looked out through the gap in the hull at the absolute void beyond. There were no stars, no obscuring gas clouds. Just an absence.

"Look!" she shouted, pointing through the ship's wound. "I saw something. Through the hole, a blue sparkle. Could that be a star?"

Jackson shook his head. "That will be the integrity field failing."

His words were a cold kick in the gut because he was right. But there *was* something out there. A pattern of concentric circles cycling through every possible color and approaching them head on.

Or were *they* approaching *it*?

Grace felt herself squeezed and pulled down inside the object, which rapidly gained depth. A *lot* of depth. And breadth. Enough to swallow planets whole. She began to circle it, stretched impossibly thinly down this vortex throat.

For some reason, she thought of her father. They had to survive this, she reasoned to herself, so that when she saw him back in 2739, she would have a tale to tell. When she was a little girl, she'd made her mother endlessly repeat her stories about the crazy things Dad had done in his youth. Now she would have one better.

*Karypsic* fell through a hole in reality.

And was reborn.

# ——— Chapter 12 ———

*Present day*

**Fleet Admiral Indiya**
**Admiral's Quarters.**
**Legion flagship *Holy Retribution***

"An attack through time," said Tawfiq's image, which had carried the scars of old wounds Indiya was sure hadn't been there before. "Thank you for making it so ineffectual that I am now well prepared to repulse any further attacks. I was impressed, actually. Not that you yourselves have the technology to move through time. Clearly you are the pawns of my more serious adversaries, but the way the prisoners I took from your time capsule destroyed themselves before my interrogators could prize information from them – that was impressive."

Indiya tried hard to ignore the invader. "Our cyber-teams will deal with this," she told Kreippil. "I'm coordinating with them now."

"That attack on Cairo twenty years ago always smelled off," said the Hardit. "An irritating worm of doubt remained, because I could never understand why you humans had gone to so much trouble to destroy the Cairo hub and then do *absolutely nothing*. Now I know. It was a feint."

Indiya glanced up at the creature on the bulkhead screen and realized with a jolt of surprise that only two Hardit eyes were staring back at her. Tawfiq's left eye was an unseeing orb of swirling pus clouds. And that snout… beneath its hair it was now puckered with old scar tissue. Years-old wounds that hadn't been there days ago.

But the more urgent mystery was what Tawfiq was trying to achieve with this conversation. There was a security team outside trying and failing to get in. Tawfiq had sealed the doors, and if she had sufficient control to do that then she could presumably have killed them. What was it the Hardit wanted more than their deaths?

"The strangest thing about time war," said Tawfiq, "is that for the lesser mortals not connected directly with the matter, your failed attempt to kill me in Victory City at the same time as your uprising in Cairo was an event that had always taken place. But *we* know differently. This was your big gamble, your one chance to outflank me, and it failed. I defeated you. And if you attempt another attack in the past, I will defeat you again, and again. My technical advisers are convinced that every time you try the same trick, it will be easier for me to detect your attack and prepare my ambush. Soon I will attack *your* past."

The cyber team reported that the attack had been isolated to her quarters, but Indiya was more interested in Tawfiq's words. The Hardit was talking as if she had no knowledge of Arun's attack. But she could lie as easily as breathe.

"Oh, I perceive you are removing me from your computer systems. I have no doubt you will succeed, but that is of no concern. This is not an attack. I just called to suggest something."

"I have no interest in your lies," Indiya snarled.

Tawfiq's eyes blinked in rotation. The chodding veck was laughing at her.

"I wasn't speaking to you," said Tawfiq. "Admiral Kreippil, you know better than most that the species name of 'human' has come to mean something far more to a diverse range of races. Even to those who have never seen a humanoid of Earthly heritage, the word human is a rallying cry for those who would throw off the shackles of oppression. The Legion fanatics need a leader to inspire them, an individual who embodies principles."

"The Purple One has divine sanction," Kreippil said without hesitation.

For once, Indiya was relieved for her friend to call her by that ridiculous title.

"Perhaps you are right," said Indiya, "but there's a difference between a special individual triggering a holy war and being its field commander.

Deities set the agenda of the universe, but it is you mortals who implement the details. You need to be wise and strong. But this human freak with the purple hair has been emotionally stunted ever since the incident in her youth when she murdered thousands on the troopship *Themistocles*. Have you ever seen her happy? Has she ever taken a lover? Does she have a hobby, a friend?"

"I am her friend," Kreippil said firmly.

Indiya wanted to scream at him to stop listening, but that would only tell him that she didn't trust his judgement, a sensitive point in their relationship.

Tawfiq blew through her long lips. "You are her friend, perhaps, but she has none amongst the humans except perhaps by force of habit with McEwan while he still lived. She runs from her own kind and hides with you because she knows she is a freak, an experiment in genetic engineering gone wrong."

Tawfiq's words spoke truths Indiya had acknowledged for a long time, so why could she feel them hollowing her out?

"Kreippil, your friend and leader, the mighty Purple One, is an emotionally stunted wreck, whose sanity is so fragile that you fear she will crack any day now. Is that not why you are inside her quarters? To watch over her in case she loses her mind?"

"With my physical presence, I seek to bolster her emotional strength," Kreippil replied. "It is true that the years have placed a heavy burden about my leader's heart." He swam before her and bowed his head. "And yet I place my trust in you, Admiral Indiya, without condition or reservation."

Relief flowed through Indiya. Pride too. Kreippil couldn't have said that better. Tawfiq's attempt to drive a wedge between them had achieved the exact opposite.

"Dear, dear Kreippil," Tawfiq sneered. "And you have been known to call *me* a liar? If you trust your purple friend, why did you conceal from her the results of your investigations into my Faithful?"

"Kreippil?" Indiya queried. "What don't I know?"

"Yes, what?" echoed Tawfiq gleefully. "Do you want to explain, or shall I?"

# ——— Chapter 13 ———

**First Fleet Admiral Kreippil**
**Admiral's Quarters.**
**Legion flagship *Holy Retribution***

Kreippil looked with disappointment upon his human friend. He had thought, briefly that she had recovered her wits when she had begun dealing with the return of the *Karypsic* as if her old self had returned. Yet how easily was her spirit broken by Tawfiq.

"The Abomination seeks to sow dissent with her lies," Kreippil pointed out to her, the need to explain himself at all in front of the wretched creature a bitter humiliation.

"Go on," said Indiya, imploring him to make everything all right.

"There is little to be said. Operational details that I did not trouble you with because they have no bearing upon the campaign."

"Trouble me now," she said. "Please."

Kreippil hesitated, suspecting a trap. But he put that down to the deep suspicion of any dealings with the Abomination. He had acted with pride and honor on this matter. He had nothing to hide. "Very well," he said. "I was tasked with understanding these so-called Faithful, the human collaborators who turned against their own kind and filled you and General McEwan with such revulsion. One of our earliest discoveries was the large number of Faithful casualties that seemed to be sustained not from wounds but from the stresses of combat. At first, we thought the cause was a very high incidence of congenital heart abnormalities and other severe organ weaknesses. We initially assumed this was a side effect of the drugs the Hardits gave their Faithful to control their minds, but then a researcher discovered the real cause."

"If you speak to the human civilians on this planet," said Tawfiq, "they will tell you dark rumors of the monsters the New Order brought with us. Monsters that snatch young children from their beds. We did bring monsters with us, but mostly those responsible for stealing infants from their beds are Janissary teams hunting for sport."

"Sport?" Indiya's voice trembled with horror. "I will enjoy your death, Hardit."

"Although, it was sport with a practical purpose," said Tawfiq. "To provide raw material."

"Malice informs the Abomination's words," Kreippil said. "Nonetheless, they ring true. DNA methylation analysis showed the average biological age of the Faithful is four years. All other aging markers confirm this. The Faithful are young children fast grown to optimal age for combat duties and controlled by constant application of mind-control drugs. They are then frozen, to be thawed when needed. It is the fast growth that causes so many organ defects."

When Indiya failed to snap out of her melancholy, Kreippil added, "I fail to see the significance. Other than the accelerated maturation, it is scarcely different from the upbringing experienced by Arun McEwan and the other Human Marines, and we fought both Imperial Marines and their Free Corps counterparts during the White Knight civil war."

"On this matter we agree," said Tawfiq. "Why, I even dosed my Faithful with the same drug cocktail we supplied to the rebels at the outbreak of the civil war. McEwan was the only one to develop an unfortunate immunity, but all the others had the exact same drugs coursing through the veins. And Indiya's comrades aboard *Beowulf* felt the calming certainty brought about by those same drugs. *Themistocles* too, of course."

Despite working alongside them for so many years, Kreippil found humans as incomprehensible as any other alien species, but he vaguely sensed a trap had been sprung. He searched Indiya's face for her reaction to the Abomination's poisonous words, but her face was utterly devoid of expression, as if her mind had retreated deep inside.

Of the *Themistocles*, she had often told him that she had perished in its destruction; that the Indiya he knew was but an echo of the young woman who had died that day. Perhaps her words had been more than hyperbole.

"When your purple friend authorized the strike that unleashed Lake Tanganyika," said the wretched Hardit, "she murdered around three million children under the age of five. How do you feel about that, Indiya? All your life you've felt the crushing guilt of the three thousand you killed when you destroyed *Themistocles*. How do the deaths of three million young children compare?"

Indiya curled into a ball, tumbling slowly in the water. "Three million," she repeated lifelessly. "*Three million...*"

Kreippil flicked his tail in anger. Why had the cyber teams not wiped away this disgusting creature? Tawfiq distorted the truth beyond recognition, and yet Kreippil had to face facts: the Abomination's words had wounded Indiya. "You did not know," he told his human friend.

"She does now," said Tawfiq. "Goddess protect me, you said. Well, I *am* a goddess. I am immortal. I have demonstrated to you that I can walk through time to smite my enemies, and within days I shall unleash a new super race of fervent disciples. You may worship me as your personal goddess, Kreippil."

"Blasphemer! I shall end you, Abomination, and the foul stain you have left upon creation. I will have your mutilated corpse stuffed and mounted."

"That's better. I wouldn't want you to give up until I had my sport with you. Your purple human is useless now. That's why I called, to suggest you take charge. Kreippil versus Tawfiq. What do you say? You know, if you conduct–"

The image of the accursed Hardit demon disappeared, to be replaced by a cyber engineer who reported the attack to have been fully repulsed. Although she kept her words professional, the way the specialist tilted her head was one of horrid fascination at the pitiful sight of the human fleet commander in whom they placed so much faith.

Kreippil held Indiya within his embrace, allowing her to sob in her human way. Between heaving gasps through her gills, she begged forgiveness of friends and rivals who had died long ago. Her second-in-command, Loobie, Kreippil remembered personally. Indiya also asked forgiveness from Petty Officer Lock, and others of whom she had never spoken to him before. Spasms wracked her body, and then the power of speech left, and she wailed like an infant.

Shielded within his embrace, Kreippil hoped to give her a little dignity, but the cyber defense team had seen everything.

"The Goddess has left Admiral Indiya," Kreippil explained. "She is to be cared for, venerated, prayed for..." He hesitated. Was he about to do the right thing? He cast away such doubts. Indiya had been fragile for a long time. Her part was now over.

Kreippil waved away the cyber specialist and opened a link to Hood, Indiya's most senior flag officer.

"Signal all fleet captains," Kreippil ordered with a heavy heart, but this dark duty must not be prolonged. "I am relieving Admiral Indiya of command. I want their sanction within the hour."

Hood saluted. "Yes, Admiral."

"I have need of revenge," Kreippil told Hood before he could disappear. "Tawfiq Woomer-Calix claims apotheosis. She calls herself a goddess."

Hood was only human, but even he looked shocked at the hubris of the Hardit abomination.

And that gave Kreippil an idea. "Do we have recordings of what Tawfiq said?"

"Standby..." Hood's image froze, but only for a few seconds. The officer was highly efficient. "Yes, Admiral. The transmission data from Tawfiq is heavily quarantined, but we have security footage showing the feed into your bulkhead view screen."

Kreippil felt guilt rot his scales. What he was about to do would not help Indiya; it would cement her hurt. He pitied his friend, and hated to hurt her, but... this was war. *Holy war.*

"As you contact the captains, circulate the exchange with Tawfiq throughout the fleet. Let our warriors know the words of the false goddess who infests Earth. Let her own words condemn her. Let a new battle cry ring out throughout the fleet. *Death to the blasphemer!*"

The Littorane tracked the messages that began flying between the vessels of his First Fleet and beyond, a new fervor sweeping across space at near-lightspeed. It affected him too, the weariness of the years dropping away, invigorating him.

Then he remembered the husk of his friend, cast away by the Goddess in her infinite cruelty and majesty. Gently, so as not to alarm her, he used his new-found vitality to spiral his tail around her, as a young parent would do to calm their young. Her mind was gone, her usefulness at an end, but as her friend he would nurture her for as long as she needed him.

As for McEwan, Kreippil had always suspected him of hubris, scarcely less offensive than Tawfiq's. The Goddess had finally tired of this human too and cast him adrift into deep time as he deserved.

The time of the humans was over.

Kreippil led now.

Didn't he?

He rumbled a threatening tone that echoed off the bulkheads.

McEwan had an obscene habit of returning from the dead.

# —— Chapter 14 ——

**Arun McEwan**
**Ancient Britannia, 319BC**

The drop pod steamed in the morning mist of a prehistoric dawn.

Arun was hardly a connoisseur of art or beauty, but even he had to admit that it was kind of peaceful dropping down to a region of rolling hills and deep woods cut through with gentle streams, and devoid of roads, cities and fortifications.

The only things flying up to meet them had been the fat wood pigeons who were now singing in the woods that started a few hundred yards away and didn't stop until the sea. No one had tried to shoot them down, and instead of rockets and artillery fire, they had been met by this grassy hollow glistening with dew, which the heat from the drop pod's hull was steaming into the air.

He sniffed. The smell of scorched grass was getting stronger.

"Hey, Springer? You smell that too?"

She dropped the equipment canisters she had been unloading from the cargo compartment and came over to Arun. "Relax," she told him, and crouched down so their faces were touching almost nose to nose. "That's an order. We're here. We're safe. On the way down we saw that the nearest settlement is miles away, and if the ground was going to burst into flame, it would have already done so. None of us have any experience with vacations, but I'm determined you won't ruin it for us with your constant fretting. So I'm in charge here. Got it?"

"This isn't a vacation."

Springer called over her shoulder to the other member of the team who had not yet left the drop pod. "Pedro! Explain to Arun how this is gonna work."

The massive Trog rumbled anxiously in his thorax before replying. "After centuries of passionate study of your species, I concur with Springer. This will be a more satisfying expedition if we obey her commands."

"You see?" said Springer, tousling Arun's hair, "I'm in charge by two votes to one, and I say" – she moved the two canisters so their handles were just below Arun's hands – "being in that chair doesn't mean you sit on your lazy ass while I do all the work. I want this pod unloaded and the burrow started by lunchtime."

Arun shook his head. "You don't get to vote on your commander of the day. We're here for one reason alone. To stop Tawfiq and the New Order."

Springer sighed and walked through the pod's open gullwing doors to Pedro, whose bulk filled one half of the troop compartment. The Trog Great Parent had explained that he had hardened his carapace for the duration of the transit to protect the unborn offspring budding inside his abdomen, and now he was loosening it prior to slithering out the drop pod under his own steam.

Arun wasn't convinced. The big guy looked stuck, plain and simple.

Springer clambered on top of her own empty seat, so she could reach up and stroke the Trog's antennae, which made him tremble with pleasure, a sight that Arun found frankly unsettling.

"I think you're a saint for sticking by him for so long," she told the alien. "We are so far back in history, Arun, that we're in a different calendar system. It's 391 BC. B frakking C. Before Christ. Before the Cull. Bring your own Cooler, and Bananas and Cream. Hell, I don't know about Earth history, but I do know that we've left fleets and armies behind. It's just us. Three friends in a drop pod. The future doesn't care whether we hurry or dally. It will be waiting for us just the same. So I tell you again, stop worrying, help unload the pod, and you *will* relax even if it kills you."

She pulled a face and Arun burst out laughing. It was her impersonation of Chief Instructor Nhlappo that she used to pull as a cadet. But Springer's face was covered in scales now, and they lacked the elasticity of human skin.

She looked as if she were suffering from piles, not a fearsome veteran instructor, the scourge of any cadet who stepped out of line.

"Yes, ma'am," he snapped off with a crisp salute. Still laughing, Arun grabbed the two equipment canisters and set his chair humming over the grass to bushes by the grass bank where they were setting up shop.

"I have always tried to be his friend," said Pedro loudly. "I do not always succeed, but that was always my intent."

Arun stopped laughing. Even for Pedro, that statement was a little weird, but then, that was the sad part of this expedition. It was finally time to say goodbye to Pedro for good.

But it wasn't time for goodbyes just yet, and Springer was right: they deserved a break. 391 BC! He stopped, realizing suddenly how much he relished the prospect of returning to the fleet in 2739 AD and telling his daughter of his adventures in Celtic Britain.

*His daughter…*

Yeah, that was gonna take a whole lot of getting used to.

Arun found his good mood dissipating, and returned to his unloading, shifting the smaller canisters while Springer lifted the heavier gear with the hoist and hover trolley. There wasn't much to unload, most of the equipment bay being taken up with the return intercalator, a featureless black box 18-feet long, and half that in width and depth.

When had he forgotten how to have fun?

He couldn't help himself. He smiled at his lover, and engaged in meaningless words of small talk, but as he did, he rolled the plan around in his mind, hunting out the dangers.

It should have been easy to relax into Springer's embrace and yield to the simple pleasure of enjoying the company of the one he loved – had always loved most, if he was honest.

Should have been. But it wasn't. Something was wrong. He'd missed something. His gut told him the plan was already unravelling but he couldn't say why.

Was it simply Greyhart's involvement? Anything to do with the veck was dangerous, and Arun couldn't figure out his game. The man from the future had insisted it was too dangerous for him to suggest ways in which the Legion could use time travel to defeat Tawfiq. Anything they might do in the past was fraught with danger – and that *did* make sense to Arun – but that hadn't stopped Greyhart dropping unsubtle hints to steer the two Legion parties in directions that suited his own agenda.

He'd practically told them to send the party back to 2717, to kill Tawfiq when she was shut up tight in her Victory City bunker while her forces were off quelling the revolt at Cairo.

But how could a small team punch through that bunker's defenses to get to Tawfiq? He had touched heads with Grace, and together they had accessed their organic battle planners, talking through their options in their rapid-fire human machine language speech – which made sense at the time, but was gibberish even to Arun when he listened back to a recording.

Indiya was with them all the way, deeper inside his mind than she'd ever gone before. The old Spacer hated the enforced intimacy of being inside his private thoughts, but without her, he would never have escaped the fugue state he was always trapped inside after accessing his planner.

When he was done and rested a little, he thought about how Greyhart had initially been helpful when Arun had asked for his help. If Tawfiq with her Night Hummer allies could maybe see through time and communicate a warning to her earlier self in 2717, where could a Legion team go that was least likely to be seen by the Hummers?

Greyhart hadn't even paused to consider. "Elstow. It's a village in England, Europe. It's a... highly eventful location. Still unstable, to be honest, but nowhere in the galaxy will be better cloaked from observation than Elstow." He'd flashed that cheesy grin – the one Arun would dearly love to wipe off his face – and added, "Plus, the Swan pub does a lovely roast dinner if you pick the right era. You want a Sunday. Definitely better on a Sunday, the slow-cooked meat will be more tender."

Then Arun had explained the plan he'd concocted with his daughter, and Greyhart had stopped spouting nonsense and started begging them to reconsider. What they proposed was too big, he told them. The consequences too dangerous.

Had Greyhart been right? Was that the worry itching at the back of his mind?

No, that couldn't be it, because he'd run through all this with Grace. And with Xin, Springer, Pedro, Indiya, and all the others. The change they were about to write in Earth's past was colossal, and the moral implications alone were immense. But it was one half of the pincer movement that the Hardits would never see coming and would give his daughter's team a better chance of coming back alive.

Pedro would finally get his chance to raise and lead his own nest. And here, by this grassy bank in a place that would be named Elstow many years in the future, was where he would start. Before industrialization and advanced technology, at a time when civilization in this part of the world meant humble collections of huts and the occasional hillfort, Pedro would forge his own alien civilization deep underground. And if he were spotted in the early years – well, it was all dragons, magic donkeys, and women with snakes in their head in this era. They would easily work Pedro into their mythical stories. And by the time people had developed radar ground mapping, seismographs and advanced targeting sensors, Pedro's nest would have hidden itself deep beneath their knowledge and spread throughout the world.

The only nagging doubt was Greyhart's heavy hint that something significant had happened here. Or *would* happen. But Greyhart refused to speak of what or when that might be.

The date that did matter was 2717, because when Grace's team made their attack on Tawfiq, Pedro's descendants would be ready and waiting. Nothing terrified Hardits more than psychotic Trog soldiers bursting through the walls in a killing frenzy. It was a shame Arun wouldn't be there to see Tawfiq's final moments, but it would be a fitting end for the vile creature.

How Pedro's descendants would then coexist on an Earth they shared with the humans was a major detail to work out. But Arun had assured the big guy that the Legion would insist on a settlement that was fair to the Trogs. He would do nothing less for the insectoids who had already done so much to free the Earther humans from the New Order. Maybe if the Earthers hadn't given up Arun's ancestors as slave tribute, he might have been more concerned about forcing them to share the planet, but as it was, the Earthers were getting more than they deserved.

*The big black box.*

He froze, and asked Barney to bring up recordings of what he'd seen in the back of the pod.

Half the pod, grandly named the *Saravanan*, was given over to the time travelling machinery. A small shielded unit, only a foot long, had brought them back all this way, and the big black box like a giant's coffin would return him and Springer to the fleet in orbit about Mars in 2739. They were sealed, both physically and by the dire warnings from Greyhart about what would happen if they were interfered with. But there was something about the larger intercalator…

*What am I missing?* he thought at Barney.

His AI showed a recording of what Arun had seen when he'd glanced at Springer winching out one of the heavier equipment crates. The panels on the black box had wobbled.

"What's the matter?" Springer asked in the here and now as Arun sped his chair back to the rear of the drop pod. By now, Pedro had managed to wriggle out of the pod to beach himself on the charred grass. The kink he formed with his antennae asked the same question.

Before Arun could answer, Springer drew her pistol, and pointed it in a double-handed grip at the bank behind him.

But she didn't fire, and he saw the intruders were only deer. Beautiful but nervous creatures, they were hesitating at the top of the bank and sniffing at these strange sights and sounds. When the animals all glanced behind nervously, he expected them to flee back the way they'd come. Instead, they ran down the bank giving the drop pod and its inexplicable crew a wide berth as they hurried past.

Arun had bigger things to worry about than the local wildlife. Telling his hover chair to raise him a couple of feet above the ground, he reached inside the rear compartment and pulled at the side panel of the black box with his bare hands.

It came away.

To reveal its true contents.

Someone has sabotaged the mission.

Someone had removed the time intercalator and replaced it with other equipment, most prominently two human-compatible cryo pods. They had no ride home. They were stranded here. Cut off from the battle with Tawfiq and separated from his daughter by a gulf of 3,000 years.

Someone had interfered. Again.

And he knew who.

"Pedro! What the frakk have you done this time?"

# —— Chapter 15 ——

**Arun McEwan**
**Ancient Britannia, 319BC.**

"I am sorry."

*Sorry?* Pedro's feeble apology didn't deserve a response.

Springer joined Arun beside the giant insectoid who'd stranded them both there. He put a comforting hand on her hip, but she didn't seem to notice. Although she was standing next to the Trog, her wide-open mouth and eyes were directed at the stowaway cryopods.

*Stranded in time, with only an ugly alien and a disabled old man for company,* thought Arun. *Yeah, I can see how that might take you a moment or two to process.*

And when she did. Then Pedro would learn the full meaning of 'sorry'.

"You've really gone and done it this time, Trog," accused Arun. "You brought the cryopods because you want us to sleep?"

"No, because I wanted you to enjoy yourselves. Removing the intercalator meant I could bring other vital equipment too that would otherwise have been abandoned. I thought you and Springer deserved time together, and I do not believe you would have seized the opportunity if you could merely flick a switch and find yourselves back in the conflict with Tawfiq. I am truly sorry I have done this to you."

"Don't tell lies. You have no regrets. I know you, Pedro."

The Trog flipped his antenna back along his head. "This, I find awkward."

Arun glanced at Springer – still in shock – and sighed. The pain in his hips was flaring up again, and he was too tired to stay annoyed with Pedro. The cryopods should be able to handle a few thousand years without a hitch… just so long as someone was around to thaw them out. It wasn't even the worst thing the big insectoid had ever hit him with. He shrugged. "Just tell it how it appears to you, Big Guy."

"I do regret upsetting you. That is not deceit. But I do not regret what I have done."

Arun laughed until the tears rolled down his cheeks.

"What is happening?" Pedro was waving his antennae in consternation. "Have I broken you? Arun, my closest friend, I have worried about your mental state for years. This is what I was trying to cure. Alas, I am too late."

"*Alas?* You're priceless, Pedro. I'm... I don't know what I am, but it is a ludicrous situation and all I can do is laugh. Look at us. I'm a broken old man in a hover chair. Springer's been dyed, lengthened, had a leg regrown, and her skin covered in alien scales. And a bloated alien giant ant – no offence – who's been heavily pregnant for centuries, is telling us young songbirds to go enjoy each other. It's hilarious. What did you expect, that Springer and I would be so overcome by the soft grass and woodland air that we'd romp naked on the virgin hills of Earth?"

*Arun...* Barney warned in the corner of his mind.

"You did, didn't you?" Arun accused. This just kept getting better. Pedro was embarrassed. It wasn't just his drooping antennae and his comical attempt to sink his fat body into the grass, but the way his words would tread carefully around his human friends until he decided he'd been forgiven.

Arun loved the big ant, truly he did, but he was hilarious when he was embarrassed. That amusement was just enough to stop Arun from shooting the interfering alien for stranding him. For now, at least.

*Arun!*

*What?* he snapped at his AI.

*Pardon me for getting involved in human affairs, but I'm just passing on a message from Saraswati here. She says to tell you that you're a selfish rat who thinks of no one but himself, except when he's having sexual fantasies about President Lee.*

Arun's laughter dried up. He swiveled his chair around and was immediately caught in the powerful glare beaming out of Springer.

"You told me that duty would never release us, that we would never find the time we deserve to enjoy each other," she said. "You told me that when we'd finally rid this world of Tawfiq and her murdering regime, that we'd slip away together. Spend our final years making up for the centuries we have surrendered to duty. Did you mean those words?"

Arun nodded.

"Then I don't know why you're laughing at poor Pedro. He's giving us an option we never really had before, because no matter how much you want to be with me, you would have spent every moment thinking about the journey home to 2739 in the drop pod. Without the downstream intercalator, we can spend as much time together as we like. We can sleep through the centuries and then awaken to duty."

She stroked Pedro's antennae, which made him sigh with pleasure. "Thank you, Pedro. I think you made a very sweet gesture." She drew his bulbous head to her, hugging him while glaring at Arun.

But her expression quickly shifted into joyfulness, her lovely eyes flashing mischief and her cheeks dimpling.

"The words of your instructors may have been lost on you," she challenged, "but I was taught to seize every opportunity with all my limbs, and it's a lesson I've learned to follow the hard way."

Her words hung there, a challenge. A challenge to both of them.

Then she walked away, striding for the grassy bank where the deer had paused.

And as she did so, she shed her clothing, stripping away everything down to her scales.

Halfway up, she turned and looked back at Arun. "Well, are you coming or not?"

He wanted to.

Oh, how he wanted to!

As she'd aged with her skin parasite, the pattern it painted on her body had darkened and softened, as had the scales themselves, which had taken on a slight sheen like ancient, yet well-oiled, leather. For the first time since he'd connived in her reinvention as a Wolf, her nakedness looked entirely natural to him. She seemed at one with the grass and the deer, far more than Arun did, even if he was still wearing his original skin.

Her patterning hadn't been designed but was a natural expression of the skin parasite combining its DNA analog with hers. The result were repeating fractal motifs that looked to Arun as if she had been rolling in abstract art. Suddenly, she appeared more like the artwork primitive people might paint on stone artifacts, her body coated with looping regular patterns of ribbons, as if an alien artist had removed the arteries from human cadavers, dyed them in woad, indigo, and ocher and then laid them out in pleasing patterns.

Centered on her navel and her nipples was a motif of three spirals that intimately interlinked, each curling into the others with no clear division between them.

He wanted to follow her up that little hill and let her lead him wherever she liked. He wanted that so badly.

But Arun couldn't. Springer's logic was unassailable – they should enjoy this time – but he didn't know how. When they were kids, he'd always fought to keep his unit from the Cull, and for himself to qualify for the next year. Then there was always the next campaign to plan for. There had been carousing, release, sex, food. But in the morning, the cares of the galaxy would claim him again. Since his earliest memory, he'd been fighting to survive. Ceaselessly. He didn't know how to relax, to be carefree. How could he? He'd never experienced such things.

Springer made a show for him of licking her lips.

He growled deep within his throat.

She tossed her head from which long twirls of auburn hair still spilled through the scales, and resumed her walk up the bank, his gaze drawn to the three-spiral pattern that nestled in the small of her back and rested on the upper swell of her behind. With her buttocks rolling with the sassy sway she was putting on, the spirals became intertwined woad snakes writhing. Beckoning.

He smacked his fist hard into his forehead. It was all right for her. They'd renewed her body. She was still strong, utterly desirable. Springer could revel in her new form, whereas he…

He looked down at the black smart fabric that fixed to the edge of his hoverchair and gently constricted itself around his waist. He'd have to take medication to dull the pain that filled his body before he could enjoy rubbing it against Springer's. Dammit! Of course they'd end up vulleying themselves raw, but it wouldn't be easy. They weren't cadets crawling into each other's racks for an exploratory look see. Didn't she understand that?

He glared at Springer who was standing on the crest of the hill, hands on the multicolored swell of her hips. Damn her!

Suddenly, she jerked in surprise – and dropped into a loose crouch.

Arun put his chair into gear. "Come on," he roared at it, but he accelerated too hard and the contraption almost tipped over, the auto-safety system shutting down the propulsion unit, making him wait while it righted itself.

*I got it*, said Barney, taking over his chair. They sped uphill, leaving Pedro stuck by the drop pod.

"Arun," said Springer, not turning her head away from whatever she was looking at, "we've got company."

# —— Chapter 16 ——

**Human Translation of Annotated Nest Archive**
**Date: 6635-154 [estimated]**
**Subject: Interrogation of Human McEwan**
**Key scents: humans~gender~friendship~historical record**

CONTEXT: The human, Arun McEwan, forever friend of the Nest by deed and by scent, was interrogated immediately prior to being placed into long-term cryogenic suspension. His human female mate was already in deep sleep by this point. The subject appeared reluctant to leave this time period and anxious about the dangers he and his companion would face if they were successfully revived. With his mate unable to overhear, he appeared grateful for the opportunity to recount his memory of the events that had taken place in this time zone.

==INTERROGATION FRAGMENT CONTINUES==

HUMAN McEWAN: So we all get to the top of that hill – well not a hill, just a little bank but with my chair and your… bloated body – no offence, Pedro – we gotta face that you and I are no longer all-terrain guys. Anyway, we get to the top, I've got my pistol ready, and there's Springer looking as imperious as Xin – for heaven's sake, don't ever tell Springer I said that – and there's a hunting party of locals bowing down like she's their goddess come to bestow favor on their tribe. I mean she does look like a goddess, what with all those beautiful patterns over her super-buff body. But she's more. She's beyond beautiful. She's perfect, and no one on Earth would look anything like her until we show up in 2739. She's not just all woman but she's all warrior too, which I think was vital to the locals. These guys were local nobility – well fed and fit for their era – but they're still Earth natives while she's from the Marine branch of the humankinds. There's no contest. One on one, she could take any of them with ease and they were all warrior enough to know that.

So they get to their knees and half bow their heads. In reply, Springer clears her throat and speaks.

They don't understand a word… at first. Of course they don't, but you already know what happens next.

GREAT PARENT: Yes, Friend Arun, I know my experience of the events, but you promised your recollection. I am finally a Great Parent, but I am still an archivist and scholar. Treat me as if I were an inanimate recording device.

HUMAN McEWAN: A microphone that keeps prompting me to say the right thing. OK, I'm hearing you, Big Guy. So Springer speaks the same tongue we learned back at the Detroit base on Tranquility-4, which is ironic because that's a descendant of English, and the place Greyhart sent us to is a little English village called Elstow. Except we're at least two thousand years too early for our languages to even begin to match up. Consequently, these guys don't understand a frakking thing.

There's consternation amongst the locals, and I could tell that because they all boasted huge moustaches that they now proceed to curl fingers through.

Then their voices grow more agitated. They stand up, and one reaches to a long straight sword decorated with grooves similar to the patterns spiraling along Springer's naked body. I can understand their reaction. First, they get the shock of meeting a goddess… but then it turns out to be a *foreign* goddess who hasn't even bothered to learn their lingo. These ancients

151

turned out to be pretty tribal about their deities, and Springer would have to go.

ASIDE: Subject at this point looks at me expectantly. I believe he is expecting a bilateral conversation, a more comforting form of interaction that he has become accustomed to. I believe he is saddened to be separated from his mate, Springer, and anxious about his return to a war zone. For a human to seek comfort in conversation with one of our race speaks eloquently of the capacity of our two species to coexist, the recent troubles between our peoples notwithstanding.

HUMAN McEWAN: So, yeah, Springer's AI, Saraswati, is as mad as a box of Khallenes, but she's got some tasty AI moves – yeah, I know you have too, Barney – but it's Saraswati who does some serious real-time linguistic analysis. Springer speaks again, and this time she's following Saraswati's prompts in her head to speak in their language. She garbles the pronunciation, but they seem to accept that deities from far away will have stupid accents.

They're what our history records as Celts, though that's not their name for themselves. Their unit commander's name is Tasciovanus, and he's enjoying some downtime after making a ruckus and stealing a few goats from a village the other side of the tribal frontier. It's hardly total war, but his raid is enough to make the village pay tribute to his tribe, who are called the Camuvellauni. Tasciovanus is smart, and we realize that he's more than the poster boy for the local mustache-growers' association; he's the king. When I'd gotten to know him a little more, I came to understand his people loved to talk constantly of war, but that was mostly bravado and the mead talking. Although the king would switch to all-out war and kill or enslave every one of his enemies if he was pushed, Tasciovanus understood that would be bad for business. From what I could make out, being a Celtic king is like running a series of protection rackets. Like a twentieth-century mafia boss, but with a thicker mustache and more swords.

Just when I think Springer's got this, Tasciovanus starts to get fidgety. He's got his priest with him, a guy in a pristine white cloak he calls his druid. Now, this druid guy is seriously stoked to be in the presence of a real live goddess and can't wait to get back and tell his druid mates. Unfortunately, that means Tasciovanus has a problem. He's just been seriously outranked by Springer, and when the priest gets to tell everyone about her at the druid club, everyone for miles around will forget that they were supposed to be paying him tribute and start paying their homage to *her*. At the end of the day, Tasciovanus can't escape the fact that he's just a guy with impressive facial hair, whereas Springer has scales and spirals, and being properly divine, doesn't need to bother with mundane details such as clothing.

Tasciovanus says nothing, but I'm sure he's wondering whether he can get away with killing the druid so news doesn't spread. In the end, he calculates that he can't get away with murder, but he's not a happy king.

Springer's one smart woman – which is one of the things I love about her. She sees all this going through the king's head while I'm still caught on the facial hair.

She commands Tasciovanus to leave her and her goblin servant (that was me, by the way). This hillock where she's standing, and the ground for five hundred hides around, is declared holy, blessed land. No hunting or warfare is allowed. She tells them they may walk her land but leave nothing but veneration, and take nothing but the joy of harmony. And if the king wanted to tell all his Celtic mates that the Goddess Phaedra was on his patch, then that was okay with her. Better still, if anyone wanted to come in peace to her sacred grove and make offerings in the stream that ran nearby, then they would receive her divine blessing.

The king doesn't like being told what to do. But then he thinks through what he's just heard, and the scales fall from his eyes. Once the druid comm network starts buzzing with talk of this living goddess, parties were going to travel hundreds of miles to do a little venerating and chuck some precious objects in the river nearby – Celts are really into that kind of thing, forever tossing swords, silver jewelry and torcs into the nearest puddle – and they would all have to travel through his kingdom to get to her. Lodgings, tithes, guest services… right there and then, I saw the concept of 'tourist attraction' being born in the Celtic mind. Springer was not only going to make Tasciovanus rich, but she was going to make him the most prestigious king in the whole of Celt-dom.

Of course, you were supposed to dig us underground, Pedro, so we would never have to meet the locals. Unpopulated area, Greyhart told us. Well, it *was* unpopulated, because we'd arrived slap bang in the middle of the king's private hunting grounds. Just bad luck, I suppose, but Springer had turned it around, putting them at ease. In fact, now that the fear of being struck down by a bolt of lightning or turned into a toad was receding, their tongues were lolling at the sight of this utterly beautiful warrior goddess.

GREAT PARENT: Were you jealous of the humans taking pleasure in the sight of your mate?

HUMAN McEWAN: Jealous? Springer was loving the attention, and I was proud fit to burst. I mean, how many people can say they go out with a god or goddess? Literally. I was more than happy to play the role of her goblin servant. I've been the center of attention for tens of trillions of people since before I left my teens. Now it was Springer's turn.

Anyway. It's my girl's smarts that get me; they always did. We needed some privacy for a while to get digging, bury the drop pod and all the equipment, and then begin our long slumber. Springer had read the king's mind and turned him from reluctant enemy to enthusiastic ally in moments.

ASIDE: Subject moves to the cryopod containing his mate and draws back the outer shield so he can see the outline of her face. He kisses her through the shield, despite the many times I have told him not to. His lips bond to the cold surface and he yelps in pain as he pulls them free. Humans can be so foolish, but that is what intrigues me to study them.

HUMAN McEWAN: You know, I laughed at you and Springer about the whole idea of romping naked in virgin hills. But that's exactly what we did for three months, until Springer persuaded me it was now or never to sleep. Sorry, friend, for doubting you. [Subject becomes emotional. Tears form and voice timbre deepens]. The time you gave us here was precious. Thank you. But now... now it is so very hard to go back to the war.

GREAT PARENT: Perhaps this will help. [Hands the human a white cube, small enough to fit in his fist.]

HUMAN McEWAN: What the hell is this?

GREAT PARENT: I do not know. Greyhart tried to give it to you shortly before we left. You were fully engaged with Springer, so I promised him I would hand it to you myself.

HUMAN McEWAN: It could be a bomb.

GREAT PARENT: It could be. Friend Arun, I do not understand the technology that brought us to this time. Nonetheless, I speculate that it enables Greyhart to kill people with enormous ease. Therefore, I do not think this object is a bomb.

HUMAN McEWAN: I don't like it. Everything about Greyhart makes my skin crawl, so maybe I'm not best placed to judge. I trust your judgement better on this, Big Guy. Should I take this?

GREAT PARENT: Yes, you should.

HUMAN McEWAN: [Takes a deep breath]. OK. Stick it with Barney in the AI cubby of my pod. Speaking of which, I'm done talking. It's time to lay to rest next to Springer.

ADDENDUM

Human McEwan entered cryo stasis within the hour.

To give credence to her magical nature in the minds of the indigenous humans, I made several appearances before them. It was no small thing to break from my labors preparing the birthing chambers in which my Nest would first grow. The urge to give birth fought with the desire to keep my offspring safe, but yielded long enough for me to return to the surface. Silhouetted by moonlight, I made an evocative vision, which they fitted into their mythology. I became Phaedra's Dragon.

They fitted Human Springer into their culture too. The whorls and spirals on her body were carved into a thousand items of jewelry and stone in her honor, the triskelion pattern of three conjoined spirals becoming the defining motif of Celtic art. Three thousand years later, and many light years distant, I saw the human Marines of Detroit base wearing decorative tattoos and unit symbols based upon the patterns of Springer's scales.

But I was no longer there to witness these cultural developments. I had waited long enough. It was time to start my colony. For so long, I had been a Great Parent to nothing more than a bloated abdomen. Now I had a nest to lead. That it would be built on the homeworld of the species that had fascinated me so long was a beautiful irony that my descendants would write many poems about.

For a thousand years, legends abounded in the culture of the British Celts – and those who came after – of the hero buried underground who sleeps through many lifetimes but will awaken when the darkest night falls upon the land. Then the slumbering hero will rise to defeat foul invaders. Later, in another age, these ancient tales were rewritten around the hero called King Arthur, but I believe Human Springer was the wellspring for that story.

In her case, of course, the tale is not a myth. She was indeed a hero, and she did rise after sleeping three thousand years to fight the Hardit invaders. But she did far more. Her most courageous act would come later still.

==INTERROGATION FRAGMENT ENDS==

# —— PART VII ——
# ALIEN APOTHEOSIS

# —— Chapter 17——

**Governor Romulus**
**Beneath the ruins of the White House**

"Who is the Voice of the Resistance?"

"How do you contact the so-called Human Legion?"

Zantoz and the Earth Resistance had worked real magic with their nano-effector factories hidden in my body, and specifically my brain. No matter how many times Tawfiq's uglies struck my head with their plastic clubs, they couldn't knock any memories out of it.

Teeth and blood, though... yeah, they were spewing forth in abundance.

Worst of all, I knew Tawfiq was crossing a line. For so many years, beatings and threats to kill had been part of her enjoyment of me, but she'd always stopped short of damaging her plaything. But now... you don't hit a guy's head so hard that bits fall off if you're looking forward to exchanging banter in the future.

My usefulness was coming to an end.

I had nothing to lose, but instead of the fighting spirit of the Wolf I had been raised to be, my inner resolve was as bare, empty and featureless as this cell somewhere beneath the White House. I knew something was wrong with me, something *false*. I still didn't understand what.

Which is why, surprisingly enough, Tawfiq ordered my beating to stop. "Fascinating," said my lifelong tormentor. "I believe you, Romulus. You honestly know nothing of the Resistance."

I didn't reply. I was too busy gasping for breath, groveling in the puddle of my own blood.

Her guards grabbed my limbs so she could safely ram her face into mine. I gagged on the stink of her breath. Guess dental hygiene isn't in the job description of Supreme Commander and Megalomaniac-in-Chief.

"Let's see if I can free your memories by other means," she said.

160

They dragged me along corridors and up stairs to areas of the White House complex that were more familiar than the torture cells – all the way back to the gilded cage of my room.

I didn't resist as they rolled back my sleeve and stuck my exposed wrist inside the drawer beneath my dresser mirror and rubbed it against a waxy patch inside.

Why would I resist? None of this made any sense.

Then I was blinking furiously as my mind came out of hiding. When my vision stopped flickering, and I looked out on a room of Hardits watching me, everything made perfect sense.

Of course, you understand even better than me. You were in this from the start, weren't you, Shepherdess?

Well, here's what you don't know. What Tawfiq revealed to me – to the *real* me – and what you need to tell the Legion. Tell them time is running out.

*Time.*

I may only be a dumb human to you, but even I'm beginning to understand – here at the end when it no longer matters – that time is more flexible, more… *mutable* than I'd ever suspected.

And yet sometimes time can be real simple. Dumb, human simple. Right now, we don't have enough of it, and that's what you need to tell the Legion.

Tawfiq's insane, but she's not stupid. Nor is she weak. She explained that we have ten days left. If we don't defeat her by then, it will all be over.

Tawfiq will become a goddess.

# —— Chapter 18 ——

**Arun McEwan**

Arun's dreams hardened.

For uncountable years he had drifted through the dream void but now he imagined cold and heat, of metal pressed against his neck, of feathery fingers stroking his face.

He imagined opening his eyes, but he must still be dreaming because he saw only swirling primeval mists.

Then he perceived a solidity forming within the vapors – dark finger-like protuberances, except these were too narrow, too long, and too finely segmented to be fingers.

A fan whirred and the mist began to clear.

Reality hardened all around.

A Trog of the scribe life-mode was flicking its antennae over him. He was inside a cryogenic pod, but it was thawing. He was coming alive.

He couldn't remember this small resuscitation chamber, but that was nothing to worry about. And the Trogs... why weren't they human techs?

Arun couldn't remember that either, but a half-functioning memory told him he shouldn't be surprised.

Then the mystery of the Trogs disappeared from his mind when he caught motion about ten feet away on the opposite wall of the chamber.

A gleaming jewel was climbing out of another cryo pod. Springer. The whorls and triskelia of her Wolf scales dripped with cryo-slime, burnishing her naked body as she plopped onto the damp floor.

Smiling, he enjoyed the slight of her slithering as helplessly as a newborn, drinking up the sight of her gradually reacquainting herself with her limbs until she waved cheerfully at him.

A low growl escaped his lips, and he knew for sure that this was not a dream because he always woke from cryo feeling seriously randy – the longer the sleep the more powerful the effect.

And he was so horny that it hurt. A lot. *How long have I been under?*

Springer somehow slithered up to sit on her shapely butt, facing him.

And smiled.

She was happy to see him – that was all – but the erotic charge that punched down Arun's optic nerve to see that woman smile was so powerful that his vision flooded with red, and he had to fight to keep consciousness.

A terrifying thought sobered him a little. Male Marines suffered statistically higher rates of resuscitation attrition than females. Was this why? Were their bodies overwhelmed by uncontrollable lust?

But he couldn't die.

Not with Springer so close.

Even the idea of her name carried enough charge of pleasure to lash his brain with electrical overload.

How frakking long had he slept?

He'd known that information before he went under. *Give it time*, he told himself. *Don't die, and it will come back to you.*

But even with his eyes clamped shut, Arun's mind was flailed by images of Springer glistening, Springer smiling with those dimples half-hidden beneath her scales, of her beside him on a Celtic hillside, the curve of her hip picked out by silvery moonlight...

*Chirp... brrp... chirp... brrp...*

What the frakk? An alert sounded behind him. From the shelf inside the pod used to store a Marine's AI.

But...

Arun touched the port at his neck and knew Barney was inside him, though still too drowsy to talk.

Then what was in the...?

He reached around and drew out a cube that fitted snugly into his palm.

It was the size and weight of a ration cube. A terrible hunger struck him, knocking the edges off his lust, but ration cubes didn't trill like that.

*Chirp… brrp… chirp… brrp…*

He gave the cube an exploratory lick… He'd tasted worse, but it wasn't food.

Springer spoke. Either her words were unintelligible or his hearing was still rebooting, because he got only gibberish. Was she telling him something vital about this cube?

The trilling ceased, to be replaced by confusing words.

"Hello. Hello, do you copy? Who are you? Speak now!"

"Unnghh," said Arun, because he remembered. This was a communication cube. It had come from Greyhart.

"Say again," said the voice.

"Unnghh," Arun repeated helpfully.

"I can make no sense of you, human. Speak with my liaison."

"Frnngk yuhh!"

"Hello," said a human voice. Male. Young but even in his semi-lucid state, Arun sensed this man had experienced a great deal in a short life. "My name is Lance Scipio, and I am an officer in the Human Legion. Do you copy?"

"Scipooh?"

"Yes, Scipio. Look, I can hear in your voice that you understand me. I just can't follow a frakking word you're saying. Take your time and then speak slowly. Imagine you're speaking with a crècheling who–"

"Scipio?"

"Yes."

"Year?"

"Say again."

"Year? What year? Now! Xin? Grace? Answer me! Indiya mission."

"Oh, perfect!" Lance said to whoever else was at his location. "The man's either coming out of cryo or is deranged. Either way, it could be hours before I get any sense out of him."

He replied to Arun. "Depends on your calendar. It's 2739 in the Terran Common Era. It's 577 years since the Vancouver Accession Treaty, 174 years since the wars started, and 298 since I'm reliably informed I started a line of Lancelings with a cute Spacer tech called Aura."

Barney woke. Arun's power of speech came back online milliseconds later.

"You can cut the crècheling drent now, Scipio. State your rank and unit."

This Scipio person hesitated, clearly reluctant to supply information that should come automatically. What was the man playing at? "We are the Rakasa Expeditionary Fleet," he said, still refusing to offer his rank.

"Idiots!" snapped a woman's voice. "Give that here."

That voice… it couldn't be, could it? Memories of his time as a cadet flooded through Arun's mind. A young Springer featured heavily in them, all dimples and wild auburn hair in a face that hadn't yet burned in a Hardit's plasma blast. The flesh, blood, and scaly edition was standing in front of him, arms crossed and head tilted as if trying to hear something she couldn't quite make out.

"General McEwan, I can't say I'm entirely surprised to hear your voice."

"Nhlappo?" said Springer incredulously.

"Nor yours, Phaedra Tremayne. Your voice has changed but it can only be you. I assume you two have finally figured out that you're soulmates. It must be like old times in Detroit."

"Never mind that," said Arun. "We've a lot to tell you. Where are you?"

"About twenty hours away from Earth. Brought a fleet with me. You remember Leading Spacer Magnetizer?"

"No… oh, you mean *Tizer*. One of Indiya's… bunch."

"You'd best ask him about the capabilities of this fleet. He built them. Where do you need us?"

Back in 2601, Tirunesh Nhlappo had slipped back to Tranquility-4 to take command of the defenses against a surprise Hardit attack. When the fighting turned nuclear, comms were fried. No one ever heard from Nhlappo or Tranquility-4 again. Everyone assumed it had been overrun by the New Order. And now, after nearly 150 years, she had turned up at the right time and place to aid in the liberation of Earth…

Arun felt as if he were a puzzle piece being slotted into a pre-ordained place – the same as Nhlappo, Scipio, Xin, Grace and all the other pieces. It was not a pleasant feeling.

"You've met him, haven't you?" Arun said in a whisper.

"Greyhart? Yeah. Nothing in my life has scared me more than that man and what he represents. He appeared mid-journey and frakked with our engines, speeding them up so we would turn up to your party on time. *On time?* Gave us this comm cube too, which has just activated for the first time, and by sounds of it right on script for the moment you wake from cryo. I'm a frakking puppet, General. I want to cut my strings."

"You and me both, Tirunesh. He is human, though. At least, I think he is, and that means we're on the same side against the Hardits for now. We'll deal with Greyhart once we've rid ourselves of Tawfiq."

"Tawfiq? She's here? Good. I've a score or two to settle with her."

The sound of a scuffle came over the communication device.

"I do not care to indulge in social small talk," said a Jotun through an electronic translator. "We have the business of war to attend to. Do you confirm you are General McEwan and in command of Legion forces here?"

"I am McEwan… but in operational control? No. Officially, I'm probably dead. Again. But I am the strategic leader, or will be once we've kicked Tawfiq down to hell. Who are you?"

"What chaotic madness are you playing at there?" boomed the Jotun. "I am Field Marshal Marchewka of the Human Legion, and I *know* I am in command."

"A field marshal, eh? Interesting, considering I've never heard of you or of that rank. Where do you come from and who awarded you that interesting title?"

"I was based at Tranquility-4, at the location you called Beta City. As for my promotion, I awarded myself that rank. We had millions of Marines in a fight for control of the planet. There was no other viable candidate to lead."

"And you consider yourself an officer of the Human Legion?"

"I have pledged allegiance to the cause. Freedom shall be won."

"Good. Because that means you report to me. As far as you're concerned, Marchewka, I *am* the Human Legion. That goes for you too, Colonel Nhlappo, or whatever rank you've been using recently. If you aren't prepared to accept my orders, you can turn your fancy ships around and head back to this Rakasa place. I will not tolerate any more splits."

"Any *more*?" queried Nhlappo. "Lee Xin took off, didn't she?"

Arun hadn't seen Nhlappo since the 26th century. Had the fate of his marriage and alliance with Xin been so obvious even then? "She did," he replied, "but we are reunited for the final battle. And you? Are you with me?"

All Arun could hear from the other end of the link was labored Jotun breathing. Marchewka made a weird noise in his throat as if gargling gravel, and then spoke awkwardly with his own voice.

"The Rakasa Fleet is under your command, General McEwan. What are your orders?"

A wave of alarm swept over the scribe revival techs.

Arun half wondered how he could tell not just the scribes' anxiety, but that they were frantically urging someone outside the cryo chamber to stay the hell away.

The Jotun field marshal was bellowing out of the comm cube, but Arun's mind wasn't yet up to multitasking. He sensed a threat looming and hadn't room to think of anything else.

Ten seconds later, with the scribes leaping around in agitation, he heard heavy footfalls approach from the passageway outside.

Ten seconds after that, a brute of a Trog filled the entrance, a second huge Trog resting its front legs on the first one so it could poke its armored head into the resuscitation chamber.

Two pairs of antennae pushed through gaps in their head armor and painted the shape of cones in the air as they scanned the room.

Arun didn't know what he was seeing, but he sure didn't like it.

In their many cultural liaison meetings back when Arun was a cadet, Pedro had described the complex lifecycle stages of his race. These brutes in the doorway had never featured in those stories. They were a new life-mode.

Their massive heads sloped up like glacis armor into an enormous crest that rippled up to a frilly edge. Two curved horns protruded over deeply recessed eyes on heads that bore no resemblance to the smaller scribes, who were jumping up and down in front of the newcomers. In fact, their heads reminded Arun of armored snow plows that could be affixed to a tank

The unidentified Trogs burst into motion, scattering the scribes and charging at Springer.

Pulling himself out of his pod as fast as he could, Arun looked on in absolute horror as the lead Trog tried to gore his Celtic goddess with its horns.

Springer rolled, and the horns missed her by inches, shattering floor tiles and digging a furrow into the stone below.

In their eagerness to kill her, the two Trogs now got in each other's way in the confinement of the small chamber. They stomped with their legs at their prey who dodged the worst of the blows but couldn't break away.

Springer was strong, and her beautiful scales also provided a tough layer of armor. But beneath these Trogs built for war, she didn't stand a chance.

Arun screamed in rage and threw himself at Springer's attackers.

# —— Chapter 19 ——

**Governor Romulus**
**Beneath the ruins of the White House**

So there I was, back in the personal chambers of the Governor of Earth, the familiar human stink of my room accented by the smell of my own fear and blood.

Tawfiq watched me intently as my memories reassembled themselves, her upper eye narrowing to a slit even though she'd been blind in that orb for years.

I was the Voice of The Resistance, a role I had performed under the direction of others; a lie as dark as the notion that it was I who ruled the Earth.

I didn't. My role was to be the betrayer of humanity.

I'd refused the chance to escape a hero on Tawfiq's shuttle, preferring to return to my reviled status as governor, because I might still be useful as a spy inside the White House.

At least, that was what I had told myself.

Tawfiq had suckered me from the start, light years away, in space near the White Knight homeworld. *Stand here next to this officer, Romulus. Say these words to this chief engineer, Romulus. Leave this package where we tell you. Do these simple things and Janna won't be hurt. We'll be gone out-system soon, anyway, and none of your human comrades need ever know what you did.*

I wasn't stupid. I knew her orders weren't as innocent as they appeared, but I went along with Tawfiq's lies at first because I was too cowardly to risk Janna's life. Before long, she had trapped me in my own treachery. Even before she brought me to Earth, I was implicit in murder. And then... my crimes were entirely explicit. I remember that astronomer who'd accidently discovered a Legion attack, and a hundred like him.

I'm no hero. Now that my mind is back in a single piece, I realize the true reason why I didn't escape on that shuttle was because I know I don't deserve a chance at redemption.

I despise myself, but there is one person I hate more.

And as my spirit was hit by the curse of remembering, Tawfiq was pressing her scarred snout up against mine, smelling every last drop of my self-loathing while my arms and legs were pinned by her guards.

I pulled myself out of their grip with all my strength to gain enough height to bring my forehead cracking down on Tawfiq's.

She dodged my head butt, though she was too slow to avoid me spitting in her eyes.

If there was symbolism in the way bloodied human spittle coated Tawfiq's evil yellow eyes, blinding her, then her guards interpreted it differently from me. I saw it as a sign of human resistance, but to them it was a sign that I was in urgent need of being beaten to death.

To my surprise, after the first flurry of blows, Tawfiq signaled them to cease.

"I require the human's head to remain recognizable. And his body is already tenderized. I do not want my meat to be overly bruised."

Tawfiq's words hit me harder than the cudgels of my guards. Many times she'd threatened to kill me, but to eat me…?

"Yes, that's right," she sneered. "Even you must have heard rumors of children snatched in the night by monsters. The monsters are Nernailner Nyrotaps – hunting wolves, if you like. Initially, we only hunted for sport, and to snatch infants to swell the ranks of Faithful, but then we learned something unexpected about the tender young of your species. Something *delicious.*"

I didn't need the long tongue licking around her chops, or the satisfied noise in her throat to grasp Tawfiq's meaning.

"My apotheosis is only days away," she told me. "My ascent to the ranks of the divine will come with the birth of a new race of super warriors. My New Corps has ample weapons and equipment, but in the first few weeks, feeding these millions of hungry new mouths will be a challenge, one for which I have kept wild humans alive for all these years. They shall become food. And you, my dear Romulus, will be eaten first. By me."

# ——— Chapter 20 ———

**Arun McEwan**
**The Nest**

Resuscitation played cruel tricks with memories.

Until Arun tried leaping onto the Trogs trying to kill Springer, he'd forgotten his legs had been amputated many years ago, after a long session with Tawfiq's favorite torturer.

He slid to the floor in an explosion of pain, but he didn't hesitate for an instant, slithering over to where Springer was dodging the stamping Trog feet. He pushed himself onto her chest and wrapped his arms loosely around her neck.

"Let me take their blows," he told her. "And when you see your moment, get out and run while I distract them. Get help. Maybe this is a Trog civil war." He paused and looked into her wild lilac eyes, which stared over his shoulder at the Trogs. The insectoids had fallen silent.

"They've stopped, haven't they?" he said.

She nodded. While he brushed away the blood running into her eyes from a head wound, she added, "I think they want me dead. But not if it means hurting you."

More of Arun's memories came back online, important ones from when he was a cadet – the agony as Pedro had forced a scent emitter into his chest, so he would be recognized forevermore as a Nest sibling.

He twisted around and stared up into two pairs of swirling antennae extruded from snow plow heads.

"Back off!" he shouted.

They obeyed, retreating to the entrance.

Springer sat up, arms around Arun who perched on her lap.

"She's with me," he said firmly. "She is of the Nest. You will protect her with your lives."

The Trogs bent their forelegs and knelt in submission. Their scent emitted a complex message of eagerness to obey, combined with the terrible acknowledgement that they had transgressed.

"General," Scipio was saying out of the cube that had toppled with Arun onto the floor. "What the frakk is going on?"

Arun couldn't answer. There was far too much happening for Arun's mind to process. All he could do was hang tight and hope his pounding heart wasn't about to explode. He'd joked with Pedro long ago that his scent implant would one day make him the warrior queen of the ants. Well, he had two big beasts in front of him waiting for his orders. If that was all he had to process, his mind could have handled it. But Springers breasts were rubbing against his back with an insistence that he couldn't ignore now that they weren't under attack. A few feet away, Nhlappo and this mystery fleet were talking out of a ration cube from the future, and Springer was nuzzling his neck, and... and then one of the Trogs spoke!

# —— Chapter 21 ——

Governor Romulus
Beneath the ruins of the White House

Tawfiq explained her plan for apotheosis in every terrible detail, relishing my horror whenever she reminded me of the part I had played in making her ascent to goddesshood possible.

A million Ultra Janissaries – the New Corps she called them – would swear loyalty just outside the White House in Victory Mall in a ceremony linked to millions more waiting in secret galleries dug beneath North America. My memories have been fragmented for years, but her words sparked a recent memory of being shown hints of a new Janissary army that would defeat her Hardit rivals, but I didn't trust my own memories. Besides, Tawfiq had lied so often to me that I didn't know whether to believe any of this, but that wasn't good enough for her. She wouldn't allow me the escape of doubt.

So she showed me. All of it.

Tawfiq had previously escorted me on many journeys through the galleries beneath the main White House complex. I had seen the factories in which Janissaries were made, and the vile tanks in which human children were fast grown into adult Faithful. There were development labs where specimens of Faithful and Janissary alike were experimented upon in the never-ending search for design improvements.

Beneath that were the secret new looms for the Ultra Janissaries. And if I truly had seen them before, it had only been a glimpse of their true enormity. Hidden deep beneath the ground, Tawfiq's secret looms stretched on for miles and were layered deep into the bedrock. I have never seen or heard of Hardits building on such a scale before. This was almost worthy of Trog architects at their most ambitious.

The fleshy outer shells of these Ultra Janissaries were already built; all they needed was the internal wiring. The existing Janissaries of the New Order were physically tough Hardit specimens, but their creation had centered on the removal of their gender, and the associated scent that underpinned natural Hardit society. As the Ottoman sultans of ancient Earth had created a corps of Janissary warriors so completely outside of society that they could not themselves become a rival to the sultan – or so the Ottoman rulers had thought – the Hardit Janissaries were so set apart from gendered Hardit society that they could be loyal only to the New Order and Tawfiq.

This new generation of Ultra Janissaries were physical giants of their race, not only on the outside with their tough hide and Marine-like muscles, but on the inside, their agoraphobia had been erased. These Janissaries wouldn't need to be drugged to fly in air and in space. But the most important internal upgrade, as far as Tawfiq was concerned, was to their loyalty.

Their minds were physically complete, but their internal connections were still being wrought. Approximately fifteen years of learning and indoctrination was being compressed into just four weeks. And they were over halfway through.

They would remain barely functioning, Tawfiq explained, able to do little more than a stumbling walk under supervision until they were awakened in an imprinting ceremony. It would be like a hatching chick imprinting their loyalty for life, she told me, adding when she saw the hope blossom in my face, that they would only imprint when given the correct codes. Codes I would never get near.

She's right. I won't, but perhaps the Legion can. They have to try.

If they don't, Tawfiq claims she's already immortal, and with her new army rising from the bowels of the Earth to strike across the stars, she will rule the galaxy forever.

Five million Ultra Janissaries, bio-engineered super warriors with fanatical loyalty and enough war materials to make them a formidable army from the get go – that's what's coming in ten days, and it's just the start.

They'll continue to crank out Ultra Janissaries by the million, and then they will build more vats. Soon the Earth will be a military factory, all non-Hardit life permitted on the planet will be reduced to farmed biomass fed into the engines of production.

I'm watched by armed guards every moment of day and night. I'm not permitted anywhere near a radio. The only person I can communicate with covertly is you, a telepathic orange blob in a glass tank. We have ten days to stop Tawfiq, Shepherdess. You must warn the Legion now.

*No.*

No? Are you crazy? They will kill you too soon enough, my friend.

*Certainly, but I will not contact the Legion.*

But… why not?

*Reality has jumped already. A foe even greater than Tawfiq is interfering in the flow of time, but his work has unclouded my vision of what may come to pass. I can see through time once more, Romulus. I foresee that if I attempt radio contact with the Legion, I will be overheard and that will prevent vital events that must take place from ever occurring.*

Vital events? Do they involve me? Is there something I must do?

*Your time is over, Romulus. I am sorry, my friend. Only the manner of your death remains for you to choose. I speak of the human, McEwan, who once swore an oath to my people. The power of his oath has yet to unleash its potential and must be protected at all costs. I dare not contact the Legion, but there is one power left on Earth who may help. The entity is hidden well. Powerful, I think. And listening always, for a thousand years or more. I will contact it.*

Who? Who is this?

*I know only its name. Hortez.*

# —— Chapter 22 ——

**Arun McEwan**
**The Nest**

"You have nothing to fear from us, General McEwan," said the military Trog lowered in submission on the revival chamber floor.

Arun looked incredulously, trying to spot the mouth parts. Pedro had always spoken through a translator device because Trogs had no speech organs whatsoever. This was no mechanical speech, though. Not any he recognized. The crazy ant even spoke with a Detroit accent.

"Both of you are safe, no thanks to this dumb drellock here." The Trog soldier gave its comrade a hard shove. "I *told* you not to get too close without a rider."

"I couldn't help it," said the other Trog. "I smelled the non-McEwan human and... I guess I frakking lost it. My bad."

Arun willed the Trogs to shut up. He said nothing, not with his spoken voice, but the creatures swayed as if stunned by the power of his command.

"Let's get this straight," he said. "I'm communicating with you through pheromones, and that's all thanks to the box Pedro stuck in my chest long ago."

"Yes, General. Your scent authority pheromones speak to us far louder than your words. Speech is a much more recent innovation in our nest but lacks the authority of scent. Your venerable scent, General, is burnished with great age. You have been of the Nest for thousands of years."

"Nest Hortez operates on pheromones," explained the other Trog.

"Hortez?" queried Springer.

"Yes, Nest Hortez. The Great Parent regretted that no trace remained of his deceased human friend to add to the Nest scent. Only his human spoken name endured. As I was *trying* to explain, your scent, General, makes you overwhelmingly powerful, second only in aura to the Great Parent."

"Pedro? You mean Pedro's still alive after all these years?"

"Indeed, the Great Parent flourishes."

"So, I'm his second-in-command. Is that how it works?"

"*His…?*"

"The great one often talks with fascination of your primitive gender assumptions," explain the other Trog to its fellow. "*He* looks forward to reacquainting *him*-self with the ancient McEwan."

"The Great Parent wishes you to command his armies. That is your purpose, and why you have been revived today. We have barely ten days left to defeat Tawfiq. If she is allowed to deploy her forthcoming army of super soldiers, then all hope is lost for the Nest and for your species."

"Not now," Arun growled. "Wait until later."

"There will not *be* a later," the Trog protested, anxiety about Arun's lack of congruence blasting out of its scent glands. "Ten days. After that there is no hope."

"No, not you," Arun replied, "*her.*" He shrugged away Springer's hand, which she had been rubbing over his chest.

"Are you copying this, Scipio?" Arun asked, grabbing Springer's hand and putting it back on his torso.

"Loud and clear, sir."

"Good. Life has a habit of going crazy around me. You'd better get used to it. I've just woken up after sleeping three thousand years with a Celtic goddess, and now I learn I've become queen and battlefield commander of an army of giant ants. Oh, and Tawfiq is going to kill everyone on the planet in ten days. Anyone up there still planning on following my orders?"

"I have already told you I shall, sir," said the Jotun, which surprised Arun, because Jotuns liked their world neat and predictable. "Nhlappo has briefed me about you, and your status report is entirely in line with my expectations. It is an honor to serve with you, General McEwan. What is your plan?"

"We go back to where it all began for me. I know Trogs – they will have riddled this planet with their deep burrows, just as we planned. In fact… *I can sense them.* We fight in tunnels deep beneath the surface, and we're going to keep going until we find Tawfiq. Then I'm going to kill her. Marchewka, I know tunnel war is not to the liking of Jotuns. Can I rely upon you?"

Across the link, he sensed the Jotun bristle with indignation. "It is indeed not to my liking, General, but the souls of my slaughtered enemies will tell you that I can wage war underground to devastating effect. We also have a contingent in our fleet who are tunnel warfare specialists. Tell me, sir, have you ever heard of a race called the Sangurians?"

"No," he replied. "Never heard of…" His mouth dropped open, to see the Trogs of all caste types flailing their antennae in agitation.

"Mader zagh!" groaned one of the speaking Trogs.

"Chodding Sangurian tunnel bunnies," said the other. "I don't believe it!"

"Sangurians, you say…" Arun grinned. "Tell me more!"

"No!" Springer shouted. "I want you to all clear off and allow us a few moments of privacy."

"Arun," she whispered into his neck, "I never mentioned this but–" He flinched when she bit his ear. "When I wake from a long cryo, I come out… *tense.*"

Without needing Arun to shape his desires into words, the Trogs marched out of the chamber, one of the scribes carrying the comm cube from which Scipio's laughter rang out.

Springer laid Arun onto his back and looked down at him from all fours. As her gaze drank in his body, her eyes lit up with an interior glow that made him ache with love for this unique woman.

"This won't take long," Arun called out to his waiting armies, as he pulled her down to kiss him.

# —— Chapter 23 ——

**Arun McEwan**
**Nest Hortez**

The new Trog caste with the killer instincts turned out to be the equivalent of an armored warhorse. Not only was the head modified, but with the natural studs and ridges on its flanks, the abdomen was obviously designed to be swung as a club. And a groove traversed the thorax near to its join with the head. When Arun allowed one of the Trogs to lift him up onto the groove of the other, it was clear this was a seat complete with a hand rail growing from the creature's carapace, flexible stirrups, attachment clips and view slits cut into the head crest that curved protectively around its rider. All of this had been programed into the creature's genetic code. Unable to use stirrups himself, Arun's Trog had a leather harness to secure him, which clipped into attachment points in the thorax casing.

As they proceeded through the Nest on the way to meet Pedro, Arun's naked butt told him something else about his steed's design. He was sitting on a natural gel cushion.

What no one could tell him was what the hell was going on topside in the liberation of Earth. Through his prolonged pheromone bullying of the scribes that accompanied them, he learned that he had been thawed a few days after the *Saravanan* drop pod had departed for Celtic Britannia, and not twenty-two years earlier in time to support Grace and the team aboard *Karypsic* in their attack on Tawfiq.

Why hadn't he been thawed earlier? What had happened to his daughter's mission? Even he couldn't get that out of the scribes.

They passed through scenes reminiscent of his time as a cadet, when he'd been ordered to liaise with the Trogs beneath the Detroit base on Tranquility-4. The creatures came in many sizes and functions, metamorphosing from one life-stage to another, sometimes going back to repeat the previous stage, and sometimes moving forward, shedding intelligence as they progressed.

In many regards, Trogs were indeed like the ants they resembled: simple creatures following rudimentary biological programming. Nonetheless when the simple creatures were combined in groups, their behavior quickly spiraled into complex patterns. When necessary, their actions were nudged by pheromone orders from supervisors at a superior level of the nest hierarchy.

At some point on the journey, he realized his hand was clasping Springer's. He couldn't tell who was gripping harder.

They rode through dormitories, machine rooms, armories, laboratories, power plants, mess halls, and far more places whose function Arun couldn't even guess.

At one point they passed through a viewing gallery that looked down on a sandy pit stained with gore. Arun thanked his luck that this wasn't in use because he knew from Pedro's descriptions long ago what this must be.

Pedro had always been obsessed about sex, and Arun's life had apparently given him plenty of observable data. The Trog's fascination stemmed from the lack of gender on his home world, where sexual reproduction existed only in obscure plants, and then only under rare conditions.

Gender baffled the species, but physical lovemaking was the terrible heart of Trog life, even if *sex* might be the wrong word for it. They built arenas, such as the one Arun was traveling through, so you could watch your nest mates busy at it.

Pedro had often talked about romance, which was the creative wellspring of their culture precisely because love between Trogs was doomed to a brief flourishing between committed pairs before being ruthlessly cut down. Once Trogs fell in love, a relentless biological countdown began until, one day, it would be that pair's turn on the sex arena floor. Lovemaking meant literally ripping into each other in no-holds-barred unarmed combat, in which reproductive organs were some of the principal weapons.

New lovers would invariably deny their fate to begin with. As the inevitability of their doom began to claim them, they would try to delay their destiny in the arena with plans that grew more desperate with every passing day, as the urge to fight slowly claimed them. They would write excruciatingly lengthy poems in which they expressed how their love was so strong, so uniquely special, that *they* would never yield to their cruel biology.

But, of course, they always did.

The act of mating was fatal for at least one of the combatant-lovers. The victor consumed their lover's corpse, whose reproductive material would by then be within them. Bloated beyond belief, they would haul themselves to the birthing chambers where they wove themselves inside cocoons. Eventually they would emerge with renewed bodies and minds, and feral younglings would burst free at the same time to skitter through the Nest.

Arun sneaked a look at Springer who basked in the warmth of his attention. For all the complexities, inefficiencies, and heartache that human love had brought him, Arun was glad he wasn't a Trog.

That was the thought uppermost in his mind when they finally came across Pedro himself in what Arun decided was a throne room.

To an uninitiated human, peering through the view-slit in his mount's armored head crest, it was a large and almost empty stone chamber in which lay a swollen giant ant. Arun knew that the low stone couch upon which Pedro was lying his bulk would have been warmed to the temperature of a warm summer's day on Tranquility. Smaller attendants, mostly of the scribe mode, fussed over their Great Parent.

When experienced through the medium of scent – which Arun could now glimpse through his pheromone implant – this almost featureless room emerged as an opulent palace woven with complex tapestries of scent art that entwined with each other in an intricate dance. Artisan Trogs were continuously weaving new threads into the artwork, layering new levels over… not just old but *ancient* threads. This wasn't static art, this was a *performance* that had been ongoing for generations!

"Arun!" snapped Springer.

A pair of scribes peeled away to reveal the cause of Springer's warning. A human child – a girl of perhaps five years old – was burying her head against the protective bulk of Pedro's abdomen, too shy to look at these strange people she didn't know. She sneaked a brave peek behind her at the newcomers before pressing her head back against Pedro. She couldn't have seen anything through her wild brown curls, because Arun and Springer were hidden behind the crests that rose from their steeds.

"Don't be scared," said Springer from Trog-back. "We won't hurt you."

Arun pushed aside the question of why the hell Pedro would allow humans in the Nest, when it was imperative that the Hardits never discover its existence. Instead, he tried to remember how he had perceived the outside world when he'd been as young as that girl. Springer was a muscular Wolf woman with freakish eyes and covered in bright scales, while he lacked limbs. Was that scary to a kid? Thank Fate the scribes had earlier found some simple tunics to cover their nakedness.

"When you see us, you may think we look strange," Arun told the girl. "That doesn't mean we're bad people."

Amazingly, his words seemed to do the trick, because the little girl took a deep breath and, with lower lip firmly sucked up into her mouth, she made herself run over to Arun's Trog. Hands planted firmly on the chitinous head shield, she peered around its frilled edge at Arun.

The girl allowed her hair to fall to one side, revealing her face... *her eyes!*

Springer screamed in horror and the girl's head shot back behind the safety of the Trog's head armor.

"It's all right," soothed Arun, and reached around to gently stroke her thick auburn hair.

But it wasn't all right. Not really. First Grace and now this... The universe was laughing at him. *Again.* And he hadn't time for any of it. He had a job to do.

The girl peeked out again, taking care to look only at Arun, and not the other human rider with the scary scream.

"We've been asleep for a very long time," Arun explained, "which makes us confused. And we're here because the Great Parent has *a helluva lot of explaining to do*, which he'd better do real quick if he knows what's good for him."

The little girl laughed, her beaming smile reaching her eyes, which sparkled with an inner lilac glow. "Hello, Pappa. We've been waiting for you to wake up for *such* a long time. Do you like my nest?"

# ——— Chapter 24 ———

**Arun McEwan**
**Nest Hortez**

"Will you *ever* stop interfering?" Arun shouted at Pedro.

"I have your vital interests at heart."

"Do you really? Didn't you think to ask me what those interests might be? Did you ask Springer? You know full well what this means... *would have* meant to her."

Arun swallowed his angry words and tried to remember that many lives still depended on Springer's identity remaining secret. Pedro knew, of course, but she was still supposed to be Lissa in this time period. The painful details didn't need to be disinterred aloud. Arun, Springer, and Xin had all been part of an alien conspiracy against the White Knight Empire – weaponized kids being built inside the Human Marine Corps under the noses of their masters. Maybe against Greyhart too. But the Corps provided a cruel upbringing which many children did not survive, and so Pedro had taken DNA samples as backup in case replacements for any or all of them needed to be fast-grown. When still a cadet, Springer had almost been killed in the Hardit rebellion on Antilles. She had survived her wounds, but her hopes of becoming a mother died in the radiation blast that melted half her skin. Or so it had been until Pedro revealed he'd mixed their DNA to produce embryos.

Arun's mind stopped rubbing its nose in the memory of dark consequences that had flowed from Pedro's interference. Instead, he watched wide-eyed as Springer dismounted and walked with tears in her eyes over to the giant Trog. She reached up on tiptoes to his antennae.

Arun couldn't breathe. Was she going to rip them out? He felt his mount tense, but it was too late to protect the Great Parent now.

Springer stroked Pedro's antennae as gently as caressing a baby. The great bulk of his thorax shuddered. The big guy still liked it.

"Thank you," she said.

"Why do you thank me, Human Lissa? Your eyes... Mine are dim but I can see you have Springer's lilac pigmentation." Was that a slight curl of amusement to Pedro's antennae as he directed them at Arun? "Your aide and consort has colored her eyes to better resemble the woman you once loved. That is a powerful gesture, Lissa."

Springer laughed at word *consort*, but Arun just hung his head in his hands. "Can we just get on with the war and deal with all this drent later?"

"As you wish. I shall brief you, and then we must resume contact with this Lance Scipio."

Before Pedro could get started, the chamber was invaded by a score of children, all with lilac eyes.

"I told you to wait," Pedro admonished. "We have downstream lifecycle business to discuss before you can meet your father."

"We're sorry," the children chorused, and proceeded to mob Arun, laughing and singing, skipping and staring.

"As you see," said Pedro, "being a single parent to so many of your kind is a challenge I have not yet mastered. It is good that their father is here to help out."

Arun flicked a glance at Springer. She was in shock, her soul melting before his eyes.

It was obvious she'd already opened her heart to these clones, but Arun couldn't. And he feared Springer was allowing herself to become vulnerable just when he most needed her to be strong.

These Nest humans had been created out of his and Springer's stolen DNA, but they weren't their children. They had been grown in a lab, not born. Were they even real people?

*Do I really have to put you straight on that point?* said Barney.

*What you need to do,* replied Arun firmly, *is to leave me be. I need to kill Tawfiq. I can't deal with this now.*

186

*I would have agreed with you, if not for one thing. Springer has clearly accepted them as her children. And that's the woman you love, Arun, like you've never let yourself love anyone before. Not even Xin. Don't forget that Saraswati and I have been riding your brains through every embrace, and felt you pine every time you're apart for more than five seconds. Arun, you're a soldier. You've stayed alive by adapting to situations as they unfold, not blindly following the scenario you originally planned for. Springer's not the person she was an hour ago. Deal with it and adapt!*

*Adapt? I can only stretch so far, Barney. I have a battle computer in my head, and an AI riding shotgun in my neck. My bloodstream is patrolled by nano-scale EMTs, and my body design is optimized for extended zero-g campaigning. I'm at least half cyborg, but most of all I'm a Marine. We were bred to train, love, fight, and die, Barney. Nothing more. We weren't supposed to have choices outside of the battlezone. We weren't supposed to have a life. Don't tell me to adapt to anything that doesn't lead to Tawfiq's death.*

*Easy, Arun. I know. I grew up with you, remember? Springer understands this life drent better than we do. Stick close to her, because when we've kicked Tawfiq's ass and the war is over, I think you'll go to pieces without her, and you'll take me down with you, buddy. You talk of leaving the military to Aelingir and Indiya and walking hand-in-hand with your love into the sunset as if it will be easy. You have no frakking idea. Trying to become a civilian will be the most difficult campaign either of us have ever fought, and you need to prep now. Go to her.*

But Arun couldn't move. This was too much.

"Your children have many talents," said Pedro, "as I shall soon demonstrate. Amongst Springer's many fine characteristics, they share some of her foresight. Individually, this ability is weak, but they can combine as nodes into a powerful array. Look, they are exhibiting signs now."

The eyes of the clones began to glow. *Weaponized children.* The sight horrified him. They all joined hands in a circle, stared just like Springer used to at something Arun could never see, and then collapsed into a heap of weeping children.

"That's cruel," Arun growled. "Look at them. They're sobbing their guts out."

"Friend McEwan. I am reluctant to correct you on matters of your own species, but I have considerably more experience with human children. Those are happy tears."

Happy? Arun looked again. Damn that ant, he was right!

As one, the kids lifted themselves off the ground and swarmed over Springer, knocking her over in a cloud of laughter.

"Mamma!"

"You're alive!"

"It's Mamma!"

Arun sighed. Springer's secret was breached and venting atmosphere, and the implications would be vast. But it would have to wait. He needed to know what had happened to Grace, and he needed to loop in Scipio.

Springer had raised herself out of the sea of her children and was glaring at Pedro, her fists shaking in rage. *Anger? I thought she was deliriously happy.* "You played God," she spat at Pedro. "You had *no right!*" She cooled slowly and spread her hands over the children. "These are people, Pedro, not Nest drones. They need to love, to feel human society. They need to meet outsiders."

"I agree," said Pedro. "And they will, but we are cut off here in Australia."

"Australia?" said Arun. "I thought we were in England."

"Not safe. We transferred you and the remains of the *Saravanan* here many centuries ago. There are large underground aquifers in this region. We buried beneath them. They shield us from observation and from the gamma beams that scoured Australia when your species was first fought over by regional interstellar powers."

"And the ants with speech?"

"We are a new stage for the Nest people," said a voice from behind.

Four more of the Trogs with the armored heads had entered the chamber. An adult purple-eyed human stood high in her stirrups, so her head was visible over the armored frills. The humans carried lances tipped with glowing blue crystals.

"We are dragoons," said rider and steed together.

They looked at each other.

"No, *we* are dragoons," insisted the human. "You're a dragoon steed."

"Steed?" The ant waved his antennae furiously. "It is you, human, who are the detachable and expendable auxiliary attachment, interchangeable with any of your kind."

"You can't possibly mean that. Interchangeable? We've been a pair all our lives."

!QUIET!

Arun flinched, same as everyone else there, including the kids. Everyone but Springer. To the members of Nest Hortez, Pedro was the drill sergeant from hell, and they'd just disappointed him. Big time. Which is why he'd bellowed, though not with his voice; he had none.

Arun tried the same trick.

!BRING ME THE SPEAKING CUBE!

Moments later, a scribe offered up the comm cube, and Arun felt a wave of relief at the prospect of speaking with another human without lilac eyes.

But before he spoke with Scipio, there was something he needed to know. "Grace," he said and looked straight at Pedro. "What happened?"

"The Nest tried," he replied, "but we couldn't get close enough. We dug vast military staging areas beneath Tawfiq's bunker, centuries before the White House was built. But the Hardits discovered them and filled them with their own birthing chambers, and then set defenses around them. We were discovered but covered our tracks through swift killings and the triggering of an earthquake that led to a partial collapse of our caverns."

"Did she die? In 2719 without your support… the mission obviously didn't succeed, but did my daughter survive?"

"I believe so."

Arun let out a deep breath. He'd barely had time to speak with Grace, but the prospect of a universe without her seemed such a barren place.

"We helped in more subtle ways," explained the Trog. "If we had risen openly against the New Order, they would have detected our movements and put their defenses on a high state of alert before Grace arrived with *Karypsic*. Instead, we sowed confusion, disrupting their communications even more than the Cairo attack could achieve, and sending false mission orders that dispatched New Order mobile reserves to the far corners of this world. Tawfiq was injured but survived. I believe the same could be said of the *Karypsic*. Since then, we have remained hidden from Tawfiq, the Legion, and everyone. With you to lead us, Friend McEwan, now is the time to fight with mandible and claw."

"Got it. You're right about one thing. This is the time, Pedro. It's now or never, and not just for you. Greyhart's supplied us with unexpected reinforcements. I hope." Arun spoke into the cube. "Scipio, you can't reach us directly. Tawfiq's erected a corrosion barrier around the Earth. You'd never make it through. Indiya's main fleet might have a solution by now, but even if she has, I doubt she'll be able to retrofit more than a handful of ships to get through. We'll have to deal with Tawfiq using the forces we already have on and under the ground."

"Not a problem," said Scipio. "Greyhart warned us about the corrosion shell."

"You mean he fixed your hulls?"

"Not exactly. But he explained that the barrier the Hardits have erected is not their tech. It was extracted from Tranquility-4."

"Tranquility-4? But we left it dead, except for Nhlappo's retrieval mission to uncover the Marines buried beneath Detroit."

"Turned out there was more than one sleeping legion, plus a host of other buried surprises. The tech comes from a long-dead race called the Makoni. Tawfiq stole their tech for her barrier and we used it for our ships, and that includes our dropships. They'll punch through the barrier, no problem."

"You're very confident."

"I am. Way I see things, General McEwan, someone's gone to a whole lot of trouble to get me and my friends here and now with the specific equipment we have at our disposal. I don't need to tell you that there are entire universes filled with easier ways to kill us. So, yeah, I'm confident. I have to be. I'll be riding down with the first wave of dropships."

"Nhlappo here, General. This Trog army, who will lead them in battle?"

"Me."

"Yes, but your commands will be heard by scribes who will then pass on your requests to the soldiers who will issue pheromone commands. Too many intermediaries. I learned the hard way not to trust allies unless they've earned it."

"Then trust me. I can issue pheromone commands directly. Pedro is the big boss, but I'm number two. I'm the Queen Ant, Nhlappo. You'd better believe it."

Nhlappo hesitated, but only for a fraction of a second. "Oh, I do," she said, and Arun could almost believe the old drill instructor was smiling. "I would believe anything of you." The humor left her voice and she ended, "But I do not trust this Greyhart person. He requested we stay cloaked until we spoke with you. We've complied even though the main Legion fleet has attempted to contact us. Do we now liaise with Indiya?"

This was exactly the sort of decision Arun had learned to offload to Indiya, Aelingir, or Xin. Even Nhlappo had proved the better field commander than Arun. But his gut told him that he was to lead his forces into battle one last time.

He looked over at Springer who returned a cautious smile that made his heart leap. Hell, this plan hatching in his mind… deep down, was this intended to impress her?

*You know what I'm thinking?* he asked Barney.

*I do.*

*Do you think I'm mad?*

*No more than normal.*

Arun grinned. "Maintain maximum stealth stance," he ordered Nhlappo. "Quantum-entangled comms only. Keep a running summary of our plans and narrow beam it to the main fleet as soon as the New Order detects you. We have ten days to kill Tawfiq. And I'm going to lead you every step of the way. Here's what we're going to do…"

# —— Chapter 25——

The New Order Hardits had built tunnels throughout Australia, but Nest Hortez had been there long before, and dug deeper, circumventing Hardit concentrations wherever possible. The Hardits had no idea the Trog nest was there. However, the downside of keeping its distance, was the Nest's poor intelligence on Hardit deployments.

Seventy-five years ago, in 2664, human biologists had begun rebooting the Australian biosphere, which had been scoured of all life during the Tusker invasion of 2155. With the conquest of Earth at the turn of the century, the Hardits had driven away the bio-scientists and declared the continent off-limits for all humans.

However, a few brave souls had refused to abandon the continent, and had risked everything to covertly keep the repopulation projects active. Discovery by the Hardits would mean certain death, and so in order to survive, the human bio-engineers had secretly mapped the sparse Hardit military presence in order to keep their distance.

Nest Hortez members had discovered these humans hiding away in the vast continent's interior, and made contact, scaring the life out of them. After convincing the humans that the giant insectoids were Legion advance forces, the Nest recruited the scientists to help pinpoint the locations of Hardit activities throughout the continent.

As the date for the Legion invasion had neared, Pedro ordered attack tunnels to be built within striking distance of Hardit anti-aircraft and other defenses.

And now that the Human McEwan was here to lead the Trog armies, he put them to good use.

At their new battle commander's pheromone signal, Trog swarm squads began swimming through the soil that separated their jumping off points from their targets.

Hardit Janissaries were well-trained and resilient fighters, but they were natural tunnel dwellers, craving the security of thick tunnel walls of soil and rock. What could be worse than for those same tunnel walls to betray them, to be the avenue of attack for a merciless enemy who could move with ease through hardpacked soil to emerge with murder in their hearts?

Nothing terrified Hardits more than Trog warriors.

In hundreds of small actions, Trogs of the guardian life-stage sprang out of Hardit walls under the direction of scribe officers.

There was no subtlety to their assault. Anything that did not smell of the Nest was to die, and die they did.

Metal-sheathed feet slashed through Hardit limbs, and decapitated their foes, locking in death trios of eyes wide open with horror.

The heads of these Trog guardians were wreathed in thickets of horns that resembled super-hardened chitinous brambles. These were rammed into flesh whether still living or not.

To the guardians, dead or dying Hardits smelled almost as repugnant as those who now fought back with guns. They did not cease until those who were not of the Nest were gored, speared, and stomped into a furry red paste. Never mind that their comrades were falling in great numbers now – the Hardit survivors of the initial attack were rallying, bringing heavier weapons to bear.

Their scribe officers cared for their soldiers, but the guardians were beyond caring for themselves. In this, the final stage of the complex Trog life-cycle, the sentience of individuals who had themselves once been scribes and engineers and other modes, was now worn away to vestigial stumps. Their former names, friendships, achievements and history were mourned by those they left behind as they had entered their cocoons at the end of the previous life mode. The guardians who emerged, dripping and restless for war, had been reduced to simple killing machines with no other function.

Nonetheless, it was a role for which they were perfectly designed.

And when they had finished their grisly task, they stood without purpose on ground slick with blood, ichor, chitin shards, bone, and spent munition casings.

They moved aside to allow their scribe officers to pass through, their minds empty until given fresh instructions.

The scribes spiked the Hardit guns with acid, shot up sophisticated targeting equipment with their sidearms, and laid charges inside barrels.

The Great Parent of Nest Hortez had intended to use the Hardits' own guns upon them, making up for the Nest's critical lack of heavy weapons, but the Human McEwan had insisted this was too risky.

According to the human, the New Order commanders might be worthless pieces of excrement, but that didn't mean they were stupid frakks. McEwan insisted that the moment you underestimated your enemy was the point when all your plans turned to drent.

The Great Parent and the Human McEwan had been locked in disagreement. No words were spoken, but none were needed.

There could be no battle for supremacy within the Nest hierarchy, not with its structure fixed so rigidly. With horror welling in alien breasts as they perceived the disagreement between the two most senior Nest commanders, the Trog warriors had begun to fidget, their minds trying to encompass the blasphemous prospect of killing the Human McEwan, despite the powerful scent that imbued his every cell.

In retrospect, many scribes remarked that this was a perfect showdown, *almost as if engineered.* When the two commanders argued vehemently in one of the principal garrison caverns, the confrontation ended in an astonishing display. The Great Parent lowered its antennae in submission, with overpowering pheromone instructions to all present that every single member of Nest Hortez from the lowliest Guardian to the Great Parent must defer to Human McEwan in all matters of war.

The unprecedented scene had imprinted so strongly on the Nest commanders that they were almost jumping out of their chitinous carapaces to do the bidding of the freshly anointed military commander. Indeed, several commanders were so overcome with stress hormones in response to the extraordinary event, that they suffered cardiac arrest and perished at the scene. For the surviving witnesses, the experience was so intense that when they passed on the scent memory to their peers, they in turn felt McEwan's power with almost the same fervor as if they had been present at the Great Parent's submission.

Henceforth, the Human McEwan was to be known as the Queen of Battle, and his military orders were paramount.

And now, with the opening act of the battle concluded, they obeyed their Queen's orders to return to mustering points and await reinforcements.

Meanwhile, high above the surface, New Order defensive platforms in low orbit blared with alarms as a surprise naval attack materialized out of the vacuum, energy beams, spinal-mount railguns, and missile swarms blasting them at point blank range.

The defensive capability of the Hardit platforms had been heavily upgraded in recent days. Although most platforms died in this initial attack, filling the skies above Australia with explosions and fiery debris, many survived.

But the attack from space had drawn Hardit attention long enough to allow the following troopships to approach the outer reaches of Earth's atmosphere. These were not Admiral Indiya's command – her flagship only being contacted by the attacking fleet as it went in. This was the Sleeping Legion, and it had arrived with a fierce lust to avenge the comrades who had been slaughtered through New Order treachery on the distant world of Tranquilty-4.

They had waited decades for this, but now it was time to bring the war to Tawfiq Woomer-Calix and finish her once and for all. And they had just over eight days left in which to do so.

# —— Chapter 26 ——

**Colonel Lance Scipio**
**Orbital drop over Australia**

Lance Scipio sneaked a sidelong glance at the woman he loved.

As a Cardamine Island Marine, Lance saw nothing wrong in giving Sashala Kraevoi a gesture of his affection, even in front of the half company sitting with them in their dropship.

But Sashala was from Detroit, and in her era people had grown up differently, with inflexible upper lips and iron rods up their backsides.

The troopship to which the little craft was clamped shuddered under the fury of Hardit orbital platforms.

"Guess the monkey-vecks have finally seen us," he said on the unit-wide channel.

A command advisory feed in his visor HUD notified him that the drop was imminent.

In a few seconds, he would lead the first wave down to the planet below. And if the techs had not gambled correctly on how to counter the Hardit corrosion barrier, a few seconds later, he, Sashala, and his entire command would be eaten down to their constituent atoms. Everyone here was thinking the same thing; they'd have to be idiots not to.

He could sense the panic beginning to twist the guts of his brave comrades. Time to raid his meagre store of stirring speeches. He hated this part of the job.

"Brother and sister Marines," he announced, "we've all heard stories of Arun McEwan. It's easy to think of him as an icon, a demigod of outrageous fortune. But I've spoken with him and he's a real man, a Marine like you and me. With the same dreams… and similar urges." That won a rumble of laughter. "And if you think the stories about him are wild, you haven't heard the half of it. I swear, the man is as mad as a bucket of Hardits on heat. And that makes him all right in my book, because whether he realizes it or not, he so obviously has Island heritage that we're practically related."

That earned a few more chuckles, though as he said the words, Lance wondered whether they were true. Then green lamps lit the compartment, signaling five seconds to drop.

"Time to earn some fresh ink, Marines," Lance shouted enthusiastically. "Forward to victory!"

The dropship clamp released, and a fraction of a second later the hangar deck retracted, and the Sleeping Legion fell into Earth's outer atmosphere.

# —— Chapter 27 ——

**Arun McEwan**
**Hidden Dragoon Army**

Arun watched Scipio's dropships descend through enemy fire and begin to flare as they entered the upper atmosphere, superheating cones of atmospheric gasses compressed by their descent. For him to be seeing this at all, the dropships must have made it through the corrosion barrier.

*They'd finally done it!*

Debris clouds provided the evidence that this was by no means an uncontested drop, but after the regional Hardit surface-to-air defenses had been slaughtered by Nest Hortez, the fire streaking up from the ground was limited.

It was a sight Arun had seen on a dozen invasions, though usually from inside a dropship weaving down to make his appointment with the LZ. Now that Scipio's wave had passed through the barrier in orbit, what was strangest about this drop was where Arun was viewing it from. Not only was he on the ground already, but he was watching it via a viewscreen secured to the back of his steed's crest, a fluted shield grown from layers of chitinous armor sheets filled with spongey layers to absorb the energy of incoming fire. Pedro had proudly explained that the frilled and fluted crest had been styled on an ancient Earth creature called *Triceratops*.

The frills along the top could pass as something from a naturally evolved creature, but then the crest descended like a snow plough in a purely functional design with deeply recessed shuttered apertures to protect the eyes and antennae of the Trog.

The Trogs had no desire for spoken names – their scent being ample identification – but when Arun named his steed Hansel, and Springer followed suit, naming hers Gretel, the unnamed Trogs demanded names from their human riders.

Arun shook away the strangeness of this bunker where his dragoons waited to play their part, and patched into the network of drones and orbital sensors. He observed the opening acts of this battle for Australia on his *Triceratops*-shaped screen.

The mysterious Rakasa fleet of troopships and escorts was taking a serious pounding from Hardit orbital defenses, but had managed to open up a wide-enough gap in space that the wave of dropships had punched through.

But the New Order were a formidable foe, and the Hardits were already redeploying their forces to close the gaps in their defenses – in orbit, in the atmosphere, and underground. But for the time being, the sky and space above Australia belonged to Arun. The Mars fleet under Indiya's command had also signaled that it was moving in to support, but was hours away if not more, and worryingly, it was Admiral Kreippil who was in command, relieving Indiya who was apparently *resting*.

Indiya's absence was a problem for the future, as were the New Order reserves. It was the Hardit ground forces in Australia that Arun had to contend with first. Legion intelligence said the Hardit defense strategy mixed fixed defensive emplacements with a mobile reserve that could deliver a crushing counter-attack to any landing zone before its defenders had time to establish their position.

In the earlier landing in the Sahara, Aelingir's assault had overwhelmed the Hardit mobile reserves through weight of numbers, and the sheer impulse of an attacking force relishing the chance to finally bring the fight to Tawfiq. But Arun wondered whether the initial success in the Sahara was at least as much due to Tawfiq deliberately leading them into her traps.

Arun watched in dismay as the Hardit mobile reserve in Australia revealed itself as it emerged from hidden underground positions in far greater strength than he had planned for. Scipio's forces coming down through the sky didn't have Aelingir's numbers and now looked inadequate. Backbone of the Hardit reserves were lightning-fast behemoth tanks with a huge main armament, secondary turrets, and a protective screen of attendant vehicles to provide force deflector screen and anti-missile defenses.

The human capital ships in orbit were trying to take out these behemoths, but energy weapons were withered by the intervening atmosphere, and missiles were easily swatted away by the attendant swarm of anti-missile trucks.

These beasts weren't so much tanks as miniature battleships the size of a shuttlecraft. They were making at least 15 klicks per second as they moved over the ground in a holding pattern to avoid offering up a stationary target. The main turrets housed a large-caliber railgun which they raised high in the sky... at the descending cloud of dropships. Despite their high-speed movement along the uneven ground, the turrets absorbed the shock, keeping the main guns perfectly aligned on their targets.

Through a camera in the lower stratosphere, Arun watched a gun bloom in fire as a behemoth spat its first shot at the upper atmosphere, leaving a cloud of burning air behind as it sped away.

Seconds later, he started hearing reports of dropships being shot out the sky. Intel had assessed that 27 of these behemoths had revealed themselves so far, and by the time Barney had told him the casualty figures from the initial tank salvo, he'd seen the fire belch again from the end of the massive railguns.

To the Hardits it must have seemed like a video game on easy setting. At this rate, none of the dropships would make it down, and without the heavy weapons the Sleeping Legion was bringing with them, Arun's attack on Tawfiq stood no chance.

But Arun was no longer the Marine cadet who'd dreamed of a human legion. He had learned to respect his opponents.

"Activate Antilles defense," he said, but he needn't have bothered. The scribes acting as aides raced to implement his order, having read his intention through his scent transmitter before the words finished forming in his mouth.

A mile away from his hidden position, a patch of desert had been labelled Landing Zone-Alpha. Buried beneath the LZ, repurposed Nest ventilation turbines spun into action, as did force beams and an ever-shifting pattern of energy shields and pressure barriers.

A slowly circling tunnel of red dust and dirt reached up into the sky, where the dropships were coming in hot and hard through the devastating fire of the behemoths. The plummeting ships fired every last piece of defensive munitions in a desperate attempt to reach the safety of the rapidly extending dirt tunnel.

With the New Order satellites and defense platforms reduced to orbiting wreckage, the tanks lacked effective targeting data. The combination of first the defensive munitions and then the unnatural sand tornado quickly degraded the accuracy of the Hardit fire.

The dropships – the two thirds who'd made it to the sand tunnel – landed at the LZ. The bad news was that they would all be clumped together into a single force concentration.

With the behemoths leading the New Order reserves charging toward LZ-Alpha, this was very bad. Every Hardit missile and shell within range would be retargeting on the LZ, a task made easier because it was situated in the shadow of the most obvious natural landmark in central Australia, a thousand-foot high sandstone brick that glowed an eerie red in the late afternoon sun.

Before the human inhabitants had been killed or driven away centuries ago, some had venerated this place they called Uluru Ayers Rock. Maybe in recognizing the spiritual power of this place, they had sensed an echo of the crucial events playing out here today. Who could tell? Certainly, Arun had learned that cause and effect was not a simple one-way flow along the river of time.

He winked at Springer whose knuckles showed white through her scales as she gripped the rail that grew out of Gretel's thorax for the use of human riders. She even smelled good to him on an inhuman level, a Nest Hortez scent marker having been inserted within her chest cavity the day before.

He had to force himself to look away from her and take in a view of the hushed assembly of human and Trog warriors hidden inside the rock. Everyone here was silently waiting for his command.

The one redeeming aspect of concentrating Scipio's units close to Uluru Ayers Rock was that Arun could predict the New Order response to the letter. True, the enemy's numbers were greater than he'd hoped, but he had planned for this outcome from the very start.

After a lifetime of being manipulated by friends, conspirators, and enemies alike, now it was his turn.

# —— Chapter 28 ——

Colonel Lance Scipio
LZ-Alpha

Lance Scipio's first impression of Earth was of a featureless drentball of a planet infested with angry Hardits. The only landmarks in the flat desert were a red zit of a mountain, and fat enemy tanks that were seriously ruining his day because they wouldn't die, no matter what he threw at them. At least the mountain wasn't trying to kill him.

He'd ordered his Marines to fire EMP grenades from a range of vintages, knowing from experience that New Order military tech was often vulnerable to ordnance long declared obsolete.

Looked like the Hardits had grown wise to that, because the tanks hadn't even slowed in the face of EM fireworks that had burned so brightly that his AI, Xena, cursed him, his mother, and his entire lineage, whether yet born or not.

But when he unleashed GX-cannon firing X-Ray munitions, doubling them up with volleys of anti-tank missiles, that was when he really started to worry. The super-tanks shrugged off the punishment, scorched and battered but with those enormous railguns still operational, and making it impossible for Lance to properly establish his position.

As for the vaunted General McEwan, savior of all humankinds, Lance checked the BattleNet tactical map in his HUD once more, but the man had yet to show up to his own battle. All he'd supplied to the party were giant ants Xena called *guardians,* which had chased away any of his Marines who'd gotten too close to them.

"What the hell use is an ally who attacks us on sight?" yelled Lance in frustration.

*Keep up with the program,* snarked Xena. *These giant ants won't attack us on sight, they'll attack us on* **scent.**

*Nice try to distract me, Xena. But that's not what I want to know. Any sign of General Bighat?*

*Negative, Lance. Dumbass General Veckface was all mysterious and vague beyond saying he'd meet us here at the LZ. Seemed to think the Hardits might be listening in – as if I of all AIs couldn't establish secure comms. Idiot.*

*I'm beginning to think we're the idiots here, Xena. Where the hell are you, McEwan?*

The sound of Sashala firing a burst of darts from her carbine brought Lance back to the here and now.

Xena too, who thought to add the tac-display overlay to Lance's HUD.

Sashala had just dropped a party of monkeys into the sand, but more of them – about six – had worked their way around Lance.

As smoothly as he could, so as not to spook the Janissaries who thought they'd gotten the drop on him, Lance drew his void-black sword made from a material strong enough to cut through six inches of ceramalloy armor plating.

His mind flashed through what he would do. He would drop suddenly into a crouch, and then use every ounce of augmented strength in his power armor to back flip high into the air, and land behind the confused Hardits, slashing and stabbing them before they could put enough firepower into him to penetrate his armor.

In reality, he did leap backward, catching a stray Hardit bullet that deflected off his armored butt, but when he landed it was directly on top of the enemy. Human and Hardits collapsed in a rapidly shifting heap of tails and limbs, of daggers stabbing at the joints between armor plates, of gunshots, and Lance's sword and fists.

But the Hardits were pinning Lance down and he couldn't get in any telling blows with his sword. Even so, as the clumsy melee continued, with Hardit and Legion gunfire exchanges close by, Lance felt the strength of the Hardit grappling progressively weaken.

He took a chance and threw them off, pushing himself up to his feet, even though that would present a better target.

Sword in both hands, he readied to deal killing blows.

But he was too late.

The Hardits were already dead. Sashala stood over them as she retrieved her throwing knives from their corpses, while giving an ear bashing to the Command Section Marines who were supposed to stop that kind of attack from happening.

Xena faded out the sound of Sashala's voice and replaced it with her own. *Hey, hero, there's a grasshopper battery signaling it's ready to fire. You want me to link them in?*

*Grasshoppers.* Mobile artillery platforms that would fire a salvo, and then hop hundreds of feet away to a new firing position. From there, they could fire almost immediately before hopping again to the next battery site.

*They will do nicely...*

Lance directed the grasshoppers against the nearest behemoth, not to smash through the armor and force shield protecting the super-tank – because the armor had shrugged off everything the Legion had thrown at them so far – but at the desert ground beneath the tanks.

The battery commander understood exactly what Lance was asking for.

Shells rained down in a narrow spread in front of the behemoth's path, carving out a deep pit that flung rust-red clouds of dirt high into the sky, to merge with the outer wall of the sand tornado.

When the super-tank ran into the pit, it hit so hard it might as well have crashed straight into a granite mountainside. With any luck the crew would be smashed to a pulp in that brutal crash.

Not trusting to such good fortune, the battery commander sent a second salvo screaming down onto the behemoth, this time ordering the shells to fan out in a semicircle behind the tank.

So much dust debris and sand was being thrown up, Lance couldn't tell what was happening, until the network of battlefield surveillance drones supplied a radar-enhanced image showing a deep pit had been gouged out by the battery fire. And there, at the base of the pit, tens of feet below the surface, the behemoth stood immobile, like a venomous hornet trapped beneath an upturned glass.

The sides of the pit were not quite sheer, but surely they were far too steep for the tank to climb.

"Get out of that," he sneered.

The grasshoppers had shown one way to beat the behemoths. Elsewhere in the battle to secure the desert landing zone, the GX-cannon and anti-tank missiles that had failed to destroy the super-tanks were proving much more successful at taking out the protective swarm of smaller armored vehicles that shielded them. Strip them away and no matter how strong the armor of the super-tanks, once Lance could hit them with every weapon he had on the ground, and with Marchewka adding her firepower from space, then it would eventually fail.

Having issued orders he was confident would beat the behemoths, which were fortunately arriving piecemeal at LZ-Alpha, Lance took the chance to assess the wider shape of the battle.

McEwan had positioned his damned giant ants in a protective crescent that curved around the eastern flank of the LZ, where all the dropships had now disgorged their contents, and were waiting for his signal to climb back up through the sand tornado to dock with the troopships and embark the second attack wave.

Ideally, the dropships would wait until he'd taken out the behemoths and their massive railguns, but the Janissary infantry was already outnumbering his Marines, and a sea of enemy troop carriers on the horizon was streaming their way. He needed that second wave here now, but if he sent the dropships up above the protective tornado – assuming they could even do that without being blasted out of the sky by the wind and sand – then they would be shot down by the behemoths as soon as they emerged out the top.

Having a well-anchored flank was helpful, but the Trog guardians were just standing there. The Janissary mechanized infantry was streaming around the Trog crescent and deploying into the gap between the LZ and the mountain. Typical Hardits – if they couldn't fight you in a tunnel, they would always move somewhere so they had their backs against something solid.

The prospect of tunnel warfare made him think of the Sangurian warriors he had brought with him from Tranquility. The war-obsessed aliens could dig beneath the Hardit position and collapse it, wreaking an underground slaughter as they loved to do.

One problem.

The Sangurians were still in space, waiting to embark on the dropships.

There were no easy options, but that was Lance's role: to peer through the confusion and risk and make the big calls. He decided to risk sending the dropships back up, and was about to issue the orders, when garbled fragments of speech filled the command channel. "*Scip… io… do you… ipio.*"

*What the frakk? Who is this joker, Xena? And how are they accessing the FC-1 comm channel?*

*Which question do you want answering first, o master? No, strike that. The signal's strengthening and if I can just clean it… standby… voila!*

"Lance Scipio. Do you copy?"

"McEwan! Where the frakk have you…? I mean, it's good to hear you, sir."

"Stow that shite, Marine. It's these ants. They've no experience of voice comms. I'm having to speak with you using borrowed Earth Army kit."

"Sir, the situation is critical–"

"I know what's going on, Scipio. Just haven't been able to speak with you until now. You see the Janissary infantry between your position and the big red rock to your west? I want you to pin them there, while wearing them down. Can you do that?"

"For how long?"

"I know Hardits. They will mass under protection of energy shields until they are at maximum strength. Only then will they have the guts to assault

Legion Marines. You keep them in place until the last moment before they attack. Then I'll hit them hard."

"Lance!" Sashala screamed.

"Where are you…?" The words dried in Lance's throat. He'd never before heard panic in Sashala's cry

He wheeled round to see what she was pointing at.

Dust was rising from the edge of the pit the grasshoppers had dug for the behemoth. A chill shiver ran through Lance's body as he watched this play out, his limbs refusing to move, his brain unable to think on anything other than that pit and what the dust signified.

"We'll assault their rear," McEwan was saying, but the Legion general had faded into insignificance in Lance's mind.

*This can't be happening,* he told himself.

But it was.

The mammoth armored vehicle levitated gracefully out of its grave, with barely a hum of power, its main turret traversing to bring that mighty railgun to bear on… *him!*

Sashala grabbed his arm and pulled.

"Run!" she screamed.

His paralysis snapped, and he used every last bit of juice in his power-assisted legs to run for his life.

# —— Chapter 29 ——

**Arun McEwan**
**Hidden Dragoon Army**

Just a few moments more, Scipio… Keep it together just a little longer…

Arun had to face facts. The battleplan was turning to drent.

Those frakking tanks were responsible. Scipio's Marines were investing all their energy trying to neutralize them, which meant the Janissary infantry had arrived largely unscathed in front of Uluru and in enormous numbers. Occasional flashes bloomed over their monkey-wolf heads, revealing the outline of overlapping energy shields as Legion artillery shells and missiles were exploded prematurely, their energies dissipating harmlessly. To their front, the Hardits had erected ceramic palisades behind which they exchanged small arms fire with the Marines.

Outnumbering Scipio's Marines, the Janissaries would be moving to the offensive soon. If the Marines had been ready to repel the attack, maybe they could prevail, but the behemoths had disrupted them so badly that Scipio's position was in chaos… or at least, that was the impression the colonel was trying to convey to the New Order commander.

Scipio had better be in more command of the situation than it looked. There would be no second chance for the Legion. Not if they were going to stop Tawfiq before unleashing her new army of Ultra Janissaries. Arun had to win this battle and decisively.

Just a few more seconds…

"General McEwan," said a voice from the back of Hansel's crest.

How the frakk…?

The image of a Legion officer stared down at him, a Jotun dressed in a Legion black uniform with rank insignia Arun didn't recognize.

"Marchewka?"

"Yes, General. I recommend it is time for you to act."

"I am at the head of fifty thousand dragoons, about to lead them into battle. Trust me, I'm about to act."

"Lead? You are like Scipio when I first met him, following your primitive instincts to lead from the front. That is not a commander's place."

"Negative, Marchewka. A commander's place is dictated by the needs of the battle, and this one will not only be decided by shells, squad tactics, or those frakking Hardit tanks. The victor will be the side that possesses the strongest hearts because they have the most belief in victory. I will lead from the front because the Legion will believe in me. I am not just a field commander, Marchewka. I'm Arun McEwan. I *am* the Human Legion. Watch from high and support me as you see fit. I'm going to be busy for the next little while."

Without waiting for a reply, Arun turned to Springer and asked, "Is it on?"

She grinned and gave him a thumbs up.

His heart fluttering with adrenaline, he smiled back. *Patch me through, Barney.*

Praying that this would work better than the voice link to Scipio's forces, Arun cleared his throat. From the top of Uluru, the powerful radio transmitters, which Nest Hortez had liberated over the decades from Earth Army equipment caches, broadcast the sound to the armies below.

"You thought I was dead," Arun said. "But I cannot die until my destiny is fulfilled, until I have won freedom for all the human races."

On the back of Hansel's crest, Arun replaced Marchewka's image with spy drone footage of the battle scene. Hardit and human alike were looking around in confusion. Perfect.

"I've beaten the emperor of the White Knights," he continued. "And now I'm going to beat Tawfiq and the New Order. I have one goddess by my side, and the avatar of another speeding here from Mars. But I don't need divine help to win this battle. I'm Arun McEwan. And I *was born to win.*"

The wafer-thin frontage of the cavern, carved into the base of Uluru Ayers Rock over the past decade, now collapsed in a spray of rock dust. Neat lines of dragoons trotted out, fifty thousand lance-wielding children of Arun and Springer paired with the same number of Pedro's children, human and Trog united in their desire to kill the New Order Hardits.

A quiet descended on the battle beyond as if a timeout had been called. Legion Marines and Janissaries turned to see what the hell was happening.

Arun grinned. He'd missed this. At the top of his lungs he yelled in a voice that would have made his old training instructor, Nhlappo, proud.

"CHARGE!"

# —— Chapter 30 ——

**Arun McEwan**
**At the head of the Dragoon Army**

An ethereal blue glow emanated from the tips of the lances held high by the dragoons (Springer had pointed out that they should by rights be termed lancers, but Pedro would not countenance a change in their title). Pedro had designed these lance tips to resemble the glow from the monofilament teeth of an SA-71.

Hansel was running at full pelt now, as fast as any running Marine in fully charged combat armor, but the combination of the naturally cushioned seat set into his thorax, and the gripping rail that grew around it, meant Arun could do more than just hold on. Through the vision slit in Hansel's head frill, Arun watched the Hardits before him lower their tails.

*Yeah, that's the fear I want.*

With fifty thousand armored nightmares wreathed in carbine blue charging at their rear, the sight must be terrifying. The sound too. Even through the din of battle, the thunder of the dragoon feet striking the ground was deafening.

Some of the enemy had moved beyond fear into the brain-emptying paralysis that could afflict Hardits in moments of utter hopelessness.

But Janissaries were bred for battle. While some froze, many more were rallying, spurred on by the sight of officers executing any who dared show acts or scents of cowardice.

Hardit rifles fired at the onrushing horde. Machine guns opened up. Plasma lances shot out. Grenades. Darts. Infantry support railguns.

And still the dragoons rode into the hail of shot and shell, the bombs and darts. The sloping head armor of these Trogs unique to Nest Hortez were chipping and cracking, but for now still protected mount and rider alike.

Crazed by fear and pain, the dragoons sped to an even faster charge, desperate to close and engage.

Lucky shots found eyeholes and blasted Trog brain matter over their human riders. Indirect fire blasted riders and steeds from above, while heavier ordnance ricocheted off the head armor of leading dragoons, to blast through the flanks of those who followed behind.

Tough though it was, the head armor of the leading ranks began succumbing to the attrition of steady small arms fire, breaking off in chunks to reveal unprotected human riders. Many of the horns that had curved over Trog eyes had been reduced to jagged stumps.

All it took was a stumble from a Trog steed taking a wound, or falling foul of the shell-pocked desert ground, and the rider thrown from their mount would be crushed to bloody pulp beneath the feet of the dragoons in the ranks behind.

Ever since Pedro had revealed he'd been playing alien god with his and Springer's DNA, Arun had tried hard not to think of the clones as his children. But when he saw the drone camera images of the trail of broken young bodies that resembled Springer as he'd first known and loved her, and he saw her tight-lipped grimace of determination on the faces of the survivors, a heady mix of pride and grief forced itself into his heart.

Fortunately, the Hardits didn't have the same drone coverage.

With the human riders hidden behind their steeds' head armor, the Hardits only saw an anonymous horde of nightmare creatures bearing down on them. They couldn't single out this human who would not die, their eternal nemesis: Arun McEwan.

The behemoth tanks fired on the charging dragoons. They were so close to the Hardit line now that the gigantic railguns tore bloody chunks out of their own troops as they fired their enormous kinetic rounds into the dragoons.

Railgun darts weighing several tons gouged lines of death out of Arun's army, but they still could not find its general.

Marchewka could.

"Leave the heavy tanks to me," said the Jotun face that had reappeared on the reverse of Hansel's crest. "But you need to deactivate the sand tunnel first."

*Do it, Barney,* Arun said in his mind, and then forgot Marchewka as he lowered his lance, sliding it into the grove cut into Hansel's crest for that very purpose.

The Hardits were close enough for Arun to see their noses glisten with dampness, and their eyes go wide with fear.

Arun picked his target.

Meanwhile, Scipio had quickly rearranged his forces to spread into a dangerously thin line that lapped around the Janissary infantry, and ordered his Marines to extend the teeth on their carbines, leaving his mobile artillery to do what they could to neutralize the behemoths by showering them in sprays of sand.

High above, Marchewka looked down on the sight of a beautiful but deadly blue flattened ring forming as dragoons and Marines united with lance and teeth to surround the Hardit army. It looked perilously thin against the thickness of the Hardit forces. Could it possibly hold against the superior New Order numbers?

Arun skewered his first Hardit, couching the lance against his flank and gripping tightly onto the thorax hand rail as the lance tip passed as easily through the Janissary as a sharpened knife through tender steak.

Hansel kept charging ahead, not pausing or deviating from pushing deep into the Hardits. Even if Arun had wanted to slow, the momentum of the lines of dragoons pressing behind gave him no choice.

Acting as a single unit, Arun and Hansel aimed for another Hardit, crouched in a firing hole. If she had kept her nerve, maybe the Janissary could have shot Hansel from beneath, but she panicked and sprayed bullets that deflected harmlessly off Hansel's sloping head armor. The Hardit stared into the onrushing blue of the lance tip... and then dodged aside at the last moment.

The lance did not strike home, but Hansel had been waiting for this and crushed the Hardit with his rear legs as he passed.

And on they charged.

As wave after wave of dragoons smashed into the Hardit infantry, the clone riders fired searing blue energy discharges out of their lances to disable weaponry and vehicles; the living flesh of the enemy was skewered, cut, and sliced by the lances as they swept past.

To the east, Scipio's Marines set about the grisly business of dismembering fleeing Janissaries with their spinning monofilament needles.

Far above, Marchewka watched the blue noose tighten, its interior flooding with red.

The senior Hardit commander knew she had the superior force, that if the Janissaries could just hold firm long enough to dissipate the impetus of the Legion advance, then their greater numbers and firepower would still tell.

Superior numbers or not, Janissaries saw the terrifying sight of Legion Marines on one side, and this nightmare Trog cavalry on the other, and instinct cut in.

They dug.

Once the first Hardit scratched away at the red desert sand, her comrades nearby raced to follow suit, throwing away weapons in their desperation that they would not be the ones caught at the rear of their flight.

But there was no sanctuary below the ground. Swarms of Trog guardians oozed out of the earth to slice through Hardit limbs before diving back down beneath the sand, reappearing a short distance away to deal more death to the fleeing Hardits.

There was nowhere to run. Nowhere safe to dig.

The behemoths were not intimidated, though. Firing constantly, they were grouping, forming an armored spearhead that would tear through this thin blue line, cutting it to ribbons. Even now, if the Hardits could break out and rally behind the safety of the giant armored vehicles, their numbers were still superior. And the Hardit commander knew reinforcements were only an hour away.

Suddenly, Hansel was through into open space because the dragoon charge had overrun the first Hardit unit and was making for the rear of a unit facing east in readiness for Scipio's attack. The rear elements of this new target were beginning to turn around, weighing up options for running.

But the Hardits were several seconds away. Arun took advantage of this pause in his killing work to survey the battlezone.

Dragoons were streaming ahead of Arun now, the foremost with couched lances and Trog horns about to hit the Hardit line. Gretel was alongside, Springer having lost her lance and replaced it with a Hardit rifle. When had that happened?

But before he could ask, a crescendo of screaming engines overhead made him look up.

While some of the Sleeping Legion's surviving dropships were spiraling up through clear skies, making for the troopships in space, others were diving at the battlefield like giant birds of prey. They were aiming... at the tanks.

The behemoths saw the threat and raised their main armament as rapidly as possible. Support vehicles and any ground forces that still maintained discipline sent up fire from cannons and missiles. A dropship exploded into a fireball, sending red-hot metal shards raining down into the desert, but the others kept coming.

The crews bailed out in what looked like jet packs, just in time... the dropships slammed into the tanks.

No amount of advanced armor or force shield could resist the brute laws of physics, not with such enormous forces in play.

The tanks blew.

When the ordnance inside exploded, adding to the already immense energies released on the impact, the giant turrets were thrown high into the air, their enormous barrels scything through Hardit bodies on their descent.

The biggest threats to the Legion's victory were now burning carcasses of metal and high-tech materials.

A small group of Janissaries who'd kept discipline throughout – perhaps an elite unit – rallied with some of the surviving lesser armored vehicles and punched their way through the encirclement to the north.

But that was all. The remainder lost all cohesion, and in many cases lost their sanity before the end.

It was a grisly business, but Marine and dragoon alike slaughtered every last Hardit except for the handful that Marchewka had urged them to take for questioning.

# —— Chapter 31 ——

**Arun McEwan**
**LZ-Alpha**

"Nice ride, sir," said Scipio to his new commanding officer when they finally met on the field of battle. The mysterious colonel, who claimed to have been thawed from a dead Marine base on Tranquility-4, seemed to be weighing up whether it was safe to reach up and shake the hand of a man atop the insectoid equivalent of a heavy tank in a bad mood. Scipio decided it wasn't worth the risk of the Trog slicing off a limb.

Arun tried to imagine how his dragoon charge must have looked to a man who had probably never seen a Trog, but soon gave up. He'd lived around Trogs ever since that day as a cadet when he'd been sent into the tunnels below Detroit on a training exercise, and came out the laughing stock of the base but with the best kill score in the regiment. "Relax, Scipio," Arun said to the nervous Marine. "It's the guardian Trogs you need to be careful around. Hansel here won't bite you while I'm around. Not so long as you behave."

The Marine standing next to Scipio came to attention facing Arun. "Permission to ask an impertinent question, sir?"

There was something about this woman that sounded familiar – as if she were a memory buried so long ago it would be unwise to retrieve. Intrigued, he nodded at her.

"Sir, have you fought Hardits before?"

He nodded grimly. "Many times."

"Good. What is the instinctive Hardit response if you humiliate them?"

"They lash out without a care to the consequences."

"Exactly."

The hot rush of victory froze to ice in his breast. Arun surveyed the scene of dead and dying Hardits, of the carcasses of the armored vehicles, and bowed his head to Scipio's comrade. "You're right. We need to get far below the surface before Tawfiq wipes away the scene of her defeat." *Barney, open a line to the Sleeping Legion commander in orbit.*

The image of a Jotun officer appeared in the viewscreen on the reverse of Hansel's head crest. "Marchewka here, General."

"Postpone the second wave of landings. Keep the dropships safe with you in orbit."

"But the second wave is already launching."

"Then send them back! Tawfiq wants to beat us here, to destroy us in a straight battle. If she can't do that, she'll settle for scorching the Earth. Within ten minutes this whole area will be radioactive hell. Let her have her fit of pique. We've no choice."

The Jotun hesitated, but only for a moment. Then she set about recalling the next dropship wave.

"Get your people down below ground," Arun ordered Scipio. "I want everyone living or dead to safety, and I want it done real fast. But leave no one left behind."

"This *leave no one behind* is human madness," said Marchewka.

"Is it? I sent Nhlappo back to Tranquility-4 to rescue the sleepers beneath the ruins of Detroit. She left her own children to go back down and defend them against Tawfiq's attacks. If we hadn't gone back for our brothers and sisters then you, Marchewka, would still be sleeping the war away beneath Beta City. It's that same human madness that got us this far."

The Jotun bit her lip, the front fangs piercing the flesh to leave ragged bloody scraps. Without mentioning her wound, she started issuing orders to her subordinates on the ground. Everyone who still had a pulse was to be moved down deep below ground. As far as they could be taken.

"Thank you," mouthed Arun, and set to work evacuating his own people from the surface, summoning worker-mode Trogs to help bring back the Trog wounded through the red mountain they had hidden within and down to safer depths. The evacuation of the humans too, both Marines and clone children – wounded, dead, and fatigued – was made possible by the workers, dragoons, and scribes of Nest Hortez. Only with the guardians did Arun keep his Nest members separate from Scipio's legion.

Arun worked silently, except where speech was necessary to liaise with Scipio. He was discovering the simplicity of pheromone commands, and the efficiency with which scribes could interpret every nuance and organize results with inhuman efficiency.

Even so, they were still on their way hurrying to the lower depths of the shelters below Uluru Ayers Rock when they felt the first explosions burst overhead.

The New Order punished the land with dirty nukes and biological weapons, but for Arun and his army, poor Australia had been no more than a starting off point. They dressed their wounds and organized a rudimentary cooperation between the Sleeping Legion and Nest Hortez. As night was falling on the burning desert sands above their heads, the leading elements were already headed west along tunnels cut long ago to reach the mass transit hub beneath the shore of the Indian Ocean.

Next stop Arabia. And beyond was the pocket of Legion forces locked up in Europe. If they could break the siege and link up with the Legion forces there, nothing could stop them.

Only one thing worried Arun as he dozed off to sleep that night on Hansel's back; their great depth below a ground that was now highly radioactive had cut off their communication with Marchewka in orbit, and beyond to Indiya's Legion fleet. Why had Kreippil taken command? Was the main fleet yet able to penetrate the corrosion barrier?

But Arun had long ago learned the knack of snatching sleep wherever he could while he was on campaign. And when Hansel took his own rest during the night, so a fresh dragoon mount could carry their leader at speed, Arun was too safely wrapped in the comforting embrace of the Nest scent to stir from his slumber.

# —— Chapter 32 ——

**United Army of Liberation**
**Beneath the Earth**

United – so long as the guardians were under tight control – Arun led the armies of Nest Hortez and the Sleeping Legion on through the tunnels beneath the Earth. They left their wounded cared for and defended but pressed on without daring to lose momentum, for there was no time for delay.

Pedro had been preparing for this day for thousands of years. Deep underground, mass transit routes, which had been mothballed since the human industrial revolution for fear of discovery, now ferried soldiers and equipment at high speed beneath the Indian Ocean and then the Arabian Sea.

Tawfiq and his Ultra Janissaries would come to life in North America, but Pedro had built the main tunnel routes long ago to relieve the beleaguered Legion troops in Europe before moving west across the Atlantic to Victory City. Why Pedro had forced them to relieve the siege of Europe first was a question Arun hadn't found a satisfying answer to. Sometimes aliens just didn't make sense and you had to roll with it.

Worse, now that they suspected their existence, New Order forces sought out the hidden Trog routes and were beginning to discover them. Arun's advance slowed dangerously because his units couldn't know whether the route ahead was clear, blocked by a collapsed tunnel, or set with booby traps backed up by a Janissary suicide squad.

All this time, joint operations between Arun's Nest army and Lance's Marines increased in sophistication, but there was no time to train together. They had to press ahead and learn how to work together as they moved.

The objective of reaching Victory City drove them on. By the time their lead elements had reached the Mediterranean Sea, they had five days and ten thousand klicks to go. The main Legion fleet was headed their way from Mars orbit, but who still lived, and what progress they had made in penetrating the secrets of the corrosion barrier, was not clear from the scattered reports from the Trog signal teams who had made occasional forays toward the surface.

In his youth, Arun could have carried on for weeks before dropping from exhaustion, but he was feeling every one of his 220-odd years now, and his life had not been gentle.

Springer drove him on mercilessly. He could see in her eyes how much her cruelty cost her, but he thanked her all the same. There would be time to rest after he'd confronted Tawfiq – one way or another.

Until then, sleep was a luxury they could afford only sparingly.

The Trogs, though, were not Marines. Only two days after the Battle of Uluru, with New Order resistance appearing to crumble, and with Sangurian and human Marine reserves on their way from Australia following later waves of landings, Arun reluctantly called a general halt beneath the Mediterranean. The enemy had collapsed the long-laid Trog tunnels here, flooding them out, but the Trogs had swiftly cut around these obstacles with new tunnel systems.

Even the digging caste of Trogs had their limits and they had exhausted the last of their energy reserves. It was time to rest.

With the Trogs and their lilac-eyed human warriors halted for twelve hours, Arun sent Scipio ahead to link up with survivors of the first Legion expeditionary force, still holding out in northern Europe.

The New Order forces were far from beaten, though.

Hidden Hardit spy systems linked to human Faithful intelligence and interpreter teams discovered this temporary weakness in the relentless pursuit by Legion forces. New Order commanders saw the opportunity and seized it.

With Scipio away fighting his way north through France, the Hardits launched their counter-attack beneath the Med.

While Arun's forces had still been concentrated in Australia, New Order senior generals had begged Tawfiq to allow them to unleash their most potent anti-Trog weapon.

Only now, with the Trogs almost in Europe, had Tawfiq finally relented – confirming the suspicions of many Hardit commanders that their supreme commander wanted loyal Janissaries to die, in order to weaken the hand of the army commanders who might one day threaten her absolute grip on power.

Spearheaded by mini-tanks with a single crewmember, elite Janissary units punched deep into the Nest Hortez encampment beneath the Med.

Sentry caste Trogs sounded the alert and tried to slice apart the invading Hardits with their enormous mandibles. Many Janissaries died in this way, torsos and limbs neatly sliced into many parts, but the mini-tanks cut a path through the sentries and beyond into the vulnerable army of sleeping Trogs. Behind them ran Janissaries armed with light weapons and bomb jackets. Speed was paramount to these teams, pressing ahead into their enemies by dodging and outrunning the Trogs while they were still slowed by sleep and fatigue. They were not weighed down by heavy equipment, because they had no intention of defending their objective against counter attack. None of them would be coming back.

As the Trogs regained their effectiveness, the slaughter they wreaked upon the Janissaries was terrible, but still the enemy pressed ahead until the senior surviving Hardit commander gave the order to unstrap the bombs that hung around their chests and detonate them.

Choking crimson poison gas billowed out through the tunnels beneath the sea. This gas was what allowed the Hardits to sleep at night, the ultimate counter to the terror of Trogs who could swim through the dirt and slice your head from your torso with a casual flick of their claws.

Developed over centuries, the payload of the gas bombs was the same plague that at the start of the interstellar war had killed the Trogs beneath Tranquility-4 – Pedro's birth world.

Pedro was a brilliant bioengineer and had spent the first few decades after his people had been wiped out re-engineering his body to develop immunity to the plague. And that immunity adaptation extended to his many children, but whether it would work was another matter – it had never been tested outside the lab. It was Trog bioengineering versus Hardit biowarfare. Which would prevail?

The Trogs caught in the poison gas attack choked, collapsed, and vomited into their narrow passageways and corridors until the poorly ventilated area reeked with alien bile.

Then they rose to their feet and slaughtered every Hardit who had dared to unleash the vile plague that had killed all but one of the Trogs of the Detroit Nest.

By the time the Janissary armored units at the vanguard of their follow-up assault smashed into Trog forces ten klicks offshore from Barcelona, eager to exploit the devastating effect of the poison attack, their enemy was not only fit for duty, but was alert and roused to anger. Even so, the battle was close fought, and conducted without mercy.

The New Order commander, General Pordsin-Ayul, had recently taken command of the European sector by virtue of demonstrating superior loyalty to the supreme commander, but she was determined to prove that she possessed as much competence as the old fool she'd replaced when they had dared to criticize the supreme commander. Pordsin-Ayul threw all her theater reserves into this attack, judging this was the critical turning point in the campaign.

For their part, the would-be liberators of the Earth knew that if they did not repel this counter-attack, they would not reach Tawfiq in time to prevent her awakening her super army.

Pordsin-Ayul was very aware of this timetable and had concluded that the most efficient way to rob her enemies of the momentum they needed to reach Victory City in time was to decapitate the Legion.

They had to kill Arun McEwan.

The finest unit she commanded was the Sil-Rhul-Thullix Brigade: elite troops with fanatical loyalty to the supreme commander. They howled with delight when she sent them ahead through secret routes to win this war, for they would have the honor of killing McEwan.

# —— Chapter 33 ——

Arun McEwan
Beneath the Mediterranean

Arun's first live fire exercise as a cadet had been in Trog tunnels. Now the Trogs were his to command, but the uneven tubular passageways they carved were just as confusing as they had been in his youth.

Human, Littorane, or Jotun engineers would have built underground defensive warrens with mathematical precision, but the Trog tunnels were so organic they almost looked like living beings. They didn't merely zigzag along a plane to thwart the possibility of an enemy slaughtering the defenders by firing down a straight line, but they snaked up and down, twisting completely around on themselves and narrowing into constrictions he would have struggled to pass through if not for Hansel's ability to cut through any obstruction – or even go off-piste *through* the ground and bypass an obstacle altogether. Bedrock still required blasting or burning through, but Trogs could swim through the deepest subsoils.

Without a Marine BattleNet feeding data into a visor HUD, Arun could not track the fast-moving events in the tunnels, so he had passed tactical command to a senior dragoon officer duo.

The Trog half was known as Batch, and the lilac-eyed woman who rode the Trog – her hair spiked up and dyed blue in an echo of a Celtic warrior – was named Escandala-2713.

His brain struggled to process the information that this clone was his daughter, biologically speaking, and was named after his mother. It was off-the-scale weird.

But Escandala and Batch had rallied the exhausted Trog army, and having robbed the enemy attack of momentum, was now pushing back.

All Arun had to do was hurry up and stay alive.

"Will you stop doing that?" Hansel snapped at Arun while they waited for the Hardit pressure to relent from the relative safety to the rear of the front lines – although the *front* in tunnel warfare was a fluid concept at best.

Arun frowned. "Stop what?"

"Drumming your fingers on my saddle rail. You're making me nervous."

"Hush," Gretel implored. "You know the Great Parent talks often of the Queen of Battle when he was merely the Human McEwan. Their first meeting was traumatic."

"I was buried alive," said Arun, snatching his hand away from Hansel's saddle rail. "It was not a pleasant experience."

"You looked at the time as if you enjoyed some of it," said Springer, voice like a devilish angel.

"Enjoyed?" Hansel spiraled antennae in amusement. "Please elaborate."

"Well…" Springer caught Arun's warning glare and shrugged. "He was so high on combat drugs that he didn't know what was going on. For a lot of the experience, he was singing. Badly. Naked, too, as I recall."

"I do not wish him to sing," said Gretel. "It might be bad for morale."

"Easy for you to say," Hansel retorted. "You do not suffer his drumming fingers."

Arun froze his hand. He'd been drumming again.

"You see?" said Hansel, waving antennae imploringly. "Please sing, great Queen Human McEwan. Take pity on me and sing."

Shaking his head – he couldn't exactly imagine Indiya or Aelingir doing this – Arun filled his lungs with the fetid tunnel air and prepared to sing.

But the song never reached his lips. The world exploded in confusion. Arun was spinning through the air, ripped painfully from Hansel's back. He felt as if hidden assailants had beaten his reinforced skull with iron bars, making it ring like a bell. Meanwhile, other little bastards were hammering away at his rib cage from the inside. He was going to choke to death with the dust and debris filling his mouth, but his lungs were so agonizingly bruised that he just held himself without breathing until he impacted the ground and grunted in pain.

He opened his eyes but saw only an impenetrable haze of dust cut through with flashes from energy weapons, and the din of a furious melee filled with Hardit growls and yelps of pain.

A huge Trog charged at him.

At first, Arun thought the creature was coming to his aid, but it was a big, dumb digger caste Trog. He braced for the giant's impact as it ran across him, but the digger knew enough to step nimbly over him. He could do with being shielded by the creature's bulk, but to guard Arun from the Janissary attack was beyond the creature's comprehension. Instead, it was leaping up into the air like a dancer. Other bulky shapes were similarly prancing, oblivious to the battle raging around them.

The air cleared sufficiently Arun to realize what he was seeing; the diggers were eating the dirt right out of the air. And the sight they revealed was not good.

Janissaries had blasted a hole through the tunnel wall and were pouring through in unceasing numbers.

He looked around, searching for something to use as a weapon, but there was nothing. He had no armor and no visor HUD, and he still could see nothing clearly, certainly not Hansel nor Springer. The hole the Hardits had blasted was no more than fifty feet from where he'd been chatting with the others. That was too close to be a coincidence. The enemy was here for single purpose: to kill him.

Arun had never felt so helpless in his long life. Rolling onto his belly, he dug his fingers into the dirt and began dragging his body away from the fighting.

He made about ten feet before he was grabbed from above and lifted off the ground. Arun twisted and bucked, flinging his arms to throw his weight around.

It did no good. He was hurled into the air and fell… directly into the cushioned area that served as a saddle on Hansel's thorax.

"Stop wriggling, will you?" grumbled the Trog.

"What took you so long?" laughed Arun as he grabbed the power lance from the bracket on Hansel's flank.

"Oh, nothing much. Just passing the time saving Springer and Gretel. Now, quit yapping, Queen of Battle, and act regal."

Arun grinned. "You got it."

Arun activated the tip of his lance and charged into the fray.

Unlike the Hardits and Trogs who could tell friend from foe by scent, Arun relied far more on his eyesight, which struggled to penetrate the still-thick dust clouds. So he trusted to Hansel's superior senses and his own quick reactions.

There… a tail appeared out the dust clouds. Arun guessed where the torso was, and aimed his power lance, thumbing a blast of intense blue light that lit up a Janissary wielding a grenade launcher. The Hardit screamed and burned.

Arun wanted to grab the launcher, but Hansel had already bounded away. Just in time – a stream of Hardit bullets flailed the space where they had been a second earlier.

Hansel wheeled and caught a pair of Janissaries from behind, their rifles up and noses probing the air to find where Arun had disappeared to.

Hansel speared one with the sole horn that remained after the Battle of Uluru, and Arun jabbed the other with his lance, the tip cutting through Hardit armor, hide, and ribs to pierce its heart.

And beyond the dead and dying Hardits, Arun saw Springer and Gretel scything through the Hardits like reapers of death.

Nonetheless, by the time the air had cleared fully, the situation looked grim indeed. Arun's Trog guard had fought back tenaciously, the old Marines and their clone children gutting hundreds of the enemy on their lances and horns, or stomping them beneath their feet, but hundreds more were still racing through the breach in the wall.

In the narrow confines of the tunnel, the Hardits hadn't been able to take full advantage of their superior numbers. Then the wall exploded as they opened a second breach. A few moments later they blew a third. Now that the stream of Janissaries was becoming a flood, the attackers made their numbers count and began separating the Trogs into isolated groups, surrounding them. Despite their formidable chitin armor, the Trogs succumbed rapidly to the sheer weight of Hardit firepower.

Although the lance Arun wielded was deadly effective, he wanted to die with an SA-71 carbine in his hands, as was his Marine birthright.

He jerked, disoriented because his memories and his reality were blurring. Consequently, he missed a Hardit, his lance merely striking a glancing blow against the enemy's flank instead of slicing through the heart.

Hansel skidded around in the dirt and dealt the slightly stunned Hardit a crushing blow with his armored Trog abdomen.

"Do you tire?" asked Hansel breathlessly.

Arun noted his companion's labored breathing and suddenly realized both that Hansel was bleeding in a dozen places, and that Arun cared. He stretched forward and gave the creature's antennae a quick stroke in the way that Pedro liked. "No, my friend. I thought I heard the report of Marine carbines. I'm sorry. I think my memories are rearing up to claim me."

"I do not hear human carbines," said Hansel as he lowered his armored head to the ground. A Hardit fusillade ricocheted off his crest, snapping jagged shards off the once-magnificent display. "However… I smell something approaching that I cannot identify. Nor can I pin down its location."

Yet more explosions blasted the walls, sending out fresh clouds of choking dust. This time the breaches were in the opposite wall, completing the encirclement of the Trogs.

Or so Arun thought. His eyes couldn't see through the dust, but his ears could hear through it. And that sound of gunfire was so familiar that he could hear it through vacuum, the laws of physics be damned.

He heard the whine of SA-71 rails charging, the soft fizz and pop as darts emerged from the business end at hypersonic velocity, simultaneous with the wet fleshy noise of a Janissary life ending. Then he heard it all over again. Controlled Marine carbine fire.

A moving shape caught his eye through the clouds. There was something different about this person – not only did the combat seemed to be focused on them, but the way they moved was different from anyone else Arun had ever seen.

He knew who this was.

# —— Chapter 34 ——

**Arun McEwan**
**Beneath the Mediterranean**

The Marine wore the same ACE-series combat armor Arun had practically been born wearing. Not only was the armor proof against the worst Hardit small arms fire – reducing impacts that would rip gaping holes out of flesh to mere brutal punches – the exo muscles of his armor were powerful enough to lift his enemies and dash them against the ground in head-pulping violence.

This, Arun knew from personal experience. But this wearer neither wielded an SA-71 – it was strapped to his back – nor ripped apart his enemies with gauntleted hands.

The Marine advancing on Arun used his powered armor to wield a black two-handed sword through the heads and torsos of his opponents with tireless strength.

And his armor was enhanced by the nimble bodyguard who used her carbine's teeth to rip apart any Janissary who worked around the sword-wielding warrior's flank.

He still couldn't recall the bodyguard's identity, but the swordsman… this was the leader of the Sleeping Legion forces on Earth, Lance Scipio, who should be hundreds of klicks away to the north.

When he'd first arrived, bearing barely believable stories of hidden assets buried beneath Tranquility-4, and then went into battle armed with a sword (what the frakk?) Arun had thought Scipio a deranged madman, and not in a good way.

Arun began to reconsider his assessment of the man.

He'd seen that desperate need to get into close quarters fighting deeply embedded into earlier generations of Marines. His old friend, Carabinier Umarov, had been so eager to close with the enemy that once within a hundred yards, he'd drop his weapons and sprint at them, screaming paralyzing battle cries, and brandishing his crescent-shaped blades. And now that he thought of his dead friend, Arun recalled that when he'd first met Umarov, the ancient Marine had referred to Arun's Detroit home as Marine Farm #3.

If Beta City was Marine Farm #2, then where the hell was Marine Farm #1? Scipio had mentioned something about *another* Marine base at Cardamine Island. Frakk it! Umarov had given him a clue to the existence of this new Sleeping Legion nearly two centuries ago, but Arun had never joined the dots.

A stray Janissary bullet grazed Arun's back. He leaned out beyond the cover of Hansel's head shield and fired lance blasts at the group of three Hardits trying to flank him.

Springer and Gretel wheeled around Arun's rear to protect his exposed flank, because Hansel was no longer able to respond to the Hardit attacks. Arun's mount was wheezing now, listing on his five remaining legs and bleeding heavily. Arun had seen Trogs recover from far worse batterings, but there was no way his friend would be able to accompany him to Victory City and Tawfiq.

Hansel set his head down to protect his rider from another wave of Hardits flowing around the swirling melee that had brought Scipio and his bodyguard to a halt. The dragoon's crest armor was flaking off in jagged sheets in the hail of incoming fire.

Arun looked through the cracks in the armor crest and fired lance blasts at every Hardit he could see. Springer did the same.

Then another wave of Janissaries made a push for their target.

Scipio was fully engaged with the Hardits to his front, but the Janissaries had changed tactics. They were pinning him in place with feint attacks, so they could overwhelm his bodyguard first.

"Never again!" she screamed, in a voice Arun definitely recognized. A pair of Janissaries brought chainsaws buzzing to angry life and advanced the cutting edges to her neck. She flew into the air, using the ability of her suit to make mighty leaps, even if that model couldn't fly in strong gravity fields. With five Janissaries clinging to her legs, she collided with the roof – which dislodged two of the Hardits – and descended toward an area of tunnel empty of anything beyond the dust-coated corpses of a Janissary and one of Arun and Springer's clone children.

Meanwhile, Scipio was on his belly in the dirt and blood, his arms stretched out behind him by teams of Janissaries. Kneeling, the two chainsaw wielders who'd threatened the bodyguard now brandished their cutting tools near Scipio's neck, looking around at Arun and lifting their long lips in a Hardit grin.

This was an execution being staged for his benefit! Even for the foul creations of Tawfiq Woomer-Calix, this was perverted behavior.

Arun pointed his lance at the group around Scipio, but the weapon was inaccurate. With the Hardits crouching so close to the colonel, he was as likely to hit the human they were about to execute.

Springer charged at them.

"McEwan!" warned the bodyguard. Arun remembered her now. Her name was Kraevoi, and she was supposed to be dead.

"Frakk!" A jolt of fear hit Arun, which in turn roused Hansel. Kraevoi hadn't landed in empty space at all. She'd come clattering down on top of a line of Janissaries who had been concealed behind an overlapping wall of shields that seemed to convey stealth concealment. Now that the shields had been scattered, their absence revealed a tripod-mounted cannon. It was in the final stages of being readied for use. And it was aimed at him.

He jabbed at the gun with his lance, but the energy blast deflected off a force shield.

A short distance away, Springer was busy jabbing at the chainsaw-wielding Janissaries threatening Scipio while Gretel stomped on those pinning him down.

Kraevoi tried to leap again, but her suit motors whirred powerlessly, drained, and the Janissaries rushed her, pushing her away from the cannon as they struck her with metal clubs that glowed blue.

Hansel stirred. He was too exhausted now to control his scent, which reeked of agony and the kind of fatigue that smelled fatal. But he jumped at the Hardit cannon.

And in mid-leap, the cannon barked.

A stream of rounds cut through the Trog's thorax and abdomen, but the great bulk of Arun's mount was too great to be blown away and he landed in front of the gun

Hansel's legs collapsed on impact, and Arun had to hang on tightly to avoid being thrown by the hard landing. He lost his grip on his lance, and was reaching for his pistol to shoot at the Janissary who'd fired the cannon, when he saw the Hardit twitching, impaled on Hansel's remaining horn.

But it wasn't over yet. Two more Janissaries raced to the gun, pulling it upright and aiming at Arun.

He shot at them with his pistol, but the plasma round glanced off the portable force shield one was using to protect them both.

The firer grinned. "Die, McEwan!" it said through a speaker on its collar.

The shield bearer activated a control on its wrist, which Arun assumed would open an aperture for the cannon to fire through.

He aimed at the cannon's barrel with his pistol.

There came a blur of motion. Gretel streaked into Arun's peripheral vision, Springer standing up in the stirrups, her lance high above her head, angled at the Hardit gun crew.

She threw the weapon at the monkey-wolves at the same time as the Janissaries fired. A split second earlier, Arun had dropped his pistol and dived for the ground behind Hansel.

Shots thudded into Hansel's flank, but the Trog gave no reaction.

Arun grabbed his pistol off the ground and scrambled around Hansel to face the gun crew. He saw the Hardits pitched forward into the dirt, Springer's lance skewering both their torsos.

And that was it. The battle was over.

Gretel was nudging Hansel with her head, as if urging her friend to get to his feet and stop messing around, but his scent was already growing cold.

Scipio was striding over to Arun, hand outstretched. "Ass saved, sir," he was saying. "Just in the nick of time."

Arun had no reply.

The bodyguard rose unsteadily to her feet and took off her helmet to reveal curly black hair and a diamond-hard stare. A tiny part of him rang with recognition to see Kraevoi after all these years. She never made the rendezvous in the operation over Beta City in the First Tranquility Campaign. Arun hadn't searched for her. Couldn't have. She was supposed to be dead.

But Arun had nothing to say on that either.

"Thank you, Scipio," Arun said tonelessly. "But you weren't in time to save everyone." He leaned forward and embraced the cracked head of his dead friend.

He told himself he was being foolish – Hansel was only a Trog with a silly name, after all – but Arun's eyes and his mind were too clouded with tears to encompass Lance Scipio or Sashala Kraevoi.

The others left him alone to his grief.

They had seen this before. All too often. It was time to end the war.

# —— Chapter 35 ——

**Arun McEwan**
**Brompton Road Station**
**London Hypertube**

According to Major Knudsir, who'd delighted in researching the hidden places beneath London, the city where the Legion's last European bastion had held out, the neat text framed within green lines had been fired into the curved tile wall of the station platform for over seven centuries. Having spent most of those years buried under a thick protective layer of dust, the tiles had come up gleaming when Knudsir, to whom command of the stranded Legion forces had fallen in the final days of the siege, came across this long-abandoned station linked to the London Hypertube network, and recommissioned it as a forward command post. Its small size and mostly sealed exits made it relatively easy to clean, sterilize, and seal off from the radiation and chemical weapon residue that blighted the city above ground.

Arun ignored the senior commanders streaming around his hover chair as they left the meeting to reconnect with their subordinates. "What would they think of us?" he mused at the station name on the wall. "Our distant ancestors who last saw those tiles as they made their way to work, or perhaps looked forward to rendezvousing in the city above with their friends or lovers. The everyday matters of lives long forgotten, names consigned to unsearched data stores, but whose insignificant speck of existence mattered back then, and still does today. Together, all those forgotten people brought us to our position today in the galaxy. What would they think of us? Have we failed them?"

Arun felt a hand on his shoulder, a hard gauntlet of ceramalloy armor plating and artificial muscles, but gently placed.

"Only if they could hear you utter that meta-existential shite-babble," offered Lance Scipio, adding a "Sir" as an afterthought.

238

Springer chuckled. "Thank you, Colonel, for saving me the bother of having to tell the old man the same thing. Again."

Arun looked up at his lover, deciding that her bright scales resembled the tiles on the wall, though her patterning was far wilder. The brown pigment in her eyes had also reasserted itself, her body obeying the instructions of its recoded DNA rather than whatever force lay deep within her that expressed itself with the lilac glow.

She seemed bemused by his attention. *Well, she'd better get used to it*, he thought, *I'll never tire of looking on her face.*

"Meetings. Conferences, strategy planning, politicking," he told her. "As soon as we've cut Tawfiq down, they will all belong to someone else. You and I will be free of the aftermath. We've done enough."

"I admire your optimism, General," said Scipio. "Personally, I believe only death will free us from meetings, but you got what you wanted back there, didn't you? Everyone on the planet and in space has agreed to back you. Marchewka, your ex-wife, the big ant we left in Australia, the space otter admiral – who seemed very disappointed to find you were still alive, by the way – and even the Sangurian warlord agreed that you are the big boss. CO of all you survey.

Arun sighed. He supposed Scipio was right, but the command meeting in the cramped cylinder of a room at the end of the Brompton Road Station had been harder than he'd ever expected. Even Scipio seemed to have noticed that Kreippil had assumed the command of the Human Legion had fallen to him, and that the human phase of its formation had come to an end. With the Littoranes at the head of this holy army, blasphemy would be driven from the galaxy in the name of the goddess.

It had been Marchewka who had frustrated Kreippil's designs for leadership, arguing the strongest that the forces aligned to defeat Tawfiq must have a single commander-in-chief and that person had to be Arun McEwan. With Kreippil's fleet still only able to project limited force through the corrosion barrier, it was Marchewka who commanded more boots on the ground and more guns in space. His words had won out.

The Final Alliance, Xin had named their coalition against Tawfiq.

The name carried a sense of its own impermanence. And although Marchewka carried the balance of power in Earth orbit, that would change. A large New Order fleet had arrived in the outer system and was using the giant snowballs of the Oort Cloud to refuel and resupply before heading in system. They would arrive too late to affect Tawfiq's plan to ascend to goddesshood, her apotheosis, but who would meet them? The Final Alliance, or Kreippil in command of a holy fleet that answered to no one but the distant Queen of the Littoranes, and maybe not even her.

Before the meeting, both Flag Lieutenant Hood, and Grace had warned Arun that Indiya had finally cracked. It was bittersweet indeed to hear the voice of his daughter alive and well, but for her to speak of his oldest ally's mental anguish.

!C o m e. F o l l o w  u s !

The Nest Hortez scribes Arun had dispatched after the meeting to update his Nest commanders had returned, jumping around the ancient tube station platform in excitement.

? W E L L ?

Springer's query came as one helluva shock. That she could understand the scribes was impressive, but for her to speak the pheromone language already was astonishing. The scars where her scent device had been inserted were still fresh. But Arun had lived with his scent implant for most of his life and could glimpse behind the words of the scribes to the thoughts themselves. Whatever had excited them so much concerned his clone children, and it had profoundly shocked the Trogs.

"I'll catch you later, Queen Ant," said Scipio with a chuckle. "I've got some… ahh… business of my own to attend."

"Okay," said Arun absentmindedly as he set his hover chair speeding along the platform. "And when you attend to Kraevoi, please tell her that when Tawfiq is dead, I want to explain what happened in Phase Guinshrike all those years ago."

# —— Chapter 36 ——

**Arun McEwan**
**Brompton Road Station**
**London Hypertube**

The scribes were so eager for them to follow that they covered most of the distance to their clone children on foot.

"Let me carry you," Springer had insisted when Arun had slowed to allow his chair to negotiate the ancient steps down from the station platform.

Arun had shrugged her away. As the CO, he needed to comport himself with a little dignity. But Springer was not one to be brushed off easily, especially where her children were concerned.

"You already have a reputation for embarrassing yourself in tunnels," she pointed out. "By comparison, to be carried over my shoulder barely registers."

There was no answer to that, and so with Arun balanced over her shoulder, they pressed on through frequent barriers of protective hazard sheets draped from the roof, past bemused legionaries still coming to terms with the idea that the long siege of Europe was finally over, and on to a passenger waiting area for the modern hypertube where the Jotun commander, Knudsir, was waiting for them. He explained that he'd ordered them here out of the way because Arun's children were beginning to freak out his exhausted Marines, and frankly they had seen enough in the past few weeks.

Scores of men and women inside linked hands and mumbled an indecipherable chant. Some stood, while others knelt on the chairs or sat in each other's laps, and all of them resembled Arun and Springer.

Springer herself pushed to the center of the crowded room, her children grudgingly parting to admit her. Over her shoulder, Arun saw a steady trickle of the clone children continue to join the group. There must have been a hundred of them or more already, and it was strange to feel so ignored by them.

Normally, he felt more comfortable around the Dragoon Trogs than his human descendants who acted as if he were a combination of deity and celebrity, around whom they tried but failed to behave normally.

Without warning, they ceased their chanting and regarded Springer and Arun in their midst with slack-jawed surprise, suddenly remembering to be awestruck so close to their hero parents.

He felt bad about it, but Arun shuddered. He was their father, after a fashion, but that didn't prevent this being super creepy.

One of the older women, her buzz cut hair shockingly white, emerged from the nervous crowd to face Arun, and gave her parents a bow. "We have foreseen," she said.

"Wait!" said Springer and shooed her children aside until she had placed Arun and herself into two of the waiting chairs. "Now, tell us your name and then what you sensed of our future."

The woman paused to think. Until their parents had awoken from their long cryogenic sleep, the human members of Nest Hortez had identified themselves only by scent. "Escandala-351," she replied.

Inwardly, Arun cursed Pedro for forcing him to endure such weirdness once again. Escandala had been his mother's name, and now that he thought of it, this woman did resemble the images he had seen of Sergeant Escandala McEwan as she had been before her death at the battle of Akinschet in 2560. Though the burning lilac eyes, not so much.

"The Hardits are the key," explained Escandala. "If you make a frontal assault with your armies, you will not reach Tawfiq in time. The Hardits will give you another line of attack that can succeed. We have seen this."

Arun winked at Springer while his daughter who looked like his mother squeezed drops into her eyes from a bottle she kept in a chest pocket. "You always told me you didn't see with your visions."

242

Springer gave him a hefty punch in the shoulder. "Escandala is being metaphorical, you drent-head." She stared her daughter. "Right? You can't tell us which Hardits, can you? You can't draw a picture or describe a scent?"

Escandala shook her head. "All I know is that they will allow you to get to Tawfiq from a direction that she won't expect."

"And there's definitely more than one Hardit?" added Arun. Around them, the other clone children were filing out of the room, content they had played their part and had nothing to add to what Escandala would say.

"A small number, I think," said Escandala. "More than one, but not whole armies."

"So you don't think it's a split," said Springer. "You don't see us aligning with one of Tawfiq's rivals to drive a wedge into the enemy."

"I don't think so, but I'm not certain about that."

Arun resisted the temptation to snap at her. She claimed they needed Hardits, but of the millions on the planet, she couldn't say which ones. He supposed it was an improvement. Until today, whenever the clone children had met in groups and tried to discern the patterns of the future, all they could say was that the campaign would end in blood. Yeah, great help. Every time, it had been the same answer. But how could they use this new insight? Within the hour, they would be heading west beneath the Atlantic for the final confrontation. They had a few New Order Hardit prisoners, but they had revealed little of use. Approaching Earth orbit, there were Hardit legionaries aboard First Fleet troopships. The Hardit mini-tankers of the 7th Armored Claw had distinguished themselves in several battles across the galaxy, and their survivors were licking their wounds here beneath London. Did Arun need to order Kreippil to land another Hardit and Wolf assault Regiment in Europe to join Arun's main force as it travelled beneath the Atlantic?

"By Tyndall, I know the ones she means," said Major Knudsir walking in from the lobby outside. "Despite the deprivations of the siege, I kept these two prisoners alive and well treated. I sensed they might have a part yet to play."

"Yes," said Escandala. "I like what this Jotun officer is saying."

"Please forgive my impertinence at addressing you, Major," said Springer, "but without trying to rationalize your choice, can you tell us what instinct provokes you to spare these Hardits?"

"Oh, that's simple. With most of the prisoners we capture, if we set them free they would simply return to their units as fast as possible and fight us, loyal Tawfiq Janissaries to the end. A few are so traumatized that they're broken beings, incapable of being soldiers again. But this pair of deserters we caught skulking in the Hypertube, still believe in themselves as soldiers, but they have lost belief in their cause. They are Janissaries, but they bear no love for Tawfiq Woomer-Calix nor for the New Order."

Springer looked pointedly at Arun, which confused him until he remembered that her name was supposed to be Lissa, and when they had first served under Jotun officers, to address a major directly, as she had just done, was to invite summary execution for disrespect. Arun, on the other hand, was now a general.

"Thank you, Major Knudsir. Your service in commanding this last European bastion against the New Order has already been honorable enough that the poets must already be at work. They will search tirelessly to discover the words that will immortalize you and your brave army. And now you provide great service again. Perhaps even more so. Major, I trust your judgement. Bring these Hardits to us here, immediately."

The major wore a Jotun model of armored combat exosuit, but his helmet was off and hanging by his hip, and Arun was amused to see Knudsir's fur stand up and his ears prick out in pride. Human-Jotun relations had progressed a long way since he was a cadet.

"Yes, General," said the Jotun, giving a human style salute with both arms on his right side. "Thank you, sir. It is my honor to obey."

# ——— Chapter 37 ———

Arun McEwan
Brompton Road Station
London Hypertube

The comm connection ended, and the viewscreen that had showed the Hardit legionaries of the 7th Armored Claw reverted to a transparent material taped to a tiled wall on which had been painted the words: "Please do not smoke".

The two Janissary prisoners gave no reaction, as if the connection to their non-Janissary Hardit brethren, who were a few klicks away beneath another part of London, was so powerful that cutting the transmission channel made little difference.

Wokmar and Shocles had stood through the entire linkup standing wide-mouthed and speechless, and they showed no signs of any change.

"Have I broken them?" Arun asked Scipio in all seriousness after a couple of minutes' silence.

"How should I know, sir? We allied with Hardit militia on Tranquility against the New Order, but that's not the same as recruiting Janissaries. We had a few Hardits join up as AuxTechs, but they weren't Janissaries either, and you know how much Hardits love tinkering with machinery. To be honest, I'm as surprised as these two monkeys to see Hardits serving as frontline Legionary fighters."

"These two we spoke with," said one of the prisoners, "they merge their scent with you humans and Littoranes and other aliens, and do so voluntarily?"

Arun read the English version of the name written in ink on the Janissary's collar. "Well, Shocles, if you're asking whether our Hardits are best friends forever with filthy xenos such as myself, Major Knudsir, and Colonel Scipio, then I'm sorry to disappoint you. Several Hardit communities – usually miners in asteroid belts and outer system shells – have joined as members of the Human Autonomous Region." He laughed to see both Hardits curl their lips in contempt. "Yeah, they like the name about as much as you. Anyway, those are full-fledged Hardit colonies who volunteered to become a part of what we are carving out from the White Knight Empire, but rest assured the individuals within those communities would rather bathe in their own vomit than be in close proximity to a being from another species. The Hardit legionaries you just heard from are something of an exception. Renegades–"

"Males," said the other one, Wokmar.

"Err, yes. I believe they are. We pair them up with Wolves, who are themselves the outsiders of humanity. They get along okay."

"I cannot believe that my Hardit brethren could cooperate voluntarily with a lesser species," said Wokmar.

"But to believe that is to believe our race is one of fools," countered Shocles. "We have seen successful symbiotic relationships between species on many of the biospheres we have encountered during our campaigns. Why, then, are you so quick to discount cooperation between species of unrelated biospheres?"

Wokmar snapped her jaws hard. "I despise your logic, Shocles. Because it is impossible to refute. The implications…"

Shocles gave Arun a long stare with her yellow eye trio. Arun knew enough about Hardits to realize that with Shocles's ears pitched forward, the longer the stare, the more carefully Shocles was considering Arun's point of view.

Time was pressing. Arun had spent over an hour talking with Shocles and Wokmar, and setting up the link with the Hardit legionaries, but he allowed Shocles another couple of minutes before the Janissary spoke again.

"My comrade talked of implications," said the Hardit. "It would be easy to underestimate their significance. And maybe not just for us, but for other disaffected Janissaries too."

"The New Order preaches perpetual war against all other species in the galaxy," said Wokmar. "We may choose not to fight a race at a given moment in time, but that is either due to a temporary armistice or because we are waiting to defeat our enemies in detail. But we are at war with all other races at all times until either Hardits are the only survivors in the galaxy, or we are ourselves exterminated."

"Our minds can encompass the possibility of eventual defeat, but of a third option, one in which we are not at war with creation, this is a dangerous and powerful new idea to us."

"Gotta love the spiritual awakening aspect, guys," said Scipio, "but our intel says your former boss is going to raise a new super army in five days. Clock's ticking and it's a long walk to Victory City. You know anything about this?"

"No," the two Hardits said.

"Just peachy," said Scipio. "Word is, Tawfiq's talking about becoming a goddess. Don't suppose you know anything about that either?"

"No," agreed Wokmar, but Shocles twisted her tail around her comrade's and gave a sharp tug.

"We are lowly Janissaries," said Shocles. "Speculation is punished severely except in senior officers and design technicians for whom it is a proper requirement of their role. I was once an officer like you, Lance Scipio, in command of several regiments. I was once allowed to speculate. We *know* nothing of new armies, but we have *heard many rumors* that Tawfiq seeks to replace us with a new breed of Janissaries with unshakeable loyalty to her and her alone. And we have heard in her own official bulletins that she intends to lead the New Order armies over the tens of thousands of years it would take to win the war against a galaxy, and we have seen her body alter but not age in the natural way. It is said, also, that she is not herself a true Janissary because she has retained her original gender. There, I have spoken a sickening mix of fact and hearsay. Make of it what you will, humans."

"Oh, I already have," said Arun. "Let's say that I have an intuition that this new super army is real, and Tawfiq is going to bind it to her in a ceremony in a few days' time. You two are going to get a strike team in close enough to kill her."

"You mean you have foreseers?" asked Shocles. "Why did you not say in the first place? You humans are so inefficient. The solution is obvious. We Janissaries are not like those of the Hardit race whom we saw on the screen – those who ally with your Legion."

Arun almost snapped back that the Hardits of the 7th Armored Claw were not allies – they were full members of the Legion – but that seemed a little too far for these Janissary deserters to stomach.

"We are stripped of gender and without that, our scent is a flimsy thing compared with the males who talked with us. In natural Hardits, scent is all. It binds us to the group, identifies those with authority. Gives us purpose and comfort. With our scent so weak, the means with which Tawfiq and the New Order impose their loyalty is a complex thing of artifice and fragility."

"What Shocles is trying to say," said Wokmar, "is that if you can capture the clothing and carcass of a Janissary officer, we can wear their scent and pass amongst their unit without notice. Only Janissaries such as us can do this. Your Legionary Hardits cannot."

"Wokmar exaggerates. If the Janissaries loyal to Tawfiq are alert to the possibility of treachery, then we would be discovered. But if we are careful, and if they do not expect strangers in their midst, then it is possible we can accomplish much."

"I'm just a simple human," said Scipio. "I don't understand these maybes and could-dos and possibilities. Can you frakking sneak us in or not?"

The two prisoners linked tails. "Yes," they said in unison.

# ── Chapter 38 ──

**Governor Romulus**
**Victory Monument**

Tawfiq Woomer-Calix was mad.

The hatred Romulus harbored for Tawfiq had burned within him for so long that it was difficult to step outside the pure loathing for the instigator of his torment, and see the Supreme Commander of the New Order from other perspectives.

It had taken this. This megalomaniac hubris. This apotheosis. The sheer spectacle that was about to play out over the grounds of what had today been renamed the Imperial Mall. It had taken all this to make Romulus realize what should have been obvious for years.

Tawfiq was insane.

For this, the most important day of her mortal life, Tawfiq looked west from the top of what had been the Washington Monument at her marble carved image staring back from a klick away. Both flesh and stone versions sat in stone chairs, and both wore identical military-style jackets.

Standing beside Tawfiq was the Janissary general who appeared to have won the battle for survival in Tawfiq's wave of recent purges. General Dine-Alegg wore a tight-fitting silvered jerkin with a metalized fabric hood on which a traverse mounted crest of precious metals ran from ear to ear. This was the uniform of a senior Janissary officer from the very earliest years of the New Order. Dine-Alegg wore Hardit clothing.

But Tawfiq?

Her jacket was in a human style. Her carved image aped the historical human leader, Lincoln, and sat upon his chair in the memorial that had once been named after him. And Romulus tried hard not to think about the floor covering stitched together from rectangles of human hide.

Humans. Humans. Humans!

The supreme commander was obsessed.

Ever since she brought him here, Tawfiq had imprisoned Romulus beneath the ruins of the White House, which had been the official residence of the president of the International Federation right up until the last holder of that office had been executed by a New Order firing squad.

Everywhere, around the planet, Tawfiq had ordered human symbols to be preserved, but in corrupted forms. She wanted every human to look out on their world and know that it had been violated personally by Tawfiq Woomer-Calix.

The New Order had fought other races, but for Tawfiq that had been the tedious practical matter of eliminating lesser species from the galaxy. Her presence on Earth was personal. She was obsessed with humanity.

And above all else, she was infatuated with Arun McEwan.

This whole spectacle, Romulus realized, was her ultimate expression of flipping the bird to the human who had thwarted her so often. Her way to mark his ultimate defeat.

The flesh and fur version of Tawfiq shifted around in her stone chair to regard Romulus through her two good eyes.

"That won't do," she said. "I want him to properly observe the proceedings."

She gestured with her tail to the ring where the golden collar around his neck was chained to the wall. The Janissary guard nearby give a salute and began to free him.

This was an opportunity.

He wouldn't get another.

Romulus had been secured to the north wall. Escape through the spiral ramp to the south seemed impossible and pointless. Tawfiq's seat had been placed to the west, beside a table set with a tasseled black cloth on which sat audio-visual-scent recording equipment that Dine-Alegg was poised to activate. Other than the two Janissary guards, the only other occupant was a Night Hummer in its cylindrical capsule. Shepherdess had warned him not to attempt mental contact with Hummers. Any of their kind who were Legion aligned would reveal themselves to him as required.

The Janissary unhooked Romulus from the wall, holding the end of the chain in its meaty paw.

Romulus grabbed his chain in both hands and pushed it down, hard.

The chain slipped out of the Janissary's grip, allowing Romulus to flick its links. Sprinting with all his might at Tawfiq, he caught the end of the chain and readied to tighten it around her neck until her vertebrae cracked. Then they would learn just how immortal she really was.

Dine-Alegg was reaching for her side arm, the guard he'd given the slip was reaching for her rifle, and Romulus was counting on the other guard to hesitate because Tawfiq was in her line of fire.

As for Tawfiq, her only reaction was to give a toothy grin, as if the onrushing former Marine bent on murder was the perfect entertainment.

Romulus raised his arms to bring the chain over Tawfiq's head, deciding at the last minute that once he had hooked her neck he would cross arms and drop to the ground, snapping Tawfiq's neck over the back of this copy of Lincoln's chair.

With a little stutter of his feet to time his jump perfectly, he threw his chain at his target, and the warmth of courage that he'd not known for so long entered his breast.

She was divine, and he was a human, the most despised race in her universe. Of course she didn't feel any threat – she was mad.

And he was… *floating*. His arms had frozen and he was hanging there in the air with his feet off the ground, arms outstretched just inches from Tawfiq's neck but locked in place. Even his momentum had disappeared.

"Perfect," said Tawfiq. "Dine-Alegg was convinced you still had some fight in you, Governor, but I wasn't sure. Watching the hope die in your eyes one last time is a fitting overture for the events that will now unfurl." She glanced at the Hummer. "Release him."

Romulus felt himself float above the hideous carpet of human hide, the metal chains in his immobilized hands rustling gently, until he was dropped to his feet at the north edge of the viewport. His muscles regained their freedom.

"You're welcome to try again," Tawfiq challenged. "In fact, I urge you to do so. My ally will sense the impulses in your head before they reach your muscles and will stop you with ease. Go on, Romulus, let me sense the hope flare in you one last time."

Romulus didn't give her the satisfaction of a reply. Instead, as Dine-Alegg ran the final tests on the equipment that would bind Tawfiq to her new army, Romulus rested his arms in the viewport and looked out on the scene below, anything to take his mind out of this room and its sickening occupants.

During his long-enforced idleness in his prison below the White House, Romulus had learned the history of this area, research Tawfiq had encouraged for her own amusement.

Which meant he could put a name to the original human incarnation of what had become today the Imperial Mall. He'd seen images too of passionate humans massing here to listen to political speakers, or simply to let their numbers speak of their support for a great cause. The last great crowd – well over a million of them – had gathered here to listen to President Horden speak, and to show their support before he flew to Vancouver to sign the Accords that would admit humanity to the Trans-Species Union under the patronage of the White Knights.

Two days later, a rival crowd had begun gathering, in protest at the same Vancouver Accords. But the protesters had been quickly dispersed, and the National Mall had not seen further mass gatherings until its Imperial successor hosted the Apotheosis of Tawfiq Woomer-Calix.

Ranks of Tawfiq's new army stood in silence facing their goddess to be in the classical Greek temple where Abraham Lincoln had once looked out from his cold seat. From the steps of the memorial, the ranks of blank Hardits stretched in a column around the reflecting pool and all the way back to the ruins of the old Capitol building. Tawfiq had claimed over a million were paraded here, and Romulus didn't doubt it.

And they weren't alone. Giant 80-foot high viewscreens had been erected to the north and south of the Washington monument, angled to look upon the giant marble statue of Tawfiq. Romulus had to lean out to get a good view, but he could see thousands of tessellated images showing more ranks of blank Hardits paraded in underground caverns around the world.

The only gap in the ranks was a hundred-meter perimeter around the base of the obelisk, which was guarded by a ring of the standard model of Janissary.

A pair of Janissary officers was parading the outside of their ring of guards. Did they realize they were about to witness the birth of their replacements? Would any of them even survive the day if Tawfiq decided she no longer had use for the unreliable old model?

For a moment, Romulus almost believed the tiny Janissary officers 200 meters below had heard his thoughts, because they appeared to falter.

But it wasn't Tawfiq high above them that attracted their attention, nor the Mark 2 Janissaries massed along the Mall, but a flowerbed about 400 meters to the northwest.

Romulus stared at the large circle of well-tended dirt in which a Hardit eye trio was painted in alien flowers.

He still remembered the morning when he'd been shaken awake by the bombs cutting through the ground in an attempt to kill Tawfiq in her bunker. They'd failed, of course. And there was nothing there now except for a deep hole that had been filled in and topped with flowers, Tawfiq's gesture of defiance to the species who had tried so many times to kill her, and yet here she was alive and about to unleash the army with which she would war against the universe forever.

Mad she might be, but Tawfiq was very accomplished in her insanity.

Today was the day she would become a goddess.

And there was nothing anyone could do to stop her.

# —— Chapter 39 ——

**Arun McEwan**
**Imperial Mall**

"Stop looking at us," snapped Arun. "You'll give us away."

"We were trained for battle," said Wokmar, "not spying. This is a coward's way of war."

"There's nothing cowardly about pulling yourself through the dirt beneath your enemy's feet in a digger Trog's wake, not daring to stop for an instant – no matter how much your arms cramp – because if you fall behind, the dirt will solidify around you and trap you until you suffocate."

Through the camera stem hidden in the flowers overhead, Arun watched as Shocles gave a half-step to the left and stamped her foot down sharply on Wokmar's, bringing an alien yelp from her companion.

"Ignore Wokmar," said Shocles, "she's lived a very sheltered life. Trust me, McEwan, the Janissaries here have no idea that they've been divulging the secrets of this place for the past hour."

*Trust.* Arun bit his lip. It was easy for Shocles to ask Arun to have faith in her, but for the CO of the Human Legion to stake almost everything in these two deserters was damned hard. Arun's trust was draining fast. What had he been thinking of to rely upon Janissaries?

"If you can't trust them, trust your instinct," said Springer, the interior light of her helmet making her facial scales gleam. Like Arun, she wore an ACE-series helmet without the rest of the suit. Tubes connected the helm with her air cylinder and power cell; a coiled wire hooked it into Saraswati via the port in her neck. Did he also look like an undead cyborg?

Another voice joined in from the back of the hollow the digger Trogs had scooped out from the dirt. "Hardits will break their word, murder their allies, and rob their own mothers," said Scipio, "and all before sitting down to a hearty breakfast. But what they won't do is tell you a lie to your face.

You need empathy to fool other people, and Hardits have as much empathy as a lump of damp basalt."

Arun also struggled to feel empathy for the Janissaries, but he saw something Scipio didn't. It was obvious to him that Wokmar and Shocles had been fashioned as tools designed for a purpose but had been discarded by their maker. Declared useless. Arun was offering them a chance to feel a sense of purpose once more, to kill Tawfiq. Since recruiting them in Brompton Road Station, their fur had become glossier, and they held their heads and tails erect.

"Let us move to a more shielded location before reporting our findings," said Shocles.

"Better make it sharpish," Arun replied. "My people are getting restless, and you know how reckless humans get when they're unsettled."

"Violently so," Wokmar acknowledged.

The two spies hurried away into the ranks of Ultra Janissaries where they rapidly disappeared from Arun's view.

"We've been spotted," said Dranjer, the missile specialist who'd been part of Nhlappo's operation to thaw the Sleeping Legion from beneath the ruins of Detroit on Tranquility-4.

"I see it," confirmed Hunter. "Human looking out from the top of the obelisk."

"It's Romulus," added Ree, who crewed the GX-cannon with Hunter. "He's watching our position."

The cramped confines of their burrow had produced a suffocating effect on the strike team, making them whisper and hold themselves still as if they needed to conserve their rather than breathe through their masks and helmets.

Now the dimly lit underground pocket seethed with motion. A dangerous, restless urge to break free.

"Stop it!" Arun commanded them. He looked around to see who was losing their nerve.

Scipio and Kraevoi were coiled springs, waiting with supreme coolness to deliver death to the Hardits overhead. As for the Marines they'd brought with them under Marchewka's command, Hunter and Ree ignored Arun, their gun assembly to hand and ready to move out, while Dranjer was lost in her own thoughts.

It was the Nest Hortez contingent who were twitching with nerves, all of them.

The four Trog dragoons – Gretel, Leon, Bwilt, and Hansel's replacement, Dane – were shaking their enormous armored heads from side to side. Their two clone-children riders – Escandala-351 and Hyper – were trying to calm them, but were only reflecting their unease back at them. And the four digger Trogs were snapping their dirt-eating mandibles as wide as a Marine's outstretched arms.

"It's you," said Springer. "They're sensing your doubt. You're their Queen of Battle, don't forget." She tapped him on the shoulder. "Look at me, Arun."

He did. But her beautiful face couldn't distract him today.

"What's wrong with me?" he said. "Am I going the same way as Indiya?"

"Not on my watch. There's nothing wrong with you, Arun. You're just placing a lot of trust in those unnatural spawn of Tawfiq. After all you've been through I'm not surprised you're finding that difficult. Don't overthink it. Trust your gut. Trust your children. They're the sons and daughters of Phaedra Tremayne – Springer as she once was – and did she ever let you down?"

"Maybe. Once."

Springer's face grew fiercer than he'd ever seen.

"But the making up afterwards." He whistled. "It was a long time coming, but by Tyndall, as the Jotuns might say, it was epic."

"Idiot," she snapped.

He grinned back. "Don't deny you love it."

Around them, the Nest members had calmed. There was even a smile on Escandala's face, though she couldn't seem to work out why.

"McEwan!" came a voice inside his helmet "I repeat, do you copy, McEwan?"

"Well?" Springer gave him a wink. "Don't keep your new friends waiting."

# —— Chapter 40 ——

**Governor Romulus**
**Victory Monument**

General Dine-Alegg leaned in close to her boss and *whuffed* down her long snout.

A moment later, the translator built into his golden collar translated for Romulus. "The equipment is ready for you now, Supreme One. We're still experiencing connection difficulties with a handful of the African loom galleries. Approximately 178,000 vessels still await the connection to your presence."

Tawfiq waved him away with her tail. "We can wait a few more moments. What of the foraging operation?"

"It launched a few moments ago. I can hear them begin."

The Hardits flicked their ears, and Romulus strained his too. Powerful vehicle engines revved in the human areas of the city to the north. Then came the screams and gunshots.

"Try to keep them alive," said Tawfiq. "Food is more enervating when it's fresh enough to struggle."

Tawfiq knew he was listening – of course she did – but Romulus gave her no reaction. The anger within still burned. With the telekinetic Hummer here, any attack on Tawfiq was likely doomed.

But Romulus remembered being raised as both a Marine and a Wolf. Neither tradition would ever give up, futile or not, and with every passing moment after rubbing his wrists against that nano-impregnated wax, he was remembering who he had once been.

He wasn't done yet.

——

## Arun McEwan
## Imperial Mall

"You copy?" said Shocles.

It was the same toneless thought-to-speech computer translation that Arun had heard all his life, but he could picture the Hardit and imagine the speaker's excitement exhibiting itself in tremors running along its rubbery lips.

"This is McEwan. Go ahead."

"The mall is filled with what you have called Ultra Janissaries. From what we can smell, they are a significantly enhanced battle-optimized version of ourselves, much as you human Marines are improvements on the human civilians who surrendered your ancestors to the White Knights."

Arun already knew that, but what he could see through the hidden camera was still shocking. This new evil was seriously boosted. Regular Hardits looked like a cross between wolves and monkeys, but this new batch were tigers crossed with bears.

"I told you that our Janissary scent is simpler than our ancestors', and that means our loyalty conditioning is correspondingly complex to compensate. Tawfiq fears rivals among our commanders. Already, purges of senior commanders are widespread. The supreme commander seeks to solve this issue permanently by creating these Ultra Janissaries who are not merely stronger, but completely loyal to her and her alone."

"I'm not so sure they are so fearsome," said Arun. "They look lifeless."

"This is what I am telling you. The individuals in the mall have not yet been activated. They will be woken and imprinted by the sight, scent, and sound of Tawfiq, binding them to her loyalty for as long as they live."

"Okay, and how is she going to do that?"

"Tawfiq imagines herself a goddess. She craves spectacle. She will look down upon her assembled new race from the top of that tower that we call Victory Monument. From its pinnacle she will issue her imprint, not just to the hundreds of thousands or more Ultra Janissaries assembled here, but to others watching underground in the looms where they were made, and in other regions of this planet. If her plan succeeds, and this new race emerges with Tawfiq as its goddess—"

"Yeah, I get the picture," snarled Arun. "But I'm not going to let her. We'll blast that tower and Tawfiq's new super race will be useless. Simple."

"An excellent strategy," said Shocles. "Assuming the supreme commander and her advisers have been too stupid to think of preparing backup systems."

Damn! The Hardit was right. Arun didn't rate Tawfiq as a general, but she was wily, and she always left herself exits and contingencies. This wasn't going to be as simple as it looked. "Okay, I'll buy it. I want more options for myself. Can you get us inside the monument?"

"There is a ground level gate on the east side, and the sliding doors you can see on the west that open from the inside. I believe we could gain entry and open the sliding doors."

"Do it," said Arun. "And thank you. I know what I ask of you is difficult, but down the centuries to come, people of all races will honor you for what you do today."

"Only if we win, McEwan. Otherwise we will be reviled as traitors, and then quickly forgotten."

"Then it's up to us to make sure we're on the winning side, Shocles. We're watching you. McEwan out."

"Well?" asked Scipio. "The suspense is killing me. Do I go in with my sword or my SA-71?"

"Both," Arun replied. "Listen up, people. New information. New plan. Plan A – steal Tawfiq's new army and use it to kill her and destroy the New Order." Beside him, he sensed Springer bristle, but he didn't stop to think why. "Plan B. Destroy that obelisk, kill Tawfiq, and then proceed as originally planned. Orbital Legion forces safe to pass through the corrosion barrier will descend on Victory City while the underground forces will advance northwest from their start lines in Florida. Any questions?"

"Just one," said Kraevoi. "When do we start shooting?"

# —— Chapter 41 ——

**Arun McEwan**
**Imperial Mall**

The doors on the west base of the obelisk slid open. Inside, Arun could see a lit open space that curled around the base of the pillar and began to rise away just out of sight, the kind of helical ramp beloved of Hardit architects.

Some of the Janissary guards on the perimeter turned around in surprise at the doors opening, but seeing no one inside, they quickly redirected their attention outward.

"I don't see our little friends," said Scipio. "This doesn't look right."

"Nonetheless," said Kraevoi, "the Jotuns have a useful saying. When you glimpse an opportunity–"

"Seize it with all six limbs," finished Scipio. "I know. There's a difference between taking your chances and jumping into a trap headfirst."

"Even if it's a trap," Arun replied, "it's still the best chance we're going to get. Remember, people, we want to capture whatever Tawfiq's using to imprint her new army and use it for ourselves. Failing that, we blow shit up, starting with Tawfiq's ugly carcass. *For the Legion! For the Nest! Go! Go! Go!*"

Before he'd finished speaking, Arun silently commanded the giant living digger machines to tunnel up and out. They were brutish creatures, so simple that they barely registered as sentients except with regard to the single topic of digging.

The strike team had snuck into the mall from the west, the diggers cutting a channel through the narrow gap between the ground and the top of the underground Hardit complex. Arun's jacket still carried the mud splatters that had dripped down as they had tunneled beneath the Potomac River. As the lead digger cut their route, those that followed with the main party sealed it, and the digger at the rear collapsed it behind them. Beneath the Potomac, a digger sealing the tunnel walls in front of Arun had explained that the dirt separating them from the riverbed was less than the thickness of a human's head, and Arun could see for himself that they couldn't dig deeper because he was crawling over armor plate shielding the top of the Hardit installation below. And yet, amazingly, the Trogs had hardened the few inches of dirt until it could withstand the press of the river.

But now they were on the attack, and the diggers blitzed their way upward in a maelstrom of flying dirt, stones, and alien limbs. Within seconds, sunlight flooded into a gently sloping exit ramp along which Marines and Nest dragoons were charging.

The Janissaries guarding the obelisk perimeter wasted precious seconds, frozen in fear by the sight of Trogs bursting from the ground, a narrow window of opportunity that was claimed by Scipio and Kraevoi who sent railgun sabots spraying into the air and hypersonic darts through the heads of the stunned foe.

While the Sleeping Legion contingent occupied the nearest defenders and set up the heavy weapons, Escandala led the four dragoons in an arc that wheeled around the Janissaries to hit them from the south.

A wave of screams rose from the civilian sectors of the city. *What the hell were the monkeys doing?*

The burrowed exit complete, the diggers stood in the open ground, as lacking in purpose as the Ultra Janissaries who gave no indication of noticing this invasion.

The familiar deadly whine of the SA-71 stung the Mark1 Janissaries into action. Arun winced as the armor crest of his new mount, Dane, chipped and splintered much faster than Hansel's had done in Australia, and in the battle beneath the Mediterranean. But Dane's crest was fresh and thick, and the lash of the Hardit rifles lasted only a few brutal moments before the dragoons crashed into the Janissary line.

They didn't slacken the momentum of their charge as Escandala led them in an anticlockwise circuit of the obelisk, rolling up the Janissary flank. Dane, Gretel and the others flicked their heads to toss the Hardits on their twin horns, high in the air. Others were dealt stunning blows under the feet of the giant insects born for battle.

Third in the dragoon column of attack, Arun and Dane pushed through defenders scattered and stunned by first Escandala who rode Leon, and Springer on Gretel. Arun jabbed his lance at Hardits within reach, and threw energy blasts at any nearby who showed fight.

And fight they did. Arun and the human riders of Nest Hortez wore black battledress. From the flanks and rear, they were immensely vulnerable. He saw Escandala take a wound in her arm that made her drop her lance.

Then he felt a sting in his back and knew he'd been hit. *How bad?* he thought at Barney, and tried to look down at his wound. He couldn't twist back far enough to see. There was a lot of blood there, but it was oozing from Dane's thorax.

*I can't tell*, Barney responded. *You're not wearing a suit, remember? Hey! Watch it!*

Out of the confusion, a low whitewashed annex appeared – the guard house protecting the east entrance that Shocles and Wokmar had mentioned.

Dane leapt, and Arun sensed his pain as his thorax wound opened up with the movement. They landed on the flat roof, Dane's six legs skittering for purchase. He found a little because as their momentum carried them over the top of the guard house, Dane made a semi-controlled leap onto the Janissary gun crew who had been setting up a heavy weapon in what they thought was the safe lea of the guard house.

Dane crashed into them and sprinted away. Arun twisted around and sent a lance blast into the weapon's ammunition boxes.

The explosion sent Dane and Arun rolling along the grass, as it did the rearmost Dragoon pair – Hyper on Bwilt – but the dragoons found their feet as easily as a gymnast, and by the time they had cleared the northern edge of the perimeter and came across the slaughter inflicted by Scipio's Marines, the Janissary guns had fallen silent. The dazed survivors throwing their weapons to the ground and stumbling to their feet with arms and tails held high.

And the massed ranks of Ultra Janissaries who could have torn the assault team limb from limb if they so chose, stood in perfect lines facing the marble statue of Tawfiq in her temple as if nothing had happened.

"Cease fire!" commanded a computerized voice from inside the base of the obelisk. "All Janissaries are to cease firing and assemble on me."

Through the sliding doors came two Janissaries, also with arms and tails raised in surrender, but dressed in the officer uniforms and scents stolen hours earlier. Arun struggled to tell one Hardit from another, but Barney was linked to the senses in his helmet and confirmed that they were indeed Shocles and Wokmar.

A third Janissary walked closely behind the two turncoats.

*That's good to know*, thought Arun, *but who's the other one?*

Alarm bells sounded in his head because this one wore the uniform of a Janissary senior officer in the pattern of the earliest years of their existence, back in the days before Tawfiq had claimed leadership of her entire species.

Not only was this officer not raising her hands in surrender, but her posture conveyed the same gloating arrogance he knew so well in Tawfiq.

"Arun McEwan," said the officer. "My name is General Dine-Alegg. It's a relief to see you finally. For a while there, I thought you weren't coming."

# —— Chapter 42 ——

**Marine Annalise Dranjer**
**Imperial Mall**

From her kneeling position a hundred yards to the west of the Janissaries who were supposed to be on their side – an idea that still needed a lot of persuading – Annalise altered the load feed to her PLS-11 shoulder launch missile system. Her HUD targeting overlay replaced the red target cluster brackets around the Hardits milling outside the entrance with colored hatching showing the estimated value of firing the new type-21 load at a variety of nearby targets. Type-21 munitions – nicknamed *Structure Destructors* – fired a sonic pulse tuned to render sturdy mortar and concrete into friable filler, followed by old school high explosive to blow it all to frakk.

Two rounds through those doors, four-second interval, and that obelisk was coming down.

"Come on, McEwan," she whispered, "give me the order. What are you waiting for?"

The answer, incredibly, was a parlay, an attempt to win these Janissaries to the Legion cause against Tawfiq.

Behind her, and on the far side of the obelisk the Ultra Janissary zombies just stood there in their hundreds of thousands like frakking robots on standby. They creeped her out. And, it seemed, some of the Janissaries felt the same way. Without their guns, and many of them bleeding from the Legion attack, some listened to Wokmar and Shocles who stood just outside the sliding door, pleading with them to change sides, though more of them were too busy looking nervously at the Trogs while they patched their wounds.

"McEwan to Dranjer. You got your pipe pointed through those doors?"

"Yes, sir."

"Thought so. Listen up, everyone. Time's running out for Dine-Alegg to come over to our side. On my mark, I want Hunter and Ree to give the downstairs a two-second tickle with your cannon. Scipio and Kraevoi, put some rounds up through the viewport on the top pyramid. Dragoons will follow the cannon burst inside. Hyper and Bwilt, you take point. And Dranjer, if you think things have gone to drent inside, or if no one contacts you within sixty seconds of Hyper and Bwilt charging through those doors, then I want you to take the building down. Don't wait for an order. Don't wait for us to get out. Just do it."

"Understood, sir. You can count on me."

"I know I can, Dranjer. You may have had the misfortune to have been raised by those degenerates of Beta City, but you're still a Marine."

"So are you, sir. Despite being one of those Detroit drent-heads."

*Will you stop the silly human talk already?* snapped her AI. *I'm trying to listen to the monkeys.*

Annalise grimaced. Solara still performed as an exceptional combat AI but hadn't come out of that last cryo sleep as her old self. She had become clingy. Jealous. But they'd been through so much together during the Second Tranquility Campaign that Annalise shut up and let Solara crank up the volume of the Hardit conversation.

"Don't you realize that Tawfiq will have no further use for you?" Wokmar was saying to her fellow Janissaries.

"What the deserters say is true," said Dine-Alegg, which won tail-twitching astonishment from her troops. "The new race the supreme commander plans to awaken today will replace ours. The traitors are right, as you must surely realize, even though you have obeyed your orders impeccably."

"Listen to the human, McEwan," Wokmar implored. "There are male Hardits on this planet who have chosen to ally with his Legion rather than bow down before Tawfiq."

"This sounds promising," McEwan said over BattleNet.

"Again, the traitors speak truly," said Dine-Alegg to the confused perimeter guard survivors. "McEwan has indeed brought along primitive members of our race as pets and servants, and they will soon die like the traitors they are." The general gestured with her tail to the massed ranks of silent Ultra Janissaries. "And although these waiting husks are the future for the New Order, the supreme commander has plenty of use for us yet. All you listening, wherever you are, note that well. Now, let me release these two scoundrels from their misconceptions about New Order politics."

"Go!" screamed McEwan.

Dine-Alegg casually shot Wokmar and Shocles in the head while her panicked soldiers leaped for their fallen weapons.

A little to Annalise's left, Hunter and Ree opened fire with their GX-cannon, sending heavy darts ricocheting off an invisible barrier that protected the double doors. Deflected rounds struck sparks off the pillar's stone and clattered off dragoon head crests like deadly hail stones.

Annalise stopped breathing as she watched the leading Trog hit the force barrier at speed. She saw the armored head snap hard to one side but make a little progress in pushing inside. McEwan's mount came at the force wall more steadily. It looked as if time was running at a hundredth of its normal rate inside the force shield, but it was running nonetheless, and the dragoons would eventually get through.

McEwan decided progress wasn't fast enough.

"Dranjer," he said over BattleNet, "destroy that building."

Fire was coming down on them from windows set along the pillar's length, but she ignored them for now. "Consider it down," she replied as she sent the first missile streaking toward the pillar.

Assuming that the force shield would neutralize any launch aimed at the door, Annalise had already shifted her aim to the corner of the north and west wall a third of the way up where the stone abruptly changed color.

*Gotta be a weak point*, said Solara. *Come on! Oh... drent!*

The missile failed to explode. Annalise sent the second Type-21 at the wall while she was still trying to figure out why.

Solara had guessed. She enhanced the view, so Annalise could see the pale blue beams flicker out from blisters set almost flush against the wall when her round was ten feet out from the target.

*Fermi beams.*

Caught in these defensive weapons that could scramble the most hardened electronics, her missile died inside and bounced off to land harmlessly on the grass.

*Move!* cried Solara.

Annalise didn't need to be told. A Hardit somewhere up in the pillar had found its mark and was sending rounds slamming into Annalise's shoulder.

She rolled hard, using her suit's motor and muscle assistance to come up forty feet away in a cloud of HUD alerts detailing the damage to her armor and the tissue of her shoulder.

*Tell the suit it can alert me when I'm dead*, she instructed Solara while she prepared a Type-62 'Muck Spreader'. *Until then, it can shut the frakk up.*

One of the great advantages to the PLS-11 Personal Launch System was the flexibility of its load out. Annalise had 82 munition types available to her, and triple that number when you considered major blast and fuse configurations. But she carried her supply tank on her back, not in a convoy of carts following behind her, which meant that if she didn't have a missile type already in the pipe, the payload had to be mixed, inserted, and configured *in the tank*.

The GX-cannon was raking the top pyramid with fire. Boss Man and Sashala were finishing off the survivors of the perimeter guard, and the dragoons were still gradually pushing through the force shield.

But Annalise had to wait while her Muck Spreaders were being readied.

A line of Hardit automatic fire spilled plumes of dirt out the ground as it sped toward her.

She waited. Then the targeting overlay turned blue and three Muck Spreaders flew out at the pillar. They burst twenty feet from the target – far enough out to defeat the Fermi beams – sending out black clouds, which were opaque across much of the electromagnetic spectrum. They wrapped around the stone walls, racing up and down like black fire until the lower five-hundred feet were wreathed in the roiling layer of darkness.

Annalise thought they looked more like a demonic cloud conjured up by a dark magician than muck, but she didn't stop to see for herself until she had jumped away from her firing position.

"I think you will find this facility is defended more strongly than you realize," said Dine-Alegg. The muck cloud had enveloped the force shield at the west entrance, revealing it to be a curving canopy that extended below ground, judging by one of the digger Trogs who was attempting to tunnel underneath.

"The anti-air defenses alone are the highest concentration on this planet," taunted the general. The speaker converting her words to human-intelligible form seemed to be coming partway up the obelisk.

*Solara, pinpoint her position. Let's hope the monkey keeps yapping…*

"This last escapade will be your final one, McEwan," said Dine-Alegg obligingly as Annalise mixed a triple-shot cocktail in the tank. The first projectile would deliver a narrow beam blast from twenty feet that would burn a hole into the wall. Then a double-header would follow up, the projectile at the rear playing the part of a launch vehicle that would push the front round through the Fermi beam grid, and carry it on through the hole where its dumb mechanical fuse would ignite the biggest blast in her recipe book.

"General Dine-Alegg to Reserve Brigade…"

*Annalise…* warned Solara.

The PLS countdown ticked down. Two seconds to fire.

*Why is that filthy creature letting us hear its orders?*

"Take McEwan alive. Kill all the others."

Annalise shrugged inwardly and unleashed the devastation she'd readied in her launcher. Sometimes your enemy was plain dumb, especially when it came to Hardits and their gloating over lesser species.

Where the two types of stone met, a third of the way up the west wall, a jet of plasma shot out from her first missile before dying in the blue Fermi beams. But it had done its job, and a moment later, the remainder of her cocktail sailed through the burning hole and blew out the wall. Shattered stone rocks fell out of the thick black cloud, but the pillar did not topple.

"All the others," said Dine-Alegg, giving that Hardit laugh like a vibrating band of rubber, "kill them!"

Her voice was coming from the pyramid at the very top of the pillar.

"I'll get you," whispered Annalise as she mixed the same cocktail to fire at the pyramid.

*Incoming!* warned Solara and snapped her human's head away from the pillar's peak and over to the enormous screen to the north on which countless underground Ultra Janissaries stared out of blank faces.

The screen shook. Then so too did the ground beneath Annalise's feet. But that was nothing to the screaming noise that drove out all other sounds. Dark projectiles soared over the back of the screen. Thousands of them.

"Follow the Trogs," commanded General McEwan. "They're digging you a bunker."

The projectile trajectories had reached their maximum height and were splitting as they fell onto the Legion's position.

Annalise ran for the spray of dirt and insectoid limbs but knew she wouldn't make it in time.

But she had underestimated the phenomenal digging ability of the Trogs. Already, the giant aliens had disappeared within their fresh tunnel.

The air churned with the screams of the incoming projectiles, and as she covered the final few strides to the Trog's hole, the ground shook with a new rumble of protest. One she recognized. Tanks. Big ones.

As she threw herself down into the shelter, she twisted in mid-air to see tanks tear through the northern viewscreen, ripping jagged breaches as they roared their way.

But it was too late anyway. Annalise was in the hole but was just a few feet short of safety when the cluster munitions exploded.

Her suit registered six hits.

Which was odd. Because if she was around to be notified, it meant she wasn't yet dead.

*It must be…* started Solara. *Be… be… bzzzrt!*

Annalise's suit failed. Completely.

Her visor was pressed against freshly tilled soil, but she could see it die because the HUD went out.

Her suit had locked out completely, rendering her immobile. If she was getting out, someone would have to unlock it from the outside. And they'd have to be quick. Already, the air in her helmet tasted stale, and the power cell in the small of her back felt very warm.

And she had lost Solara.

The ground shook with the approaching tanks.

Then a thunderclap punched through the air and screamed so loudly that without the active acoustic dampening in her dead helmet, Annalise screamed with it.

But it wasn't another salvo of the EMP projectiles.

This was something different.

# —— Chapter 43 ——

Arun McEwan
Stuck below the Tawfiq Monument

Dane tensed his body and redoubled his efforts to push through the force bubble before the screaming black rain fell upon them. Arun felt his mount try to shake his way through and then… he felt a brief suction on his back and he was inside, but for Dane there was no hope.

The projectiles bounced off the invisible bubble. On Dane's abdomen, which was caught on the outside, they found their target. They were black disks that tottered on his carapace like oversized game counters, but then extended spider-like legs that gripped Dane and held on.

And did nothing.

Or so it appeared to Arun at first, but then he looked around the battlefield. Tanks were bursting through the viewscreen to the north, supported by waves of Janissary infantry. Scipio's Marines had no reply, having dropped lifeless. Their suits were not reporting the Marines had died; the suits had gone off-line altogether.

*I'm okay*, said Barney.

"As am I," Dane confirmed.

Gunshots shifted Arun's attention to the interior of the obelisk. Escandala was firing a pistol up the ramp, which curved away out of view to Arun's left. A volley of Hardit rifle fire answered, ricocheting off Leon's head shield.

Frakk it! They needed to break free and kill the Hardits inside. Dane pushed even harder, but it was like walking through almost-set glue.

Hardit shouting came down the ramp. The tanks and infantry support outside were moments away from being able to shoot the stuck Trogs in their insectoid backsides, and that annoying analytical machine in his head couldn't stop wondering how Dane had just answered him as if he could hear Barney speak in the neck port that plugged into Arun's brainstem.

To cap it all, with the noise descending from the heavens, it sounded as if the Janissary tanks and infantry had just called in air support.

Hyper was throwing lance blasts up the ramp, but the Hardits were hugging the outer curve of the ramp as they fired, and the clone warrior couldn't get the right firing angle.

Arun's first veteran sergeant had taught his cadets that when it all goes to drent, Marines put their faith in the two sturdiest pillars of reliability in the galaxy: their comrades, and their SA-71. Well, Arun wasn't toting a carbine these days, but he *was* packing some old favorites. "Flash bang," he warned, as he began tossing grenades up the ramp from a collection he'd strung to the attachment points that grew from Dane's thorax.

Springer was also following old Sergeant Gupta's advice, and had used the cover of the flash to jump from her mount, her lance clipped to Gretel's flank, so she had both hands on her SA-71, which weighed a ton without the muscle amplification of a combat suit.

When Arun followed up with a frag grenade, she edged around Gretel's head crest and let her carbine do the talking.

"You've got to kill Tawfiq," Arun shouted above the shattering din coming from every direction. "The Trogs are stuck and were not getting out in time." Fresh Janissary corpses tumbled down the ramp. "Springer, take Escandala and Hyper, and finish this."

Their two children obeyed, climbing down from their mounts, and covered the ramp with pistol and lance. Springer didn't. She walked over to Arun and rendered her visor transparent as she looked up at him.

The scales on her face pulled taut, shrinking the concentric rings around her eyes into deep wells of compassion.

"You look ridiculous," he told her. "Zombie Marine." She didn't, of course. Not to him.

"Later," she said, and almost smiled. Then she turned and led their children up the ramp.

"Come on," Arun urged the four Trogs struggling through the force barrier. "The Nest never gives up. Keep pushing!"

The dragoon mounts had hardly been slacking, but they jerked under his admonishment as if stung by squadrons of bees.

It seemed their efforts would be in vain, though. Because when Arun turned around he saw three tanks a short distance away on the edge of the Ultra Janissary ranks – who clearly hadn't come alive enough to move out the way of an armored vehicle.

For some reason, their main armaments were elevating rapidly in their turrets, but it made no difference because Janissary infantry flowed around the tanks, cautiously approaching the obelisk. Some trained their rifles on the dragoons stuck in the force field like giant bugs in amber, but their main attention was on the hole the diggers had dug into the ground nearby. It wasn't the Trogs they could see that terrified them. It was the ones lurking underground they could not. A flash reflected off the sloping armor of the tanks. Arun craned his neck and saw a gleaming spark break cloud cover and come in hot from the south.

"General Lee-McEwan to General McEwan, you copy?"

Arun grinned like a maniac. "Grace! You wonderful girl. You been wanting to say that since forever. I know you have."

"I plead guilty. What do you need, Dad?"

"First task: waste this horde of angry Hardits to the northwest of the obelisk. Watch for their armor. It's in anti-air mode."

"Don't worry. Sit tight and wait. I know what I'm doing."

I hope so, he thought as a swarm of missiles broke cloud cover in hot pursuit of his daughter in *Karypsic*.

The Hardits outside began shooting at the vulnerable dragoon mounts. At the same time, the sounds of railgun fire, Janissary rifles, and screams revealed that their dismounted riders were engaged in hot killing work higher up the ramp.

# Chapter 44

**Governor Romulus**
**Victory Monument**

His eyes had lost the super-sharpness of the X-Boat ace he had once been, but Romulus knew a lost cause when he saw one, and the whatever-the-hell it was over the southern horizon, starting to line up for a strafing run, was not going to make it. Missiles were almost up its tail and that was just the start of it. Tawfiq was reveling in his reaction as she explained the giant viewscreen to the south of the obelisk was a concealment emitter. An armor-reinforced infantry company had hidden behind the northern shelter, but to the south were her hidden anti-air assets.

Hellspewers were charging up, ready to emit focused beams of pure energy mined from the quantum substrate.

"It's hardly worth the bother," said Dine-Alegg, "but I know the supreme commander appreciates despair in you humans. You see the hellspewer battery, but there are also SAM emplacements around the city. The air defenses around this position are the heaviest in the history of this planet." To Tawfiq, she added, "Supreme One, there are further human air assets headed our way across the Atlantic."

Tawfiq sat with her arms stretched along those of the chair in imitation of her statue. Her eyes were closed as if connecting to deeper planes of existence than the mundanity of space-time.

"Is there any need to delay?" she asked.

Romulus wasn't looking her way. He made himself watch the crew of the brave Legion aircraft meet their end as the missiles converged on... *empty air.*

He blinked.

And the aircraft had transformed from a dark blob on the horizon to an attack craft coming in off the Potomac River with all guns blazing.

"It would be wise," continued Dine-Alegg. "Interference from the hellspewers could–"

The aircraft had traveled ten klicks in an instant!

His vision had lost its sharpness, but Romulus still had the implants and gene programming of a Marine, and that meant his brain could appear to slow down time so he could properly evaluate his environment in order to select the best course of action. That was why Marines made the ultimate pilots, after all.

He saw the ionized gases streaming from the quad cannons in the aircraft's nose. Smaller cannons mounted in belly turrets were spitting rounds at extreme fire rates. And he saw how beaten up this bird was, this... what was it, a souped-up dropship?

He could never forget pulling multiple sorties flying Phantoms off his old carrier, *Lance of Freedom*. While he'd grab a snack and a drink in the cockpit, the hangar rats would not just re-arm and re-fuel, but patch the worst of his X-Boat's wounds until his flight was ready to rejoin the fray.

But if his Phantom had suffered this kind of damage, he would be told to park it out the way and get his ass in one of the spare birds. A scar along its fuselage had been crudely plated over, and a name had been hand painted near its nose: *Karypsic 1.1*. The aircraft was painted black – except for three stubby nacelles secured with weld patches that were still wearing their yellow primer coat. They hadn't even had time to paint the dropship after a mission it looked as if it had barely escaped from. Where the hell had it been?

A ghostly hand reached out of the ether to twist and pull at his entrails. He would have vomited if the reflex hadn't been removed. And he would have whooped for joy at this wonderful discomfort if it weren't so painful. It was the same feeling he got from the trans-dimensional wash of an X-Boat.

He glanced at his tormentors – his turn to gloat for a change – but the Hardits hadn't yet reacted. Hadn't even realized the dropship had winked out of trouble and reappeared just where it needed to be.

Tawfiq still had her eyes closed, but Dine-Alegg was looking at the equipment on the table in front of her mistress that would transmit her scent and image to her new army. And Romulus had been around Hardits for long enough to know when one was up to something. What was Dine-Alegg plotting?

The Hardits showed no signs of experiencing the trans-dimensional wash, but the Hummer did. The orange fluid in its tank reverberated as if a pressure wave had just ripped through it.

Then the sonic boom hit the room like a giant tiger clawing at the air and ripping at their lungs. Now the Hardits took note! They practically jumped out of their pelts.

Romulus ignored their panic, enjoying the sight instead of the *Karypsic 1.1* flying over the north of the city leaving smoking ruins of tanks and infantry in its wake. She rose into an inverted loop. Surface-to-air missiles lifted from the city to greet her.

Hellspewer beams crackled through the air, vaporizing the screen the battery had hidden behind. They were the Hardit development of one of McEwan's earliest innovations: dismantling the engine from an interstellar spacecraft and pressing it into service as an anti-aircraft weapon to devastating effect.

Beams lit the air in beautiful plasma shades of purple and blue. The energy lances converged, blockading the aerial intruder's path with an interlocking lattice of high-energy death that no aircraft could possibly evade.

*Karypsic 1.1* gave the hellspewers a wing-waggle salute and disappeared…

…To reappear a few klicks to the south, where she completed her loop and came in for a second run.

*Your enemies are coming for you, Tawfiq.* Romulus smiled. *This is the last day of your existence.*

His smile froze. Whoever was outside gunning for Tawfiq weren't his friends either. Would it be *his* last day too?

# —— Chapter 45 ——

**Arun McEwan**
**At the base of the Victory Monument**

"Dad, you still hanging in there?"

Explosions ripped through the ground to the south of Arun's position. The hellspewer beams extinguished.

"I'm here," he replied, and then added, surprising himself, "Your mother?"

"She's too busy politicking in orbit to save the Earth. Where do you need me?"

The *Karypsic* streaked away to the north, her lower shield shrugging off the weak Hardit fire from the wreckage of the hidden unit Tawfiq had unleashed. Arun wondered how much of the relief he was feeling to see their destruction was really to hear that Xin wasn't here.

"The obelisk," he said. "I need the equipment it houses to remain fully functional, but every Hardit inside to be a corpse."

"I'm on it, Dad."

"And I have five Marines on the ground outside in dead suits. Cut them out before they suffocate or their power cells blow."

"On it. More help's on its way. Aelingir got down safely over Europe with a small fleet. She's picking up troops and will be joining us once we soften up the defenses here."

Suddenly, Arun's world jolted and he grabbed on tightly to Dane's thorax handrail as he finally cantered inside the lower level of the monument, stepping carefully over the Janissary corpses and trying not to slip on their blood.

"Are you badly wounded?" Arun asked, mentally expanding the scope of his question to encompass the four Trogs, all of whom had now forced their way through the barrier.

278

"Bloodied," Dane replied, "but I remain functional."

With the other three confirming the same report on a scent level without words, Arun inspected Dane's abdomen. The carapace was badly chipped, and he counted seven wounds where rounds had penetrated. Leon and Bwilt were as bad; Gretel worse.

"Our bodies are designed for battle," Dane explained. "Our organs have multiple failsafes, and our blood flows through a packet-switching circulatory system designed to survive multiple wound channels of the types inflicted by Hardit rifles and Legion railgun darts."

"Wait, Pedro designed you to hold your own in a fight with humans?"

Dane didn't answer with words. His scent said the answer was so obvious it would be humiliating for the Queen of War to hear it spoken.

Gretel jumped around and rushed back to the force bubble. "What are they?" she asked, pointing her antennae at the sky.

Black shapes floated through the air, headed for the obelisk.

"Friends," said Arun. "I think. OK, we're disturbingly fit. Let's go help out the others."

He lost his grip on Dane's rail and was flung back against his strange seat as his mount leaped up the ramp to rejoin their fellow Nest members.

———

**Sergeant Kraken**
**Far Reach Strike Team, Arrow Squad**
**Above the Imperial Mall**

Mader Zagh!

Kraken's team was coming in blind. Some kind of anti-electronic frakk-up field had nixed the micro spy drones they had thrown at the obelisk. It had also killed the grenades they had fired through the existing breach Stafford's sharp eyes had spotted through the fading clouds that wreathed their target.

Bleeding off his lateral speed, Kraken gave the breach a burst with his carbine and flew inside.

When no gunfire rose to meet him, he thought that just for once it would be an easy entry. As he crossed the threshold and entered the mess of stone debris, his HUD lit up with threat alerts. Janissaries were standing inside with their backs to the outer wall, waiting to shoot the legionaries as they sailed in.

But these Hardits weren't used to Far Reach Marines.

Kraken lashed out with his boot as he came in, hitting a Hardit hand and the rifle it was gripping too.

Like any Marine, his natural fighting environment was the void of space. The ACE-6 armor couldn't exactly let you fight planetside the same way, but it got passably close.

He accelerated in toward the inner wall of the ramp, angling his trajectory sharply upward so he actually landed on the overhead, high above the heads of the Hardits, and on bunched legs that sprang him down onto them like a missile with his carbine teeth extended and buzzing for blood.

The results weren't pretty. And when Fallaw and Stafford followed up with their own assault cutters, the defenders were reduced to a messy pile of meat underfoot within seconds. Kraken had a minor bullet wound to his left thigh, and Fallaw a bayonet wound to his right. BattleNet reported bleeding staunched and suits resealed.

"They weren't expecting me to bounce off the overhead like a boarding action," advised Kraken. "Next lot of monkeys we meet won't be so easy, so stay alert."

Fallaw and Stafford acknowledged, and they advanced cautiously up the ramp to join with the teams who had breached and entered at higher points. It was only wide enough for three abreast, and every step of the way, the enemy could be waiting for them behind the inner curve. Fallaw took point, following his sergeant's orders to not use spy drones to peer around the corner, because doing so would likely reveal their position to the enemy. If both sides surprised the other, Kraken was counting on his team to win out because one-on-one human Marines were superior.

Meanwhile, Kraken watched the rear, throwing BattleNet extenders at the walls as they went. The gray burrs stuck to the walls and beamed enough sensory data that BattleNet awareness stretched below to the areas they had already covered.

"Boss says any Hardit in this building needs to be a dead Hardit," Kraken reminded his team. "Let's see if we can oblige her without killing her father. Got it, Fallaw?"

"Don't kill the Old Man," Fallaw replied. "Got it, Sarge."

"Make sure you do," said Stafford, "because if any of us kill General McEwan the paperwork that will descend on the LT's ass will put him in a serious state of discombobulation."

"I think Stafford means that a heavy duty reaming will be–" Fallaw held up a fist and everyone halted, alert to a new threat.

A moment later, Kraken's HUD updated to paint probable threats waiting for them around the inner curve of the ramp. His pulse pounded in his helmet. They knew what to do. That didn't make it easy.

Warnings to show Stafford and Fallaw's rapid heartbeat increase flagged too. "No, shit," he whispered. He'd have to get that seen to, but for now he snapped his carbine to his back and activated the null zapper on his gauntlets.

"Go!"

At his command, Fallaw sent a brace of grenades up the ramp while Stafford rushed around his outside, sending a four-second burst of darts into the waiting Hardits.

While Fallaw advanced past Stafford, Kraken was fully concentrating on the flashing red cylinder that was his HUD highlighting the grenade the Hardits had thrown at *them*.

He leaped at the deadly weapon as it rolled down the ramp, bringing his left hand outstretched above his head. The only other thing to do was hope.

The null zapper, or Blast Containment Field Emitter (Personal), was an adaptation of the static force shield technology that had been in use in the White Knight sphere of influence since long before the Earth even knew it had become a regional political issue.

The invisible force projection was short and curved beyond the gauntlet like a catcher's mitt. Luckily, this time there was only one grenade and Kraken didn't need to snatch it from the air.

He caught it in the null zapper's field and angled his hand downward.

The grenade exploded, directing its force down to blow a hole through the floor. Dust and debris blew outward, hugging tight to the ground, but Kraken already had his head up and was alert to new threats.

His two team mates were dealing with the Hardit ambush, and there were no more grenades to handle for now.

Kraken blew out a breath and allowed himself to relax... just in time for new threat indicators to erupt into this HUD, which decided they were so significant that it imposed its own custom overlay view to show a 3D map of the local battlezone.

"Contact behind!" he shouted and turned to face the new threat, carbine ready.

They'd advanced up four circuits of the tower and checked carefully for surprises all the way, but they hadn't been careful enough. Hardits were streaming out of a doorway concealed in the inner wall of the ramp. More threats were advancing up the ramp from farther down.

Hardits and Marines exchanged fire, filling the ramp with flying rounds and deafening noise.

Kraken was hit in the leg, but before his HUD could tell him the damage, he jumped and stayed high so the others could fire underneath him.

They would need all the carbines on their attackers as they could get. A dozen of the enemy were blazing away.

Kraken saw their surprise to see a Marine float above their heads. And he saw them raise their aim.

All three Marines were firing away, and several grenades were flying through the air toward the Hardits. But they hit an invisible barrier and rolled down to the ground. The monkeys had their own defenses against grenades!

The grenade explosions lifted Kraken against the overhead, buffeting him so he couldn't get a good aim.

Expect the unexpected, he'd always been taught, and he certainly didn't expect what came next.

Some kind of blue plasma blast slammed into the Hardits from behind. The reverse of the force shields that had protected them from the grenades now told against the enemy, catching the blast and reflecting it back at them. At the same time, grenades were lobbed through the concealed entrance and the gorgeous sound of an SA-71 sang its sweet melody, mowing down the Hardits from their rear.

"Hey!" Kraken called to his team. "The Old Man's come to save us. Just like the good old days."

Then his body decided to notice the multiple wounds that were hurting like hell, and he fell onto the ramp with a clumsy impact.

"Ungh, Sarge?" warned Stafford. "She don't look like the Old Man to me."

# —— Chapter 46 ——

Sergeant Kraken,
Far Reach Strike Team, Arrow Squad
Inside the Victory Monument

The two parties sized each other up.

When he'd been briefed to expect friendly Marines under the command of General McEwan, Kraken had expected to find the Old Man and his team in obsolete-model ACE combat armor. The three who'd saved their asses were human, and even had the build of Marines, but they didn't dress like them. At a stretch you might call their dark blue fabric clothing a form of battledress, but to be honest it looked like the kind of dirty overalls an Aux worker and their fleas might wear. The older woman carried a pistol and grenades, and the younger man a frakking lance! At least the Wolf woman who seemed to be in charge carried an honest SA-71, but it couldn't belong to her any more than the Marine helmet, spouting tubes and wires, which she wore without a suit.

"What are your orders, Sergeant?" she demanded.

"I don't report to a damned Wolf in a stolen Marine's helmet. Who the hell are you?"

She removed her helmet, and his body tensed.

Wolves freaked Kraken out. Anyone who said they weren't scared of the human attack dogs was lying because they were feral. Insane with no morals. No boundaries. No remorse.

This one's eyes glowed fiercely but it wasn't the usual berserker bloodlust passion, and… they were actually glowing. There were absolutely-frakkin-lutely glowing purple like ionized moist air. And her two weird companions had lilac eyes. And the lad with lance? Toss out his lilac eyes and replace with brown ones and there standing before him was the young Arun McEwan.

284

*Frakk!* He knew who they were.

*Frakk!* This would change a lot of things, but not yet. Tawfiq had an appointment with death that needed to come first.

"My apologies, ma'am. We are to clear this building of Hardits but prevent destruction of equipment. We're linking up to take the ramp before…"

"Arrows here," called out Stafford and Fallaw as five Marines joined them down the ramp, led by Corporal Malinga.

"They're friendlies," said Kraken, indicating the Wolf and her two comrades, "though I wouldn't get too near in case they bite."

"LT wants you to hold a three-Marine perimeter here," said Malinga. "'We're headed out that breach to assault the east viewport from the outside."

"And why hasn't he told me himself?"

"He's still at top. No signal."

"Ahh." Made sense, Kraken thought. The plan was to lock the top of the tower up tight with jamming and signal barricades.

As if the day couldn't get any more bizarre, four mammoth Trogs trotted up the ramp to the obvious delight of the Wolf and her two human companions. The aliens had armored heads shaped like tank turrets, and a rider leaned into view from behind one.

"Arun!" cried the Wolf.

The man rendered his helmet transparent and there he was. The Old Man himself. Arun McEwan.

If Kraken had harbored any doubts about the Wolf's identity, they were swept away by the look that flashed between the Old Man and his lover.

Then the intimacy was gone, and the two old companions were all business.

"Where's the officer in charge?" McEwan asked Kraken. "We need to take the top now."

"Lieutenant Chey is aware of that, sir. He has the matter in hand."

Fallaw and Stafford joined Kraken in blocking the way up the ramp. Frakk, those Trog beasts were enormous! The humans had leaped into a slot cut through the middle of the three Trog segments and disappeared behind the head armor.

"Stand aside," commanded the Old Man. "I've a score to settle."

"No offense intended, General McEwan, but you can kiss my ass. You've proven yourself countless times, and we all owe you our lives, but none of that makes you a part of my team."

He was all right that McEwan. He nodded his understanding without a fuss and led his strange band back down the ramp. "We'll guard the lower floor, Sergeant."

"Thank you, General. Give our regards to Plasma Squad. They should be there with your disabled Marines by the time you get down the bottom."

"Did that really happen, Sarge?" mused Stafford when the general's party had disappeared out of view.

"Yes, Andrew, it did. You just met a living legend riding a Trog into battle. If you can't dine out on that for the rest of your life, then you haven't been listening to a word I've taught you since you transferred into the Arrows."

Fallaw gave half a laugh but seemed lost in thought. It wasn't difficult to figure out why.

Arun McEwan hadn't been the only legend they'd just encountered. But the other one had been very publicly put to death.

After today, the galaxy was going to be a very different place.

# —— Chapter 47 ——

Marine Bryan
Far Reach Strike Team, Vengeance Squad
Top of Victory Monument

The scene of carnage stuffed Bryan's guts with disgust. And yet, it also resonated with hope.

She was back in the same open space lined with human hide at the top of the obelisk. Only days ago, she had escaped by jumping into the *Karypsic*, though years had passed as far as the Hardits were concerned.

But this time, it had been the Far Reach team who enjoyed superior strength. The Janissary guards were all dead, and a quick glance out the western viewport showed Tawfiq's forces were a smoldering wreck. The strange new updated Janissaries filled the mall in enormous numbers, but they seemed too drugged up to care about her team.

Maybe she would be able to go home after all. Meet up with her cousin's family in one of the Far Reach colonies. *Settle down.* It was too strange a concept to process, but it *could* happen. Only this morning it had seemed impossible.

"Our usual spot, I think," quipped O'Hanlon, indicating the place where they'd set up the GX-cannon days or years before.

He had to shove an empty stone chair out of the way, which screeched in protest, but yielded so she could fix the tripod while Jintu got the targeting system organized.

She'd done this a thousand times, but maybe her optimism had jinxed the gun set up because the tripod feet locking indicators refused to show green.

Typical.

She lifted the tripod and swept clean the floor beneath with the side of a boot. Shell casings, stone chips, and a Hardit fang formed a ring of debris she had cleared.

Still the damned thing wouldn't lock down into the floor.

"Is he sightseeing again?" she asked Jintu, a little angry that O'Hanlon wasn't helping with the deployment of his own gun.

Jintu didn't reply – perhaps she had been a little harsh – and she got down onto her knees to give the situation a closer inspection.

A splash of dark fluid on the cleared floor gave it away. The hydraulics for one of the foot claws was leaking the last of its content, probably severed by shrapnel.

"It's no good," she said, "we'll have to settle for suboptimal stabilization."

What was wrong with O'Hanlon?

She looked up at him, about to give the corporal a piece of her mind, but then she realized that if O'Hanlon wasn't acknowledging, then her comms must have failed.

But when she rose to her feet and looked around the scene, a cold fist slowly twisting inside told her she had more to worry about than a failing comm signal.

The LT, O'Hanlon, Jintu and all the others were checking equipment, setting up fire positions, or huddled in conference as before, but *no one was moving*.

Had she been caught out of time?

Her HUD reported good life signs and excellent BattleNet connectivity, at least within this room. So why had everyone frozen?

"Vengeance-8 to all call signs. Please respond."

Nothing.

The LT had been trying his damnedest to block any signal coming out of this space, so the lack of response wasn't entirely a surprise. But that still left her dealing with this alone.

Bryan couldn't bear to look her comrades in the face, to touch them, so she rushed to the viewport instead and looked outside. Black smoke was

288

belching from the ruins of the tanks. A pair of wounded Janissaries were helping each other off the battlefield. *The world on the outside was still moving through time.*

She took a deep breath of courage and walked up to O'Hanlon, who had been caught in the process of talking with Jintu, both his arms out in the kind of expansive gesture so typical of her gun team lead.

"Sorry, O'Hanlon." She gave him an exploratory shove. He moved. Just a fraction, and then a force resisted her. It wasn't the corporal pushing back; it was more as if he were caught in a web of force.

Swallowing down the waves of dread, she undid his neck seals and lifted his helmet off and stared into John O'Hanlon's nightmare face. His eyes were bulging yet unseeing. The muscles stood out on this neck like cables, and his mouth was tearing open his face in a silent scream. There was movement, though. She put her ear to his mouth and, yes, he was breathing. Very faint but it was there.

Bryan had been on stealthed missions in the void of deep space that lasted days sealed tight in her suit with only her own voice for company. But she'd never felt so utterly alone as that moment.

She bumped foreheads with O'Hanlon. "Stay alive, John. I'll be back for you."

Her plan was to race down the ramp to make contact with the other Marines. And if they were frozen too, then she'd get out away from the signal jamming and contact *Karypsic*.

Only two strides across the obscene leather floor, she heard the vibrating buzz of Hardit laughter and spun around.

Three Hardits and a Wolf human stepped into the room from… nowhere. It wasn't a hidden alcove. Before declaring the room clear, they'd checked interior and exterior dimensions of the room matched expectations.

One of the Hardits had a pistol aimed at her chest, and another a rifle. Would her armor shield her long enough to break their necks? The human wore a golden chain around his neck. He had to be the traitor, Romulus.

"You have given us priceless moments of amusement," said the Hardit with the pistol, whose elaborate dress suggested it was an officer.

She hesitated, her Marine mind giving the illusion of slowing down time as she sought options. Her GX-cannon over to her left wasn't assembled. Corporal Joshi's crew had their cannon ready to fire over by the eastern viewport, but it would cost her several precious seconds to reach it and ready it to fire.

There were SA-71s around, but she'd have to rip them out of their Marine owners' grip. The plasma pistol at her hip was a better bet, but the fire rate was slow.

And the guns the Hardits were carrying? She didn't recognize the pistol, but she did know that Hardits didn't enjoy their gloating until they were sure of overwhelming odds over the lesser species they had bested.

They were confident their weapons would defeat her armor.

She would hit them the hardest and fastest way available to her. With her suit propelling her at maximum thrust, she would barrel into the two armed Hardits and grab, twist, rend, and slam until either her enemies lay dead with their necks broken and skulls crushed… or she did.

Her mind spooled time back up to normal speed.

As she took her first step forward, she gasped. Another figure revealed itself. A Night Hummer in its tank. Her training warned of the aliens' telekinetic power that could result in a short savage repulsive blast.

She felt inky black fingers on her neck. Probing her. Choking her. Violating the back of her mind and pushing deeper to claim her will.

It stopped, leaving her teetering on the precipice of losing control.

"You humans are so predictable," said the unarmed Hardit, who walked over and studied her as if she were an art exhibit. Its snout was badly scarred, and its upper eye was blind but nonetheless resonated with evil. "I knew that if you ever came back, you would return here, so I laid a trap with the help of my foreseer friend."

*Quick! Gotta think!*

The moment that ugly Hardit tired of her gloating, Bryan knew she would be frozen like the others. If she tried to fly at them, she'd be locked out of her mind. What could she do that might win an edge?

She ignored the Hardits and turned to regard the traitor, Romulus.

His face was distorted in horror. She recognized that look because she was sure it was mirrored in her own face. He was no willing ally of the Hardits; he wanted to strike them down but felt helpless with despair.

"Traitor!" she screamed and ran at him. "Traitor! How could you do this?"

The grip on her mind and neck released just a little. Enough to permit this amusing display.

Bryan grabbed Romulus by the shoulders and kneed him in the groin.

As he grunted in pain and slid down the wall, she punched him in the gut and watched him curl up in agony.

"You should be rewarded," said the Hardit she assumed was Tawfiq. "When the time comes, make her death quick. See, I am generous even with my human slaves."

Bryan refused to give Tawfiq the satisfaction of a reaction. She stood at attention and felt the Hummer's constriction around her neck squeeze, and then everything went black.

# —— Chapter 48 ——

**Governor Romulus**
**Top of Victory Monument.**

Romulus groaned.

The Marine had pulled her punches but they still hurt like hell.

He guessed he deserved all that and far more, but it was worth it. And not just for her timely demonstration of the quick thinking and cunning he'd once taken for granted. A reminder of what it had meant to be a Marine.

He clutched at his lower abdomen and edged the knife she had craftily handed him deeper into the waistband of his pants. Standard human-issue Mark 2 Marine combat knife. Not the poison-tipped crescent of the Mark 1, but the six-inch straight blade Mark 2, which could cut through his chain or tear through a Hardit's guts but was right now a hair's breadth from nipping open his femoral artery.

For the benefit of his audience, he grimaced, hiding the smile on his face, because the Hummer showed no signs of noticing what was in his mind. The bubbles in its tank were flowing so fast that they were blurring.

*Maxing out your super brain, aren't you? Nothing spare to waste worrying about me. Just you wait, pal. You'll get yours soon enough.*

But there was someone Romulus needed to kill first.

The Janissary guard had locked Romulus's chain to the wall and was laughing at his prisoner.

Dine-Alegg and Tawfiq had dismissed him from their minds and were at the west viewport, Tawfiq taking her place on her seat while Dine-Alegg checked the equipment that would broadcast her signature. The general glanced over. Not at Romulus but at the guard, who showed no sign of noticing the officer's scrutiny.

Romulus felt the knife press against his belly and knew his opportunity would soon be here.

He would be ready to seize it.

――――

**Arun McEwan**
**Ground Floor. Victory Monument.**

"Hey, what's up with them?" growled the Far Reach sergeant at the dragoon mounts who had all simultaneously angled their antennae out the open double doors.

So far, the task of cutting open Scipio and his Marines from their dead suits, and bringing them to safety inside the monument, had distracted the NCO from her distrust of the giant insectoids.

"Trouble," Arun replied and rode outside for a clearer sniff.

He could no more understand Hardit pheromone language than the sergeant could that of the Trogs. But he knew a signal had just been given. A powerful one.

The Ultra Janissaries had changed. The stationary ranks stretching out beyond the pool to the giant statue of Tawfiq had their backs to him, but those backs were now straight, and with ears and tails pricked up. If he could look upon their faces, he guessed he would see the light had come on in their eyes.

The hundreds of thousands of enemy soldiers were alert and waiting for instructions.

Arun wheeled Dane around and led his dragoons up the ramp, scattering Far Reach Marines out of their way.

"What the hell do you think you're doing?" shouted the sergeant.

"Saving us all," Arun shouted over his shoulder.

Behind him, he heard a man shout, "Forward to victory!" His cry was taken up by other voices. The sound of bare feet slapping on the ramp pursued the charging Trogs from lower down the ramp.

It seemed Lance Scipio had the same idea.

―――

**Governor Romulus**
**Top of Victory Monument.**

Dine-Alegg drew her pistol and shot Tawfiq.

The supreme commander shrugged off the round that shot through her without interaction, like a passing x-ray, but her general seemed to have expected this because she was already flying at her with a knife in her hand and her tail around Tawfiq's throat.

The Janissary guarding Romulus raised her rifle and weighed her chances and her loyalty.

None of which mattered to Romulus. His moment had come.

He drew the knife passed to him by the Marine who was still nearby, hands frozen halfway to her throat as if trying to break a chokehold. The blade cleaved his chain and then pierced all the way through the guard's neck and out the other side, wedging itself stuck in the Hardit's throat.

Romulus released his grip on the knife and grabbed the dying guard's rifle.

Tawfiq and Dine-Alegg were grappling on the floor beside the stone chair, oblivious to his freedom.

Romulus in turn ignored them for the moment and emptied the magazine at the Hummer's life-support cylinder.

Supersonic bullets with explosive tips flew out the muzzle at the alien.

He was out of practice, out of an ACE suit, and the rifle lacked the recoil dampener of the SA-71 pattern carbine that was his Marine birthright. The barrel tracked upward until he was blowing chips out the roof, but the first three rounds had been on target.

They still were.

The rounds spun impossibly slowly. They pushed through the air at a glacial pace, slowed but not stopped, nor showing signs of succumbing to gravity.

What the frakk would it take to kill a Night Hummer?

The rival Hardits had noticed him now, but the priority was still the Hummer. If he could kill it, he would release the room full of Marines from their strange stasis and the human numbers would tell. He threw the rifle to the ground and, bracing his foot in the dying guard's head, he reached over and drew out the knife, releasing a fountain of Hardit blood.

Maybe it would be down to the Mark 2 Marine blade to end the alien monster?

He heard human voices – from the ramp leading up from the base of the monument. Heavy footfalls too, as if warhorses were approaching!

Romulus panicked. He stepped forward into the pocket dimensional alcove.

He heard three carbine shots, followed by an instant of blinding white light and noise, then a pressure wave that clawed at his lungs.

But only for a moment, and then he was in an unreachable place, cut off from the space and time of the pyramid at the top of Tawfiq's obelisk. His head ringing, he sat down heavily, blood froth around his mouth but confident his heavily enhanced physiology would patch him up to return to the fight to rid the galaxy of Tawfiq.

Knife in hand, he watched events unfold from his impossible hiding place.

———

**Arun McEwan**
**Top of the Victory Monument**

While Springer, Escandala, and Hyper charged into the room, Arun hung back to take in the situation.

The flash bang had cleared to reveal the Far Reach Marines as frozen as Kraken and his two comrades had been when Arun found them on the way up. Springer had aimed her shots carefully, but the blunted dart rounds rested lifeless on the soft brown floor beside Tawfiq and Dine-Alegg who grappled each other for a knife.

Force shield. Had to be.

Should have fired at the formless amoeba in the life-support tank. Bullets and shrapnel were already flying at the night Hummer, but it seemed to have selectively slowed time to stave off the ring of projectiles.

"Take out the Hummer," he commanded his team, but the alien had other ideas.

As Hyper and Leon crossed an invisible line, they were wrenched out of their thorax seats, clutching their necks as if wire had been strung across the room at neck height.

This had to be the Hummer's work, though, because Springer and Gretel advanced to the center of the room without incident.

The two clone children clutched at livid red wheals on their necks, but their wounds didn't look fatal, so Arun left them and followed Springer into the room.

She had her teeth out in the end of her carbine and raised the weapon high to strike down against the Hummer cylinder.

But she didn't.

Her arms wavered under the gun's considerable weight and she roared with anger but could not bring those assault cutters to gnaw through the Hummer's tank.

Arun didn't hesitate. He aimed his lance at the Hummer and… dark fingers of alien malevolence entered his brain. The Hummer sought to control him, to bend his will to its design, but it could not. He felt it project its will with renewed vigor, persuading him that his entire body was seething with the realization of Springer's absolute betrayal. Springer must die for her filthy crimes. He must kill her. *He must. Kill…*

"I'd rather die," he hurled back in defiance. Whether it was the complexity of his movement through time, the organic computer in his head, or the strength of his love for this woman, Arun knew the Hummer could never make him hurt her.

A sense of delicious irony oozed from the alien creature. Arun saw his moment and with a sudden burst of will, he jabbed his lance in the direction of the cylinder, but still, the Hummer's grip on his brain prevented him from firing.

Then he saw what had amused the Hummer. Springer was slowly traversing her aim. Her scales gleamed with sweat and she was grunting through a jaw clamped shut, but the Hummer's control was too strong for her. She aimed at Arun's heart.

"Please!" she screamed.

He heard her rails charge.

"Don't make me!"

Staring death in his face, an instinct for self-preservation rose up and threw off some of the Hummer's mental blocks. He used his scent emitter to order the Trogs to intervene. He realized he'd been so engaged with his own mental battle to notice the Trogs were also caught in the Hummer's psychic web. Their pheromones screamed self-loathing as they disobeyed their Queen of Battle's commands and stood by to let him die.

Springer was still fighting the alien's control, gasping in horror. The bullets and shrapnel were still crawling toward the tank, they would not be his salvation. They were too far away.

An incongruent smell of hot oil and brass licked the back of his nose. "I swore an oath," Arun insisted, acting on intuition supplied by the battle computer in his head, which Greyhart had implied might help him to resist the Hummers. His eyes bulged with the effort to speak aloud under such psychic pressure, but he had to. Speaking was the *human* way. "I swore to nurture and protect your race," he groaned. "I swore to give you a homeworld. I have not forgotten. Ceres shall be yours. I will honor that, if you allow me."

The icy fingers of darkness pushed harder into Arun's head to snuff out this human arrogance forever.

Arun let it in suddenly, abandoning his mental struggle so abruptly that the Hummer stumbled blindly into the depths of Arun's mind. And the inside of Arun McEwan's head was a deeper and more complex place than any human this Hummer had encountered.

His last gasp defense was to lure the alien into his memory of that day as a cadet when Arun had first encountered a Hummer on a mined-out micro-planetoid, and secured allegiance in return for an oath that Arun would provide a homeworld safe from the White Knight Emperor.

It worked.

But not as he'd hoped.

The Hummer hadn't forgotten Arun's oath, it just didn't care. But his other memories of Night Hummers – including the ones on Ceres who had secured his promise that this would be their new home – confused the hell out of it.

The psychic link ran in both directions, Arun realized. For the first time, he was beginning to sense a Hummer's emotions, because the alien was too shocked to lock him out.

As Arun cautiously probed the psychic link into the alien's cylinder he came up against such intense mental anguish that he gave up and retreated into his own head. The Hummer was screaming in agony in an attempt to process what it had seen inside Arun's mind.

"You, McEwan, have allies amongst my people. That is impossible. That faction was destroyed."

"No," said Springer.

Had she spoken aloud or in her mind? Arun couldn't tell but she was back. That's what mattered.

*Arun, you aren't...* Barney was back too. *I've been shouting at you, but you couldn't hear. What the frakk's happening?*

But Arun hadn't time to reply. All his mental effort went into lashing Gretel with all the considerable power of his Nest scent to fight off the Hummer's control, even if he killed her in the attempt.

"You had the available data all along," Springer taunted the Hummer. "You just interpreted incorrectly. Believe me, I know all about that."

Screaming with effort, Arun wrenched his body free of the creature's grip. Just a little. Only enough to twist his head to look at Springer, and see she had done the same thing to look at him.

All they did was gaze upon each other, but the connection that bound them had run so deep for thousands of years that it was palpable. It was too strong for the Hummer to break.

Springer grinned. Give her enough time and Springer would bounce back from the darkest adversity with those dimples on her cheeks and her heart bursting with optimism. That was how she had won her name, and with her on his side, Arun knew he could never lose.

It was like a taut cable snapping.

Gretel jumped so high in the air that her crest cut a score into the roof. Dane cracked his mandibles in anger.

And the shrapnel and bullets awoke from the alien's spell to accelerate into its tank.

Spider cracks formed, but it wasn't enough. Still the Hummer was in Arun's mind.

"At last," came the translation of a Hardit voice. Dine-Alegg had won her fight with Tawfiq, who sat dazed on the floor, trying to staunch the bleeding from the side of her head. Dine-Alegg ignored her ousted leader and took her place in the stone chair.

"Tawfiq is not yours to kill," Arun roared at Dine-Alegg and before he realized what he had done, he had shot a lance blast at the Hummer.

Plasma arced inside the tank, boiling the circulating fluid around the orange blob that was the Hummer's core.

The tank exploded.

Steaming fluids sprayed over Dane's headshield, joining the sticky mess of corpses and bloody debris on the floor.

Freed from the dead Hummer's grip, the Far Reach team were released, slumping groaning to the floor, the creature that had held them now a wizened orange sponge twitching in its own juices.

Arun advanced on Dine-Alegg, but Springer beat him to it.

With Dine-Alegg adjusting the equipment that would imprint herself on the Ultra Janissaries waiting all over the planet, Springer dismounted and stalked around the outer edge of the room to get a firing angle at the two surviving Hardits.

Arun froze, not wishing to miss a millisecond of this scene about to play out. Because if Springer had walked around the force field with such ease, it clearly didn't extend all the way to the wall.

Tawfiq saw her nemesis, and brandished her fists, revealing that her right ear had been severed by Dine-Alegg, who herself was too intent on the controls to notice.

"I don't suppose you recognize me," Springer told Tawfiq.

Finally, Dine-Alegg looked up, saw the threat, and went for her gun.

Springer blew the general's head off with a burst from her carbine.

"You took away my name, and gave me a number," Springer told the growling Hardit. "It wasn't even unique to me. You just wiped the blood off the last Aux slave to die wearing that number. But I haven't forgotten. I can never forget. Aux slave number 114 reporting for payback, Mistress Woomer-Calix."

Tawfiq thumped her chest an instant before Springer opened up.

Her fire discipline was good, dart after dart was aimed perfectly through Tawfiq's center of mass… and kept going to blow chunks out of the floor behind the supreme commander.

The darts refused to interact with her.

Tawfiq laughed, though the pain was clear in her strained grunts. She scrambled with difficulty to the lip of the viewpoint where Arun gave her a blast but with his lance that sailed through her into the air.

Tawfiq jumped.

It was 600 feet up, but Arun knew in his gut that this wasn't suicide.

Springer balanced herself over the lip and sprayed the air with darts.

"Can't see her," she reported after ceasing fire. "She's gone stealthy. Aelingir is here, though. She's brought Marines, Wolves, even some Legion Hardits. Why the frakk did she do that, Arun? Arun? What are you doing?"

By the time she looked back, Dane had thrown Dine-Alegg into the room thick with Hardit corpses and stunned Far Reach Marines. In her place on the stone chair, she had sat her Queen of Battle.

A sense of destiny was slamming into Arun with brutal force. He detested what he intended to do next. But he was sure he had been born to this all along; he'd just never figured it out until now.

He had to take Tawfiq's place before someone else did.

Dine-Alegg had readied the controls. All he had to do was use them.

He thought of himself. The way he looked. The things he had done and the people he'd loved. Dead and alive. He encapsulated all of this inside his essence and transmitted it through his scent emitter. Finally, came the words. "I am Arun McEwan of the Human Legion and Nest Hortez. I command you. I bind you to me."

# —— Chapter 49 ——

Arun McEwan
**Top of the Victory Monument.**

"Uhh, General McEwan, sir," called a slightly breathless voice from the ramp, "you need to disable the signal barricader first."

Scipio and his team had arrived. They wore just their gray under suits and were mostly carrying only side arms. "Beats me, General," said Scipio who had his black broadsword in both hands. "I don't know what that is either, but Dranjer knows what she's talking about."

"Marine Dranjer had the sense to extract that information from the Far Reach squad at ground level," Kraevoi commented.

"It's the size of an eyeball," explained Dranjer. "Spherical and you'll get a small electrical shock if you touch it."

*An eyeball!* The hollowed-out space inside the pyramid had become a seriously crowded place with four Trog dragoon mounts and their riders, and the Far Reach Marine team struggling to come to. He counted at least a half dozen Janissary corpses but they were difficult to count as they were in so many parts. Then there was the Night Hummer in a litter of splinters and steaming fluids, and now Scipio's team. This could take all day.

"Scipio," he ordered, "assign one of your people to check the Far Reach team are okay – maybe try to bring one round to tell us where this damned barricade thing is." He gestured to Hyper and Escandala who were on their butts rubbing their necks. "And another to check on… my *children*. The rest of you, on your hands and knees and start looking."

"Roger that, General." Scipio shot him a wink and then looked away quickly just in time for Arun's view to fill with a very angry Springer, helmet off so he could get the full effect.

"What the hell were you thinking?"

"Them!" Arun pointed outside. From Tawfiq's chair, he had a perfect view of the hundreds of thousands of Ultra Janissaries waiting to be commanded. And somewhere out there was Tawfiq.

In the grass to the north, Jotun-led Marine teams were setting up a fearsome line of fire power. Legion aircraft were keeping the skies clear. But even if Aelingir and Grace could withstand the overwhelming Hardit numbers here in the mall, there were millions more around the world ready to waken. Human screams reached his ears from the city. They were quickly shut off.

This wasn't over yet.

"It's not the right approach," snapped Springer. "Even if it were, I know it shouldn't be you."

She stormed off to check on their children, leaving him to stew in her words.

If not him, who? Maybe Escandala? She had a strong scent identity, and unwavering loyalty. Better her than the first Hardit to tap into the imprint mechanism of the waiting armies.

Someone must have switched off the signal barricader, because Arun's HUD sprang into life.

The tactical updates, com requests, and vast ocean of BattleNet data were too overwhelming to take in. But Arun was never alone. He had Barney, who summarized the status in a few whispered messages and allowed only one voice transmission through.

"Karypsic Actual to… Father! What the frakk's going on?"

Hardit stink hit Arun from the equipment pointing at him on the table. "We're okay, Grace. We've taken the tower, but Tawfiq escaped. Stay alert."

"Understood. I have bombing solutions for the Janissaries I see in the mall. I can't dust them all, but the sooner I start, the more damage I'll do."

Barney couldn't translate the pheromone signal that now issued from the broadcast equipment, but it seemed a surefire guess that it was announcing it was now ready to transmit.

"Move away from that equipment, McEwan! Now!"

It was Romulus!

What the hell…? It didn't matter. Arun didn't listen to traitors, and however Romulus had appeared out of nowhere, it only proved the situation was so fluid that Arun had to seize his moment while he could.

He leaned forward and spoke into the equipment. "My name is–"

"I'll kill her!" screamed Romulus. "Say another word and I'll slice her pretty neck. Her scales are tough, but are they tough enough for a Mark 2 knife? I don't think so."

Arun twisted around upon a nightmare scene. Romulus was lifting Springer up onto her heels with his blade cutting a crimson line into her neck, a knife that was covered in the blood of another victim. Blood still dripped from scaled arms that disappeared into nothingness. His head and shoulders thrust into the real world, the light of madness in his eyes, but of his legs and lower torso there was no sign.

Arun told himself to keep calm. "If you hurt her, you'll never get out of here," he told the traitor, but as he spoke doubts crept in. Between Scipio and the dragoon mounts, it was true Romulus would never get as far as the ramp down, but part of him wasn't *in* the room. Perhaps he was in some kind of portal and could reappear in another location out of reach?

But Romulus laughed at him, and the sound chilled Arun to his core because it carried the manic edge of someone who had lost all hope.

Scipio drew his sword.

Romulus pulled back on the knife. Just an inch, but Springer was straining her neck, her head tilted back. Even so, still the knife was cutting deeply enough that the blood ran freely down her neck.

Scipio froze.

"I don't expect to get away," said Romulus. He added darkly, "Nor do I deserve to. But I do want you to listen, Arun McEwan. Destroy the equipment. I've been Tawfiq's plaything for years. Nothing good can come from her, and those waiting Janissaries are her creation. Nothing good can come of them either. Destroy the equipment!"

"I can't let it fall into the wrong hands," said Arun, trying to hold back on the anger welling up inside. The veck was already hurting Springer, but if he cut her badly...

"Destroy the equipment or I destroy *her*."

"Even if I did what you ask, someone will build their own and take control for themselves."

"Not before you kill them all." Romulus laughed. "You're too soft, McEwan. You have cannons and aircraft and ships. Even a nest of Trogs, I hear. Kill them before they spring to life. Seek out the underground Janissary looms and murder them before they are born. You're right to fear another taking Tawfiq's place. Clock's ticking, McEwan. Destroy the equipment and start the killing. Now! They're only Janissaries. They deserve to die. Every last one throughout the galaxy, and it needs to start here. Today."

Arun remembered the way Shocles and Wokmar had come alive when he'd given them a new sense of purpose. He pictured one stomping on the foot of the other as they bickered and grumbled, just the same as the people he'd grown up and spent his life with.

"No," Arun said calmly. "Hardits are not monsters. Those altered Janissaries out there are still innocents. If we murder them, we're no better than Tawfiq. Besides, there's a New Order fleet skulking in the outer system. And I've got a feeling that when the White Knight Emperor learns the identity of the woman whose life is in your hands, he's going to be mightily pissed off. We need to demonstrate adamantine strength to him."

In reply, Romulus jerked Springer backward. "Believe it or not, McEwan, I'm trying to do the right thing here. It's all I have left. I've nothing to lose. So believe me when I tell you this is your very last chance. You move away and you..." He nodded at one of Scipio's Marines. You know how to set up and fire a GX-cannon?"

"Yeah."

"There's one half-assembled by the west viewport. When McEwan is out the way, you finish setting it up and shoot the broadcast equipment on that table into oblivion. Make a sudden move or point the cannon my way and I'm dead. But *she* dies with me."

"Okay!" Arun shouted. "We'll do it." He gave Scipio's Marine a searching look and felt a flood of relief when the man gave him a simple nod as if to say *not planning any tricks here.*

If Romulus had threatened anyone else, Arun would have hardened his heart and gone ahead with the imprinting. He'd meant every word he said, but now that he had been tested, he knew he would sacrifice everything to save Springer.

As Dane plucked him from the seat and walked him away, Arun went cold with shock to realize he wasn't so very different from the traitor. Romulus had betrayed everything and sided with the devil herself in order to save Janna. That had to have been the threat Tawfiq held over the younger man. Arun would have done the same for Springer.

Suddenly, disembodied hands reached out of the nothingness behind Romulus and grabbed the knife. Romulus held on, but the sudden attack gave just enough of an opening for Springer to slam the back of her head into his nose with an audible crack.

Blood gushing from his face, Romulus lashed out with a kick to his assailant's shins that won a cry of pain from her, but when he followed up with an elbow strike seeking the vulnerable points on her head, Sashala Kraevoi easily dodged his attack. She slipped around his side to emerge with Springer safely inside the pyramid room.

By the time Romulus had recovered his balance, Scipio had his strange black sword to Romulus's own scaly neck, with several armed Marines to back him up. Not that he needed them. He flicked his sword point, scoring a dripping red line across Romulus's neck.

"Is there any reason to keep this traitor alive?" Scipio asked.

"Only for his trial," Arun replied. He noticed some of the Far Reach Marines begin to sit up and take notice of the surroundings.

"Does he deserve one?" Scipio questioned.

Arun stared into his face. Romulus looked as if he would welcome a final release. It might be a kindness to spare him a drawn-out legal process and end him here. But not this way. Not with the anger he heard in Scipio's voice.

"He will pay for his crimes," Arun said, "for they are far too great to ignore. But Tawfiq forced him to choose between his duty and the person he loved most in life. Are you so sure you would have acted differently if Tawfiq had forced the same choice upon you, Lance?"

Scipio glanced at Sashala and turned white. He lowered his sword a little.

One of the Far Reach Marines rose to a kneeling position and pointed to the west viewport. "What the hell is she doing?"

Springer had taken Arun's place on the stone chair. "You were right about the Ultra Janissaries, Arun," she said. "Except for one thing. It needs to be me."

She looked into the recording equipment and cleared her throat to speak.

# —— Chapter 50 ——

**Springer**
**Victory Monument**

"You don't have to do it," Arun was pleading.

She shook her head, releasing drops of her blood onto the chair. "You've carried enough burdens, Arun. Any more and you'll crack like Indiya. And I don't want this burden on my Nest children. No, it has to be me."

"But… our future. Slipping away together to leave all this behind…" His words faltered. Not because they were so hypocritical – dear Arun never saw his own failings – but because he knew they were a lie. The universe hadn't finished making demands on them. It never would.

"My wonderful Arun, we *did* have our time together. Back in Celtic Elstow. And it was beautiful."

"No, let me–"

"Shut up, Arun. This is hard enough."

She allowed herself a sigh for the lost future that had never really been theirs, and projected the essence of her Nest identity through the emitter in her chest. "My name is Phaedra Springer Tremayne. Know my image, scent, and name. No one shall command you unless it be on my authority."

A mistimed jumble of her words was flung back at the tower from speakers throughout the mall. Springer's image superimposed upon the giant statue of Tawfiq facing her from the far side of the reflecting pool. Human on Hardit – it made for an awkward mix.

The blank Janissaries in front of her swayed.

It was a reaction of sorts, but was this going to work?

*Of course it will, dear,* chimed Saraswati. *You say the words and I'll translate into scents they understand. So long as you stay clear of higher level mathematics and romantic poetry for now, we'll be fine.*

"Face me," she commanded, trying to visualize her intention and project through her scent transmitter.

They did.

Hundreds of thousands of Ultra Janissaries turned about and looked up at the tower, awaiting her command.

Just two words and the response had been immediate. She couldn't deny there was a dark side of her that relished the feeling.

*And that's why that useless boyfriend of yours must never taste such power. You know he could never handle it.*

*Please pipe down, Saraswati. Like I told Arun, this is difficult enough as it is.*

The cuts in her neck were now a burning line of pain, but she had something to say that couldn't wait. "You were conceived in hate, but you are born in dignity. Your lives will be respectful and respected. But first you have a task. Find the one known as Tawfiq Woomer-Calix. The two-eyed tyrant. Seize her and bring her to the statue carved in her image. Then you will march out into the city and separate those who wish violence upon each other. Humans and Hardits. Humans and other humans. None shall war upon each other today."

The Janissaries looked up at her, unblinking. Unmoving. Had they understood any of her orders?

*Go!* she thought. *Do it! Execute!*

They kicked into motion.

With each passing moment, she learned more of the awakening beings, and they of her. Although they looked identical from her position in the chair, it was clear that they were predisposed to hierarchy, the better to carry out her orders. Officers for want of a better name – she didn't want to impose on them the same military strictures she had experienced growing up – began organizing teams to search the area by sight, scent, and touch.

The scent from so many of these new beings, each an individual eager to explore their relationship with her, was overpowering. The responsibility more than she could handle. It wasn't just unconditional obedience they gave her, but trust too. They were babies. Never mind that they were infants stuffed with muscles, bodies designed to withstand severe trauma, and a working knowledge of military tactics, they still depended on her. She knew then that she would never call them Janissaries. They deserved a better name, but that would have to wait.

Behind her in the tower room, the humans went about their business. Romulus was pleading that he was the Voice of the Resistance and should be spared. Arun and Dane were right behind her chair, her lover silent and closed, but her Trog Nest sibling offering her gentle scents of support. Bwilt and Leon were soothing their wounded riders, and Scipio was talking anxiously about the Legion officer on her way to make contact. And the pounding in her heart was not slowing. Her hands shook.

*Easy, dear. Nice and slow. Take some deep breaths. It will become easier, I promise.*

*Thank you*, she said, and meant it wholeheartedly. Saraswati would never let her down. Would never misunderstand her in ways that Arun sometimes did.

He'd always been at the center of the war. The responsibility had scarred him, was close to breaking him, but he'd never known solitude like her long years alone, sent away on diplomatic missions. Now she was the mother to thousands in Nest Hortez. And as of a few minutes ago, to millions more of these innocent beings, these… *unbound*.

The Unbound. Yes. She would not fail them.

Nor would they disappoint her.

The scent message came up to her seat from the Imperial Mall below – something else that deserved urgent renaming – Tawfiq had been captured. They were taking her up to the temple on the far side of the pool. Others began advancing into the city, understanding that whatever evil was raising humans screams of terror must cease.

"It's almost done," she told Arun. "My people have caught Tawfiq. Arun? Say something."

"Then we've won," he replied, though the sorrow in his voice suggested anything but victory. "And now the consequences begin to play out. Here, in this room. Nhlappo's arrived."

# —— Chapter 51 ——

**Remus**
**Halfway up the Victory Monument**

"Wait for me," Remus called up the endless ramp.

A few seconds later, Janna trotted back down into view. She put her hands on her hips and gave him a look of exasperation. "Do I need to find myself a younger lover? Stir your bones, we're almost at the top."

Remus ground to a halt and pointed at the rifle slung over Janna's shoulder. "I get to carry the mini gun on my back, not that toy you're carrying. I don't want to turn up breathless."

Janna shrugged. "Why should we care? So long as your big gun gets a good field of fire, no one cares that the scaly hide of the man who's carrying it is burnished with hot sweat. No one but me, Remus. Come on, shift your ass."

Remus wasn't so sure. The major who had sent them here had been evasive, as if she were acting on her own dubious initiative. And if they wanted big guns up here, they would have deployed GX-cannon. But Janna had already disappeared around the curve in the ramp and Remus ran after her.

Three more circuits of the tower later, and Remus bludgeoned into Janna's back, sending her staggering forward into the open space at the top of the obelisk. He looked up and saw immediately why Janna had frozen on the threshold of this room.

In some ways, the scene was overstuffed with details, like the aftermath of a lengthy and exceptionally violent party. McEwan was there sitting on a Trog, and that man in his under suit with the sword was Lance Scipio. There were legionaries too from Xin's traitor faction, although the ones they'd met on the way up acted as if they were on the same side as the Legion. The corpses of Hardits and even a Night Hummer were strewn on the floor among spent rounds and a *lot* of blood.

But two details burned so brightly that everything else faded into irrelevance.

Mother was here.

So was Romulus.

His brother noticed them first, eyes wide in... In what? Fear? Shame?

Remus searched inside himself for his emotions. It seemed like the right thing to do – to react in some way – but he was completely numb. And that was good. He didn't want this to be happening. He didn't want to be a part of whatever *this* was.

Janna wasn't like that. Remus was a Marine wearing Wolf scales, but she was a Wolf through and through. She launched herself at Romulus, screaming curses.

She punched him hard, but not on a weak point of his body as she could so easily have done, but on his chest.

His brother winced but stood his ground. He hadn't tried to block her blow.

Her shoulders shaking, Janna unclenched her fist and held her palm over the point she had struck.

The fingers trembled. Did they recall a happier time when they often enjoyed tracing the furrow down the center of that man's chest?

She lifted her elbow slightly as if to run her hand over his breast once more, but her palm bent back and would not touch Romulus, his brother's betrayal pushing her away with an invisible force like repulsing magnets.

Janna's head dropped, and she stalked off to disappear into the crowded room.

Remus looked away and noticed his mother had been watching him the whole time. Field Marshal Nhlappo she was called now. Her last message had been in 2601, but it had only been in the last few years that Remus had finally come to terms with what everyone assumed was her death.

She had removed her helmet, and he saw that the face of the woman who had raised him had aged, but she looked healthy. He found he couldn't summon happiness to see Nhlappo. Couldn't even think of her as his mother – not yet. Romulus had numbed him too much for that.

Nhlappo gave Remus a curt nod and turned her attention back to Romulus.

She was a Marine to her very core, and as such the SA-71 in her hands was such a natural organ of her being that Remus hadn't noticed it until he caught her hands trembling. It was a weakness that lasted only a second before she brought herself under control, but Remus had seen it and wondered what it meant.

So too had his brother.

"I am the Voice of the Resistance," said Romulus, starting to panic, his chest heaving. "I told Shepherdess to warn Hortez. I don't know who that is, but the Hummer said Hortez was our only hope. And I sent Tawfiq's shuttle through the corrosion barrier to Indiya. Could have ridden it out of here myself but I stayed planetside out of duty. Duty to Earth. That's the reason you're here, isn't it? Indiya worked out how to get through the barrier. Tell her the message she received was from me. Ask Squadron Leader Dock. I bet he guessed it was from me. *Please.*"

"Indiya has been relieved of her duties," said Nhlappo. "From what I hear, even if she does recover, it will not be a speedy or easy process."

"Relieved?"

"Indiya has lost her mind."

"We will establish these facts," said McEwan. "You have crimes to answer for, but you will have your chance to do so. You will be treated fairly."

"Fair? I didn't ask to have my X-Boat shot from under me. I didn't choose to be tortured, my mind trapped in a web spun by Tawfiq's Hummers, and Janna threatened if I didn't cooperate. Don't speak to me of *fair*, McEwan. If you believe the galaxy could ever be fair, then you're delusional."

"And you're a coward," said one of Xin's Marines. "You claim to be a secret resistance hero, but you'll say anything to save your skin. Shall we bind your wrists and send you into the city to face the verdict of the civilians? Eh, Governor? Will they free you from your bonds, or choose a different fate for you?"

"That's enough," snapped McEwan. "I will permit no more talk of mob justice."

"I believe in you," Nhlappo told Romulus.

"You... you do?"

"I am your mother. You were not born mine. It was Marine Phaedra Tremayne who saved you from the New Order concentration camp, and it was I who raised you and your brother as truly as I raised my own son who died on Tawfiq's orders. As your mother, my love for you is without condition."

"Thank you, Mother."

"I know little about this Voice of Resistance, but I hear the truth in your words." She swallowed hard. "But others will not. You have already been tried in absentia and found guilty of treason. General McEwan says you will be given a fair hearing to establish new facts. He means what he says, but we both know you will not face justice, Romulus. You can only ever face retribution."

"No!" Janna ran to him. She moved again to place her hand on his chest, but she was still repulsed by his aura of treachery, and she let it slump to her side.

Romulus pushed her away and stood proudly in front of his mother. "They are right to find me guilty," he said, his voice resolute, prideful. He smiled, a fleeting echo of the fighter ace swagger that had once been his hallmark. He glanced at Remus. But if he had sought forgiveness in his brother's eyes, he did not find it there.

Nhlappo looked across at Remus.

He shook his head, but he wasn't sure what he was trying to convey. Romulus was right about one thing, though. The soldiers in this room had not suffered directly from the governor's betrayal, but even so the hatred for this traitor seethed in the poisonous air. If Romulus stepped outside into the mall, his death would be drawn out, humiliating, and certain.

Romulus cleared his throat and spoke clearly. "Try, I beg you all, to remember the good I did before Tawfiq took me down to hell. And learn the truth of what I have done on Earth in resistance to her plans. But the deaths of thousands of innocents stain my soul beyond any hope of redemption. I await my judgement."

"They will make an example of you," said Nhlappo.

"No," said McEwan. "We won't."

She raised her carbine.

"Nhlappo," McEwan ordered. "Put down your weapon."

"I love you," she whispered to Romulus, "and I give you… *absolution*."

There was no doubt in Remus's mind that his mother would fire, but when she did – two rounds through Romulus's heart – it felt as if the darts had pierced his own. His legs collapsed beneath him and he slumped to the floor at the same time as his brother.

"No!" Janna screamed and rushed forward to catch Romulus as he fell.

The anguish in her eyes unlocked Remus's limbs and he too came forward.

He wasn't the only one to spring to life. A Wolf Marine on the far side of the room roared in anger, which attracted the Trogs to form a protective arc around her. "There will be no more killing today," she shouted. "Except one. And it ends with her. The wars are over."

As Mother looked on as lifeless as a cold statue, Remus went to his brother.

Janna was kneeling, Romulus's head in her lap, caressing his head. Remus straightened his brother's legs and arms so he looked a little less crumpled.

It was all he knew to do.

# —— Chapter 52 ——

**Springer**
**Victory Monument**

The scene behind her was so paralyzingly sad that she turned her back on it. Couldn't deal with it now. She owed it to everyone who had fallen to end this properly. Only then could she stop and take in all that had happened. She didn't have time to feel.

She sensed Arun and Dane's presence behind her and could smell their absolute support.

Arun understood how she felt.

And now that the fate of planets depended on the decisions she made, she in her turn finally understood the man she loved, and all he had borne over the grinding years of the war.

Springer encouraged the sorrow to sink beneath the surface. Anger welled up in its place. Hot, energizing, and urgent.

Aelingir was linked into Tawfiq's broadcast equipment, and was relaying to Kreippil and Marchewka in space. When Aelingir had punched through the corrosion barrier, she had only a dozen multi-use dropships to command. Springer had thought all that effort to get a corrosion-resistant craft up from Earth had been to little avail. But Aelingir's paltry strength was because the Legion fleet had concentrated all their efforts in upgrading their space-to-ground missiles to fire through the corrosion barrier.

Janissary military installations around the world had been hit. The defenders sent reeling and then neutralized by her Unbound rising from hidden galleries deep below, an operation that had been largely peaceful.

The New Order Janissaries had not formally surrendered, but they were offering cooperation for now. So when Aelingir said the transmission relays were in place for Springer to speak to the world, it was the Janissaries who made it possible. Her words and scent would be picked up by Hardit-manufactured equipment and broadcast around the world and into near space using more Hardit equipment.

The camera on the table before her emitted a scent to indicate it was recording.

Behind her, someone broke into sobs. She shut off the sound from her mind and spoke.

"There has been enough killing. There will be no murder of prisoners. There will not be lynchings on the streets. Collaborators will be brought to justice. Legion justice not mob justice. There is only one who deserves summary retribution. Let her death be an end to it."

She unclipped the lens from the bank of equipment and pointed it out through the view port.

The monitor screen wrapped around the lens showed the image change, the focus shifted first to the reflecting pool and then a little farther on, past white stone steps to the Supreme Commander of the New Order who struggled in the cruel grip of those she had created to serve her, and who now lifted her up for all the worlds to see in front of her own statue.

Maybe the camera sensed Springer's intention. Whatever was driving it, the image zoomed in close on Tawfiq's face, capturing the blind upper eye and the scarred snout trembling with fear.

"Rip her apart."

Despite the dwindling anger keeping her going, Springer couldn't feel satisfaction at Tawfiq's demise; she was too drained to celebrate. Nor did she feel disgust at the sickening spectacle as the Unbound grabbed her limbs and tail. The latter came away quickly, but her legs took several minutes before the many strong hands could finally detach them from her hips.

The deed was crude. It was savage. And it was the opposite of the divinity Tawfiq had been expecting.

Then the Unbound started to smash up Tawfiq's statue.

"Leave the seat untouched," she ordered.

When she was satisfied they had understood and were obeying, Springer slotted the lens back into its original place and returned to her stone seat.

"People of Earth, hear me. We are the descendants of the slaves whom you sold to save your skins. I personify what became of those Earth children. Altered. Manipulated. Burned, and yet forged anew. Now the children have returned, and we are not impressed. The Earth shall be home for all humans in the widest possible meaning of the term. We have fought for centuries to win our liberty from terrible slavery, and we are not going to swap that for a new servitude to the old humanity."

She paused. The moment was hers to claim, but what she was about to say could not be unsaid.

Springer fought the urge to turn around on camera and ask Arun his advice.

*That man of yours sends a message via his crude AI*, said Saraswati. *He says to keep going. Speak whatever's in your heart and he will back you. He's right, of course, but it means nothing. Even a broken McEwan will be right twice a day.*

She smiled at Saraswati's little joke. "Let the killings end with the death of Tawfiq Woomer-Calix. I declare the Liberation of Earth, the full establishment of the Human Autonomous Region, and the end of the system known as the Cull. The wars are over. Any who wish to continue them will answer to me, Phaedra Springer Tremayne, Marine, proud member of Nest Hortez, deputy ambassador of the Human Legion, and protector of the Unbound."

She rose and unsnapped the camera again, redirecting it at the bloody scene on the far side of the reflecting pool where Tawfiq's statue had already been tipped from its seat and had smashed into a dozen pieces.

"I am told a great human leader once sat there on that stone chair. We will replace him, and you, the people of Earth, will choose who will sit there."

She played the camera over the mall, along those Unbound who had remained there, and over to the detachment of Legion Marines who included six-limbed Jotuns and Hardits. Then she panned across the scene of destruction behind her in the obelisk, dipping around Janna's back to keep Romulus from view but lingering on the Trog dragoons and their human Nest siblings. "Trogs, Jotuns, Legion Hardits, my loyal Unbound, and many more people have fought against the White Knight and New Order tyrannies. Night Hummers too have made this possible and we have sworn to provide them with sanctuary, and they shall have it here in the Solar System on the airless rock of Ceres. I hear reports of Sangurians setting up a burrow in Australia. Earth is no longer only for you. You must learn to share. That is the price I demand in recompense for selling my ancestors as slaves. It is not negotiable."

She replaced the camera one last time and glared into its lens.

"But there are benefits to sharing this system with new friends, advisers, and allies. No more will Earth beg its masters for scraps of airless rock on which to establish worthless colonies. No more will Earth's people do the hard work of early terraforming only to hand over colony planets to the White Knights. Humans of Earth, we give you the stars."

She shut off the equipment and slumped into Tawfiq's stone chair, utterly spent.

# —— Chapter 53 ——

**Arun McEwan**
**The Monument**

Nhlappo was staring blankly at her son's body, the weapon that had ended him still in her hand.

It was too much.

Arun moved closer to Springer, his heart still pounding with horror, disbelief, and admiration

He remembered Sergeant Gupta's advice. When everything had turned to drent and little made sense, trust in the things that will never let you down. And Arun trusted in his love for this woman who'd snuck into his life when they were still novices, and now sat alone in that cold stone chair, her head bowed and shoulders trembling.

Even so, though he hated the poisonous taste of the words escaping his lips he couldn't stop himself from saying, "Springer, what have you done?"

# —— PART VIII ——
# THE JUDGEMENT OF NHLAPPO

# —— Chapter 54 ——

**Springer**
**Temporary Legion HQ**
**Washington, D.C.**

"I need him alive," said Greyhart, "but he cannot remain here on Earth with you."

Springer took a long look at the man from the future, who wore a blood-spattered woolen military greatcoat over t-shirt and jeans, and wondered whether she should alert the Marines standing guard outside.

His mood swings made the man difficult to read, but Springer had never seen him so devoid of humor. She decided it would be better if the guards outside continued to believe she was sleeping peacefully in the cot hastily installed in what, ironically, had been the Australian embassy building in another era.

That didn't mean she was about to agree to Greyhart's demands.

"I've already told Nhlappo no," she said, sitting up in bed. "You get the same answer. I can't leave Arun. Not after we found each other after spending most of our lives apart. We deserve this."

"Do you?" Greyhart suddenly peered intently at something on the ceiling. "I suppose you do. I make it a policy not to comment on domestic politics or local morality. Such a messy business, both of them. McEwan's necrosis is spreading fast. I know you Marines pride yourselves on your robustness, but even you have your limits, and he has pushed himself far beyond them."

"Don't beat about the bush, Greyhart. Speak plainly, and then leave."

"McEwan is dying."

"I know!"

"But do you really? It's been a week since Tawfiq's death and almost that since you saw McEwan. Tomorrow, when you meet with him in orbit, you will have to confront how rapidly he has declined since you last saw him. His deterioration will only accelerate."

"Which is why I need him here with me," said Springer. "If he hasn't long to live, then I will nurse him through his dying days. I'll do more than that. I'll enjoy him, and he will find peace in an echo of the time we spent in Elstow long ago. When he departs this life, I'll be there at his side holding his hand so he knows he is not alone. In his last moment, he will know that he is loved."

"Admirable, Springer. I'm sure I would be in tears if I cared. Look, I need desperately to back off from this endless cycle of intervening in the affairs of your time period. Just to remain here is excruciating pain, and yet I cannot let go. McEwan has not delivered all the things I require of him. I need him as much as you – though admittedly for differing reasons. I can't leave this to chance. I try not to dabble but sometimes I cheat to get my way. I have no choice. I *must* have your Arun."

"Cheat?" The man squared his shoulders and looked straight at her. "Greyhart, are you saying you can keep him alive?"

"Oh, yes, of course I can. I can do better than that. I can cure his pain. Even regrow nerve endings. If he wishes, your existing technology can regrow new limbs or attach prosthetics. Or I could do it myself."

"He doesn't need to get out of his damned hover chair to be the most wonderful, capable… Oh, frakk you!"

Greyhart was the most patronizing veck in the galaxy, and every instinct made her want to tell him no. Whatever he wanted: no! But if she refused what first Nhlappo and now Greyhart were asking, she would lose Arun. And if she bought into this devil's bargain with Greyhart, she would lose Arun anyway. What the hell was she thinking? This choice wasn't hers to make.

Greyhart held up a finger. "Just one caveat. This is important, and I shall hold you to it. Whatever you choose to do or not to do as a result of this conversation, it is imperative that McEwan must never learn of what we said here. The truth would be devastating for him, and for countless others too. This *cannot* be his choice."

"I'll think it over."

"You shall not! This window of opportunity is fast closing. I need your answer now."

Springer thought again about the guards outside her room as she lifted Saraswati's pendant from under the pillow. They couldn't harm Greyhart, but they might be able to chase him away. "You can shove your high-pressure selling up your backside, Greyhart. I don't believe you."

"Your confidence in me is of no consequence." He raised an eyebrow as she donned the pendant. "I desire only your actions. You must agree to Nhlappo's plan and you must make it succeed. Only that way can McEwan be rewarded."

"You're wrong. Trust is important. How do I know you will heal him?"

"Logic. I need him fit and strong to carry out the further actions that I require of him. He is no use to me dead. But if he remains here with you, I have no reason to intervene and cure him."

"No? How about a sense of decency? Is that by itself not a reason to intervene? Arun is a good man and he has suffered a great deal. Let compassion be your guide. Do something good without asking for something in return."

"My every action affects the lives of countless trillions. My inaction likewise dooms trillions and sustains more. I cannot account for the life of a single individual. Whether you believe this or not, the opportunity we could exploit has almost moved beyond our reach. You must decide. There is no need to speak, because I will see the influence of your decision."

How could she possibly decide? She didn't know what Arun wanted and she definitely didn't trust a word that came from Greyhart's lips.

Greyhart took a deep breath. He sounded very satisfied as if the very air in this damp old building was hearty sustenance. "Very well," he pronounced. "The decision is made."

"No. No, it isn't. I haven't made up my mind."

He eased into that patronizing smile of his. "You have. You just don't know it yet."

*Frakk him! Saraswati, get those Marines in here!*

"Remember," said Greyhart, his finger pointed at her heart, "not a word."

The Marines roared in, screaming curses at maximum speaker volume at whoever had dared to threaten their charge.

The shouts died away as they swept the empty room.

"Stand down," she told them.

They brought their carbines to port arms.

"It was just a ghost. A spirit from the future." She bit her lip and growled with frustration. "But it was real. We have enemies I do not know how to fight. Not yet."

The sergeant of the guard saluted. "Springer, ma'am, I recommend posting two Marines in your room to keep watch as you sleep, and adding more to the corridor outside."

She took strength from their reaction. Sergeant Kohn didn't think she was making a fuss over a bad dream. He believed her and hadn't hesitated in making what some would think a forward suggestion, because he took his duty to protect their Springer with the utmost seriousness.

When she'd revealed her identity to the galaxy, Springer hadn't thought the Marines would care about her. About what she represented in the Legion's relation to the White Knights – sure, that mattered a great deal – but she herself had only been a footnote in Arun's history in the minds of most Legionaries.

Worse, she expected her former brother and sister Marines to call her a traitor for disobeying Arun's orders and setting herself up as a new Tawfiq.

But that hadn't been the way veterans such as Sergeant Kohn saw it. Already, some were addressing her as *the Springer*, as if her nickname was a formal title.

And the longer they had served, the more likely they were to treat her as a totem of a new beginning.

Which she could not be if Arun remained.

Damn Greyhart! He had wormed his idea into her brain.

And if Arun departed… would Marines like Sergeant Kohn turn on her?

Damn Greyhart for making her think these thoughts!

The Marines tensed, unsure whether she was under psychic attack, reliving trauma, or about to unleash a tongue lashing at the forwardness of Kohn's suggestion.

She understood their uncertainty. It was the same she felt every night she was with Arun, watching over him as he screamed in his sleep.

"Good idea, Kohn. Post two guards with me every night until I say otherwise. What happens farther down the corridor I leave in the hands of the captain."

"Roger that, Springer, ma'am."

She nodded and shuffled back under the blankets to sleep. Before her head hit the pillow, she knew she had made her decision. And with that release, she reached for the sleep she needed to keep herself fresh, because tomorrow was going to be the most difficult day of her life.

Under the watchful gaze of her Marines, she was asleep within moments.

# —— Chapter 55 ——

**Arun McEwan.**
**On board** *Holy Retribution*

How were the Unbound to be fed? Who commanded the fleet if the inner planets needed to be defended from the New Order fleet still threatening from the outer system? Was it even theoretically possible for Sangurians to listen to reason, and if the only reason Xin and the Far Reach ships had come was to defeat Tawfiq, why were they still here?

It had been only eight days since the events in the Imperial Mall – or Liberty Mall as the local civilians were now calling it.

Arun had expected there would be interim details that needed agreeing, but they were now lurching from major issue to full-blown crisis, and on a heading for worse.

Already! Eight days!

Floating by the bulkhead outside the conference room, he watched as the last of the key players and their teams filed out, and was reminded of something Del-Marie had picked up from Bloehn. As the sole representative of the people of Earth – at least until a better arrangement was worked out – the old International Federation Defense Force sergeant said he felt like he was watching great powers carving up a conquered land.

The Earther stomped out the room, clumsy in his use of the charged pathway. Arun caught the eye of Del-Marie who had left in Bloehn's company. His old friend floated over to join Arun.

"Still worried about what Bloehn said?"

Arun smiled at his former cadet dorm buddy but didn't reply. With his elegant cream robes, and just a hint of white in his neat beard, Del looked the part of the experienced diplomat he was: body worn, but mind still sharp. Ambassador Del-Marie Sandure had kept out of the way during the Battle for Earth. Not anymore. This was *his* time.

"It's a matter of presentation," said Del. "We can fix this."

"And Japan?"

The mask slipped; Del seemed to age decades. He'd survived on his own once, cut off behind enemy lines for years. At times like this it showed. "The recent trouble in Japan—"

"Trouble? The civil disobedience and riots – that's what I would call *trouble*. The brutal way Aelingir suppressed it was something else again. All she's achieved is to destroy lives and infrastructure and fan the flames of resentment."

"You know Jotuns. We grew up with them, Arun. Remember? Aelingir possesses more empathy for humans than any Jotun I've ever known. She loves us almost as much as her own people. But as a *race*. She only values the individuals she knows personally. I sat down with Aelingir and spelled out the moral angle of killing hundreds of civilians, but she doesn't get it. They're just individuals she doesn't know and they're gumming the works. So she clears them away. She's an alien for frakk's sake. Don't ever make the mistake of thinking your alien friends are humans just because you want them to be."

"And you should stop making excuses for Aelingir. There can't be another Japan."

"You're right on that last point. But I'm not excusing anyone, Arun. I'm pointing out the problem. And I'm talking to the solution. Earth is a human planet. It requires human governance. I know you want to retire, but Earth needs you."

Arun looked away, back to the conference room where the last delegates were leaving. He couldn't look Del in the face because he couldn't do what he asked. Someone else had to lead the Legion now. If Arun tried, he'd crack like Indiya.

Springer floated out into the passageway with Xin alongside. Today was the first time Springer had left the planet since she'd taken charge of the Unbound and later took the surrender of all New Order personnel in the inner system.

An aura of civility dampened the enmity between the two women, but even so Arun imagined he could smell the ozone in the air from the charge building up between them.

*Olfactory hallucination,* said Barney. *It's a known side effect of the pain medication you're taking.*

"I'll think over what you said," Arun told his ambassador, who nodded and floated away.

It was Springer whom Arun had really been waiting for. They hadn't spent any time together for over a week. Although she gave him a wave and a smile, they seemed forced. Arun's heart soured further when she walked off to meet with Kreippil and Nhlappo, and it was Xin who floated over to his position at the bulkhead.

"Walk with me?" she said. "Well, *float.* I meant no offence. Sorry."

Already, Springer was gesticulating passionately to Kreippil and Nhlappo. Barney tried to clean up the sound, but he couldn't make out what they were discussing.

"Are you with us, Twinkle Eyes?"

"Factions. Alliances. Secrets." Arun shook his head sadly. "Do we really have to go through all this again, Xin?"

He saw her looking at him with compassion in her eyes, and he remembered a time when much of the strength and the cunning that had kept the rickety alliance of the Human Legion together had come from this woman.

"You thought it would all be over with Tawfiq's defeat," she said. "It didn't work that way when you beat the White Knight Emperor, and it doesn't now. In our little part of the galaxy, we've broken the way the universe works, but it will reset into a newly hardened form soon. The responsibility is ours to make sure it forms in the way we choose. No one could fault you for leaving that fight to others."

"Others like you, I suppose?"

"I've come too far to give up now. We're alike, you and I, Arun. Always were. We cannot rest until we know that we've done our best." She looked away. "Indiya was the same too. And, Arun… everyone in that conference could see how labored every movement you make has become. We could hear the rasp in your voice. I don't want you to die, Arun. Nor does Grace. But if you keep pushing yourself, we'll lose you. This isn't something you can put off until it becomes convenient. You need medical attention. Today, Arun. You don't have a tomorrow."

*Listen to her*, insisted Barney. *Every day I beg you to seek help. It's like she says, one day soon, there won't be a next day.*

Arun ignored them both and glanced at the others. Kreippil had walked off to leave Springer and Nhlappo deep in conversation, with Del-Marie waiting a respectful distance away, presumably to discuss an issue with his former junior ambassador who now represented the most powerful fighting force on the Earth's surface, the Unbound.

But it was Xin who had voiced the starkest truth. Barney had been telling him for days that the fight to defeat Tawfiq had kept his body together far longer than should be possible. But now she was gone, he was fading fast.

He couldn't deny the truth. But the Legion was still divided, the Earth was a combustible mix, and from his poison-choked moon, the Emperor watched all through malevolent eyes. Arun couldn't afford to die. There was still so much to fight for.

He hauled himself away, hand over hand, along the grips recessed in the bulkhead. Xin chose to follow him the same way, rather than use one of the charged walkways. They passed through a blast door and stopped on the far side.

"I need to understand," she explained. "You faked Springer's death, and you let me believe you had sacrificed her to the Cull. That's why I left. That's why your daughter grew up without her father, because you wouldn't tell me. Why?"

"Tawfiq had infiltrated us. The Blood Virus was in Romulus, and who could tell how many other people?"

"But you should have told me. I was your wife. I still am. You should have told *me*."

"Tawfiq would have heard from her spies. And even if she didn't, she would have seen your opposition to the Cull moderate when you understood the Emperor and I were dancing around each other's lies. I couldn't afford for the Emperor to learn what I'd done so soon."

"Soon? We're talking about the White Knights here, Arun. For them, a thousand years into the future is like next Tuesday for us. When the Emperor learns that your new Cull means nothing more than a respray in Wolf colors, it won't just be a war between the Human Legion and the Empire, you will be in breach of treaty obligations, the one thing that can unite the Trans-Species Union against you. Even you can't win a war against the entire galaxy."

Arun made himself look Xin in the eye despite the shame smearing his heart. "I'm sorry. I know I can give you only words, but what we had between us was precious to the end and I shattered it. I did what I thought was my duty to my people, but I burned the one closest to me, and I am sorry, Xin."

"You didn't do your duty. You made the wrong decision. If only you'd talked to me first. And now the victim you saved has rewarded us by revealing herself to the Emperor. You and I will be dead before the retribution comes, but you've doomed us, Arun. Our entire race. All of our descendants will die because you broke a treaty obligation before the ink on it had even dried. *You should have confided in me.* You and Springer like to talk of noble sacrifice – how about asking her to go to the Emperor and put herself at his mercy?"

"Xin, I didn't break a treaty. If I had, then Springer and I would be en route to the Emperor now. Pleading that if we surrender our lives that he might forgive our transgressions."

Xin looked like she had swallowed a bee.

Even though he had wronged her, and despite the itching at his eyes that enticed him to curl into sleep and never wake, Arun couldn't help grinning to see Xin so flummoxed. But then his face hardened. He knew Xin of old.

She didn't seem merely surprised but was realizing she had miscalculated. Her plans had gone off track.

What plans?

"Del hit it out the park with his treaty wording," he said, studying Xin's face for her reaction. "The Cull is all about transformation in pursuit of accelerated change. That's the White Knight obsession it's supposed to venerate. Change doesn't have to mean death. Del's wording is a masterclass in vagueness. Springer emerged from her Culling with a new body, new skin coating, new DNA, and a new name. If I say that's a sufficient transformation to satisfy White Knight tradition, then that's up to me. And if the Emperor finds out and says it isn't, then that's up to him. The wording of that clause is so infinitely malleable that no third-party will ever say it's broken and go to war to save the Trans-Species Union from chaos."

"You magnificent bastard. But you're only confiding in me now? You could have told me the moment you showed up on *FRS New Frontier*."

"None of it would have meant anything if Tawfiq–" A muffled bang resonated up the passageway from past the blast door. He frowned. Was that a gunshot?

Xin's face went white with horror. "Del!" she murmured. And then she was away, back through the blast door and pushing herself along the zero-gee passageway as fast as any Spacer.

Arun pursued her, although his strength was fading and she left him in her wake. It was just as well he was dosed on pain dullers because his body would scream in protest later, but he made it to the area outside the conference room.

"Keep back, Arun!" warned a Far Reach Marine with an arm locked around Springer.

Springer? The layers of fatigue sloughed away and he surveyed the scene properly.

The half dozen Far Reach Marines wore identical black combat armor, but he recognized the voice of Estella Majanita as Springer's assailant.

A young woman was applying a medical patch to a wounded man secured onto the walkway. She looked over her shoulder at Arun, wide-eyed.

*Not you too, Grace.*

"Ambassador Sandure is hurt," cried Grace. She was still in the dress uniform she'd been wearing in the conference room. She looked as horrified as Arun felt.

He saw another unarmed person floating unconscious.

"Nhlappo is just tranquilized," said Majanita, warning him back with her carbine. "Del would have been too, if he hadn't tried to play the hero. He's always looked up to you. More fool him."

Arun tried to catch Springer's eye, but Majanita was interposing her armored body. "What do you want?" Arun growled.

"That depends," Xin answered, "on the truth of what you just told me."

She made a sudden grab for their daughter, gripping Grace around the shoulders and pushing off the walkway to float closer to her Marines. "Sorry, my dear. But as C-in-C I'm temporarily relieving you of command."

Grace screamed in fury, but she could only kick her legs against empty air.

Then the Far Reach team vanished.

No, not vanished, he realized. *Teleported.*

And they'd taken Springer.

Del's arm was badly burned, but Grace had applied an auto-tourniquet and nano-field patch to the wounds. Arun squeezed his friend's hand, whose half-open eyes flickered in response.

Barney patched through to CIC. "This is General McEwan. Interim President Tremayne has been taken by a Far Reach snatch squad. Don't let them get away. Also, medical team to Deck 31 frame 17B. Ambassador Sandure has been shot. Field Marshal Nhlappo is unconscious."

It was Kreippil himself who answered. "You let them take her? Stay where you are. I'll deal with the Far Reach traitors."

"Don't power play me, Admiral! Where are *New Frontier* and *Expansion*, the Far Reach ships?"

A pause. "Still in Mars orbit."

"That's too far to teleport." Arun frowned. Was it? Everything he knew about the technology had come from unreliable sources. But his gut said he had been told the truth. In which case… "They must have *Karypsic* nearby. Blockade it!"

A squad of Littorane Marines showed up within the minute, suited up and ready to do harm to any who would hurt this new vessel of the goddess, because that was how the Littoranes were seeing Springer now: as Indiya's spiritual successor.

"Let's hit the airlock," said Arun.

"Our instructions are to repulse intruders," replied the shoal leader.

"They teleported away. I think they must be really close. Come on, with me. I'll grab an emergency pressure suit at the airlock and join you. I have a special connection to Phaedra Springer Tremayne. I might sense her location in ways others cannot."

"That is outside mission parameters, sir."

"I'm Arun McEwan. The only reason any of you are here today – the reason this ship even exists – is because I broke mission parameters to create the Human Legion. And so did Springer. Now, let's go rescue her."

The Littoranes looked at each other unhappily.

"For the Goddess!" shouted the shoal leader. And then they were racing for the airlock with Arun struggling to keep up.

# —— Chapter 56 ——

**Springer Tremayne**
**Aboard *Karypsic 1.1***

"*New Frontier* and *Expansion* signaling ready to jump," said a voice over a bulkhead speaker. "First and Second Battle Fleets leaving Jupiter cloaking shield."

"Copy," Xin replied. "Initiate jump when ready." She looked wistfully at Springer for a few seconds. Was she looking for a reaction to the revelation that there were Far Reach fleets close by? Springer didn't give her one. "You should have killed me when you had the chance at the Second Battle of Khallini." For a moment, Xin looked away and her eyes glazed over – concentrating on something Springer couldn't hear. "You're too soft, and you made Arun soft too. You would have been the death of us all."

"What does she mean?" Springer asked of Grace, who was strapped in beside her, and appeared to be just as much a prisoner. "And why does she sound like she's reciting an overly rehearsed speech she no long believes in?"

A voice in a bulkhead speaker warned of a time jump in three seconds.

"I can only answer the first question at this time," Grace replied.

*Depressurization!* screamed Saraswati in her head.

Springer didn't question her AI; she evacuated her lungs and shut her eyes.

The time jump initiated and for the third time in her life, Springer experienced the vacuum of space without a pressure suit. Her belly swelled, and the bronchioles in her lungs began to burst. A prickling sensation came to her eyes and mouth as their moisture boiled into space.

And then she was safe again.

Springer opened her eyes on a giant pressurized bubble filled with air, and very surprised Far Reach personnel spinning about inside this balloon. Of *Karypsic 1.1* there was no sign. It had disappeared, replaced by the bubble which hung in space just a few hundred feet off *Holy Retribution's* enormous port bow.

*Most of that didn't really happen*, Saraswati assured her. *It was over so quickly you just remembered the pain of what should have come next. Maybe none of it did. Frankly, you can make up whatever version of reality suits you best, because none of it makes sense. Which does rather point the finger of blame, don't you think?*

"Guess your friend, Greyhart, didn't want you abusing the toys he gave you," Springer shouted at Xin. "Did you void the warranty on his time engines?"

"Friend?" Xin looked at her like she was insane. "Greyhart is a bigger threat than Tawfiq ever was. But, yes, if it pleases your petty mind, I believe you are correct. Greyhart has just given us a lesson. His time intercalators only operate when he says so."

Long before the air could run out, the area of space around the bubble was swarming with Legion X-Boats. Littorane Marines arrived with rescue gear and overwhelming firepower.

And with them, armed with a plasma pistol and an emergency pressure suit, was Arun.

Her heart leaped to see him, but though she would always love him, the words she had exchanged with Nhlappo after the conference sliced through any thoughts of joy.

Arun had no formal command authority over the Littoranes – he never had – and look how ready they were to follow him.

Look how ready Arun was to *lead*.

Arun. Xin. Arun. Xin.

She looked around at the Far Reach team. Grace was different, but the others would follow Xin through an event horizon and back. Colonel Lee had been their hero, and as President Lee it was no different. And now, it seemed, there were Far Reach military fleets about to reveal themselves in the Solar System.

Arun. Xin. Arun. Xin.

Nhlappo was right. The galaxy might be big enough to contain both of them, but the Human Autonomous Region was not.

But that wasn't the reason for her betrayal

*I don't think 'betrayal' is a healthy framing for your decision.*

*Shut the frakk up,* she told Saraswati because this was a personal betrayal of the man she loved.

Arun closed and pressed his hand against the flexible material of the pressure bubble. Grace gave Springer a shove so she could meet him at the interface, and touch her fingers to his across the insulated material.

Inside the bubble of his helmet, he was grinning. It was the same cheeky expression of the boy she'd known long ago, but it was painful to see it in a face grown so stretched with gauntness it looked as if his smile would surely tear his skin. And if she ever gripped him again in her arms, she feared she would crush his frail body to powder.

*I love you,* she mouthed, but she was ashamed of the tears forming bubbles over her eyes. She kicked off against Arun's mass and scrambled from Marine to Marine to seek refuge in Grace's arms.

"I understand," said Grace. "Nhlappo's sounded me out too. It stinks, but I don't see any other way. And so soon too…" Her voice caught, and for the first time, Springer considered the hurt it would cause this young woman. "I told Nhlappo no, but when I saw you support her. I mean… my mother…" Her face clouded. "You love him most of all, Springer. If you can endorse the plan…"

"I can't speak openly," said Springer, gripping Grace's shoulders, and noticing Xin watch them intensely, "but hear this. I'm doing it all for your father."

It seemed to be what Grace needed to hear. In a voice taut with pain, Grace replied, "Thank you."

# —— Chapter 57 ——

Arun McEwan
Isolation cell. Deck 41. *Holy Retribution.*


The inside of a Littorane cell was not an environment Arun McEwan had expected to experience just days after the fall of Tawfiq. Perhaps he should have seen it coming.

The amphibians were more comfortable in water, so naturally the cells were not designed to be flooded, which meant that instead of leaving the prisoner to float, there was a stretchy mesh fabric attached to one bulkhead to serve as a sleeping pouch. The bad news was that with his wrists cuffed, it was going to be near impossible for Arun to wriggle free of the pouch and float across the cell to take advantage of the water fountain or zero-g toilet. He didn't intend to humiliate himself trying in front of the dark bulges in the overhead that housed the cameras.

He was on the point of trying anyway when the door slid open.

"What is the meaning of this?" he demanded from the pouch.

Kreippil floated in. So did Nhlappo. Neither spoke.

"Is this a coup?" Arun challenged.

When he first heard of Indiya's absence, Arun had feared Kreippil would seize control of the fleet in the name of his goddess, but in the first virtual conference in the wake of Tawfiq's death, when Springer's recoded brown eyes had glowed lilac with passion, Kreippil had seen it as a sign of divine favor. In Springer, he had found his new *purple one.*

"This is me maintaining security and order on my ship," Kreippil replied. "And reminding you that you have no authority to order my personnel about."

"The Admiral speaks for himself," said Nhlappo in a monotone. "As do I. And what I'm about to propose… yes, you could call it a coup."

Arun stared at Nhlappo, trying to figure her out. She'd sided with the Wolf mutineers on *Beowulf* many years ago, but that had turned out to be subterfuge. Maybe. He'd never been entirely sure of that. And then there was the business a few days before with Romulus.

*To kill your own child…* it was such a horrific concept that Arun struggled to call it by its name. *Murder.* Not that anyone had suggested bringing charges against her – not in his hearing, anyway – but how had this business wounded her?

Frankly, Arun didn't know how to talk to her, and for a long while Nhlappo didn't seem capable of speech either. But when she did break the silence, it wasn't in the monotone of someone so damaged by recent trauma that they were not truly alive.

"I made the right decision," she stated. "I don't ask for your understanding, even less your approval. I knew Romulus better than he knew himself. The guilt of his crimes would have killed him from the inside, even if you didn't offer him up for a show trial or mob justice. Now he's gone and I have my own guilt to bear. And what is it we have won with our sacrifices? Within days. *Days*, McEwan, that's all it's taken and already Xin has plotted a coup, and you have acted as if you have the right to command every being in the Legion. Aelingir is slaughtering civilians, and there's not enough consensus to deliver anything even if we could agree on a way forward. All the while the New Order is waiting for us to fall apart completely before wiping us out. How long do you think they need to wait? Eh? Another month?"

Disgust filled her face and she looked away from Arun. "It will take less than that before we're at each other's throats. We've traveled too far to let it all fall apart now."

Arun balled his fists but his anger had nowhere to go. *He* wasn't plotting coups. That was Xin's department. All he wanted was to slip away with Springer and find a little peace. But first she made herself responsible for millions of Unbound, and now everything else was turning to drent. There was so much left to do! It was unfair, but he could never talk of unfairness to the woman who'd shot her own son. So he said nothing.

With a sigh, Nhlappo turned back to Arun. "The Legion Council," she said. "The Human Autonomous Region and the civilian authorities we've established on liberated worlds. We've winged all of that while the war was still hot. Now we have to act as if we have won. We must decide how to organize ourselves, and that means *politics*." She spoke in a monotone once more. Arun had the impression that Nhlappo wanted to disappear even more than he did. It was duty drawing the words out of her.

"I'm a soldier, McEwan. As a rule, I despise politics and politicians, but I detest even more soldiers who assume political power when there are others better suited for the role. It is my firm belief that soldiers should only intervene in civilian matters when the politicians screw up so badly that we are left with no other choice. I find that President Lee has proven herself unworthy. And you too, my friend, are no longer what the survivors of the war need and deserve. Even if you could be restored to health. You leave me with no other option."

Was she going to kill him too? Arun couldn't help but flinch, but he refused to beg for his life.

"You have your loyalists," she said. "If you rallied the Legion to your personal colors, many would follow, assuming your health permitted you to live long enough to do so. Xin has her loyalists too. Neither of you will accept the other taking control of Earth or the Human Autonomous Region. While one faction exists, the other is critically destabilized. Even if we executed both of you – and Kreippil, Marchewka and I have discussed that – doing so would only create martyrs. You and Xin. This cannot work with you both here, and so we need a radical solution. General McEwan, will you accept banishment, taking your followers with you far outside the Human Autonomous Region never to return? Will you willingly leave Xin with free rein to do what she wants?"

Kreippil interposed himself between Nhlappo and Arun. "Your part would be played out, General. But I and many others would not let Xin Lee have *free rein*. I'm not planning on rising her up to be a tyrant empress."

Nhlappo nudged the Littorane out of the way. "If you accept banishment, Arun, then these matters will no longer be your concern. You must let us go free to make our decisions and our mistakes as best we can. You must withdraw yourself completely. Will you accept this fate?"

He couldn't dismiss Nhlappo out of hand. Not after what she had done. So he shut his eyes and rolled the idea of banishment around his mind to see if he could cool it down from burning injustice to something he could actually think about rationally.

And he couldn't. The idea wouldn't settle in his mind because of who he would be forced to leave behind. He was not prepared to abandon Grace so soon, and as for Springer, their separation was impossible to contemplate. Not again. And he couldn't take her with him if it meant abandoning everything they'd fought for to Xin.

"Not going to happen," he told Nhlappo. "I'm not going to make it easy for you."

"Xin Lee gave the same reply," said Kreippil, "though she didn't have to think about it."

"Which is why I'm going to recommend a third option," said Nhlappo. *Now* her voice was strained. "You, Xin, and all your supporters shall be banished on a one-way journey to a location far outside of the Human Autonomous Region. All who fought Tawfiq in this system will get a vote to decide your fate."

"How about a fourth?" spat back Arun. "Reject your illegal coup and stop all this talk of banishment. Let's carry on as before and make it work instead of giving up when the going gets tough." He shook his head, disgust welling up at this betrayal. "I don't trust votes. Too easily rigged. At least you're admitting this is a coup, Nhlappo. You didn't, Kreippil. Is that because you're the one making the grab for power?"

"No, not me." The Littorane thrashed his tail excitedly. "A madness took me, and I thought myself a great leader. Worse, I imagined I had divine sanction, may the Goddess forgive me. I am a soldier like Nhlappo. To lead a people in peace is very different to commanding a fleet during war. Neither I nor Tirunesh Nhlappo are worthy of that task."

"If not you, then who?"

Nhlappo looked appalled, and Arun's insides twisted.

"I'm sorry," she said.

Arun knew exactly who she had in mind.

# —— Chapter 58 ——

Arun McEwan
Conference Room, *Holy Retribution*

The oval conference table slowly span about its longitudinal axis, delivering just enough micro-g to settle its delegates into their chairs, perches, or whatever suited their physiology. It was the same room where earlier that day, Aelingir had been subjected to a dressing down for his handling of unrest in Japan. The same room Arun had hung around outside, hoping to catch a little time with Springer, only for her to be snatched by the Far Reach squad.

But the salient point he had failed to see earlier was the way Springer had been plotting with Nhlappo, Kreippil and others Arun had once called friends.

In their previous meetings, delegates had been carefully positioned around the table to avoid an us-and-them dynamic.

Not this time.

Arun and Xin sat on one side, arranged in opposition against everyone. Nhlappo, Marchewka, Grace, Kreippil, Aelingir and Bloehn ranged against them, and sitting directly opposite him, Springer.

Arun's defocused gaze was locked upon her, seeing through her but unable to look away.

He felt so very tired.

Security inside and out of the room was ferociously heavy, but without Springer at his side, Arun lacked the strength to fight this coup.

On his way here from the cell, Springer had intercepted his party and taken him to one side for a little privacy, but the moment he saw the steaming tears in her glowing eyes, he knew their time together was already over.

345

"I'll never stop loving you," she had told him. "I've loved you since we met in novice school. I loved you through all those years I told myself I wanted nothing to do with you. Remember that, Arun. No matter how much you hate me, I will never stop loving you. But Earth is a mess, and it's a combustible mess. If we aren't careful, we will soon see civil war. The Sangurians will fight the Trogs. The Hardits will fight them both. The Littoranes and Gliesans are already bickering. Marines and Spacers of the Legion will square up to the humans of Earth in mutual recrimination and suspicion. And the New Order is a force that will rise again if we're weak enough to allow it."

"I never imagined it would be easy," Arun had snapped. "But it will be ten times easier facing it together. You and me, Springer. We've done so much together. Let's do this too. As a team."

She had glanced inwardly then. It was a unique look she had, and it meant she was reflecting on her foresight. Her visions. That damned place where Arun could never follow her.

"I'm not sure I trust my foresight any more. But I trust our children. They see many futures, but in the ones where the Earth and humanity prospers... you aren't in it, Arun. If we stay together... it all crashes down in flames, and quickly. We had our time in Elstow. I hope that one day..."

Springer's words had tailed off, and by silent agreement they decided there was nothing left for either to say to each other.

So now, Arun hunched in stony silence, allowing the events of his betrayal to wash over him. Those who sat on the opposing side of the table were speaking as if the vote had already taken place, and the decision made to banish the two former Legion leaders. They'd even decided upon a name for the history that they intended to write: the Judgement of Nhlappo.

But there was one detail that itched under his skin, burning him until his focus return to the room and the one opposite him. He spoke up. "If Xin and I are banished and we both depart the Human Autonomous Region, what's to say Xin's fleet won't just turn about after a few years and come straight back to play havoc?"

"Ahh, I was wondering when we'd get to that question," said a man now sitting in the vacant seat to Arun's left. He wore beige fabric pants tucked into socks, and a peculiar dark jacket with a high collar trimmed with lace. Other than a rearguard of graying hair over his ears, and a fulsome mustache, the man was completely bald. Arun was sure he'd never seen this man before in his life, but this could only be Greyhart.

"Well done on dealing with Tawfiq and her Night Hummers, by the way."

"And this banishment," cried Arun. "Is that part of your plan? The Judgement of Nhlappo. The name has Greyhart written all over it."

Greyhart wagged his finger. "You know, Mr. McEwan, I can't possibly comment on such matters. I've just popped over to let you all know that if you want to go ahead with this banishment, then I can help you out." He held out his hands in a placatory gesture. "I'm not vote influencing. The decision is entirely up to you. I'm just offering to help out with the practical details. How to make a banishment stick. A trip that's guaranteed to be safe – well, probably – but definitely one way."

Greyhart flicked his gaze to the side, as if remembering painful memories. "I have a daughter myself. Dear Mary… But I'm separated from her by time. Your separation from your daughter and others, though, McEwan. And for all those who choose to follow you. That I can make a little easier to endure."

347

# —— Chapter 59 ——

The scores of ships in their docking cradles made Springer feel sick to her core every time she saw them. Every week she made herself come up here. She detested doing so. But still she came.

At least in recent weeks, as they awaited the final upgrades, the ships had begun to look proud to her now, despite the close guard they were kept under and the freedom denied their crews. It was those crews who had named their collection of vessels the Perseid Pioneer Fleet, and said they would seek a new existence together far beyond the boundaries of the Trans-Species Union in the Perseus Arm. And they would do so together: Arun's followers and Xin's.

If only such cooperation could be relied upon without the need to travel nearly 7,000 light years away.

"Pilot, take us in close to *Lance of Freedom*."

The other occupant of the passenger compartment put a comforting hand on her shoulder. "Hey," said Grace, "believe me, I understand your need to beat yourself up, but in a week's time they will be gone, and we will still be here. The Settlement of Vancouver was better received than I'd dared to hope. Remember that, because the Settlement alone has justified all that we're doing here. Don't self-flagellate so much that you stop realizing the future is depending on you, Madam President. This is the most important campaign you will ever fight."

If she hadn't felt so hollowed out by the sight of the light carrier rapidly filling the observation viewport, Springer would have laughed at the irony of taking advice from this woman of all people.

Marchewka, Nhlappo, Aelingir, Kreippil, the military forces of Nest Hortez, and the newly reconstituted Earth Defense Force all reported to Grace Lee-McEwan. Under the Settlement of Vancouver, the President of the Human Autonomous Region was forbidden to issue direct commands to any military unit, but Grace was Chief of Staff of the Human Legion, and that meant she reported to Springer. Every serving member of every military branch was to swear a personal oath of allegiance to Springer as the embodiment of the office of President. Those in the Solar System had already done so. And when it was time to pass that office to a properly selected civilian replacement, the personnel of the Human Legion would renew that oath to its new holder, sanctifying the vow with the most binding statements appropriate to their religion and culture.

And Springer – she shuddered at the thought – would swear fealty to the White Knight Emperor like a feudal vassal, but it would be a charade to fulfill the letter of treaty obligations signed by General Arun McEwan, and many centuries earlier by President Horden in the Vancouver Accords. The difference between the two men was that Horden was a beaten supplicant pleading for humanity's continued existence, whereas Arun was dictating terms as victor.

Well, Springer and the Human Legion were even stronger now and the Emperor knew it. He'd even sent a message of congratulations to the new President of the HAR.

"We'll need to rebuild our carrier fleet urgently," Grace reminded her as they swept over the opening to the *Lance*'s main hangar. Through the hash of the force shield, Springer could make out partially disassembled X-Boats, waiting to be unlocked at the far end of the one-way journey out to the Perseus Arm.

"Your objections are noted," Springer told the younger woman curtly. "However, this is not transportation to a penal colony. Who knows what they will find out there? Our region of the galaxy is a vindictive and dangerous place. Why should the Perseus Arm be any different? Don't forget that the Legion voted to banish Xin and Arun for the wider good, but all those who travel with them volunteered."

"True. But when you agreed to supply them so generously, President, you critically underestimated how many would volunteer to go. Nearly 23% of human personnel. It was a critical error of judgement. You can still change this."

"Marines can never retire," whispered Springer sadly, and thought of the person she cared for most in the universe who was somewhere aboard the warship they were passing over. If duty didn't chain her to Earth, she would order the pilot to dock with the *Lance* immediately and leave with Arun on the Perseid Fleet when they departed in a few days. But it could never have been retirement for them. For those bred under the stewardship of the Jotuns in the Human Marine Corps, there had been no such concepts as retirement or civilians. You were a Marine for life until you were no longer useful, and then you would be spaced by your alien officers. If you survived one campaign, you would simply be put on ice until you were required for the next mission.

And that was what she was doing to Arun, Xin, and all the others. Giving them a new mission. One that required them to cooperate, not fight each other. They would keep going as Marines until the end, whereas those left behind had to fight to become something new.

Civilians.

The idea made Springer's flesh crawl.

It wasn't meant to be easy for her, though. It was the job of those who stayed behind to make it easy for the next generation.

And it had been her personal task to make it easier for Arun. With a new purpose and healed body, that was preferable to fading away in a hospital bed, wasn't it?

She half-expected Saraswati to argue with her, but they'd said all there was to be said on the matter of Arun. He'd undergone secret medical procedures and was already in deep cryo. She could only hope and pray that Greyhart had kept his side of the bargain.

Grace interrupted her thoughts. "I'm not asking for them to go into the dark defenseless, but you should force them to swear a binding oath of allegiance to you, *and* tell Greyhart to adjust the time setting so they don't arrive in Perseus for centuries."

Springer didn't disagree with Grace's advice, but it was Greyhart she needed to convince, and he had whispered with silvered tongue into the right ears to make this Perseid Fleet a reality.

And his parting gift was to equip the entire fleet with one-way time intercalators. They would travel back into deep history, at around the time the glaciers on Earth were retreating after the last ice age, and set a course for where the Perseus Arm would be thousands of years hence. Where it would be *today*.

Then they would sleep, coasting through the void as civilizations began to rise and fall on Earth. Toward the end of their long journey, alien powers would pierce the barriers hiding their presence and reveal themselves to the humans of Earth in a rush to possess the fruits of human invention. And still the Perseid Fleet would fly cold and secret across the immense gulfs between the stars, skeleton crews awakening every century or so, just to keep the fleet in good repair before returning to cryo.

A few days after setting off from Mars, Arun's fleet would arrive where Greyhart wanted them. The journey would be over ten thousand years for Arun, but that was of no interest to the man from the future.

Oh, he was an arch manipulator all right. Even now, Springer couldn't discern the joins between Greyhart's meddling and the free will of the other players. That business with the *Karypsic* disappearing, never to return. Had he planned that from the beginning?

"Ma'am?"

"Sorry, Grace. What were you saying?"

"I think you should give us a chance to rebuild the Legion on our side of the galaxy, by telling Greyhart to delay their arrival. Otherwise in a few weeks, a significant part of the Legion's naval strength is going to wake up seven thousand light years from Earth and dismiss us as an irrelevance."

"Let them," Springer retorted.

"With all due respect, it's a mistake to have two Legions operating out of rival bases of operations thousands of light years apart. One day, both Legions will meet. It will be millennia into the future. Maybe more. But it will happen."

"Enough! Your opinions are already noted, Lee-McEwan. Do not repeat them."

"Ma'am."

Springer softened. Her chief of staff was supposed to be an ally, not a lackey. "I admire you enormously, Grace, but you were not there when the wars began. You and I are separating ourselves from those we love most, but we do not do so out of cruelty, and they will come to realize that. Our comrades setting off in that fleet are Marines and Spacers. They do not know how to be anything else. Better by far to send them off to their final mission with hope in their hearts and the honor of taking many of our proudest ships with them. If our distant descendants should ever encounter theirs, then the manner of the Perseid Fleet's departure may prove crucial."

Springer stared in cold silence upon Arun's ship for long minutes before ordering Grace to join her in sealing her pressure suit, and then evacuating the air from the passenger compartment.

With helmets kissing together, they talked privately through the vibrations of the faceplates.

"Arun led us to freedom from alien tyranny," she told Grace. "With your mother's help," she added tactfully. "But we have a more dangerous foe to face than Tawfiq and the White Knight Emperor. Long ago, Indiya spoke of space-time being edited by the Amilxi ship, *Bonaventure*. It's a future that has not yet happened. Some of those people about to leave in the fleet will return in our past. Greyhart has made all this possible because he has a purpose for them. I don't know what that means. I don't know a damned thing, Lee-McEwan, but I must assume we are facing hostile interference. We must prepare for time war."

"I agree, Madam President. It won't be easy. So far, we've played around the edges with what Greyhart has decided to allow us. The potential for time war… it scares the crap out of me."

"And so it should. But we have to try, and here's where I want you to start. Greyhart's people are from the future, and if they're operating in our present, it's a safe bet that they're doing so in our past too. Find them."

Grace considered for a moment. "Elstow?"

"My thinking too. Greyhart told us the Hummers wouldn't see us arrive there because so much disruption had already occurred in that location. I looked for signs when I was there in Celtic times and found nothing. Investigate every rumor, legend and coincidence about that place. Listen for the silences where history falls silent. Look for absences and gaps in the historical record throughout the Earth, but most of all, Elstow. I *will* find your secrets, Greyhart. And you will pay for making me push Arun away again. I'm coming for you."

# —— Chapter 60 ——

**Imperial Pleasure Grounds**
**White Knight Homeworld**

"Die, McEwan!"

The Emperor drove his thumbs deeper into his arch-enemy's throat. Only a faint rattle escaped the vile human's windpipe, but the pleading look from his bulging eyes was sweet, eloquent submission.

The creature's desperate entreaties entered the Emperor's mind across a telepathic link.

He pulped its head and watched the rest of its body slump into the thick umber clouds covering the valley floor. In his hands, he still held the bloody plating that had forced a convincingly human form upon the Kurlei slave's head.

Its torso still looked human but wasn't even convincingly male. And real humans were not telepathic.

His imperial gaze took in the litter of corpses strewn over the ground. The flekk clouds obscured the details, aiding the work of the mutation engineers, surgeons, and prosthetic artists. The fourteen ruined corpses all resembled Arun McEwan, but the real one had escaped him forever.

Worse still, the Human Legion had also evaded his claws. They had deployed hidden assets against the Hardits at Earth. Far from destroying themselves in the battle, they had emerged stronger than ever.

But humans were short-lived creatures who lived for the moment.

He had time.

And so, it seemed, did the humans.

The secret to time, hidden under his nose all the while.

But he knew it was there now.

And he would possess its power for himself.

"Remove these corpses," he ordered the underlings waiting nearby. "Prepare a fresh batch for tomorrow."

"Your Elevance, we have real human prisoners now. Would it please you to enjoy their deaths tomorrow?"

"Humans? Why was I not informed? Summon the heads of the experimental mutation clans. There are powerful secrets locked inside that vermin species. I will plunder their DNA until I possess them."

The Emperor howled in victory at the scattered bodies of these faked enemies. "You haven't escaped me yet, McEwan," he cried. "When I learn your human secrets, I shall reach into your past. And there I shall watch you die."

# —— Chapter 61 ——

3 years later...
also
12,000 years later...

**Arun McEwan**
*Lance of Freedom*
**Zhooge System in the Perseus Arm**

Hot water saturated Arun's hair and sluiced away the dried-on cryo fluids. He marveled at the complex patterns made by the streams of soapy water running down his body. Drips cascaded from his knees and onto his feet.

An hour after waking from his final two-thousand-year sleep, and Arun's world was still filled with things he could perceive and understand on their own, but not quite connect together. The way the water fell, though... he was sure this was significant.

Seven thousand light years from home – a vastly greater distance than the extent of the Trans-Species Union – and Arun was standing in a coasting spaceship with hot water falling down from a shower head and dripping down legs planted firmly on a slightly angled tray that channeled water down a hole.

*Down* a hole!

Even the strangeness of his hairless legs with skin as smooth as a baby's didn't register on the weirdness scale as much as the artificial gravity. After all, when he woke from long cryo, he would usually forget he'd lost his legs and promptly fall over, but he had never forgotten life in zero-g. He was a Marine. He'd been born, raised, trained and engineered for a life without gravity.

The high priority comm alert chimed in his cabin.

Sighing, he switched off the water flow and pushed off through the drip containment field to coast through his cabin over to the comm station.

And fell flat on his face.

"Damn!" he growled, rubbing at his jaw. "Forgot the gravity."

The comm chime mocked him.

"All right! I just got out of cryo. Can't you give me an hour to get my head straight first?"

He walked over to the comm screen.

*Incoming message. Audio only. Channel 114. Accept?*

At least he wouldn't have to grab clothes first. "Accept," he said and froze. That number! Channel 114. The call had come from the people he'd left behind. From the people who'd cast him out.

"McEwan, go."

Silence.

"McEwan here. You are unreadable. Say again."

But there was nothing.

*Barney, what the frakk is going on?*

*Comm handshake is established, but there's no associated data transmission. Why not?*

*How the frakk would I know? We've just finished a 12,000-year journey. 7,500 if you take account of time dilation. Greyhart sent the fleet into the deep past so at journey's end we would catch up with the moment of our departure from the Solar System. If I understood how chbit polarized entangled comms worked, maybe I could tell you why we can't talk with home. But I can't. When Earth encountered the TS-U, humanity's science said entangled comms could never work without breaking the no-communication theorem.*

*I know. They were wrong. But we've never figured out why. But we've loaded up with comm blocks entangled with home. We should be able to talk with Earth and Khallini across an instantaneous comm link. No one's ever talked across 7,000 light years, though.*

Arun made full use of his new limbs and gravity to punch the bulkhead hard. "We're cut off. Greyhart said we'd be able to speak with home and I believed him! I'll never hear Grace's voice again."

*You told me you never wanted to speak with home again.*

*This is not the time, Barney. Seriously, not... the... Wait!* Arun had brought up the transmission info detail, and there spinning on the comm screen was some kind of callsign glyph.

He peered at the screen. It was a golden sun around which a ring of planets orbited. He blinked away some of his cryo confusion and looked more carefully. The planets were familiar. He recognized Khallini. And there was Shepherd-Nurture too, and Earth. Obscured by the circling planets, a silver number was embedded in the sun. 412. He straightened his back. The 412th Tactical Marines. It was the old regimental banner he'd served under as a cadet.

As had Springer.

*That callsign glyph. Barney, don't you get it? We've never seen it before, which means it's new information. It's not audio, but if home can transmit information to us via the carrier signal we can figure out a way to carry voice. Right?*

*Listen!*

Breathing. Arun heard the sound of human breathing catching on heavy emotion.

"I didn't think you'd answer," whispered a tiny voice.

"Springer?"

"I called every day for three years. You never picked up."

"Uhh? We've only just arrived."

"We made contact on the day you were supposed to arrive. Furn answered. He was... not welcoming."

"Furn?" Arun tried rubbing sense into his head, but it was still too thick with cryo glue.

*Greyhart piloted one ship himself,* Barney explained. *It was due to make pickups on Khallini, where Furn was imprisoned, and the Far Reach proto-colonies too.*

"So I tried a direct call to you, Arun. And kept trying. It wasn't easy, knowing you didn't want to hear from me."

"What? Why wouldn't I?"

A minute ago, Arun couldn't have said whether he'd rather hear from Springer or wring her treacherous neck. Now he'd heard her voice, all the anger flaked away, and he knew there was nothing more in the universe that he would rather listen to than that sweet voice.

"Don't stop, Springer. Every day. I want to hear from you every day."

"You don't know how good it feels to hear you say that. All day long, the galaxy dumps its most intractable problems on me. Forget Earth and its many problems for now, there's corruption in our core worlds on a scale we never suspected. I've formed an intelligence agency to–"

"No! Stop, I can't hear any of that. Sorry, Springer, it's too raw. I can't – and *mustn't*. I have to spool my old mind up to face my own challenges. I can't let it snag on yours. Far Reach and Legion Loyalists. Our fleets are combined, but now we're here, do we split again? Where do we settle? I have to face these new challenges and you yours. One day, we could be each other's closest advisers. Not today. I just want to hear your voice. That's all I can cope with for now."

"Grace sends her love."

"No! It's all too raw for me. Not yet. Not even Grace."

"I should go, Arun. Leave you to thaw in peace."

She was right, but Arun shook his head forlornly. Then he laughed, forgetting she couldn't see him. "Don't go," he said.

"Let me help you. I hope." She sucked in her breath sharply. "Greyhart and the Hummers have confirmed something Grace found out years before we met her, something Xin tried to tell me when she snatched me from *Holy Retribution.*"

"Why are you telling me this? I don't want to hear."

"Because I think you *need* to hear it. The planner AI inside your daughter's head is able to run projections *backward*. Every time she re-runs the history of the Legion's formation with the two of us being happy together, we're wiped out before we turn the tide at Khallini. She sees only a handful of scenarios in which you and Xin become the axis that gives the Legion the ruggedness it needed to survive. Try to reconcile with Xin, Arun. We all owe her our lives."

"Do we? Or is it Greyhart we should thank for piloting us through dark waters to the version of history that suits his purposes. Man, I hate that creep, even if he did patch me up. I'm healthy again, Springer. More than healthy."

There was an awkward pause – it seemed that Greyhart was not a topic Springer was willing to discuss – before she changed the subject. "How's Indiya?"

Arun smiled because the news there was good. "I spent a lot of time with her on my last watch. That was two thousand years ago, and if she survived cryo then I find I'm looking forward to getting to know her as a friend. She's practically a kid again, confused to be inside a middle-aged body. All her memories since the first mutiny on *Beowulf* and the destruction of *Themistocles* are… Well, not exactly *buried*. She remembers it all, but she says it's as if it happened to someone else. I like the sound of her laughter, Springer. I need to be around someone I knew from the early years who can remember how to laugh."

His words dried up, and the weariness that had seeped deep into his bones shuttered his eyes and threatened to shut down his body.

"I slithered out of my pod less than an hour ago," he babbled in an attempt to stay awake. "I'm so lonely, Springer. Now that I've heard your voice, all I can think of is you, but the words won't connect in my head. Not yet. I love you and I hate you, but neither as much as I want to go back to sleep, but you know the resuscitation techs always say to keep awake, and – look, this is all too complicated. Can you just be with me a while in silence?"

Springer hesitated, but when she did reply, he could hear the dimples in her smile. "You know, Arun, I could tell from the beginning that you'd just thawed from a long cryo-sleep. I just couldn't bring myself to believe it."

"No. Brain's still fuggy. I don't follow you."

"Impaired cognitive function is not the only effect long cryo has on you. I remember what you were like when we woke up in Australia after a 3,000-year sleep, and it appears that nothing's changed."

Arun paused. "How do you know?" he asked sheepishly.

"The new legs suit you, by the way. Greyhart did you proud on that score. They're still too smooth though. Shame I can't come over and roughen them up."

Arun's face flushed hot and he swallowed hard. Excitement began melting the glue that had locked his eyelids tight.

"Maybe I can do something to help your resuscitation tension," said his lover. With the faintest of hums, the sound of a holographic projector activating crashed through Arun's awareness.

He opened his eyes.

"Phaedra Tremayne!" He had to stop to clear his throat. "You appear to have forgotten your clothing."

# —— Epilogue ——

Seven Years Later...

**President Tremayne**
**HAR Government Complex**
**HAR Federal Territory of Former Australia, Earth.**

Springer waved away the Gliesan senator and was rewarded with an angry wing shake.

"I value your support, Senator Gjen-Hyush. I always have, but my mind is made up. I shall stand down after my ten-year term of office, and hand over to an elected successor."

"In an election that is deeply flawed. New Order raiders are still active in the fringe worlds. Corruption remains stubborn in the core. We are asking people to vote who have no tradition of democracy. Absolutely none. You cannot unravel the cultural scarring from thousands of years of White Knight imperial rule in just a few years."

"This is the first step. Dangerous and uncertain, but it must be made. I'm a Marine, Gjen-Hyush. I move when the time is right, not when everything is neat and certain."

"So was I, President. That does not excuse rashness."

Springer sighed. She'd miss the stubborn Gliesan. They'd been political sparring partners many times, but the respect had always appeared to be mutual. "In a thousand years, Gjen-Hyush, we will be long forgotten. Maybe my name will be remembered, but the real me behind the name will be rewritten to suit those who follow and then lost forever. As for the minutiae of government, they will be forgotten within the decade. But the stories we write now – the grand gestures – they will set the tone for the Human Autonomous Region unto the far future. We allowed the backbone of our navy to depart in the Perseid Fleet and nearly paid the ultimate cost when the Muryani sensed our temporary weakness. But that gesture will be remembered. In the same way, I will hand over power after ten years because that is the commitment I made in the Settlement of Vancouver. The ability for power to transition peacefully is a key test of a robust society, my friend. History will judge us on this first transition within the HAR. What kind of precedent would I set if I didn't stand down as I promised?"

"Noble words, President. I never doubted that you are courageous and principled, but maybe you are naive and irresponsible too. It is a fine line, and history will also judge which side you stand on."

Her piece said, the senator bowed in the formal Gliesan way, with wings slowly extended to their full extent. Springer saluted, and Gjen-Hyush departed her private office, hopefully in friendship.

*You see*, she told Saraswati. *It only reinforces the importance of the book project. And its difficulty. All I thought I had to do was order an official history to be written.*

*Is that an apology?* asked her AI sweetly.

*You were right all along, Saraswati. I admit it. I should have listened when you said how much work this would be.*

*Would you like me to summon Councilor Hood from his labors?*

*We both know he's waiting outside. Just get the poor man in here.*

After Hood arrived, Springer gave him the courtesy of looking through the first printed draft for five minutes before telling him it wasn't good enough. The truth was that she'd arrived at that conclusion within seconds.

"The problems start here," she said, opening the book at the title page. "The Annals of the Human Legion. Book 1: The *Beowulf* Mutiny 2566."

"The title does have the majority approval of the steering committee, and subsequently backed by focus group."

"Then I apologize, Hood, because I have failed in my duty to steer the steering committee. That's going to change. The title is far too dry. Too academic."

"Then you need to help me to understand so I can serve you better. Because right now I see that as matching your orders, ma'am. You told me to deliver as accurate and balanced a story as we could piece together."

"*Story,* Hood! Stories hold more than facts and dates and events. Stories hit you *here*." She thumped her chest over her heart. "And it is just as well they do, because if Arun hadn't sold his story to us and the Littorane Queen, and all those who joined the Legion in its earliest years, it would have been snuffed out and already forgotten. You and I would be dead, Hood. It is stories that won our freedom, and stories that our descendants must remember as a bulwark against the potential tyrannies of the future. Arun was not an academic. Back in 2566 he was a cheeky no-hope greenhorn with a belief that anything was possible, and a kind of naïve charm that many of us couldn't resist. That title isn't him at all. I want something less academic, something simpler."

"You want the kind of thing a young Arun McEwan would have called it."

"Exactly."

"OK. Perhaps a call sign, or your squad name."

"Yes, something along those lines." Springer paused because it still wasn't what she needed. "The galaxy needs to understand Arun better," she told Hood. "It is *his* story, after all."

"Ma'am? I seem to recall that you were there too."

"Of course I was. As were all the millions dead or yet living who played vital roles but the story will not find room for. Yet it was above all Arun's story. Always was. Park this draft and go write the story of who Arun was before *Beowulf.* Start your account one year earlier."

"Ma'am, it would be dangerous to idolize the man. You said to present a balanced history… I mean, a balanced *story*."

"And that is exactly what you shall do. Write him the way he was at the beginning – as a lovable idiot. And start his story in the Trog nest below Detroit at the most embarrassing moment of his long life."

Councilor Hood allowed himself a smirk. "I think I know the incident in question, ma'am. And do you have a suggestion for the title of this new volume?"

She grinned so deeply, she could feel the dimples pitting her scaly cheeks. "Damned right I do. We'll call it... *Marine Cadet.*"

*Arun and Springer as 16-year-old novices. The artwork (by the wonderful Vincent Sammy) is for a forthcoming novella called MARINE NOVICE.*

# So, the Battle of Earth has ended. What next?

Arun's flown into the sunset – or so it seems – but there are plenty of adventures to be enjoyed in the Human Legion Universe and beyond.

**The Human Legion** — If *The Battle of Earth* was your starting point for the tales of the Human Legion, you could go back to the beginning with *Book1: Marine Cadet*. Or if you wanted to get straight into the action where Arun, Indiya and the others rebel against the White Knights, then *Book2: Indigo Squad* makes an excellent entry point. Find out more at the Human Legion page on humanlegion.com. Join the Legion while you're there and receive bonus Human Legion short stories.

**The Sleeping Legion** — Can't get enough of the Marines? Lance Scipio stars in this series of four novels and more, written by army veteran JR Handley. Find out more at the Sleeping Legion page on humanlegion.com. Join the Legion and receive a Sleeping Legion prequel novella.

**Revenge Squad** — Frontier world adventure featuring a veteran of the Battle of Earth, whose boss is Laban Caccamo! Find out more at the at the

Revenge Squad page on humanlegion.com. Join the Legion and receive a Revenge Squad novelette.

**Four Horsemen Universe** — Join a merc outfit. See the galaxy. Kill the bad guys and get paid. I've written a novel and several novelettes in this bestselling mercs & mecha series from Seventh Seal Press. Join the Legion at humanlegion.com and receive one of my Four Horsemen Universe novelettes.

**Chimera Company** — This is my latest project under development, and tentatively set to launch at the end of 2018. It's set 7,000 light years and 3,000 years after the events of The Battle of Earth in the Far Reach Federation. For fans of the classic Star Wars movies.

# Enlist as a Legionary today!

Receive free eBooks!
(Summer 2018: The Sleeping Legion prequel novella: 'The Demons of Kor-Lir', Revenge Squad novelette: 'Damage Unlimited', Human Legion short story: 'Hill 435', and Four Horsemen Universe novelette: 'Thrill Addict'.)

Read de-classified Infopedia entries!

Be the first to hear mobilization news!

Get involved with the telling of the Human Legion, Sleeping Legion and Revenge Squad stories!

Receive bonus content such as maps, author's notes, and author readings.

Experience a gruesome end as a redshirt.

HumanLegion.com

Made in the USA
Coppell, TX
03 October 2021

63415688R00215